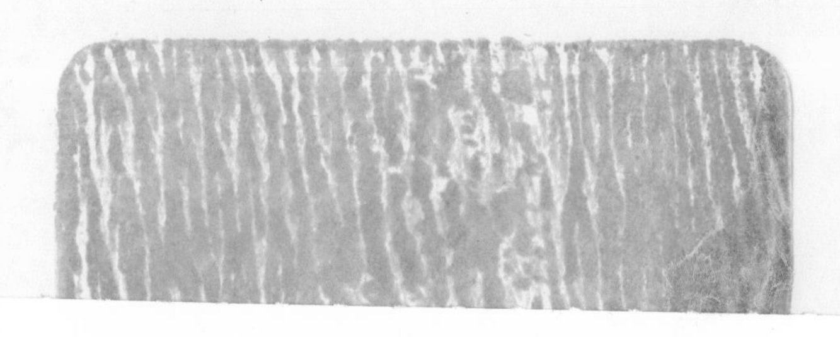

The War Babies

Gwen Davis

By Gwen Davis

THE WAR BABIES

SOMEONE'S IN THE KITCHEN WITH DINAH

NAKED IN BABYLON

THE WAR BABIES

Coward-McCann, Inc. New York

Published on the same day in the Dominion of Canada by Longmans Canada Limited, Toronto.

Library of Congress Catalog Card Number: 66-13116

Printed in the United States of America

TO DON

The War Babies

I

THE afternoon the bazooka was fired at the UN, Bo asked one of the other guides to cover for her, her last few minutes on duty, so she could be home in time for the call. There was still a great deal of excitement around the UN Plaza after that morning's demonstration, but she tore her way through the last die-hard picketers and TV cameramen and newspaper reporters, and managed to catch a cab uptown. In spite of traffic, she was upstairs and in her apartment by seven minutes to six. She sat down in the chair by the telephone and waited.

At precisely one minute after six the phone rang.

"Hello, Daddy," Bo said.

"Luanna? Is that you?"

"Of course it's me, Daddy," Bo said.

"Then you're all right?"

"I'm *fine*."

The sigh at the other end of the line was a little too heavy. "Thank God," he said. "You could have been killed."

"Oh, please don't overdo it, Daddy. It was just some piddling little bazooka or something and it plopped in the East River."

"The radio said people inside the building might have been killed and maimed—God knows what."

"That's if it hit, Daddy," Bo said patiently. "But it plopped in the East River."

The sigh came again, more weary. "You could have died."

"Well, I didn't," Bo said. "That's the important thing. I've never been in better shape in my life. The United Nations still stands. Life goes on."

"My little girl," he whimpered. "Dead."

She started to stop him, but as he seemed to be enjoying it so, she let him go on for a moment. It was, she realized immediately after, a moment too long.

"I want you out of there," Mr. Bowman said. "I want you back here in Cleveland with me and your mother, where you'll be safe."

"Oh for heavens sake," Bo said. "In Cleveland I might get hit by a taxi."

"At least people wouldn't be firing atom bombs. We don't have that sort of thing."

"Oh, Daddy, it was a pathetic little missile. It couldn't even make it across the river."

"Then get another job. Some place else. I don't want you working there."

"You know how many girls would love to have my job? Thousands and thousands of girls apply as guides, and they took me. Do you have any idea how keen the competition is?"

"That's fine with me. Let them take the other ones," Mr. Bowman said. "The ones who want to die young."

"Nobody's going to die," said Bo, annoyance leaving her voice, warmth creeping into it, encompassing him in the reassurance. It wouldn't hurt, letting him know that he wasn't going to die so fast either.

"I hope you're right," he said heavily, and on the other end of the phone, so many miles away, she was sure he was holding his heart.

"What else can they expect?" he said, after a moment. "Playing patty cake with those Commies. You start playing patty cake with Commies, first thing you turn your back, they shoot missiles at you."

"If there's one thing it wasn't," Bo said, "it wasn't a Communist."

"How can you be sure?"

"The people demonstrating were anti-Communists. Cuban ANTI-Communists. They were protesting the appearance of a Cuban COMMUNIST. So the people who shot at the UN from behind were the same ones who were out in front. The ANTI-Communists."

"They'd like you to think that."

"Who?" Bo said.

"Those Commies."

"Daddy, you don't begin to understand."

"Don't you start explaining to me, young lady. You work for ten weeks at the United Nations, and you're all of a sudden an expert in international affairs. You can't tell me about foreigners. I was dealing with foreigners before you were born."

"I know, Daddy," she said in despairing tones, and held the phone a little way from her ear while he went into his regulation speech about how he built his manufacturing company up from nothing at the start of World War II, him, just a small-time spare parts guy, making it into something colossal for his not even conceived yet much less born baby girl to inherit, something to grow into, in spite of the pressures of the early forties, in spite of cutthroat tactics from foreign competition until full war took them out of the picture. Him, Axel Bowman, all by himself, in Cleveland.

"Don't start telling me about foreigners," Bowman said. "I've been dealing with them since before you were born. There's nothing you can teach me about wops."

"Spics," Bo said into the phone, smiling.

"What?"

"Wops are Italians," Bo said. "Like dagos. The people today were spics."

There was a long silence. "When did you start talking like that, Luanna?"

"I never did," Bo said. "But if you're going to make noise like a bigot, I want you to use the right terminology."

"Don't you dare call me a bigot," Axel said. "I never even joined the country club."

"You should do what I did, Bo," Mary Kate said, when she got home that evening from class. "From the day I knew I wanted to be an actress in New York, I kept a scrapbook of every murder, rape, and sex crime in Cleveland. Especially Shaker Heights. The papers get much muckier when it's the better part of town. Anyway I had this big book just gorging with fiendish clippings, and the moment my parents opened their mouths about what happens to young girls in New York, I presented it to them."

"That wouldn't do any good with my father," Bo said. "He'd probably want to lock me in the bathroom."

"Some of the better sex abuses take place in bathrooms," Mary Kate said, and went in to shower.

Bo laughed as Mary Kate closed the door so her roommate would know the remark had been appreciated. But the truth of the matter was Mary Kate could afford to be contemptuous of parental over-concern, both emotionally and financially. Her money had been left to her in trust by an extremely wealthy grandfather. But there were no pictures of Bo's grandparents in the annals of Cleveland's important citizens. As Bo remembered them, vaguely, they had been tiny, frightened people, leaving no more an impression than they had a legacy. Her father's chronic protestations that he was "a self-made man" seemed to refer not only to his financial status but his biological origins, as though he had sprung, full grown, from the debris of the small parts industry.

Whether or not that was what he meant to imply, the fact was he had been a good parent to Bo. There was no doubt in her mind that she did love him, and wanted to give him as much pleasure and as little grief as possible in life. And if he hovered like an anxious hen around the head of his grown chick, Bo could be annoyed, but also understanding. Outright defiance of people who cared for you, no matter how extreme the degree, was not a part of her makeup.

Besides, working as a girl guide at the UN paid only eighty-five dollars a week, and she could hardly afford to live on the East Side of New York, even with a roommate, on that kind of money. Not that she was grasping, but as long as it gave Axel Bowman so much pleasure spending money on his daughter, it would be selfish and foolish of her to get herself cut off financially for the mere sake of rebellion.

At nine o'clock she called her father and apologized for being rude on the phone, promised him she would be extremely careful the following day and leave the premises immediately if there were any further signs of terrorist attacks on the UN. Then she had Mary Kate get on the line and tell Mr. Bowman that yes, Bo looked just fine, she'd never seen her in better shape, and no, there wasn't a sign of the slightest bit of damage inside or out.

"More's the pity," Mary Kate whispered, but Bo reached over and covered the mouthpiece with her hand in time to keep the words from going to Cleveland.

Early in the morning, there was an air of isolationism about the UN that cynics and political apologists found ironic and amusing. Partly it came from the hostile front that all modern metropolitan superstructures present in the cool light of dawn, unbroken by trees or fields or nature flowing free: all angles of the building were clean, all curves in complete balance, each surface of stone and cement and glass without the flaws that spelled history, or tradition long entrenched. Partly the feeling of coldness came from the emptiness around the UN buildings: the river behind, the Plaza on one side, the garden on the other—giving, with all its precision, an impression of barrenness, even in summer. But now, in winter, there was little to tell the early visitor without guidebook that this complex of buildings, as distinguished from the Seagram's Building on Park Avenue, or the Pan American Building above Grand Central Station, was the headquarters for most of the hopes and dreams of the world. One of the few clues to that complexity was the semicircle of poles that, in a few hours, would have raised upon their staffs the Flags of All Nations.

At seven-thirty A.M., the first day Security Police were admitted to the building by the night custodians; after changing into their uniforms, the security police would hoist the flags into place. By this time, traffic was beginning to move on First Avenue, and the city, like the United Nations, would begin to stir into action. At eight-thirty the delegates who were planning to speak in that day's session of the General Assembly would begin to arrive, studying their speeches in the empty council chambers.

By nine-fifteen the Plaza outside was humming with the day's visitors—reporters who were to cover that day's calendar in the General Assembly, students who had been following a particular crisis in the Security Council and had come early to ensure their getting a place in a limited visitors' gallery, or tourists in New York who were at the UN for the first time and were anxious to be off on their guided tours, impatient at discovering that the girl guides did not begin their rounds until ten o'clock.

The girls who worked as guides were as varied in hue and spirit as the Flags of All Nations, now mounted and streaming in the breeze off the East River. And like the eleven architects who had joined their creative abilities and personal talents on a committee to design the three buildings comprising the United Nations, the girls carried unique characteristics and individual style everywhere, behind the deceptively homogeneous façade.

As there had to be some semblance of order, the girls were put in uniforms—a little richer navy blue than worn by the Waves, a little less attractive in cut than sported by airline stewardesses. Skirts were the current knee-length, black leather pumps had a half-heel, not so much to minimize the shapeliness of calf as to accommodate the many hours of walking the girls had to do. It was not the wish of the Visitors Service to strip away evidence of different origins in race and custom; but neither did it want a world's fair of separate pavilions parading around in the guise of UN employees.

Once the girls had been minimally standardized, differences were allowed to flourish above and inside the uniform, just as special rooms and halls within the UN superstructure had been given over to separate architects. Breasts were allowed, and even encouraged, although they were, by and large, hardly stressed by the style of the jacket, and the white middy blouse beneath. A bachelor of arts degree or its equivalent was required: preference was given those girls who spoke at least three languages, two of them fluently, except in the cases of especially bright American girls, in whom conversational ability in two tongues was a rarity. Still, since applications were most numerous among American college graduates, they had the most difficult time being accepted. As no more than fifty or sixty girls were employed at one time, those who had the best chance of being accepted as guides besides those with unusual ability or political connections were girls from foreign lands who seemed most like Americans.

Not that it was the intention of the Visitors Service to stuff the girls into an acceptable American mold: part of their charm for visitors was the disparity of race, customs, and background. Nor did the office minimize sexuality: the morale of UN employees demanded some prurience, as evidenced by the popularity of the "Miss Carpool of the Month" feature in the *Secretariat News*. Which only went to prove, a former editor said, that no matter how high the seriousness of purpose, life, or more precisely sex, goes on.

The one other restriction had to do with coiffeur. No matter how beautiful or impressive hair was, it could not hang loose if it fell past the collar of the uniform. Guides with the most resplendent of manes had to pile them up or twist them, neatly, if the aura of respectability was to be maintained.

In the case of Ursull Hernan, a magnificent-looking Argentinian whose hair, blackly uncoiled, fell well below her waist, the restriction was a tragedy; not so much to Ursull, who seemed unaware of her personal splendor, but to Bo, who thought beauty of that caliber should be displayed, especially for sightseers. As for Bo's own hairdo, having the decision taken out of the realm of fashion dictates, or the whim of a current boyfriend and made into a rule, was a great relief for her. Bo considered herself highly expressive, although she was not always sure the expressiveness transmitted itself to her face. As a result, she had a habit of punctuating her conversations with her hair, tossing it for happiness and sheer animal high spirits, whipping it—staccato, sideways—for anxiety and eagerness, and jerking it downward to indicate sadness, confusion, etc. When it was cut short it fell all together and didn't get tangled with the many emotions. And pale copper bangs properly framed her best feature, deeply brown, richly responsive eyes. But loath to admit she had enough vanity to want the most flattering hairstyle, Bo found a rule simplified everything.

It was the reason she had always been able to give for major decisions: not staying out too late from the dormitory, refusing to sign out to a fake address on prom weekends, and not giving up her virginity. "It's against the rules," was all she would say, not wanting to admit she had anything like a personal preference.

The sudden disappearance of an undergraduate rulebook, coming with her diploma the previous June, had presented some minor problems over the summer in Cleveland. But she dealt with them, substituting variations on the theme, "Daddy would be furious." Still, at the age of twenty-one, the phrase began sounding a little hollow, even to her. So she was greatly relieved, on taking her job at the UN, to find that there were a number of fairly inflexible ordinances for the girls working as guides. They came in very handy, especially when dealing with those who did not work at the UN. The least of these, by her account, dictated her hairdo.

"Why don't you let it grow?" the young man had asked, reaching over and touching it with his hand, trying for an unwarranted intimacy in the back of a darkened Gatsby's. Her date was an attorney, and a mistake.

"It's such beautiful hair . . . Soft . . . soft as silk."

Good as gold, thought Bo. Black as pitch, cold as ice, clear as crystal, stiff as a board. Or, pitch-black, ice cold, crystal clear, bored stiff.

"It's against the rules," she said aloud, and tossing off his hand and the compliment with one gesture, she told him how it was also against the rules to be at work any later than nine-thirty in the morning, when the girls got their briefing on any questions that visitors might come up with that day. So she had better get home and go right to sleep.

And when, at her door, he asked her if he would be able to see her again, she smiled sadly, as if to imply that that, to, would be against the rules, what with the seriousness of the world situation, and her job. The young man was undoubtedly obtuse, as he seemed not to get the message, closing his eyes and zeroing in for her lips. She managed to turn her head at the very last moment, so he enjoyed only the briefest rapport with her earlobe.

"But . . ." he ventured.

"You're sweet," she said, patting him on the chin. "Sweet . . . as sugar." And scuttling inside the apartment, Bo closed the double latch behind her.

Her father was foolish to fear her leaving Cleveland. The whole world, if one was selective, was equipped with locks, and rules.

Ursull Hernan had about her an air of such subdued majesty that speculation had arisen among the girls, gossiping in the Guides' Lounge, that she was displaced royalty. Despite the thick black abundance of her hair, her skin was startlingly fair—almost white—so there was little possibility of her being an Inca princess; her cheekbones, although high, were not Slavic enough to qualify her as a runaway Romanoff; and, to the best of the girls' knowledge, Ursull had never attended any of the finishing schools in Switzerland for royalty, even oblique, in good standing. So the Guides' Lounge geneologists, lolling on the blue plastiscene sofas in between tours, decided that in all probability, she was the descendant of a long-ago liaison between a crowned conquistador and an Argentinian maiden.

Actually, it was one of their kinder speculations about those whose backgrounds were vague. Almost all the girl guides, European, African, and even Asian, had tried adopting at least that characteristic of their American co-workers that Birgitta, a twenty-four-year-old Swede, mockingly labeled "Instant History." Every American girl, Birgitta asserted, came equipped with an emergency kit containing a capsule, which, when added to Coca-Cola, burst into a full and complete life story.

In spite of the truth of the joke, there was something very winning about the candor of girls like Bo, about whom everything there was to know was known. And although such forthrightness was literally foreign to most of the girls, they tried, in that aspect at least, to become more like the Americans. For most, it was difficult, and for some it was impossible. Ursull Hernan had never felt at ease discussing her background, her family, even her schools, where she had been taught, among other things, that to talk about yourself in polite society was distinctly impolite.

So in the presence of one of these "cow" sessions, Ursull would excuse herself and volunteer to take out an extra tour, for Birgitta, who was feeling languorous, or Kiiko, whose tiny feet were hurting, Hillary who never tired of "dishing," or Marie Claire, who was always getting caught in autobiographical lies but was nevertheless most willing to talk about herself. Ursull's departure was never taken as a rebuff.

"She's very aloof," Bo would say, more praise than censure in the explanation.

Others who hesitated to discuss their backgrounds did not fare so well among the girls. Rehahnee, who cleverly avoided being stuffed into the rather sexless navy blue guide's uniform by pointing out to the guide supervisor that visitors to the UN would enjoy being shown about by a girl in a sari, and dodged minimum makeup rule by attributing her heavily kohled eyes, beaded lashes and jeweled nose to religious traditions, characterized her silence about herself as Asiatic diffidence. But as the other Indian and two Pakistanis did not veil themselves in mystery, and since Rehahnee earned the same eighty-five dollars a week as the others but maintained residence in a five-hundred-dollar-a-month apartment-hotel, the girls figured she was involved in something unsavory. For a while they had given her the benefit of a half-doubt: she was perhaps a kept woman. But as Birgitta had cleverly pointed out, any man keeping somebody wouldn't want her working around a place where she could constantly seek out so many other men. So the tacit assumption, now, was that Rehahnee was a hooker.

But the wish to conceal something was not considered the cause of Ursull's reticence: shy majesty, Bo called it, when Ursull made her usual flight from the dormitorylike camaraderie. This particular morning, however, escape was not so easy. Having already conducted two foreign-language tours, Ursull, legs up on a plastic coffee table, her head resting on the back of the leatherette settee, opened her eyes to find herself physically in the midst of an amiable argument between Bo and Birgitta.

"But you are a grown woman," Birgitta said, from the couch on Ursull's right. "How can you allow him to treat you as a child?"

"That's how American parents are," Bo insisted, at Ursull's left elbow. "You can't expect them to be as liberal as Swedes."

"My parents are extremely conservative." Birgitta chewed on a strand of blond hair she had worked loose from the sleekly coiled twist. "It is my unwillingness to indulge their conservatism that forces them to think liberally. So they mature, and I mature, and then we can trust each other as mature adults."

"You can't put down my father for worrying when a bomb goes off. He's overprotective."

"Because you let him be," Birgitta said. "You want to be overprotected but you're ashamed to admit it. So you let him overprotect you."

Ursull glanced hopefully over at the supervisor's office. Pauline, the older woman in charge, was instructing the new Italian guide to shave her legs in deference to American grooming taste. Her legs would be seen by many tourists. What she did under her arms was her own business.

There was no sign that Pauline was going to hurry any of them out on another tour. Ursull closed her eyes, and feigned exhaustion.

"It's been that way ever since I can remember," Bo insisted. "If I so much as crossed the street by myself when I was small, they had a breakdown. It got so that the first time I tried—and the light turned red—I felt paralyzed. It was like my father or mother, holding my hand, kept the light green."

"You prove my point," Birgitta said. "The special wonder of Americans. They argue and argue, and if you let them talk long enough, they prove your point for you."

The signal sounded for another guide on the main floor. Ursull anxiously jumped to her feet, but the Italian girl, newly fortified with grooming tips, was already out the door. Ursull saw Bo and Birgitta looking up at her. There was no longer any way to pretend she was asleep.

"Well?" Birgitta said.

"I beg your pardon?"

"What do you think?"

"I'm sorry," Ursull said. "About what?"

"Weren't you listening?" asked Bo.

"It wasn't my conversation," Ursull said.

"Birgitta said that education was more important in Sweden than protecting the daughter, and that parents sent daughters where they would learn most."

"Yes?" Ursull said.

"And I said that was fine for Sweden, but most American families didn't think that way. And then she said that wasn't particularly the Swedish attitude, it was the attitude of all the better classes in Europe —England, even South America. What's your opinion?"

"If education is important to the family, I would imagine Birgitta is right."

"Are your parents very old-guard South American?" Bo asked.

"They have pride in education, if that's what you mean."

"Well that wasn't exactly . . ."

"You, Bo," Ursull said. "Where did you go to school?"

"Miami University."

"That is not so near to Cleveland." Ursull smiled.

"This Miami University is in Oxford, Ohio," Bo said. "They wouldn't have dreamed of letting me get as far away as Florida. Anyway, then Daddy couldn't have driven down every weekend with extra blankets in case it got cold."

Ursull laughed. "Excuse me." She pulled her jacket down over her hips and started to climb over Bo's outstretched legs.

"Why are you going?" Bo said. "We only just started to talk."

"Another tour."

"You just came back," Bo protested, lowering her legs so Ursull could get through.

"They're expecting a lot of foreign-language visitors this morning. I'll see you later."

"Damn," Bo said, after Ursull had gone. "For one mad moment there I thought I was going to get a piece of personal information out of her."

"Why is it so important?" Birgitta said.

"How can you begin to know people unless you know *about* them? I really like Ursull, I consider her a good friend, but I'm not even sure she likes me."

"Of course she likes you."

"Did she tell you?"

"People don't have to tell people everything," Birgitta said. "She likes you."

"Then why doesn't she talk about her family, and her schools, and . . ."

"There are people who don't enjoy talking about themselves."

"That's silly," Bo said. "I mean, here we all are in the catbird's seat. We have a chance to learn to know each other, and through each other the whole world, in a way . . ."

"In a very particular way . . ."

Bo went on, unhearing. "But how can we begin to know the world unless we really understand each other, each other's attitudes and feelings? And how can we do that unless we really talk to each other?"

Birgitta smiled. "They who can, experience; they who can't, talk."

"You think I talk about myself too much?"

"No. No, Bo, I don't think that at all. I enjoy you."

"But?"

"But . . ." Birgitta tucked the renegade lock back into the twist behind her head, and smiled. "I can't help thinking that if there were something a little more interesting going on in your life, you wouldn't be quite so eager to talk about it."

The main floor tour area seemed much more congested with people than on an ordinary weekday morning. Besides the standard assortment of schoolchildren whose teachers were trying to herd them together, there was an unusual number of tourists and sightseers waiting around for their group number to be called. It occurred to Ursull that the surplus might be security officers in street clothes mingling with the crowd to assure themselves that there would be no repetition of the previous day's violence. But then again, she realized it might be that very bomb scare that had brought out such a number of curiosity seekers. It seemed paradoxical that the majority of the onlookers were making their first visit to the UN, drawn by the very violence it existed to guard against.

Ursull made her way across the terrazoed floor toward the Dispatcher's Desk, when a group of children, being informed by their teacher they would be eating lunch first, burst gleefully out of control, screaming "Coffee shop, coffee shop!" In order to avoid being physically caught in their lunchtime enthusiasm, Ursull stepped back toward the line of people waiting to buy tickets for the tour. When the children had passed, told firmly by their harassed teacher that they should hold hands and stay together or there would be no dessert, Ursull tried to make her way forward in the line.

"You'll wait your turn like everyone else," said a lady in front of her, without turning to look.

The line had re-formed behind Ursull, so rather than make her apologies all along the way she decided to wait her turn, and be passed by the checker.

A man with a camera strap pulling against the red back of his neck shouted impatiently, and turned to his wife in disgust. "Damned nonsense," he said. "Come all the way here from Illinois."

He pronounced it with the final "s," Ursull noticed, like "noise." That meant either that he was a native of the state or illiterate. She would have to ask one of the American girls, phrasing it carefully so it wouldn't seem insulting.

"Stand in line like it was some damn Radio City Music Hall . . ."

"Well, I told you I'd rather go there, Henry," his wife said. "But you will have your own way."

"I didn't feel like standing in line," Henry said.

"What do you think this is?"

"I know damn well what it is, Emma." The back of Henry's neck got redder. "All I can say is they better have a pretty good show, make a man stand in line and pay a dollar."

"I wanted to see Cary Grant," Emma said.

"The more I think about it, the madder I get," said Henry, the back of his neck bearing him out. "Make a man stand in line and pay a dollar, for God's sake. If those Ruskies would cough up their dues, then Americans could get in here for nothing, the way they ought to."

The line was moving more rapidly toward the cashier. Henry turned slightly and caught sight of Ursull, watching him. "Oh, are you . . . are you Russian?"

"No," said Ursull.

Henry looked relieved.

"But wouldn't you have been embarrassed if I were? Excuse me." She pressed her way gently through the remaining people in front of the cashier.

"What are you doing in line?" the cashier said.

"Public relations," Ursull said, and passed through, leaning back over the rope to the couple from Illi*noise*. "By the way, even if the Russians did pay their dues, you'd still be charged. This money goes toward the salary of the guides. And the tours are not part of the assessments. I'd like them to pay, too, but that wouldn't save your dollar. Enjoy your visit," she said, and smiled.

At the tour desk Elena, a Belgian girl acting for the first time that week as dispatcher, placidly announced the number of the next group leaving. People rose from the benches and moved toward the glass doors. Elena covered the microphone and the placidity left her voice as she turned to Ursull.

"Thank heaven, am I glad to see you. I had a special tour booked at 11:15—a group of German industrialists—you know how prompt they are, and at the last minute I forgot, and sent Renata out on a regular tour. She should have been back by now, but she's always slower in English. Do you mind taking them?"

"Of course not," Ursull said. "Where are they?"

"The group in the corner. The ones that look so annoyed at being kept waiting."

Ursull smiled and went to the center of the floor, toward the low double-doors leading to the entranceway. The voice of Elena ricocheted from the loudspeaker across the ceilings as she announced the departure of the German-speaking tour No. 40. The group on the benches in the far corner arose, and made their way toward the doorway like passengers at an airfield.

There were about twelve of them in all, and Ursull waited inside the glass doors as Charlene collected their tickets and introduced them to Miss Hernan. Once they were quiet, Ursull smiled and introduced herself again, in German.

"Guten Morgen, meinen Herren," she said, giving her name, dwelling lingeringly on the "Ursull," so they would feel at home with the rich Germanness of it and not be put off by the nameplate on her left breast pocket, which read only U. HERNAN. Most of the men she judged to be in their late thirties and early forties, with the exception of one who seemed considerably younger than the rest, a strikingly handsome, tall lean blond, who was watching her intently with yellow-gray eyes.

Ursull had never been particularly impressed by blond men; there was something vaguely effete about them. But the structure of this young man's face was so strong there could not be construed even the vaguest hint of femininity. She left the fine structure of his cheekbones for the scale model of the United Nations she was now pointing out to them, and set out on her tour.

"You will notice," she began, "the fine flow of the architecture. . . ." She looked up and saw him nodding rapidly, his eyes watching her face, and nowhere near the place where her fingers trailed. She could feel the redness rising to her cheeks, and continued with the speech, to which, she thought, she had best devote her attention. It was very difficult moving serenely along the terrazoed corridors. The eyes of the young man stayed always on her, even as she urged her group to look at the fine rug, hung like tapestry on the wall, donated by Iran, and the mural which depicted war, the horrors of the past, and the hope for the future, free from disaster, that the Spanish artist, fled to the Dominican Republic, saw the UN symbolizing.

She fixed her glance on the oldest, least attractive member of the group, directing her speeches almost exclusively to him, to keep from looking at the young man. But as she moved down the hall pointing out through the glass window the peace bell donated by Japan, composed of melted coins of 60 countries, she knew that he was beside her, and dared not look to her right.

"And how long have you been in the United States?" she inquired in German of the ugly man at her left. She asked it with great warmth. The young man need not on any account think that she was coldly Prussian in nature: he should be aware only that he was greatly embarrassing her. A visitor to the UN, she wanted very much for him to understand, should not stare at a guide as if she were a half-naked chorine in a Broadway play. Especially when the girl wanted very much to look at him in the same manner, but was far too well brought up to do so.

The ugly man was telling her most of them had been in New York for almost a year, and she smiled at him as if that was the most enchanting thing she had ever heard.

"We are all of us industrialists," the man was going on, unleashed by her obvious eagerness to know everything about him. "I myself am with a very important company."

"And the others?" she asked.

"More or less." The man shrugged off his compatriots.

"And what do you do here?" She had been foolish to ask. He began telling her in great detail of their program of study of American business techniques. She was greatly relieved when they finally reached the temporarily deserted chambers of the Security Council.

"Of course you know," Ursull motioned them to seats in the gallery, "that the Security Council meets usually at the request of a nation or a committee or in emergency situations, when there is an active threat to the peace."

Ursull looked up as a second group of tourists entered the chambers, conducted by Rehahnee, clad this morning in a sari of crimson and gold. The blouse beneath was pale pink silk, with a bare midriff, open at the throat, and, it appeared, the bosom as well. "I will now explain to you the function of the Security Council," Rehahnee said, in her overprecise English, grasping the rail behind with both arms, so her breasts strained against what little material concealed them. In meticulous diction Rehahnee began belting them with the briefest possible summary. Her information was so clipped and her body so embarrassingly full, that few ever thought of protesting when her tours would come to an abrupt end after as little as thirty-five minutes. Most of the tours lasted anywhere from forty-five minutes to an hour, depending on how alert and interested the group was. But few if any of Rehahnee's visitors bothered her with questions, not wanting to look at her any more directly than necessary. She leaned back against the balustrade, the jewel in her nose glittering, looking like a semipornographic illustration for *India Love Lyrics*. It was clearly going to be a whirlwind tour.

Ursull had no objections to the girls who would occasionally speak of "whipping" a group through because of tired feet, or an important appointment, or just general exhaustion. But it did strike her as unfortunate that the world's most important organization should be made consistently uninteresting, and dismissed so quickly, merely because a guide wanted to have more time in between tours to appraise the men in the delegates' lounge.

"I would assume that tells you everything about the Security Council you need to know," Rehahnee said, having told them little or nothing.

Throughout Rehahnee's shorthand discourse Ursull had been making her own explanation in German. She was never discomfited by the speeches of one or several other guides going on at the same time. For a few weeks she had worked as simultaneous translator in a booth with four other girls speaking different dialects including Chinese, and she had learned to shut out everything but stupidity.

"So in the temporary and welcome absence of a Suez or Cuban or Congo crisis," Ursull continued, "anything which resembles—much as we do not like to use the term—a warlike situation, the Security Council is not meeting today. And as grateful as we are for its existence, we are relieved that it is not in session."

She stopped briefly as the other group rustled to their feet and snapped pictures of the room, as Rehahnee urged them not to dawdle. Ursull noticed the couple from Illinois. It was sad, she thought, with all they could have learned, that they had ended up on Rehahnee's tour.

"By the way," Ursull said, switching to English, and raising her voice so Henry and Emma might hear her. "According to the UN charter, the Security Council is the only organ empowered to send forces into a troubled area. As I am sure you all know, the Soviet is in arrears for payment to the peacekeeping forces, because they claim that since the UN forces were sent to the Congo, Sinai, and Cyprus by the General Assembly and *not* by the Security Council, sending them was illegal—a violation of the UN charter. Whether or not this is so has got to be decided. The important thing is"—she saw that Henry and Emma had paused at the top of the aisle—"*not* to become confused. The Soviet has paid its membership fees to the United Nations. What they owe is money for the peacekeeping forces. But they *have* paid the rest of their dues. I'm sure you were all aware of this, but I just wanted to review it for you so you didn't get confused."

Directing her attention back to the businessmen in front of her, Ursull noticed a slightly perplexed look on some faces. "Excuse me," she said, recapping briefly in German what she had said. And then, drawing her explanation to a close, she threw the floor open to questions.

The lectures she addressed her groups were usually so complete and comprehensive there was little room for confusion on the part of her listeners. So it rather surprised her to see the hand in the back row.

"Yes?" Ursull said.

It was the very beautiful young man. "How many permanent members are there again, and how many temporary?"

She had deliberately told them that, twice. The young man could not be that stupid. He was much too intelligent-looking to be that stupid.

And then she realized. From his grin, he had asked the question merely to force her to look directly at him. His eyes were more yellow now than gray as he smiled at her obvious embarrassment. His teeth were disgustingly even and white. Perfect teeth in a man she considered as uninteresting and without character as blond hair. It was ridiculous that any man combining so many traits she considered unappealing should be so attractive.

"There are five permanent members," she said coldly. "And six temporary members. Eleven in all."

"I see," he said, smiling even wider.

"Are you sure?" she said. "Perhaps I could say it again for you if you find it too difficult."

"No, I think I can remember it now."

"Good," Ursull said, ashamed at having shown her annoyance. She took refuge in smiling at the ugly man, and was rewarded by a grateful smile that repelled her completely. "If there are no more questions, we will go on."

Leading her group to the shortcut through the stairwell Ursull collided with Kiiko Hana, a distraught expression on her usually serene little face.

"You're going the wrong way," Ursull said.

"Oh no." Kiiko lowered her voice even more than her usual near-whisper. "I get so mixed up trying to remember not to forget to show the Trusteeship Council, I forget to show the Economic and Social." Kiiko shook her head. "You won't tell anyone?"

"Of course not." Ursull smiled, waved her group forward. "Come this way, please."

"How could she forget the Economic and Social?" The blond was beside her again. "Didn't you say it was among the most important?"

"I did." He was so close to her as they walked that she could smell his cologne. She didn't like cologne on men, especially as sweet as the scent he carried, and was no less annoyed by the fact that, like everything else, it was good on him. Almost, if one had not such a splendid sense of control—exciting.

"That was, I believe, the room where the pipes and all the fixtures on the ceiling are left showing and utilized as a part of the room's décor, by the Swedish architect."

"You remember very well," Ursull said.

"You said he had been severely cirticized, but it was a question of personal taste, and you for one found the acoustics the best in the building."

"You have an amazing memory," Ursull said. "Curious that you found it so difficult to retain the number of permanent members."

"Perhaps that is because you were obviously so much more excited by the Economic and Social Council."

"The Security Council is as important, if not more."

"Perhaps," he said. "But you are obviously more excited by the possibilities of peace than the possibilities of war, so it is not as important to you. So not to me either."

He was smiling again. Besides everything else, he had a cleft in his chin. The man was impossible. "If you would be good enough to take your place with the rest of the group, perhaps you won't mind my giving them the tour as well?"

"But you haven't answered my question."

"There are five permanent members."

"Very good," he said, smiling his approbation, "but I meant what I asked you before."

"What?"

"How could she forget to show the Economic and Social Council, when it is so very important to you and me?" His eyes were even brighter now, as if mirth took the gray out of them, leaving nothing but the dark gold.

It was obvious he could tell exactly the effect he was having on her, shifting his shoulders beneath the light tweed jacket so that she could almost see the texture of his muscles. He was thoroughly enjoying her discomfort. If there was one thing she despised more than a physically perfect blond man, it was a man who was completely sure of himself. But she was, after all, on duty, and it was her duty to explain. "The Trusteeship Council was closed for redecoration, and has only been reopened a short time. It is easy to forget to show it again. A special effort to remember one thing sometimes makes you forget something you know as well as your own name."

"Ursull . . ." he said slowly.

She turned and made her way down the steps.

"She must not be very bright," he said. "At least, not as bright as you."

"She happens to be an extremely clever girl." She could feel the color rising to her white cheeks again, she hated him so, and hoped that he would not notice and mistake it for something else.

"She is Chinese?"

"Japanese," said Ursull.

"And you, of course, are German."

"Of course not," Ursull said.

Disappointment shadowed the gray back into his eyes. He was so obviously subdued and saddened by the discovery that she was not a German that for the remainder of the tour he stood quietly and did not look at her. By the time they were at their next to last stopping place she considered that perhaps he was not such an impossible young man after all, but had merely been showing off in some imagined camaraderie to a girl he took to be a countrywoman. Confusion was becoming to him, much more so than smug perfection. As his eyes traced the path of the perpetual motion pendulum hanging from the ceiling, she allowed a note of warmth to enter her voice along with the information that it had been donated by Queen Juliana.

"Any questions?" she said, almost hoping that he would look at her, with some inane inquiry. But he was silent.

"Then if you will come this way," she said, leading them toward the elevators.

He hung back, still watching the movement of the great magnetic ball.

"Please," she said, a smile there for him to see if he decided to look at her. "Come this way."

"There is a magnet in the base?" he said, frowning a little against the sunlight reflected from the river beyond the windows.

"Yes," she said.

"Then it is not in fact truly perpetual motion."

"I suppose not," she said. "Are you an engineer?"

"I have studied engineering," he said.

"The elevator . . ."

The other eleven men had entered before them, and there was room for only one more.

"You go ahead," she said to him. "I will take the next elevator and meet the group downstairs."

Just before the doors closed the ugly man stepped out of the elevator, foraging through his pockets as though he were looking for something. The doors closed behind him, and they were alone.

"Did you forget something?" Ursull said.

He smiled at her, gap-toothed. "Only the opportunity to speak to you of other matters."

"Excuse me?"

"I was wondering what you do with your time when you are not giving these exceptional tours?" He was buttoning and unbuttoning his vest, in small pale-fingered nervousness.

"I would imagine what most girls do who live in New York."

"So I would hope," he said, buttoning.

He was even more unattractive than she had observed before, and obviously stupid in the bargain. Apparently he had mistaken her seeming interest for actual interest. The boredom that was now so clear on her face had no effect on him. He was insisting they should spend time together, get to know each other better, could they not in fact have dinner together that night, he would wait for her outside the UN. Ursull had no wish to insult or embarrass him, but he was becoming annoying.

"Ah, Ernie!" she said, with much obvious delight to a passing man. "How wonderful to see you!" She spoke with a good deal more enthusiasm than she normally showed anyone, especially Ernie, whom she had known for months but had never gone out of her way to greet. And Ernie, being apparently far more subtle of mind than the German, took the greeting for what it was meant to be and fell in at once beside her, waiting, with the two of them, for the elevator.

"Ernie works with us at the UN," Ursull said.

"You work here?" the German man said, obviously annoyed at the intrusion.

"Yes," Ernie said.

"Are you a delegate?" Ernie shook his head.

"You have no uniform."

"That's part of the job," Ernie said, flicking his tongue dryly, looking up at the arrow indicator for the elevator. "I'm with the Security Police. A lot of the time we work in plainclothes, just to keep an eye out for the girls."

"I see," said the German, whose mouth seemed to have gone as dry as Ernie's.

"I'm sure you do," Ernie said, and smiled.

The red arrow lit up above their heads.

"Not that we expect any trouble," Ernie said. "But you never can tell when some disturbed person will mistake politeness for something else."

The door to the elevator opened.

"You want me to go downstairs with you?" Ernie said.

"No." Ursull smiled. "I'm sure everything will be fine now."

"I'm sure it will, too," Ernie said, nodding his head deferentially to the German, who stepped into the corner of the elevator farthest from Ursull.

Downstairs, in the basement by the elevator, the group was waiting for her. Ursull greeted them like long-lost friends, apologizing for the time lost in elevator-waiting, and then pointed out the souvenir shops, the Dag Hammarskjöld Memorial counter at which they could buy mementos, the UN stamp which could be mailed only from inside the UN, and the coffee shop.

"This will conclude our tour," Ursull said. "I hope you have enjoyed it."

The blond young man was looking away, and she was beginning to be as annoyed with him for ignoring her now as she had been at the attention he had previously paid her. It was one thing for him to be disappointed at her not being German: for him to be offended by it was ridiculous. She lingered for one last moment, trying to give him an opportunity to speak. But he made no move forward, gave no glance in her direction, no indication that he wished to make it a more personal farewell.

"Good-bye," she said, turning quickly so she could not glimpse the last-minute regret that might show in his face, if he were not so obviously stubborn. Pigheadedness in a beautiful blond man who was so sure of himself that he could not take even a slight disappointment was intolerable. She was better off not even knowing who he was.

"I am Gerd Kraben," he said, falling in with her quick step, directly beside her

"Yes?" Now it was she who did not look up.

"I wanted to introduce myself to you."

"And so you have," she said. They were in front of the doorway marked with the legend, *Visitors must not go beyond this point.*

"You do not recognize the name?" He seemed more hopeful than assured.

"Should I?"

"Kraben Chemicals," he said, formally presenting a verbal calling card.

"Ah yes, I think I have heard of it," Ursull said.

"It is the most important manufacturing company in Germany." It was a fact he stated, not proudly, just a fact. "A German would have known the name at once."

"But I told you I wasn't German."

"I didn't believe you."

"Why should I lie?"

"Not lie." Gerd shrugged. "I thought . . . possibly . . . I thought possibly you were—what do you say here—testing? . . . No, teasing, that is it, teasing me."

"Why should I want to do that?" Ursull said.

"I don't know."

He was not at all sure of himself anymore. She would have very much liked to relieve him of his discomfort, but it was not, apparently, in either of their natures to yield too easily.

"I thought perhaps . . ." His eyebrows, furrowed, were strangely dark above the pale gray eyes. "I thought if you recognized the name, I would catch you."

"At what?"

"I have never heard anyone speak more perfect German. I was sure you were from Germany."

"But I told you I was not," Ursull said. She was becoming impatient with him again. She wished that he would smile, or ask her a question that would permit her to smile. Anything but this labored lingering on nationalities.

"Well," she said, annoyed with herself as well as him, "we can't all be German, can we?"

Then she went inside.

She stood for a moment, just beyond the doorway, hoping he was not as cautious as she feared him to be, wishing there was in his nature enough spontaneity to fly in the door after her. But he was a German, and could no more move in the face of that militant warning—*Visitors must not go beyond this point*—than he could breathe.

It was a shame, Ursull mused, and then, deciding to dismiss him from her mind, went past the series of open cubicles in which earnest secretaries typed their correspondence, back to the Guides' Lounge.

Most of the girls were either giving a tour or out for lunch: the room was almost deserted, a random heap of out-of-place sofa cushions, piled to accommodate weary heads or nestle under tired toes, discarded copies of various UN publications, Coke bottles, coffee containers, a few half-open pocketbooks slung aside. Disorder in their personal surroundings, Ursull had noted, was something all the girls picked up quite easily from their American sisters. Even Kiiko, meticulous little Kiiko, was piled in a haphazard clump on the far sofa, her skirt well above her wonderfully round knees, the wax wrapping that had covered her sandwich thrown carelessly on the floor.

"You look so tired," Ursull said.

Kiiko looked up without moving her head. "I can't move." The hand that held the sandwich moved automatically up over her chest and to her mouth as she bit off a piece of bread and chewed, trance-like. "I have done only two tours and I feel like it is five o'clock."

"Maybe you ought to eat a proper lunch," Ursull suggested.

"I could not walk to the cafeteria," Kiiko said wanly.

"Are you sure? I'm going. Come with me."

"I can't," Kiiko said, moving her head wearily. "I would like to, but I could never make it."

"Still, if you had something warm to eat . . ."

Kiiko sighed. "My mother said I would never be able to work. She was right."

"I ran into your friend Ernie on my tour."

"Did he bother you?" Kiiko said.

"Oh no, on the contrary. He helped me get rid of a tourist who was becoming a little too friendly."

"Oh, I am so pleased for him," Kiiko said, a smile playing on her lips. "He is always so busy lurking around my tours, afraid that someone is a molester . . . it's nice that he finally managed to find one." Kiiko's English was still far from perfect, and she spoke slowly, trying to avoid the typical Japanese mispronunciation of English words. It was inevitable, and part of her charm, that she seemed to choose precisely those words that stressed her linguistic shortcomings. Visitors were sometimes baffled, then amused, to hear her constant references, over the scale-model representation of the UN, to "those beauties," thinking she had chosen some slang American way of expressing her approval of the organization and its architecture. It was usually not until the third quarter of the tour, when she asked them to please step this way to "the beauty" that housed the General Assembly, that they realized she was speaking of buildings.

Almost all people who had gone on one of Kiiko's tours were delighted by her: everything about the girl was appealing. She stood no more than four feet eight inches tall, a fact she had thought for a long time she could conceal by making herself a foot and a half taller with hair. For the first six months she had worked at the UN, her long black hair had been piled in an elaborate beehive on top of her head. One of the girls had finally told her that, if anything, the height of her hairdo emphasized her shortness; and the next day, she had appeared with soft black hair cut straight across the bottom, down to her neck. Everybody complimented her extravagantly, especially Ernie, who said she looked even tinier and more fragile and in need of his even greater protection.

"Maybe now that he's saved you from a fate worse than death," Kiiko said, "he will get a new fixation and begin following your tours."

"I don't think so. He is completely loyal to you."

"I don't mind," Kiiko said, a smile glimmering her dark eyes. "He is so funny."

"You really do like him. I thought so," Ursull said. Kiiko was always protesting Ernie's attentions to her, but never in a voice louder than a whisper, and not to anyone who might tell the supervisor. Ernie's obvious crush on Kiiko was a source of much amusement to the girls, but Ursull did not laugh with them. It was her feeling that Kiiko, for all her whispered protests, shared his feeling.

"Of course I like him," Kiiko said. "I like him very much. It is a shame he isn't younger and prettier."

"Why?"

"Then maybe I could like him more."

"I like men to be more mature," said Ursull.

"Ernie is not mature, he is only older."

Ursull smiled. "Perhaps you like him more than you think."

"The inscrutable Oriental?" Kiiko raised her sparse eyebrows. "We are not inscrutable to ourselves."

Ursull smiled. "Are you sure you don't want lunch?"

"Thank you," Kiiko said. "But my feet also are not inscrutable. They tell me how they feel, all the time."

Ursull got up and started to walk out of the lounge. She was vaguely sorry that none of the other girls were around, and Kiiko was tired. For some reason she felt like having company while she ate lunch, and that was rare for her. Lunch, like everything else she did in New York, was a serious business to be done for its own sake. Food was to be taken slowly, seriously and solitarily, like facts. Ursull had never been one to go in for communal studying: pre-examination preparation had to be done alone to be absorbed, and she supposed it was the same with eating. She did not disapprove of the orgy of sociability with which most Americans surrounded their noon hours. But lunches which lay light on the belly, and shading the afternoon in a martini haze, were foreign, not so much to her nationality, as to her nature. When the day was over, when it was time for dinner, that was occasion for affability and wine. She had not had very much of either since coming to New York, but that was all right too—she was here strictly as part of her regimen.

Today, though, she felt she might enjoy looking up from the dish at someone. It was a shame there was nobody around.

What surprised her as she came out into the basement promenade was not that Gerd Kraben was still there, but that she hadn't expected he would be.

"But if you are not German, then what are you?" He did not even smile, or wait to see if she was alone.

"Have you been waiting here all this time?"

"I could not go in, the sign said. I thought eventually you would come out."

"That was very clever of you."

"If I was so clever, you would never have gone inside."

"And you waited all this time?"

"It was not so long."

"It was long enough." Ursull smiled. "You waited all this time for me?"

"Yes."

"Well then I think you might begin by saying hello."

He started to smile, and then thought better of it. "You are beginning another lecture tour?"

"No." Ursull shook her head. "But this is a very casual country, and unless you want me to think I am very important to you, you should try to seem casual."

Now he smiled. "Very good, I like that. Hello."

"Hello," Ursull said. "Now. Was there something you wanted to know?"

"Oh yes." He tried to stand easy, matching the air of his country-style jacket, but ease did not sit as well on him as his clothes. "What country are you from?"

"Argentina."

"But that is impossible." It was not disappointment. It was a statement of fact. "I have never heard more beautiful German spoken by anyone. If you were not German, how could you speak like that?"

"Perhaps I am very brilliant. Perhaps I have a magnificent ear for language."

"I have considered all those possibilities, and even accepted them. I think yes, you are brilliant, and you have magnificent ears . . ."

"Ear . . ."

"That too. Even so, you could not speak like that, unless you were German."

"You insist?"

"I insist. I am a stubborn man. If you continue to say no, I will have to *make* you German so I can prove myself right."

"How could you make me German?" Ursull said.

"Marry you." The smile was gone now, and he was looking at her solemnly, but the yellow glint of laughter was still in his eyes.

"Well, must we get married right away?" Ursull smiled up at him. "Or can we have lunch first?"

He clapped his hands like a little boy, and cried Bravo and Wunderschön. Then clasping her tightly under the arm, he let her lead him to the cafeteria.

"God, I can't believe how you eat," Bo said, picking listlessly at her salad as Birgitta finished off another portion of stew.

Birgitta swiped at some runaway gravy with the corner of her hard roll, pushed it into her mouth. "You see it. It should be easy to believe."

"I don't mean that. I mean how can you eat a lunch like that every day? I could no more put away such a big lunch . . ." She looked under a lettuce leaf, and wrinkled her nose in displeasure as she unearthed a grapefruit section.

"Perhaps," Birgitta said, "if you would order something you liked, you could manage to eat more."

"I wouldn't dare," Bo said. "I'd weigh four hundred pounds."

Birgitta thought about that for a minute, and then went back to eating.

Bo narrowed her eyes speculatively. "When you eat, do you feel as though you're feeding some inner hunger, or . . ."

"Yes," Birgitta said. "A great inner hunger."

Bo's eyes were shining, and she leaned forward, listening intently.

"It is called appetite," Birgitta said, and laughed.

"Oh."

The sun danced coldly on the East River, and rays bounced up through the window and mingled with Birgitta's pale yellow hair, and with her laughter. "I am so sorry, Bo. I wish my eating habits could tell you more about me. I know how it disappoints you, my being so simple."

"You're not simple," Bo said. "No one is simple. Especially you."

"Whatever can we do about Birgitta?" Birgitta said. "She is such a big healthy girl. She eats, she sleeps, she enjoys! Surely something must be wrong with her."

"She just has great gusto, that's all."

"I'm not so sure." Birgitta looked around surreptitiously, lowering her voice. "I've heard it said she has lust for life."

"So?"

Birgitta shook her head. "It has to end badly. Keep an eye on her left ear."

Bo laughed, and then leaned back in her chair, lighting a cigarette.

In the middle of the cafeteria, she saw Ursull carrying a tray, looking around for an empty table. She started to wave to her, then saw the man. "Don't look now . . ."

"Where?"

"Over by the cashier. Ursull. And she's with a man."

"He is as beautiful as she is," Birgitta said. "How nice."

"Do you suppose he's a relative?"

"I hope not."

"He's pulling out a chair for her. In a cafeteria. Can you imagine anything so *gallant?*"

Birgitta shrugged. If she could, she didn't seem to care to express it.

"Well, let's hope he's exciting," Bo said earnestly, forcing herself to look away from the couple. "I think it's time Ursull had a romance. She's been in America almost a year."

"She's here to perfect her English," Birgitta said. "And to learn something."

"Well, we're all here to learn something. That doesn't mean we can't have a life on the side." Bo looked up nervously, remembering that Birgitta had mocked her, before, for using that exact phrase. Life, Birgitta said, was not something you had on the side. It was first and while and during, and everything else might be on the side, but life wasn't. But apparently she hadn't noticed her slip.

Still there was no harm in getting Birgitta on another track. "How's Olaf?"

"He is Olaf," Birgitta said, chewing. "He doesn't become more interesting or less."

"You sound bored with him."

"That is probably because I am bored with him," Birgitta said. "Olaf is going through a very boring period. He studies, he moans, he writes his family. Perhaps when he gets his degree and goes home to Stockholm and becomes an engineer he will become more or less, but right now he is the same."

"When is he going home?"

"June, I suppose. After his final examinations."

"Aren't you . . . aren't you going with him?"

Birgitta stopped chewing. "What for? I find him boring in my own apartment. Why should I go all the way to Sweden?"

The fact that Birgitta and Olaf were living together was no longer a source of shock or even mild amazement to Bo. True, when she had first learned that Birgitta and her nice clean-cut Swede were living together she was mildly scandalized. Birgitta had been the first girl Bo had known, personally, who was living with a man; but she supposed all that would change as she met more New Yorkers.

Birgitta had set her straight about the living-together business. The time came when men and women slept together, even in America, so separate beds was conspicuous waste. Especially in separate apartments. It was profligate of a young couple to maintain two residences, and a false sense of morality was no excuse for wasting money on rent paid only for the sake of appearances. Besides, the really dirty part was one of them having to get up from a nice warm bed to go home.

If Bo had not quite accepted Birgitta's way of thinking, she could at least understand her point. Though Bo could hardly imagine herself sporting carnivorously on the unconnubial bed, if Birgitta was going to, Bo supposed there was no additional harm in its being in the man's apartment. But this was something else again—this talk of deadly boredom with a man you were living with. It was all Bo could do to keep from asking.

"I have to ask you," she said, losing the struggle. "How can you speak so disinterestedly of a man you're living with?"

"You mean if we were married it would be okay, being tired of him?"

"I didn't mean that at all. If you're so bored, why don't you move out?"

"It's my apartment." Birgitta allowed herself to smile.

"Then why don't you make him move out?"

"Why?" Birgitta asked seriously. "He's a nice boy. It isn't his fault he is dull. He was always dull. Unfortunately the shine of romance has worn off his surface, and I see how dull he is now, but that's not his fault. He hasn't changed. It's only my feelings that have changed. He still pays half the rent. And half the food. We have been friends for a long time, and if he had to move now, it would be very hard on him. As it is, it's convenient. With the money I save, I can buy clothes, go out—meet other people."

"You *don't* go out with other people . . ."

"Why not?"

"But you're *living* together!"

"Bo, do you have a roommate?"

"You know I do."

"Are you this indignant when she goes out?"

"Don't be ridiculous, Birgitta. It isn't the same."

"Why not?" Birgitta raised her milk to her mouth and smiled over the rim.

"Well, for one thing, we're not . . ." Bo hesitated. "Oh I see. You're not . . . sleeping together anymore."

"Oh yes. I have only one big bed."

Bo swallowed. "I mean you're not . . . you don't make love anymore."

"It depends how I feel," Birgitta said, her eyes laughing at Bo's growing discomfort. "Sometimes we do, sometimes we don't."

"You're deliberately trying to shock me," Bo said angrily.

"What for? That gives me no pleasure. Making love, that gives me pleasure."

"With a man you don't love anymore? When you're seeing other people?"

"Why not? He still has a wonderful body, that doesn't change either."

"How can you . . ."

"Bo, dear Bo . . ." Birgitta took a great gulp of milk, and then set the glass down on the table. She touched the top of Bo's hand. "I don't try to shock you. I only try to tell you. You say it is your wish to know, so I tell you. I have a great appetite. I enjoy. I do not love the food. I have no passion for it. But if it is there, and I am hungry, I eat. Is that so terrible?"

"It sounds greedy."

"Yes, that I admit. I am greedy. But am I terrible?"

"No," Bo said. "That's the worst part of it. You're not terrible at all. It frightens me sometimes how reasonable you make it all sound."

"That's good," Birgitta said, gently. "That's very good. If I can make it sound reasonable, perhaps you won't be so afraid to make one tiny mistake."

In the subterranean passageway on the way back to the main building Bo, with a worried expression, paused, and pulling Birgitta out of the mainstream of pedestrian traffic, she turned and faced her squarely.

"The only thing is . . . I must have misunderstood."

"What?"

"You're not actually . . . doing it with anyone else while Olaf is still with you?"

"When I was in love with him, of course not."

"But now?"

"Now . . . everything is changing. One night *coquilles,* another *fettucini.* Would you like the same menu, every time you dine, unless you were in love with the dish?"

"And Olaf?"

"If I feel in the mood . . . *smörgåsbord.*"

In spite of herself and everything she had been brought up to believe, or make believe she was believing, Bo laughed. "I don't know how you can talk so lightly about love."

"Love is a very light matter," Birgitta said. "Except to the Wagnerians, and the people who have never had it."

"Maybe it's lightest to the people who have had it a lot but haven't really had it at all."

"Ah, Bo." Birgitta sighed. "I almost wish you would stay unworldly. You are so hopelessly romantic."

"Am I? Maybe I'm more realistic than you are. We'll see."

"How?"

"I'll keep my eye on that left ear of yours," Bo said, and whirled through the revolving door.

II

ABOUT three and a half blocks from the UN buildings there was a small grotto of a bar serving good hot roast beef sandwiches, where Ernie could be fairly sure of not encountering any UN personnel. Not that he minded them on their own ground, but his job was so completely full-time that he savored an hour free from reminders of duty, except for those in his own head. Mostly the clientele were second-rate newspapermen and inconsequential daytime drinkers—people without much sense of responsibility, which helped better than anything to remind him how great his was. There was also a smutty-mouthed radio writer named Baimbridge who used to be a teacher at a fancy Southern girls' college. But as far as Ernie was concerned, he wasn't interested in any of them. All he knew he wanted was a nice quiet place to have lunch: the low cavelike ceilings sopped up their meaningless conversations, and the pinky-black darkness quieted his soul, while the food soothed his insides.

According to the bartender the place had been very big during prohibition, and the cellars down below that were now only storerooms had housed many a wild party and gang shooting, public and private. Ernie liked that: it helped his conviction that mayhem and violence were everywhere, even underneath a dark little bar where nobody made trouble at the moment, and three thick slabs of rare roast beef on French bread was only eighty-five cents, because most of the customers did nothing but drink, and he was one of the few serious eaters.

Today, seated in the tiny booth behind the dust-lidded piano that nobody played much anymore, Ernie was already halfway through his second sandwich. The episode by the elevator that morning had disquieted him: not that the little man with the nervous buttoning of his vest would have been any problem; Ernie could have broken him in half without much effort if he had really tried to make trouble for Ursull. The part that made him nervous was how easily the man might have broken Kiiko in half, if she had been giving the tour, and Ernie hadn't been there. He didn't know if it had been the ugly visitor's intention to break any girl in half, but Ursull was an Amazon compared to Kiiko, and what might be meant only as a vile embrace could snap the little girl in two, Ernie was sure.

Kiiko would laugh if she could hear his thoughts, laughter like the tiny Japanese good luck glass, rippling in the breeze of a rock garden. So Ernie tried laughing, too, but it stuck in his windpipe at the thought of her fragile little throat, snapping like a twig in a wind it was not built to withstand. He wolfed another bite of the sandwich, to calm the gnawings inside him.

"Well, if it isn't the keeper of the poon," Baimbridge said, stumbling past the curve of the piano, clearing an arc of light dust on the piano top with his elbow. He came to a lurching rest in the seat opposite Ernie.

Ernie looked up. He had long ago learned that ignoring Baimbridge was no solution. Baimbridge ran off at the mouth like his sponsor's products ran over in the sink, and the more you pretended he wasn't there the louder he got. It was better if the filth was taken in only by him, Ernie had decided. The fewer people that knew about his job, the better, and he was sorry he had ever told Baimbridge, trying to impress him back when Baimbridge told about all the soap operas he had on the air.

"How are you, Ned?" Ernie said.

"More important, how is all that many-splendored nubbly?" Ned Baimbridge curled his mouth over the edge of his drink and spit part of his laughter into the glass. He was a rank man, with fat features in an otherwise moderate-sized face. His lips especially hung three times larger than they should have for the size of his chin, which belated anatomical development he had often explained to Ernie in great detail. "And how do you keep your pants from splitting, you Pasha of pussy?"

"I told you my job isn't just watching the girls," Ernie said. He could feel his cheeks reddening, and that was bad. Baimbridge just got worse if he thought he was embarrassing you. The thing to do was just sit there, calmly, like it was all rolling off your back, and then Baimbridge would get disinterested and stop. Eventually. "I look out for the delegates and visitors, and see that there's no trouble. Like the demonstrations Friday . . ."

"Of course, Ernie boy, of course. And when I taught at that little college in the dell, my job wasn't just keeping my eye on the girls, either, although I did that of course too, which accounts for this moderate bulge of thyroid beneath my brows. My job was filling their young minds with the glories of literature and syntax, and not watching their glorious little muzzlies shifting on those cruel wooden chairs. But I did both, and more . . ."

"I know," Ernie said. "You told me."

"Then why should it shame you? Why, all I had was a few classrooms full of freshly ripened ass, some of it not even diddled much less plucked, from the local Southland, and it was my pleasure to go through those months with a perpetual hard on. But you, my enviable lad, daily confronted with nubile nubbly from all over, guardian of international frizzly . . . where's the remorse in a slightly stiffened joint?"

Ernie had been moved to beat up on Baimbridge the first time he had let loose his flow of sewage. But that would have made it an incident, and memorable to the loose-lipped man, and he seemed to have so little in his life that was memorable, adding to it would have been a mistake, and would have made him worse. Besides, there were no ladies present to be insulted by his language, except Kiiko who was present always in Ernie's thoughts, and as long as he stayed away from the UN, Baimbridge could do no real harm to her. Hitting him might have inspired him to go to the UN, and then Ernie would have had to kill him.

As it was, it was better to just let Ned Baimbridge go on, not letting him know that kind of talk upset or excited Ernie. It didn't excite him in the way Baimbridge would like to think: what made him excited was the evidence that there were people around who were filthy and vile, so it was right to be constantly alert and protective of Kiiko, no matter how much she giggled and whispered he was silly to be so concerned. He was right to be concerned. Ned Baimbridge proved that to him, almost every day at lunchtime.

"Worldwide cunni," Baimbridge said. "It sings on my lips like whisky in my brain. It is no wonder you must gobble up those sandwiches after a morning close to those zesties. You are a great man, Ernie, possibly one of the great men of our time, to devour only the flanks of a cow. Had I your control, I would probably be one of the outstanding full professors of our day. Did I ever tell you of the afternoon I was caught, and subsequently dismissed?"

"Many times."

"It was spring, naturally, a season for young rubblies that is like no other, with the possible exception of fall when their alert little butts are firm from summer swims and tennis and their thighs are tight with horseback rides and limited clover rollings with neighborhood swains, and occasional free abandon with summer help who won't be there at the cotillions to tell that they've had a piece, or a secret coon behind the woodpile. Autumn they come into the classroom still vaguely tinged with the sweat of their exertion, and that's a smell gets in a man's blood and in his nethermost muscle. But spring —well, then they're fresh all over again, even the ones who aren't, and their juicy little jimnies are as twittery about what's coming as the robins are. Well, there were these two, I couldn't make up my mind which one it would be, one a buttermilk-breasted freckled jouncy whose nipples had to be the palest pink, I knew that, even if she didn't lean over quite far enough in her little chiffon blouse, and this other one was tiny and dark . . . so oddly dark I could have sworn her grandmammy jangled with some jigaboo. . . ."

Ernie looked hollowly at his plate. The sandwich was gone, so he could no longer lose himself in concentrating on the food. He did not wish to hear what Baimbridge was saying. Being tiny and dark did not make the other girl like Kiiko. This man could never go anything to harm Kiiko, nor could any other man as long as Ernie was around. Still it made him more uncomfortable than any of Baimbridge's other vileness, hearing about the tiny dark girl in the classroom in Carolina, and he wanted to shut the words out of his ears. But there was nothing left to concentrate on, and he couldn't manage another sandwich.

He tried staring at Baimbridge's features, studying the face without hearing the words. His fleshy lips were curling around the dirty story like it was a big piece of pie, and Ernie despised him. The bartender was always telling Ernie not to pay any attention to Baimbridge, that he didn't really mean any harm, and a couple of hours of talking garbage-mouth was his only pleasure in life, sort of a refuge from the sweet mealymouthed crap he was always dishing out for the soap operas. "Treacle," Baimbridge called it, which was why he said when he came to be with his buddies in the bar he preferred to sit down and talk titty. The thought of writing anything was inconceivable to Ernie, so he could grasp how tough it might be for a man, doing three soap operas at the same time, under different names; and he could understand too that a man must be pressed, to consider people who came to the same bar at lunchtime as "buddies." But he was hard put to feel even the remotest twinge of pity for Baimbridge, since the reason he had to do three soap operas at once was to make enough money for alimony to the wife who had left him, support for the child who would be forever disgraced as a result of the scandal, and payoff to the family of one of the girls. The other one had long since gotten married. Ernie hoped it was the tiny dark one.

"So there they both were, at one time, sitting on their pulsing twingies in my office, with dusk closing in on the magnolia blooms, outside, and not a soul—so I earnestly believed—in the faculty building. Now I've explained to you about my eyes, grown slightly bulgy from looking, as I've explained to you my theory of muscle development in the adult male."

"You've explained," Ernie said.

"There's not a muscle in the body, even full grown, that can't be enlarged and articulated by constant tension, manipulation and exercise, as the latissimus dorsei is by weight lifting—not the least of which is a man's whang."

"I have to go," Ernie said, starting to get up.

"Such has never been my wish, however." With both his arms he reached over and, grunting heavily, pulled in the wheel-borne piano leg, closing Ernie in with the keyboard. "I wouldn't want to jolt their little jinglies with an outsize prong. However, I could never stand skinny-lipped people, even when they were me. They always looked constipated. So early in my adult life I resolved to change what was, presumably, a fully formed feature."

Ernie put his hand on the piano case, and with what looked like the slightest flicker of his wrist, sent the piano rolling back to its original position alongside the bar. "I have to go," he said, getting up from the table, and leaning over the bar to pay his bill.

"But I haven't finished my story." Baimbridge got up rockily, and came to a shuffling halt beside Ernie. "You'll miss the punch line . . ."

"I've heard it." Ernie held out a bill.

"Including the coming of the tight-twattied Dean of Women?"

"Including," Ernie said, as the bartender took his money.

"That's a shame," Baimbridge said. "It's a sensational story."

"I expect you'll tell it again."

Baimbridge rapped on the bar with his empty glass, and Charley the bartender refilled it with the bottle in his right hand, giving Ernie change with the left.

"Lucifer's fall," Baimbridge lifted his glass, "was not, as philosophers and Bible thumpers would have us believe, from the stars into the fiery cauldrons of hell."

"Thanks, Charley." Ernie tossed some coins onto the bar.

"Welcome."

"It was, rather, a headlong dive into a vat of sweet juicies." Ernie was around the front of the bar, and almost out the door. "ERNEST!"

He turned briefly. Baimbridge held his glass high, toasting. "Round up those tinglies, boy. Get in there and muff them for me."

"Whyn't you do it yourself, Professor?" Charley said.

"Would that I could, lad. But I must back to the evening falling on the office of Dr. John, who has a consultation with the Widow Reems, late of New Hampshire. He suspects it's appendicitis, little dreaming that her neighbor's husband has been tiddling her twat."

"They let that on TV?" Charley asked.

"Only on nighttime," Baimbridge said.

Outside the bar, Ernie felt a little dizzy, and had to steady himself by leaning his arm against the cold stone of the red brick walkup beside the bar. Coming out, as he did, from the soothing semidarkness into the glare of midday was always a shock to his eyes, and sometimes the front of his brain. But today the quiet anger and excitement of the morning run-in with Ursull's tourist had left a knot inside him that not even two sandwiches could untwist. And the putrid ramblings of Baimbridge had oozed like molten lead gravy on his insides, making even more indigestible the horror. And horror did exist. It was everywhere, outside them, and inside some of them, waiting only to get out, like it had with Baimbridge. Kiiko would not laugh so quickly if she could hear Baimbridge, and it wouldn't hurt, the next time she laughed and told him he worried for no reason, to bring her here to lunch, and let her find out for herself.

The thought jolted him even more than the sunlight and the cold air. He would sooner die than have her ears be touched by any of that, cut out Baimbridge's tongue and die himself before it would touch her. That he even could consider the possibility of exposing her to anything like that, even for a split second, made him almost physically ill. Still, he knew evil existed, and Kiiko, Kiiko of all people in the world coming like an angel risen from ashes, just so he could protect her, Kiiko of all people should know it existed. Not that he would ever let it touch her, not ever again. But she should at least understand his fear.

All through their lunch together, Gerd was doing his whimsical best to behave himself with Ursull. Before they began to eat, he had stopped at the newsstand outside the cafeteria, to buy *The New York Times*, and during the meal, whenever he would find himself staring curiously at her, or when a question would begin to cross his lips, he searched the face of the newspaper for an article they could discuss, and questioned her about her views of the situation, or expressed his own. After a while she began to laugh, and told him he didn't need to be that impersonal, but he assured her it was his wish to be only the way she wanted him to be.

"I am thirty-two years old," he said, turning to the theatrical page. "What plays have you seen this year?"

"I'm twenty-one," she said smiling.

"I didn't ask you," he said solemnly. "What about the new Arthur Miller? Is it any good?"

"I haven't seen it yet," Ursull said. "I imagine it would be worth seeing."

"You imagine," Gerd said. "I see. Does that mean you would like to see it?"

"Yes."

"Good," Gerd said. "We have established that much. Would you imagine seeing it Saturday to be good?"

"Very."

"And do you further imagine you could see it in my company?"

"Why not?"

"Come now," Gerd said. "I wouldn't like to see you become overly sentimental about it."

Ursull laughed.

"And they say we Germans have control of our emotions. Amazing, that a girl of twenty-one who speaks such magnificent German and has such admirable control should be Argentinian. I had always heard that South Americans were hot-blooded and tempestuous."

"All right." Ursull reached across the table and took the paper away from him. "The seminar on *The New York Times* is over."

"But we haven't even spoken about the editorials."

"I am twenty-one," Ursull said. "I am five feet nine inches tall . . ."

"Superb. I myself admire height in a woman. And I am six foot two. We will be the handsomest couple at the Arthur Miller play."

"I was educated in Buenos Aires, Cambridge, Massachusetts, and in New York at Columbia University, where I received my master's degree, in French."

"Swiss!" Gerd exclaimed. "That's it, of course, you're Swiss."

"I am in New York to perfect my English—my formal speech is good, but I still have some difficulty writing fluently, and speaking in the vernacular. When I have conquered this, I shall return to my home in Buenos Aires, where I was born."

"Come," Gerd said, reaching for the newspaper, "we will discuss the editorial."

"And where," she said, holding the paper away from him, "I will once again join my mother and father, who are German."

"Aha!" Gerd said triumphantly. "You see? I knew it. I knew you were!"

"There is, in Buenos Aires, an enormous colony of German people, who speak only German and think only German. They are marvelous people, including my own parents, but I have never understood why they cannot acknowledge there is a rest of the world. Why is it so important that everyone be German?"

"But it's not important at all!" Gerd said happily. "The rest of the world can be what it wants to be, and that's fine. It was only important that *you* be German."

"Why? I am the same person, whatever I may be. I look the same, I think the same, I feel the same."

"But if you are German," he said, and the laughter left his lips, as he reached for her hand, "then you are a countryman of mine. And it becomes very important to you to take care of a fellow countryman." His fingers were warm on hers, and softly dry. "And now that I have found you, you will take me under your wing, you won't let me be alone. Not anymore."

"Is it my solemn duty as a German?"

"It is my solemn hope, as a man."

Later that afternoon, Ursull sat in the Lounge, her stockinged feet tucked under her hips, smiling vaguely and not even looking uneasy when Bo and Birgitta started talking to her. Bo was not very subtle, asking about the young man, but Ursull didn't mind. On the contrary: she seemed to welcome the chance to discuss Gerd.

"Oh yes," she said, in a strangely soft voice. "He is very handsome, and quite bright. His father owns Kraben manufacturing, so I imagine he is very well-to-do also."

"Well," Bo said, "what more do you need? When do you elope?"

"Oh, don't be silly," Ursull said, but a happy redness seared her white cheeks, and she almost giggled.

Pauline, the supervisor, called over and told Ursull she was wanted up on main to take a French group.

"Oh what a shame," Ursull said sincerely. "I was hoping we could talk for a while."

Bo stared after her in genuine amazement.

"What's the matter?" Birgitta smiled.

"The Princess of Chauantapec? Seeking conversation with the girls of the tribe? What's going on?"

Birgitta sat back, and looked at her watch. It was almost five o'clock: she pulled big tortoiseshell hairpins from the coil at the back of her head, and let her pale hair fall free. "How many tours have you given altogether, Bo?"

Bo shrugged. "Four, five a day . . . five days a week . . . ten weeks. About two hundred and fifty, I guess. More or less."

"You know the Persian rug in the main hall, donated by Iran? The one on the wall?"

"Of course. It's part of the tour. I always point it out."

Birgitta nodded. "And what do you say about it?"

"What we all say," Bo said. "What we were all told to pay special attention to as of special interest."

"Sometimes, I suppose, when we point something out two hundred and fifty times as a point of interest to strangers, we stop hearing what we say, because familiar words cease to have meaning."

"Like what?"

Birgitta sat up stiffly, and lowered her arm, as if she were indicating something high on the wall. "Somewhere in that enormous intricately patterned rug, ladies and gentlemen, there is a small mistake. The weavers put it there deliberately, as a token of their humility, to remind themselves that only Allah is infallible."

"I could never find the place," Bo said. "Could you?"

"You don't have to see it," Birgitta said. "The important thing is, the error is there. Ursull is looking to gossip."

"I don't know if I get you."

Birgitta stretched. "Only Allah is perfect."

BIRGITTA, as a rule, did not like parties. But since, as another rule, she did not dislike them until she had been to them, when Marie Claire said an Italian movie producer boyfriend was giving a party Friday evening, and they needed an extra girl, Birgitta said she would be delighted to go. As it turned out, the party was in a Park Avenue apartment, owned by an elderly millionaire who kept putting his hand on Birgitta's knee, telling her he "dabbled in" real estate. There was no sign of a movie producer, Italian or otherwise, although from time to time conversation would drift back, over the heads of the crowd in the living room, that they were expecting Marcello Mastroianni. Most of the women were young and beautiful, in a high fashion model, skinny shoulder blades way; the men were older and not particularly attractive. Marie Claire had not even appeared yet, and it occurred to Birgitta that she might have simply heard about the man giving the party, invited Birgitta for moral support, and then not had nerve enough to come herself. Birgitta felt vaguely annoyed, but not uncomfortable, she had been to enough parties to know that a tall blonde by herself was always welcome—a little too welcome, it would appear, from the hand of the aging Lothario seated beside her.

He had greeted her warmly at the door to the penthouse, exclaiming that it had been too long since he had seen her, and she could hardly disagree, since they had never seen each other before. When she asked if Marie Claire had arrived yet, he assured her Marie Claire would be along any minute, although Birgitta was sure he had never set eyes on her either—and said he was sure the lovely lady would be much more comfortable inside. He had proceeded to see to her personal comfort by leaps and bounds, and occasional furtive pinches, seating her in a booth in his private bar, built by his private architects and decorator to be an exact replica of Shepheard's. "Booths, palm fronds, Egyptian décor and all. How about that?" he said. "Cost a small fortune."

"Wouldn't it have been cheaper to go to the nightclub?" Birgitta said. "It's only six blocks away."

"Seven," he said, snapping his finger for his butler, who was done up like a Nubian. "Besides, I don't always like the crowds there. Prefer to stay here, and pick my own people. Anyway, what's money?"

"Not much to you, apparently," Birgitta said.

He laughed and put his hand on her knee again.

"I'll have a vodka Gibson," Birgitta said. "And the gentleman will have two Scotch and waters."

"Two?" He looked at her curiously.

"One for each of your hands," Birgitta said. When the Nubian brought the drinks, she knocked one of them into the man's lap.

"I'm so sorry," she said, smiling sweetly. "Your dinner jacket."

"That's okay. I have more inside."

"Of course, I should have known."

She watched him go out of the room, waving coyly at her with little-boy fingers next to his old man's eyes, and smiled, pleased, as he tripped slightly at the threshold. The truth of it was that she enjoyed dirty old men, if they were old enough not to appeal to her, and dirty enough so she could feel free to insult them at some point during the evening. Dirty old men always flocked to young, robust Swedish girls—as if they thought by the very strength of the girls they would be regenerated. Either that, or they confused emancipation with nymphomania, and the thought of the perennially poised Nordic pelvis made it seem easier, and certainly quicker, thus restoring them to the category of active lover. If that was their only wish, as it seemed to be, she wondered why they didn't deal strictly with prostitutes, who God knew were much more perennially poised. But then, she supposed, most men liked to imagine they could still get it for nothing, except the very rich, who seemed to enjoy even more the hundred- and two-hundred-dollar call girls, liking to think they could afford it.

But where, Birgitta wondered, would the call girl be who was high-priced enough for her host this evening? The apartment was enormous, and done in the most excruciating and expensive bad taste. He had not stopped with his private facsimile of Shepheard's at the end of the bar. About six feet beyond there was a small, round dance floor, shrouded in Egyptian tropical leaves, and beyond it a jukebox, with bubbling lights in its red and yellow sides, playing frug and watusi records. A thin dark girl in a *Vogue* magazine discothèque dress, fringed black at the bottom and cut well above the knee, frugged solitarily and unceasingly on the dance floor, and Birgitta wondered if she, too, had been included by the designer as part of the décor. It was all ridiculous: still, Birgitta did not feel like leaving just yet. She would have a few drinks, and then go. Right now she was not up to moving. The old man was a bore, but he could be handled, and she didn't feel like beginning anew with the crowd she had seen outside.

"Did you miss me?" He bobbed over to the booth seat beside her like an anxious rabbit, whiskers fluttering slightly under his large nose. He was wearing a moss green velvet smoking jacket, with lighter green lapels, and there was a taupe Paisley handkerchief in the breast pocket.

"What a beautiful jacket," she said. It was, actually. Olaf would have looked fine in it. It was a shame it had to hang from such thin shoulders.

"Do you like it? I picked up a few of them, my last trip to Hong Kong. You know the *Caronia*?"

"Not personally," Birgitta said.

He didn't seem to be wondering if she were joking or not. As a matter of fact, he didn't seem to be listening to what she said at all. He had established everything about her that he wanted to know, by way of her knee. But apparently there were some questions to be asked. "How's your drink?"

"Empty," she said, wide-eyed. "I wonder how that could have happened."

He snapped his fingers at the Nubian again, and indicated her empty glass. "Yes, I go . . . maybe, two . . . three times a year."

"Drinking?"

"To Hong Kong, on the *Caronia.*"

"That must be very exciting."

"Ships are a bore, as a rule, but they call this one the millionaire's cruise. Lot of good business talk, good card playing. And beautiful women. But none like you!"

"Not if they're beautiful," she said with mock coyness, and smiled her thanks to the waiter. He had brought her second Gibson on the rocks, in a deep glass that she could barely manage with one hand. It was at least a triple: the host, apparently, took no chances—with décor, or women.

"Are you kidding?"

"I don't know," Birgitta said sweetly. "What do you think?" She plucked a tiny onion from the depths of the glass and poised it sourly between her teeth.

"I think you're adorable. That's what I think." He moved to kiss her puckered mouth, and she let the onion fall into his open shirt-front.

"I'm so sorry," she said, as he foraged around for it. "It's my caps. I'm not accustomed to them yet."

"What?" He was digging very busily. He was apparently thinking more about the cold onion against his skin than about her, although he hadn't forgotten her completely. She knew that because he kept reaching in between the buttons, not wanting to open the shirt in front of her, not giving her a chance to see the shriveled old-man skin above the tiny pot that was his middle.

"I said I'm not accustomed to them yet. The caps."

"What do you need caps for? You have beautiful teeth." He had found the onion, and relaxed, sighing.

"That's what I told the Contest Master, but he said we all had to get them if we were to become movie stars."

"Contest master?"

"Miss Solar System." Birgitta drank deeply from the glass. "You know, girls from every country in the world . . . and any place else, too, I suppose, if they could get here in time." She looked at him blandly. "Well, I joined the contest back home in Sweden—"

"You're Swedish!" he said. "I could have told you the minute you opened your mouth you were a Swede."

"Yumping Yimminy," Birgitta said.

"You were telling me about Miss Solar System."

"Well, the winner was supposed to receive a movie contract, so the Contest Master said we all had to have our teeth capped."

"Poor little girl," he said, and rubbed his hand against her hair. "And after all that, you lost."

"Not at all," Birgitta said. The waiter had brought them both drinks: his in a small whisky sour glass, and another triple for her. "I won first prize: Miss Solar System, and a trip to Hollywood."

"But that's wonderful," he said.

"Not really. We came on a freighter, across the North Sea, through the Panama Canal, to San Diego. But when we got to Hollywood, no one had even heard of him."

"You poor thing," he said. "Heard of who?"

"The Concert Master. He came with me on the freighter of course, and when we got to Hollywood and registered at this dirty motel, no one would even speak to him. He swore it was all a big mistake, that he had a letter of credit from Ingmar Bergman, but I knew he was lying. It wouldn't surprise me if he made up the whole thing just so he could take some poor young girl for a ride." She sighed. "It certainly was a *long* ride. All that pitching and churning. . . ."

"That's terrible," he said. "That's just terrible." His hand moved down her shoulder.

"Isn't it?" Birgitta said earnestly. "And the worst of it was that he was at least forty-five years old."

He blanched. "That isn't so old."

"It is now," Birgitta said happily, draining the first triple, and starting in thirstily on the second.

"Well," he said. "Well." He seemed to recover slightly, and his hand began its journey up her arm. "And what are you going to do now?"

"I don't know," Birgitta said. "I can't possibly go home. What would I tell the newspapers?"

"I mean what are you doing? How are you getting on? How do you support yourself?"

"Support *myself?*" she said.

He squeezed her upper arm. "I'm going to help you."

"That's very kind," Birgitta said. "I don't know why you would want to be nice to me."

"I have a lot of friends in the motion picture business, and I'm going to see to it they give you a hand."

"Where?" Birgitta said.

"As a matter of fact, one of them is bringing—we're expecting Marcello Mastroianni."

"I heard," Birgitta said.

"Now a little later I'm going to send all these people away . . ." He was nuzzling her ear.

"I wouldn't want to take you from your guests," Birgitta said.

"That's all right. I don't know half of them anyway."

"Then why couldn't you have gone to Shepheard's?"

He dragged his sandpapery lips against the side of her cheek. She turned slightly. "What will we do later, just the two of us?"

"Well, first, we're going to have a little supper sent up from Twenty-One."

"Wouldn't it be easier to go there?"

"I like them to send up to me. They do it all the time."

"I suppose it *is* more expensive that way." Birgitta sighed.

"And then we're going to have a long talk about your future. Hardy!" he called to the bartender.

The girl in the black sequin fringe dance dress was still chugging away, and a few of the men had wandered in from the buffet table in the foyer to watch her. No one spoke to her, or joined in the dancing themselves. They just watched, as she gyrated, a glazed smile fixed on her face, sent occasionally, according to the direction of her thrusts, toward one of them.

He saw Birgitta staring at the dance floor. "You like my place?"

"It's a stunning jukebox," Birgitta said.

"That's nothing. Next month I'm getting Scopitone."

She looked at him blankly.

"Scopitone," he said. "That new French thing. Pictures, like television, of the singers and things while the record plays. They're putting them in at some of the newer discothèques around town. Sparks, places like that. Maybe even Ondine. It's really catching on."

"You mean Shepheard's is becoming passé?"

"A little," he said.

"What a shame." She sighed. "You'll have to tear all this down."

Hardy brought the new drinks. "Oh none for me," she whispered. "I'm liable to fall down right here."

"Well if you do, we'll take good care of you." He buried his face in her shoulder.

"Oh dear," she said, as her hand knocked her glass into his lap. "Now look what I've done. You got me so excited I couldn't see what I was doing, and I am a little high."

"That's all right," he said, a thin line of perspiration beading his brow.

"I suppose now you'll have to go and change again, just because you got me so excited."

"No . . . no . . ." he said, reaching for the bar-towels Hardy had brought over. "I'll stay right here. I wouldn't leave you for anything, you little angel."

"You're sweet to call me little," Birgitta said, watching the feverish mopping he was doing on his trousers. "Actually I'm five feet seven and I weight a hundred and thirty-eight pounds."

"Don't worry about that. Fella in the next room, doctor friend of mine here at the party, he'll take care of it in three weeks. Bright young man, give you a couple of shots and have you down to a hundred twenty in no time."

"I don't know if I'd want that." Birgitta took a deep breath. "You see my breasts alone weigh eighteen pounds apiece."

He stopped the mopping, and looked up at her, red-faced and fascinated. "Eighteen pounds apiece?"

"That's right," she said shyly.

"But how could you weigh them accurately . . . I mean . . . they're connected."

"That's true," Birgitta said. "But my father is a world-famous scientist, and he has a method."

"Still . . . eighteen pounds . . . I mean, an accurate measurement . . ."

"Well, that's no problem to him. He's a great Swedish endocrinologist. Perhaps you've heard of him. He's been doing these wonderful experiments with aging male monkeys, and their parts. Putting the bounce back in their balls?"

He looked, suddenly, like the jukebox, with its multiple bubbling lights. "I hope I haven't shocked you. But after all, he is a scientist."

"Shocked me? Don't be silly." He looked at his watch. "I'll start them leaving in about a half hour. Then we can really talk."

"But it's so unfair," Birgitta said. "You know all about me, the beauty contest, my father . . . and . . ." She held her hand modestly over her bosom. "And I know almost nothing about you, except you are responsible for this . . . incredible apartment."

"What do you want to know?"

"What do you do for a living?"

"I told you," the hand was back on her knee, "I dabble in real estate."

Birgitta began to feel bored. He was beginning to repeat even his dull lines. She took his hand off her knee and placed it, firmly, on his own thigh, where a few slivers of ice still clung. "I am not real estate," she said, and started to get up.

"Where are you going?"

"Home," she said. "I'm tired of this party."

"But what about my friends?" he said anxiously. "They're going to help you get into movies."

"I have already been in movies," she said.

"Really? Have I ever seen you?"

"I don't know. You might have a little difficulty recognizing me. We were all naked and wore masks." Her face had assumed a sullen expression. She was really most anxious to get out of there.

"You're kidding!"

"Congratulations," Birgitta said. "May I get by?"

"No! I don't want you to leave. I like a girl with spirit."

"I don't think so," Birgitta said, pressing his legs aside with a deceptively slender thigh. "I think you just like a girl."

She got out of the bar as quickly as possible. At her last glimpse of him, just the other side of the doorway, he had begun frugging with the girl on the dance floor.

Birgitta laughed to herself and walked through the living room, ignoring the glances of the men; she did not flatter herself that the looks were meant especially for her. It was only an automatic reaction to a new feminine presence in the room. Anything, just let it be fresh. Well, not fresh, necessarily, just fresh to me.

She turned in disgust and went to the entrance foyer, looking for the maid with her coat. And then she smelled the food. She peered through the gray-figured doorway: it was right there, an enormous table in the dining alcove, filled with all kinds of hot and cold platters. Not too many people seemed to be inside, and although Little Shepheard's was through the second doorway, he wouldn't be able to see her for the palm fronds.

Why not? thought Birgitta. The least she could get out of it was a free dinner. And she was hungry. She was usually hungry.

No one was serving at the tables. Everything was laid out very neatly and nicely, and she made her way past the couple in the doorway. A blond girl sat weeping solitarily on the Louis XVI settee in the corner; a balding man stood staring into the fireplace, although there were no logs in it. But Birgitta paid no attention to them. Her thoughts were entirely on the food, although she did notice a superb back on the man standing by the buffet table.

"What's good?" she asked him, picking up her plate.

He looked at her coolly, silver-eyed, and turned away, refilling his glass with a bottle of Scotch from the mantelpiece over the empty marble fireplace.

"I asked what's good?" she said again, and smiled at him.

"Try the white meat," he said, and wiped his lips with a coffee beige hand.

She was in no mood to argue or be particularly friendly. But Birgitta didn't like to be slighted by anyone, unless she had made the choice.

She picked up a napkin and began forking pieces of cold cuts onto her plate. "If you don't like this food, there's a man inside, I think he owns this apartment—who would be very happy to order up some dinner for you from Twenty-One. But then," she looked over at him, "I don't know if you're that kind of a girl."

He smiled, and the whiteness, even against the rich dark of his skin, was amazing. "You're pretty clever."

"I like to think so."

"You don't seem like that kind of girl yourself. Who are you?"

"Birgitta Nils." She bit into a piece of fish. "Who are you?"

"I'm the party Negro."

"I see."

"I hope so. This is a very 'in' party, and in order to be really 'in' nowadays, you must have at least one Negro, fairly dark, fairly well dressed, and fairly articulate. Well, I'm him."

"What do I call you? Party, or Negro?"

"Don't do lines with me, lady, that might make me upset, and then

I won't look happy, and then I won't get any calls to come to more parties. I'm supposed to make my hosts look enlightened, so I've got to stand here looking serene. If you upset my serenity, I might get a black look, and then I won't get any more calls."

"Why are you so nasty?" Birgitta said.

"Why should it bother you?"

"When I go to parties I'm usually the one who's cutting. I don't like anyone cutting me, regardless of race or creed. So why continue?"

"Well, to tell you the truth, ofay honey, I don't like to be patronized. Especially by white-haired chicks who try to be friendly because I stick out like a sore thumb. A sore black thumb."

"Actually, it was your back I noticed," Birgitta said. "Your sore black back. Only I couldn't see anything but the lines of it through your sore gray jacket. You'll excuse me now, I'll just finish my dinner, and then I'll go home alone, if it's all right with you."

"It's fine with me," he said.

"Splendid. You're making a mistake, not even tasting the salmon." She smiled.

"You're making the mistake." He glared at her. "This isn't a party in Greenwich Village in the Thirties. This is a penthouse on Park Avenue, in 1965. And you're no young Jewish intellectual."

"Neither are you," Birgitta said. "I suppose that's why you're so angry." She put down her plate, and walked out of the room.

The maid, sorting through the warm brown minks and the long-haired "fad" furs, the kit foxes and the snow leopard in the hall closet, for the thick weave, bright blue alpaca Birgitta had previously regarded as her "good" winter coat, chattered to herself softly.

"If you can't find it," Birgitta said, "I'll take one of the others."

"No, that's all right, dear, here it is."

"What a shame," Birgitta said, slipping her arms into the sleeves. And thanking the maid, she went out into the private foyer, and pressed the button for the elevator.

The door to the apartment opened behind her. It was the young Negro. "Birgitta?"

She turned.

"I wish you wouldn't go."

"You have a peculiar way of showing it."

"I'd like to apologize," he said. "I wasn't really angry at you."

"No?"

"I'm used to people patronizing me at parties. The hell of it is, I came to this one, and no one even bothered to be patronizing. Sons of bitches ignored me completely."

She smiled, and pressed the buzzer again.

"Won't you stay?"

"No," she said. "I've had enough of this party."

"Then at least," he shut the door behind him, "let me see that you get safely downstairs."

"There's an elevator man. I'll be all right."

"Not necessarily," he said. "You think you're waiting for the elevator. But our host for the evening owns the building, and this elevator has a breakway back. Young girls who enter alone find themselves trapped in his private bedroom."

"Is that true?"

"I don't know, but it's a hell of an idea."

She laughed, and agreed to wait for him while he got his coat. All the way down in the elevator, he kept tapping the back wall, and listening and nodding. And they both laughed.

Once they were on the street, she said yes, it would be thoughtless of him not to offer her at least a cup of coffee. They walked toward the West Side, to a place called The Crêpe, where they could get fancy pancakes. And walking, they talked.

His name was Mason Williams, he was a staff reporter for *American Crisis*, a magazine he described as "sort of the tawny version of *Newsweek*."

"It's a little slick," he said, "but very Serious Negro. Sort of like the fellow you see on the street who could be passing if he wanted to, but still puts Dixie Peach on his hair instead of Brylcreem."

She looked at him a little confused.

"Keeping in touch with his roots," he said, and then, noticing the expression on her face, smiled. "Oh I forgot. Just cause you're so hip, doesn't make you an American. Dixie Peach is a Harlem pomade."

"I figured that out," she said. "You're not quite so easy."

"You, *non plus,* Swedish lady. What are you doing here, with your golden awareness?"

"I'm working at the UN. I've finished my Ph.D. in political science in June and I stayed to go into diplomatic work."

"You working for your legation?"

"I'm a guide," she said. "It's a beginning, and later on I'll try to go to work for one of the subcommittees."

"You sound like you're filling out a scholarship application. 'When I grow up, world, I'd like to be a cowboy.' Maybe you know a friend of mine there. Quilo Harabey? He works with the Trusteeship Council."

"I don't think so," Birgitta said. "Where's he from?"

"The old country. Africa."

She didn't answer.

"They're doing a lot of things with decolonization now, aren't they? I asked Quilo if I could come sit in on a couple of sessions. I told him I wanted to pick up a few pointers, so I could start working out the problem of the decolonization of Harlem."

Again, she said nothing.

"Yeah," Mason said sullenly. "I got about the same response from him. You'd get along well with each other. Neither of you have a sense of humor."

"Maybe it's you," she said.

"Me? Don't be silly. I tickle myself pink. Dusty pink."

"I don't think I feel like having coffee," Birgitta said. "Maybe you ought to just call me a cab."

"Okay," he said. "You a cab!"

She smiled.

"I apologize," he said. "What can I do to win your favor?"

"I don't want to hear anymore what you hate. Is there anything you like?"

"No. There are a number of things I love, though."

"Such as?"

"Strawberry pancakes, blueberry blintzes, Errol Flynn. He was my kind of hero, poor bastard. The last of the great swashbucklers. Some buckle, and a lot of swash. He would've liked that, the breakaway elevator bit. Would I had thought of it in time. He would've liked you too. In the elevator especially."

"I wouldn't have liked him."

"Oh yes you would've. You probably only saw the aging Flynn. The young one would've killed you. He killed me. I saw *Robin Hood* six times on Forty-Second Street. I really dug him, you know. He had such happy contempt, I never even thought about his being white."

He said it with no malice, so Birgitta felt the stiffness go out of her, and a bubble of laughter worked itself free.

"Sometimes I wish Norman Mailer would've got hung on him instead of us duskies. Now that would've been a sexual fantasy worth immortalizing."

The wind whipped up colder as they crossed Sixth Avenue, and she shivered slightly, and pulled her hands tight in the deep pockets of her coat.

"You don't like Norman Mailer, or the myth about Negro sexuality?"

"I'm cold," she said. "I shivered because I was cold."

His arm came up from his side for a moment, and reached out as if it had no connection with him, and were only a protecting arm, wanting to shield her from the wind. And then, he remembered something, and staring at his hand with cool anger, he shamed it back to his side and into his own pocket.

"What's wrong?" she said.

"I don't know." He grinned, awkwardly. "You must have a little of the old Flynn about you, yourself. For a minute, there, I forgot you were white."

"Well you mustn't do that," she said. "Better to let me freeze to death."

"We'll be there in a minute," he said. "You'll be warm enough, soon."

IV

IN spite of her father's fear of foreign entanglements, Bo had long ago given up hope of finding romance in the UN itself. Most of the attractive delegates, in a plausible age group, were accompanied to New York by their wives, and in certain instances, great hordes of children. If Bo had any thought at all of getting involved with a married man, which she certainly didn't for her first shot, Birgitta had been quick to set her straight: the clichés of the "back-Rue" romances were already reserved for the secretaries, who had been conditioned for that sort of thing along with their typing and shorthand courses. No married diplomat worth his salt was about to get involved with a dewy-eyed idealist, which all the guides were considered more or less to be: it was one thing working for the good of your country toward the betterment of the world; but there were not many positions to which a guide could aspire without additional training, and to work that hard for so little money or hope of advancement was more dewy-eyed than necessary.

So among the eligible delegates, that left mostly the Africans. And no matter how far north their province, Bo could not really work herself up into believing that any of them really looked like Omar Sharif. As for the rest—well, not that she was prejudiced—but she knew for a well-rumored fact that most of them dated professionals, girls who regularly came in from New Jersey or Canada, provided by a hospitality committee that had nothing whatever to do with the UN.

So all in all, though she had not dismissed completely the thought that something magnificent could happen to her at work, at five o'clock exactly, when the last tour of the day had been given, Bo was one of the first dressed and out of the building. There was never any hope in not hoping, but lingering was foolhardy.

The day, for December, was unusually mild, so Bo, without undue hardship, was able to put into effect the vow she was forever taking to start going home from the UN by bus. At the stop on the corner of First Avenue and Forty-Fourth Street, two young mothers with heavily textured stockings, one pair a red and black diamond-patterned wool, and the other ribbed, disconsolate green, waited, holding a baby apiece, while three other small children stood tugging at the grown-up skirts, peeking at each other around their mother's legs. The two women chattered animatedly, seemingly unaware of the children attached to and playing around them: the expressions on their faces were terribly intent; they carried hand-lettered, well-worn BAN THE BOMB signs. Each of the babies had a HELP ME GROW UP button pinned to the front of its snowsuit, and the toddlers dragged STOP THE WAR IN VIET NAM placards around the maternal calves that served as a temporary playground. Neither of the two mothers could have been much older than Bo herself, a realization which depressed Bo slightly, since, in spite of their youth, and by virtue of their children, she supposed they would have to be considered women, and Bo still thought of herself as a girl.

Still, everybody could not be categorically lumped together, by age: that was why a seventeen-year-old girl from Iowa was an abysmal failure playing St. Joan: the fact that Joan of Arc really had been even younger was beside the point. A seventeen-year-old girl in France was a woman; Joan of Arc was a peasant, and peasants her age had already been out in the fields, humping a great deal and whelping a lusty infant or two. That was what Mary Kate had told Bo, while rehearsing the trial scene for acting class, and Bo thought there was a good deal of merit to her argument. Mary Kate had no intention of humping merely for the sake of artistic veracity, she had gone on to say, especially since Joan's sexual energy had been diverted into her voices. But the truth of her argument was there notwithstanding: seventeen-year-old French girls were women, and seventeen-year-old American girls were just that. So the same would hold for twenty-one-year-old American girls, Bo thought. Unless of course—her eyes skipped guiltily to the pair of mothers at the bus stop—they had been humping and whelping.

But then, they were another class, peasants like the French Joan, denied the benefits of higher education and higher income extended to Bo. Still, they carried signs, and seemed aware, so there was the possibility they continued to think even while doing it. For a moment there even occurred to her the slightly incredible possibility that they had been college girls like herself, who had spent midsemesters conceiving instead of going to double-features. It was a devastating thought, and one to which she did not cling for long—humping was what they had done and all they had done, and now that they had reaped the fruits of the flesh, they were engaging in intellectual endeavors as a guilty afterthought. It was conceivable that a Swede her own age and a French girl and even Kiiko, if Japanese girls did that kind of thing, might wallow in a bed of lust and read books afterwards, with some degree of sincerity. But not a young American. No, the thinking awareness was recent, and peripheral: these girls, with their placards and premature broods, were hard-core Humpers.

Obscenity, on a mental level, came with comparative ease to Bo. Her actions were above reproach, and her conversations, though occasionally on the earthy side, were far from foul-mouthed. But early in life she had abandoned Orphan Annie, with her "criminies" and "gee whillikers" for the cartoons with more enjoyable reactions like "Bz#L*+&Ky@-!!!!!" in a balloon; and later on she had turned in disgust from the honey-mouthed heroines of fiction usually portrayed in the movies by Natalie Wood. Innocence, she thought, was one thing, oppressive naïveté quite another. So she had developed a lusty laugh, the ability to listen to a longshoreman without blushing, and read and retain a phrase that seemed to say it well, albeit graphically. So while she might not participate in vile acts, and vulgarisms did not yet fall with ease from her moist little mouth, she did have what she was pleased to consider one of the raunchiest minds in captivity. Thus she could face squarely, but hiply, the undeniable fact that these girls were humpers. That these *women* were humpers.

The bus pulled up to the No Parking Zone, and the two women got in ahead of her, dragging their noisy ménage. The bus was a little crowded from the afternoon coming-home rush, and no one offered a seat, a throwback gallantry which, though unusual, was not unheard of in New York. One man looked as if he were considering getting up for a moment, but then, noticing the signs the girls carried, relaxed in his seat. They were all fairly well jammed together, Bo and the humpers, and as the driver instructed everybody to move back in the bus, she found herself carried toward an ill-suited couple who doubtlessly worked in the same office and thought they were meant for each other.

"Look at those beatniks," the man said to the girl beside him. He was paunchy and rosy-cheeked, with rimless glasses probably meant to make him look more intellectual but which succeeded only in enforcing the impression that he was a thirty-year-old grandfather. The girl was tiny and much too thin. Her wraparound coat barely covered a chiffon blouse with a frill around the neck and down the front, a style Bo had not seen anyone wearing since the last movie version of *Little Women*. She was giggling helplessly, tiny bosoms quivering thinly, like junket, under the pale pink material of her slip, which could be seen quite clearly through the blouse, and was also admirably suited to Marmee, or at best, Meg.

"Two little beatniks," he said again, and the girl piped in a skinny asthmatic breath and passed a few more giggles, as if that was the cleverest thing she had ever heard. "Think they're so hep, picketing the UN," he said. Bo clutched the overhead metal for support, while the girl wheezed away.

It was a shame, Bo thought, that that shriveled little probably secretary thought he was so clever. Anybody who had to be insulting to impress a girl was pretty pathetic, but not quite as pathetic as the girl who thought that the words "beatnik" and "hep" were *hip*.

"Dragging their poor little kids to make a fuss outside the UN."

Bo realized with a start he was talking about her *amies de passage*. In spite of their textured stockings and their picketing, she had not stopped to consider them Beats. Humping was not restricted to Bohemia.

His voice was becoming louder, as he got pinker-faced and more sure of himself, and Bo felt herself growing increasingly uncomfortable. The two poster-carriers were directly to her left, and although they were still talking a mile a minute, if he kept it up they couldn't help but realize his verbal darts, though blunted, were aimed at them.

"Haven't even washed themselves, much less those children, for who knows how many years, and they're going to change the world."

The two mothers stopped talking. Bo felt a little ball of embarrassment jiggling in her stomach to the tempo of the bus's movement. He was an insufferable boob, and she felt only contempt for him, and sympathy for the mothers: whether they were humpers or Beats or perhaps just vaguely uncombed, much less unwashed, they were at least trying to do something while all he could do was look fat and pink.

Well, he washed, there was no doubt about that. She had never seen anyone more like a rosy, scrubbed middle-aged baby. She wondered if his mother, now nearing seventy, laid him out every night on a giant white terry towel and scrubbed his fat pink duff. Certainly somebody did and constantly. There was no doubt about it—he was an anal compulsive, who held his thing with a towel when he peed and washed his hands for a half hour afterwards. The most he ever did about the state of the world probably was call up David Susskind on one of those television shows and say that he thought the U.S. should drop a bomb on Red China and get rid of those dirty little people once and for all.

She was getting increasingly angry at him, and the girl for giggling, and the mothers for paying any attention to him at all, though they were obviously far too intelligent to take his remarks seriously. But somehow that thought upset her even more— If they were intelligent, and screwed around, and the fat man and the secretary were stupid and wouldn't dream of doing it, what did that do to her entire argument? Especially since she was now no longer clear on what her original argument had been.

Bo suddenly felt deeply depressed, and not being able to pinpoint her depression—whether caused by him, stupidity in general, Joan of Arc, anal compulsion, girls having babies and being women, or what—depressed her even more. She had not gotten on this bus to work out the problems of the world. She did that all day. All she was doing was trying to save eighty-five cents.

It was not worth it.

At the next corner she pressed open the metal doors, and stepped down into the cold evening air. "Taxi!" she yelled.

Alonzo Paccielli, once he had pointed out to Bo that his meter had not yet been fixed to start with the new thirty-five-cent minimum, and the cabfare would be ten cents more than that registered on his clock, did not trouble her with any additional dialogue. Park

Avenue, as they turned north from Fifty-Fifth Street, was anesthetically ablaze with the yellow lit Christmas trees dotting the islands between the uptown and downtown lanes. Bo had heard about the Christmas trees, and looked forward to their being turned on—but she wasn't aware the decoration, much less the illumination, had begun. And now that she saw it, she was singularly unimpressed, much less unmoved.

"Why did they only use yellow?"

"For what, lady?"

"The Christmas tree lights."

"For accidents. So the drivers shouldn't think they were traffic signals."

It seemed a highly unsuitable reason: surely no one could confuse the sober round red and green at the corner with a conic blaze of reds and blues and greens and yellow (as a part of, certainly, but alone?) in the middle of the hedged-in darkness in between streets. Still, it was thoughtful of them to want to do anything at all, even in dull yellow, and she wasn't feeling worked up enough about Christmas to be other than momentarily disappointed.

Her father had wanted Bo to come home for the holidays of course, but Bo had explained to him sweetly and patiently that it wasn't like school: you didn't work ten weeks and then get a parole. Then he started working on getting her to come for Christmas weekend, or New Year's weekend, telling her as an added inducement that Mother Bowman was making an especially luscious turkey. Neither the turkey nor the phrase "Mother Bowman" were especially tempting: her father had become particularly folksy since Bo got to New York, and she had the feeling talking to him long distance that her home, unbeknownst to her, had been transported to Lincoln, Nebraska; her mother, a trim blond clubwoman in designer's suits, being referred to as "Mother Bowman" would have given her as much of a turn as it did Bo. As for turkey, Bo had never liked it; there was too much meat, not terribly tasty and usually dry; for days afterward everybody lived on turkey sandwiches, and wondered guiltily if they shouldn't make the carcass, if they ever came to it, into soup. Because of the people starving in India, and all. Why turkey had remained so long the national dish for winter holidays was beyond Bo: true, the Pilgrims had eaten it, but they had been pretty hard up, Thanksgiving or no Thanksgiving, and had had to make do.

All she told her father however was how it absolutely broke her heart to have to say no, especially at the thought of Mother Bowman making that luscious turkey (actually they had two in help, but as Father Bowman didn't mention them neither did Daughter Bo). But it was no that she had to say, as she was very absorbed in her work, and she just couldn't see flying to Cleveland for either of the weekends, what with the little time she actually had free for her social obligations, which were more or less in a business vein, she said, cloaking it in intimations of cocktails at U Thant's. Her excuse, or that part of it, was the truth: her obligations were as much business as they were social, since she had no concrete plans whatsoever.

Plans or not, she had no intention of giving up her first Christmas in New York City: nor was she about to panic at the prospect of no definite prospects. At home, or even at college, she would have been in what was then described as a perfect swivet if she hadn't known by the fifteenth of December what her plans were for every night of the Christmas holiday, up to and including New Year's Eve—what they were, and more particularly, with whom. But here it was, the twenty-first of the month, or . . .

"What's the date today, driver?" she said aloud.

"Tuesday," he said.

"No, the date," she said.

"I'nt know. I think it's the twenty-first. Friday's Christmas."

"Then today's the twenty-second."

"So you know," he said. "Why ask me?"

It was the twenty-second of the month. She felt a queasy dip in her stomach, like when an elevator comes to too abrupt a halt. It was the twenty-second of December and there was no man she knew or had even been told about in whom she felt the least interest. She had no dates whatsoever for any night of the Christmas holidays, up to and including New Year's Eve. Still, she was not an adolescent, with the immature American fixation about a date for New Year's. She was a bright young career girl, working for the most important organization in the world, in the nation's most exciting city.

Anything could happen, momentarily, that could change her entire life. That was the special wonder of her job, and New York. She had seen that, for herself, first hand: only two weeks ago Ursull had drifted around on a regal Argentinian cloud, not quite touching earth. And now she was blushing and stammering and telling Bo, actually telling her in detail, about her dates with Gerd, asking simpering American questions, like "Do you think he could be interested in me?"

"Well why not, for God's sake?" Bo had said. "You're a brilliant, beautiful, exceptional girl."

"Do you think so?"

Did *she* think so? Bo nearly collapsed. For almost three months she had been hovering around Ursull, hoping for some sign of approval. And now here was Ursull, begging for it from Bo. Still, Bo was very cool about it. All she had done was cross her legs and light a cigarette, exhaling matter-of-factly, like Bette Davis.

"Anybody would be crazy who didn't," Bette-Bo said.

Bo sat back in the cab and smiled. Any day, something unforeseen could happen, to any of the girls. Even Birgitta, whose daily exploits would read like the high-points of the careers of all the Playmates of the Month combined, had been exposed to sudden and dramatic change. Birgitta, with one man stashed in her apartment, others sniffing around the edges, now, quite unexpectedly, grown pensive and thoughtful because some young Negro writer didn't want to have an affair with her, but even so, thought she should get Olaf out of her apartment. Birgitta, of all people, brooding about morality, because a man she liked didn't want to get into—but still had an opinion about—her bed. A Negro.

Bo shook her head. Not that she was prejudiced or anything. But looking for a change didn't mean Bo was soliciting anything quite that extreme.

"What you say, one-fourteen?" the driver said.

Bo looked up. "One-sixteen. It's the next brownstone on the right."

He pulled up the additional three yards and stopped the clock. "That'll be seventy-five cents."

"I thought the meter said sixty-five."

He slumped his head in disgust. "I went through all that in the beginning. The meter . . ."

"Hasn't been adjusted yet. I'm sorry. I forgot." She foraged through her pocketbook, and found her change purse, and drew out ninety cents.

"Merry Christmas," the driver said.

"Oh," said Bo, and dropping the change back in the compartment, took a dollar from her wallet. "Merry Christmas," she said.

The small cranking self-service elevator shuddered toward the fifth floor of the building, and Bo took a deep breath, trying not to look out through the mesh of the elevator cage. In the beginning, when she had first moved into the apartment with Mary Kate, it had terrified her, ascending that slowly and being able to see every floor as the elevator creaked upstairs. Then one night Marie Claire had come home with her from the UN to dinner and told her it was exactly like the *ascenseurs* they had in Paris. So Bo had regarded the elevator suddenly as chic. That night Marie Claire had related tales of her exciting life with her father, a French diplomat, and his Egyptian mistress and how they had all had to flee Suez at gunpoint, for Algeria, where they had also been victimized and Marie Claire had been twice raped by Arabs during uprisings. The next day Bo had repeated the adventures to Birgitta, who smiled a lot, and then told Bo Marie Claire had never been outside of France before coming to New York to stay with a maiden aunt and improve her English, so she could go back and work for her father, one of the most important wholesale jewelers in Paris.

"But why would she say all that?" Bo asked.

"Who knows?" Birgitta shrugged. "Perhaps she's embarrassed because her life was so uneventful."

"Uneventful? How could living in Paris be uneventful?"

"Oh, I don't know," Birgitta smiled. "Perhaps, to a person born in France, having a father who's a jeweler in Paris seems as exciting, oh . . . say . . . as growing up with a father who manufactures spare parts in Cleveland."

The elevator clanked to a tortuous stop. Ever since talking with Birgitta, Bo hadn't been particularly friendly with Marie Claire. As a tribute to her own liberality, however, Bo continued to regard the elevator as chic; but she still considered it frightening. Pulling the heavy metal accordion gate aside, she breathed with relief as she got out on the landing.

There was no sound from inside their apartment, but just the same Bo buzzed once to give the all-clear to Mary Kate before turning her key in the lock. The light in the bedroom closet had been left on, but the living room was completely dark. Bo felt her way toward the convertible sofa, and the telephone table with the lamp. It was after six o'clock, but as Mary Kate hadn't been home, Bo's father doubtless would have been phoning every fifteen minutes since the prices changed. The apartment felt a little hot, and smelled stuffy, so Bo went to open the window and get some of the air wafting off Lenox Hill Hospital.

"Damn," she said, stumbling across an ottoman that had been shifted from its normal position. She reached to turn on a floor lamp, but it, too, had been moved from its accustomed place. One of the glories of these converted townhouses, she told Mary Kate, was the absence of those horrible overhead fluorescent lights that were everywhere in new apartments. She had delighted in the absence of wall switches; but with the advent of early darkness on winter days, and Mary Kate's latest penchant of rearranging furniture to block every scene she rehearsed for acting class, Bo was no longer so sold.

"Damn it to hell," she said, as the edge of the coffee table bit into her calf. "Shit," she said, being alone, sitting on the floor, the better to press her bruise. Then the phone rang.

"Keep your pants on, I'm coming." She waddled across the floor on her buttocks in the darkness, and still holding her leg, lifted the phone from its cradle with her free hand.

"Hello, Daddy," Bo said.

"Luanna? Are you all right?"

"Not a bomb fired at us since the eleventh, Daddy. This is the twenty-second."

"I meant—you sound odd. A little out of breath."

"I just came in the door, I didn't even take off my coat yet, and I hit my leg."

"What?"

"On the coffee table, Daddy. Just on the coffee table. It could happen in my own home. My home in Cleveland, Ohio," she added hastily.

"Mother Bowman's all set to take the turkey out of the freezer tomorrow, Luanna."

My home in Topeka, Kansas, Bo thought.

"It'll be all beautiful and glazed for Christmas Eve dinner. You think you could change your mind and come?"

"Christmas Eve is Thursday, Daddy. I have to work all day. I'd love to, but I can't possibly."

"And Christmas Day?"

"I can't. I'm sorry."

"We were hoping to fly in and surprise you for the weekend, your mother and I."

Having taken her gingham apron off, from over her Chanel suit, Mother Bowman had apparently, like a distaff Superman, changed back to "your mother." Bo, smiling, heard only the end of his sentence.

". . . country club."

"What?" Bo said

"We were going to surprise you . . ."

"I heard that part. What was that about a country club?"

"Well it's the first formal dance since we joined, so your mother feels we ought to put in an appearance."

"At the country club? When did you become a member?"

"They had a meeting of the Board of Directors, and decided to amend their ruling barring certain religious minorities—"

"Jews," Bo said. "You can say it."

"So once they did that, of course we couldn't keep turning down their invitation. After all, it was, in a way, a gesture to me: they know I've opposed their methods, even though some of my best friends were members, because they arbitrarily rejected so many of my business associates, who are among the wealthiest and most cultured citizens of the community. And some of my best friends. I took a stand, Luanna, and I believe it has paid off. It was certainly worth the effort of these years, playing golf on the municipal course. And *their* clubs. I always said I would play at their clubs, but I would never join one until they could play at *mine*. Now, they'll be able to. It makes a man feel good, to know he's wanted so badly they come around to his more liberal way of thinking."

He took a deep breath. That meant he was waiting for some approving comment. "That's wonderful, Daddy," she said. "I'm certainly proud of you." Her leg still hurt, and her butt was getting cold from the uncarpeted part of the floor by the sofa-bed. "They must have really been anxious for you to join, changing the rules like that. Still, I can't help thinking the only people left in town who can afford six-thousand-dollar membership fees are Jews."

There was a sharp intake of air. "You have no cause to say that, Luanna. You know that isn't true. Not in Cleveland."

"Daddy, I'm really so pleased, and I'd love to go on talking to you, but I've still got my coat on. I haven't even sat down yet."

"That's all right. You get yourself settled, and I'll just hang on."

"No, that's not necessary, really. I'd rather just take my time and slip into a hot bath with a little warm milk." Actually, she felt like having a Scotch, but there was no need pointing that out to him. "I'll talk to you tomorrow."

"But I haven't told you yet about New Year's," he said, and she felt her heart move down to the vicinity of the bruise on her leg.

"New Year's?"

"We can't come Christmas because of the dance. So we're planning to fly in and surprise you New Year's. Of course, it won't be that much of a surprise, if we tell you we're coming. But we didn't want you to make too many dates, a pretty young thing like you might be grabbed up by all those New York bachelors."

"But I've already been grabbed—"

"What?" There was genuine alarm in his voice. She had phrased it badly.

"I've made plans." Panic flowed through her, and into her voice. More panic than she had allowed herself at the thought of having no date filled her at the prospect of a New Year's date with Father. "All sorts of plans." Axel Bowman would want to take her to the Starlight Roof at the Waldorf, or to hear Guy Lombardo, if he was still alive. "I have three cocktail parties, and a dance . . ."

"Where?"

"All over. The embassies."

"Foreigners? Don't you spend enough time with foreigners, you have to be with them New Year's?"

"Actually"—she leaned her head back against the couch, to support her lying—"my date isn't a foreigner . . ." The back of her hair touched against something on the couch. She froze. It was something warm. She reached back over her head, and her fingertips touched an arm, a big arm, and the flesh of a naked chest.

"Luanna? Luanna, are we still connected?"

If she hung up, he would call back, and if she didn't answer, summon the police long distance. If she screamed, as she wanted to do at that very moment, he would also summon the police. If the man (flat-chested woman?) on her couch had a perfectly simple explanation for being there, she would never be able to explain it to her father.

"What?" he would bellow. "A naked man (flat-chested woman) in your apartment? You're coming home, young lady!" And she would have no choice but to go, there being something fairly concrete to a father's objection to such a circumstance.

If, on the other hand, the person on the couch were a rapist or a murderer, by the time the police got there it would be too late anyway. All things considered, she had best get rid of her father as quickly as possible.

"I'm still here," she said. "I just dropped my cigarette."

"I certainly hope you're not overdoing the smoking."

And a lot of harm it'll do a raped, murdered woman, Bo thought. "I have to go now, Daddy," she said aloud.

"But what about New Year's?"

"I can't. I have a date. He's . . . he's a dental student from Pittsburgh."

"Well, that's not too bad," Axel Bowman said. "It's only an hour from here by train. And he could always switch over to medicine."

"That's right, Daddy. He's been thinking about that. I have to go now. Love to Mom," she said, and hung up the phone.

Her fingers shook as she reached for the lamp cord on the telephone table and the light went on. It was a man, a young man, and he was naked, Bo noted with only mild relief, just to the waist. In the hand farthest from her, he held a half-empty bottle of beer, and he was grinning.

"Jesus!" Bo said, and started shaking violently.

"Not quite." He raised himself on his free elbow. "I'm Alec Ingells."

"I don't care who you are," Bo screamed, fear shattering her voice. "What do you mean, lying there in the dark, not saying a word, naked for God's sake, eavesdropping on my conversation, giving a person a heart attack, and who knows what all."

"Maybe you better sit down," Alec said.

"Maybe you better tell me what you're doing here, lying in the dark, not even saying anything when a person comes in. Just what do you think you're doing?"

"Preparing." He took a drink of his beer. "Making my adjustment to the character. Mary Kate and I are doing a scene tomorrow in class."

"Where is Mary Kate?" The fear and fury were ebbing and she could see once she wiped the tears away from her eyes that he was really kind of attractive: dark, coarse hair, but not so thick that it looked scruffy, well-built arms and a smooth nice chest, if you liked that sort of thing and didn't mind men sitting around your apartment half-naked in the dark. "Where's your shirt?" she said.

"Which do you want to know first?"

"Where's Mary Kate?"

"She went down to Lexington to buy a slip. Don't you want to sit down?"

"Just don't you be so concerned about me," she said.

"I can't help it. You're hysterical."

He was smiling. Some fucking nerve. "You have some nerve," she said.

"I'm sorry if I scared you," he said.

"Adjustment," she said. "You lie there making your adjustment, and let me come in and trip and hit myself and talk on the phone . . ." She stopped, embarrassed, and wondered if she had said anything she was sorry he had heard. No. How could she. All her conversations, like her thoughts, were totally innocent.

She went to the sideboard they had gotten from the Salvation Army, sanded and stained and made into a bar, and nervously poured herself a Scotch. "Feeling a naked man in the dark. How am *I* supposed to adjust to that?"

"I don't know, honey." He laughed, and took another swig on his beer. "But if you can't work it out, you've got a Big Problem."

"What's she have to go buy a slip for anyway? I have plenty of slips."

"I know," he said. "I looked through your drawers."

"You what?"

"Strictly in the interest of art."

"Well, you *do* make yourself at home," Bo said. "I certainly hope you found something to catch your fancy."

"Afraid not." He sat up and dangled his one foot over the edge of the sofa. His feet, too, were naked, and unlike most men's, quite nice-looking with long, well-shaped toes, if you noticed that sort of thing. Bo hadn't seen many naked men's feet in winter, so she did.

"We need one of those full slips, you know, the old-fashioned kind, with a camisole top, like. Your underwear's cute, but it's a little too swinging for Stella. I mean, Stella swings but only in relation to Stanley, not underwear-wise."

"I'm sorry if my lingerie displeases you."

"I didn't say that. I said it was cute. It just wasn't right. Would you mind closing the window? I'm a little chilly."

"I'm *so* sorry," Bo said. "How thoughtless of me. But then, most young men sitting around here usually have clothes on."

"We're doing a scene from *Streetcar*," he said.

Bo closed the window, one hand steadying itself on the Scotch glass. She finally had to put it down to take off her coat.

"You've got a cute body," he said.

"It was my distinct impression that even Marlon Brando wore an undershirt."

"I don't own one," he said.

"Not even torn?"

"I don't like the way they feel new. I have very sensitive skin." He rubbed a big hand across his chest by way of illustration. "And washed ones always smell Clorox."

"She won't find a store open at this hour," Bo said. "Why didn't she at least leave the light on, so a person wouldn't have a heart attack? How come she didn't tell me there would be someone here?"

"We were supposed to rehearse at my place, only my roommate is boffing a married lady and she was coming over tonight. We would've stayed there anyway—there's a separate bedroom and I thought banging from next door would help the scene, very French quarter, thin walls, sex and all. Mary Kate said she wouldn't mind, but Married Lady was nervous, so we split. You an actress, or what?"

"What," Bo said.

"You're much prettier than Mary Kate. Better body, too. She'd make it a lot easier on Broadway if she looked like you."

"She has talent." Bo put some ice cubes from the kitchenette refrigerator in her glass, and sat down in the corner they called the dining room. "I don't."

"Oh, I don't know." Alec Ingells stretched out the dangling leg and bent the knee on the couch, and rocked his hips slowly, lolling in the most deliberate manner Bo had ever seen.

"I thought you were pretty cool there with your old man."

"I beg your pardon?"

"That was a pretty fair reading, considering you were nervous about finding me on the couch in the dark, and lying at the same time. You worked through that very well, for a non-pro."

"Worked through what?"

"The fear, the uncertainty. That bit about the orthodontist."

"What do you mean 'bit'?"

"The story about your dentist friend. Not that it was a great story, but considering how terrified you were, you delivered it very well. I thought you were a for-sure actress."

"If you are referring to my date with the dentist, that happens to be the truth. I've known him for years, he's a very nice fellow and he's studying at Columbia."

Alec laughed. "Poor reading. Very poor. You have regained your amateur standing."

"I'm going to take a bath," Bo said. "If you don't mind." She turned, annoyed. "But then, of course, if you do, I suppose you'll just break down the door."

"What are you really doing for New Year's?"

"You already know. You *heard* me tell my father."

"Because if you're not busy, I thought you might like to spend it with me."

Bo turned her head, slightly. He was sitting up now, and the sneer was gone from his face. Without the assumed expression of the wise-acre, there was something quite sympathetic, and even a little sad about him. Not pathetic, necessarily, just this side of wistful. His shoulders were very broad, but the lower part of his chest was slim, almost skinny, so the flesh seemed hard put to stretch across that wide expanse of back and arms. In clothes, she supposed, he would look deceptively broad, but knowing a big man tended to slightness further down gave you kind of an advantage. He was at least twenty-five, and, objectively, almost handsome. The fact that he was paying for acting lessons, and was not even part of a free professional acting group, indicated to Bo that he had only recently taken up acting; otherwise, at his age, with his looks, he would certainly have gotten a part by now, or at least have achieved professional standing.

Probably he had graduated from college, as she had, majoring in something useless like English. Then he had taken a crack at his father's business, which was pretty successful. All at once in a fit of melancholy he had seen how meaningless it was, and deciding to strike out on his own, had cast aside his education, his breeding, and his father's money to begin acting, and find his identity. That accounted for his attitude. The ones with the most background and training were, when they embarked on rebellion, always the surliest, and the most gross.

All of these and other speculations about him could have been crystallized into truth merely by Bo's asking him questions. But she hadn't made up her mind yet if she cared to talk to him.

"Why?" she said.

"Why what?"

"Why should you want me to spend New Year's with you?"

"I don't know. I hate New Year's. Everybody gets such a dumb fixation about it having to be special, they get all worked up for weeks before, and depressed for days afterward."

"That's true," she said thoughtfully. It was exactly what she had been saying to herself coming home in the cab, though not so completely worked out.

"We don't know each other at all, so we wouldn't work it up into a whole big thing," he said.

"I hate whole big things," she said.

"You're a pretty girl, nice body, quick—a little bit smart-ass, but that's all right. It's my fault. I scared you."

"It's kind of you to see that," she said.

"I think I'd like to be with you. And I think you'd enjoy it."

"What would we do?" Her acceptance would not be contingent on his program for the evening, but she had heard Mary Kate moaning a lot about the ONLY party on New Year's being one at the Strasbergs'. EVERYBODY would be there, the Wallachs, the Robards, Shelley Winters, and Mary Kate too, no matter what she had to do to get there, or she would fling herself under the wheels of a taxi outside Downey's. Bo didn't care one way or the other about the party. She liked the Actor's Studio people well enough, but it was fine seeing them on stage and playing *Password* once they became universal. But Alec Ingells had something a little special about him, so it was conceivable he was a friend or even a protégé of the Strasbergs, and she was not about to go to that party, thus pushing Mary Kate even farther under the wheels.

"Nothing special," he said. "I haven't accepted any invitations. I don't want to make a whole big thing."

"No," she said. "Of course not."

"I thought we could just wing it," he said. "Maybe some pizza or a couple of drinks and then you could come up to my place and get laid."

"Thank you very much," Bo said, on the threshold of the bedroom. "But I'm afraid not."

"Why?"

It was clearly not the occasion for "it's against the rules."

"I might not like your underwear," Bo said, and locked the bathroom door behind her.

HE was afraid for her. No matter how much and how often Kiiko told him there was nothing to worry about, Ernie could see how helpless she was, and could sense the tragic vulnerability of which she was not aware. The world was rife with potential danger, and everyone was hideously exposed; but she, with her heritage of horror and pathos, lay naked in the center of the target. If she did not have the sense to cower and try to cover herself, Ernie could attempt it for her. Certainly he could tremble—that was the most important thing. He could be afraid for her.

All his life Ernie had never been afraid for anyone: people he loved were afraid for him—they were always telling him how afraid they were for him, but he had never understood why. "Don't be afraid to make friends," his parents had told him when he was a very small boy. And although he was fond of them, he thought it the silliest thing he had ever heard. Friends were to play with, and playing was for fun. He had a great deal of fun, playing by himself, and as long as his own games were enjoyable he saw no need to learn new games, where other people had to play too. Especially since he might get hurt. He knew that, because his mother told him not to be afraid of making friends, and that meant he shouldn't be afraid just because she was.

His mother was a little woman, nearly a foot and a half shorter than his father, and she cried a great deal when she talked about her own parents, when she told him about the wonderful wedding to his father, where all the girls in the neighborhood had been, eating their hearts out because the groom was so tall, the best-looking policeman in Brooklyn. She also cried when she paid the bills, when the girl next door had a baby, when her sister Maureen said she and her husband were leaving Brooklyn and moving to Long Island. Ernie's mother kept saying to Maureen how wonderful that was, and how happy she was for her sister, crying the whole time. Aunt Maureen tried explaining to Ernie that his mother acted like that because she was very high-strung, but Ernie hadn't understood at all. His mother was only a little taller than Ernie himself at the time: she wasn't high-anything.

When his father got shot trying to arrest a suspected bootlegger, they gave him a hero's funeral. On the way home in the limousine his mother kept hugging Ernie to her sparse bosom, flooding him with hot tears, telling him not to be afraid, they had each other, and the policeman's fund would take care of a hero's boy even if there was a depression. "Your father wasn't afraid," she said, "and he wouldn't want us to be afraid." Ernie wasn't the least bit afraid, he was a brave kid, all his father's friends at the cemetery told him that. He had never been afraid for his father: nothing could happen to such a big, powerful man; now that something had, it was too late to be fearful.

When the Japanese attacked Pearl Harbor, Ernie was in the eleventh grade. Until that time he had given relatively little thought to a career: he had no particular wish to become a policeman, and although his grades were good, had shown no special aptitude for a particular field. Now that there was such certainty about his future, he began spending a lot of time in the Erasmus Hall High School gymnasium, so his muscular development could catch up with his height. The better shape he was in, the more chance he would have of selecting his branch of the Armed Forces. In the spring of 1943, the day he turned eighteen, two months before his high school graduation, Ernie enlisted in the Air Corps.

His mother cried a lot, and said she was afraid for him, but Ernie himself felt quite elated. The prospect of war was much less frightening than college, where he was not at all certain he would be accepted. The Air Corps sent him to flying school, but he wasn't quite good enough, and flunked out. He was so disappointed and so icily determined to succeed that his commanding officer recommended him for bombardier training. By late 1944 he had achieved such an impressive service record that he was chosen to be one of the bombardiers of the 509th Composite Air Group.

For a hero who, in his neighborhood, was now considered single-handedly responsible for ending the war, as he had flown with the boys who dropped the big one at Hiroshima and Nagasaki, nothing was difficult: local merchants and small factory owners wanted him as an employee; mothers with unmarried daughters wanted him for a son-in-law. Girls had never been much of an issue with Ernie, one way or the other, but it was becoming to a hero to have a pretty girl on his arm—and as good a means as any to getting the mothers off his neck. So from the ranks of contenders he chose Eileen, a silent, yellow-haired girl who never gave her family any trouble. After his release from the Army Air Corps he went to work as head salesman for a bicycle company (what father could resist buying his boy a two-wheeler from a hero like Ernie?) and he and Eileen took a small apartment on a Brooklyn street sporadically shaded with trees.

Eileen started having bad labor pains a month earlier than they had anticipated, but she finished doing the dinner dishes before she would let him call a taxi, and then packed a small valise herself, all the while biting her lower lip. At the hospital, before they wheeled her into the delivery room, she pressed his hand damply and told him not to be afraid; hundreds of women had babies every day. He knew that himself—and had no intention of being afraid. Eileen, quiet thing that she was, was very strong. That was why it was so surprising when she died.

Her regular doctor hadn't been able to get there in time, and Eileen, not knowing the resident, hadn't bothered to tell him she'd just eaten dinner. When they gave her the anesthetic she aspirated the food into her lungs and drowned, right there on the table. That was how the resident had explained it to Ernie, trying to make it as simple and painless as possible, so Ernie could understand. But Ernie couldn't understand any of it. He was hard put to remember why they had even come to the hospital, until the doctor told him the baby was dead too.

"We cut in to try and save it," the doctor said. "But we couldn't have done anything. She had a congenital birth defect."

"Eileen?"

"The baby. A girl. We'd have to do an autopsy to make sure . . . if you wanted. But it looked like a ventricular defect . . . The heart . . . Her heart couldn't keep beating with the trauma. You want us to do an autopsy?"

Ernie shook his head.

That night he went home and tried to sleep in the double bed Eileen's family had given them as a wedding gift. But bad pictures kept flooding his mind. The next day he moved back in with his mother.

The company gave him a month off to recover, but Ernie didn't feel like going back to work when it was over: the prospect of selling bicycles to little children disturbed him. His boss sent deep regrets but explained that as it was the height of their season, what with summer and bicycles, he had no choice but to find a replacement. Ernie didn't mind: he had some back pay in the bank which he and Eileen had been saving to buy a car, and his mother got enough from her widow's pension for the two of them.

For more than a year he lay around the house, listening to daytime serials on the radio. After a while he tired of the radio and started reading: there were too many books he hadn't read, to make a dent. So mainly he looked at magazines. Those his mother would not enjoy having around the house—like *Life*, and *Collier's*—he felt guilty about buying. So he spent most of his time in the dentist's waiting room. The dentist was his cousin Archie, with intellectual aspirations and copies of *Harper's* and *The Nation.*

Archie did a lot of reading about psychology, so he didn't mind Ernie's hanging around. "We must try to understand what he's going through," he would whisper to uneasy patients as he tilted them back in their chairs. "He's still in a traumatic shock."

The first time he ever stole a magazine from Cousin Archie, Ernie was puzzled: he didn't remember even picking it up, much less leaving the office with it tucked under his coat. Cousin Archie prided himself on his honor system: patients never took magazines from his anteroom, which was why Archie didn't even stamp the covers with his name, like some of his stingier colleagues.

Looking at the periodical in his hand, Ernie felt embarrassed and ashamed. When he saw which magazine it was, he felt stupid. It was several months old, and he had already read it. But he pulled down the shades in his room anyway, switched on the bedlamp, and fixed the chair under the doorknob so his mother couldn't come in and find him. Then he started to read the article a second time.

It was a special report on the aftermath of Hiroshima, in congenital birth defects on pregnant women. All women who were carrying at the time of the explosion, exposed to massive radiation, had aborted. Outside the dangerous zone, some had continued pregnancy. Of the babies that did live some were born normal. A lot had been born dead, but that was expected. There were a number of congenital birth defects: cleft palates, interventricular and interauricular septal defects, renal canals connected to anuses, infant girls born without vaginas, and infant hermaphrodites. But those babies the doctors were most interested and fearful to see were those conceived after the nuclear blast, whose parents had been exposed to radiation.

Ernie tore the magazine, page by page, into small pieces, and jamming them into his pockets, carried them to the bathroom, where he flushed them down the toilet so his mother would not know he had been a thief with his own cousin. He dropped them into the bowl a few pieces at a time so the plumbing wouldn't get stopped up and regorge the horror. In between, he waited for the tank to fill with water, so they would be good and gone.

Outside, his mother heard the continuous flushing.

"Are you sick, Ernie?" she called through the door.

"No, Ma."

"Why is the door locked?"

"I locked it."

"You want me to come in and hold your head?"

"No, Ma, I'll be all right."

"I'd be happy to do it, Ernie."

"No. Go away."

"Well, don't get mad about it. There's no reason to be ashamed. Anybody can throw up, Ernie. You don't have to be ashamed to vomit in front of your own mother."

The magazine was thicker than Ernie had imagined. He was in there flushing most of the night.

The next day, he went out looking for work. What had for so long immobilized Ernie was confusion: life and death and birth and sex had never seemed particularly puzzling to him. And then, for no reason, as the result of an ordinary act of nature, Eileen had died. He had never brooded about death, his father's or strangers—certainly not that far-away population beneath him that he had exploded: a person couldn't get worked up about all those people without names or faces. But Eileen was strong and healthy and uncomplaining, and for no reason she had died. That was the thing he had never understood. Now, though, it was all quite clear to him. The baby had killed her with its congenital birth defect. And the congenital birth defect had been planted in the baby by him. It wasn't only that he had been part of a mission that killed living people: he had wiped out and mutilated unborn babies, and for that God could not forgive him. So God had punished him by twisting his seed—making it grow hideous inside Eileen, and that was what had killed her. Now that Ernie was no longer confused, he could try to start doing things again.

But almost two years had passed, and the bombardier of a big B-29 was no longer a celebrity around town or even the borough. As a matter of fact, now that all the reports on the destruction were coming out, people were beginning to feel somewhat guilty about the bomb, and wanted to think about it as little as possible: they certainly didn't want one of the boys who dropped it working for them. He thought about joining the police force, but an ex-war hero and widower would have looked silly going back to Erasmus Hall, and the police couldn't waive their requirement of a diploma even for Ernie. So he worked at a series of jobs: gas station attendant, car park, soda jerk, movie projectionist, and body mechanic in a big garage by the Bridge.

Mothers with unattached daughters didn't bother him anymore: he had no future, and entirely too much of a past. His own mother left him alone, fussing over him only at meals, when she watched every mouthful he took with tears in her eyes and a smile on her mouth. The rest of the time she was content just to have him around, as long as he left his door open so she could hear his breathing.

When the United Nations buildings were opened in Manhattan, and he went to apply to the security police, his mother was a little fearful that he might want to move to Manhattan. But he never spoke of leaving. He just went to work in the morning and came home at night the same as he had done with the garage and the soda fountain. He seemed a little happier, and he dressed with a little more pride on the days he wore the uniform. But he always came home.

Ernie's mother was not a worshiper of earthly heroes. She was admiring of Mr. Roosevelt for stopping the depression, and grateful to Mr. Truman for ending the war. But it was God she had to thank for saving her her son.

Ernie, though, was no more grateful to God than God had been forgiving of him. God had punished him for being an unfeeling human being—incapable of compassion, or even fear. He had never been able to anticipate disaster, and so, had never been afraid. Now for the first time, he was afraid—deeply afraid—but he did not have God to thank for it. He had Kiiko. He was afraid for her. She had made him a human being, and that was something that even God could not do.

When he had first seen her, over a year before, he had thought his heart would stop beating, he was so unbelieving and so frightened. He knew at once she was Japanese, and when he asked her where she was from, the answer, as he knew it would be, was Hiroshima. She was no older than his own daughter would have been, and that made her one of the children in the article, conceived after the blast. So she was the baby the article had written of, an unborn child he had not murdered. He could not see the physical defect he was sure existed, no matter how he studied her. But if there were to be any peace for him while he lived, he had to protect the human being who had miraculously been spared by him, and who had been spared to be his salvation. He feared for her safety as he feared for his own soul. And gradually, in his mind, they became the same.

Ever since Ernie moved back into the apartment with his mother, she had kept a telephone only to stay in touch with her sister Maureen. Everything she needed, the grocery, the doctor, a clothing store, her dentist and nephew Archie, were within a two-block radius, including and especially her son. She had often thought of having the telephone removed, as it seemed an unnecessary luxury, especially since Ernie never made a call. Once Ernie started phoning the girl all the time, she was sorry she hadn't obeyed her impulse to get rid of it.

"You in love, Ernie?" she would say, mocking, so that he knew that she knew it was impossible.

"No, Ma," he answered.

"You going to moon around a girl, you ought to hang around her house. You never were one with words."

"I'm not mooning."

"You sound like you're mooning."

"Were you listening?"

"I have better things to do than listen to you mooning. Maybe you think I don't have better things to do, but I have interests. What's she like, this girl you're mooning over?"

"She's a baby," Ernie said. "I don't even think of her like a girl."

"Well, there's nothing wrong with your wanting a girl."

"I don't need one. I've got a girl."

"Who?"

"You, Ma."

"Silly. Now where you going?"

"I've got to make a call."

"Again?"

"Her line was busy before."

"If a girl can't wait for your call, you shouldn't bother with her. If you were my young man, I wouldn't waste a lot of time talking to other fellows."

"I'm not her young man, Ma. And she can talk to anybody she wants to."

"Well, I only hope she lives in Brooklyn. Does she live in Brooklyn?"

"No."

"Then it's a terrible waste of message units. Especially if you're not interested."

"I am interested."

Fear gripped her throat.

"But I'm not in love."

She didn't believe him. It was not surprising. Ernie didn't believe himself.

Two days before Christmas he decided he would ask Kiiko home for Christmas dinner. He didn't mention it to his mother, and by noon he had still been unable to mention it to Kiiko. So at lunchtime he had a whisky and water at The Grotto, and two beers with his roast beef sandwich.

"Hoo-ha," Baimbridge said, moving toward Ernie's booth. "How moves it, oh Sultan of squish?"

"Go away, Baimbridge," Ernie said softly. "I'm not in the mood for you today."

"Fiddle-dee-tit," Baimbridge said. "I'm not in the mood for myself either. But as there seems to be no escaping me, we should both be resigned."

Ernie took a long swallow of his beer.

"And how are all our little coozens from across the sea?"

The whisky and beer had not yet gone completely to Ernie's head. But they were, apparently, in the vicinity of his vocal cords. "Fuck off," he said.

"Would that I could, Ernest lad, but I've precious little time. Have you done all your last-minute Christmas scroffing?"

Ernie got up to go.

"Shall I wish you the joy of the holidays, boy, or will you be here on the bearded boy's natal day? Trader Horny behind the bar there has promised a free turkey dinner to all of the regular lonelies."

"I don't like turkey," Ernie said. "I'm eating Christmas dinner home."

"Goose?" Baimbridge said. "Or furburger?"

Ernie left the bar. The air outside was clear and cold, snapping him back abruptly from the slightly warm and foggy haze that had begun to envelop him. He quickened his step as he crossed to the UN plaza, trying to escape the whip of the wind coming from the East River, unimpeded by buildings, blowing as free as if it were in the open country, and not at all like it had only a block to go before being captured in alleyways and broken against the fronts of skyscrapers. That was the difference between Ernie and the wind: it could behave as if it were anywhere; but Ernie always knew exactly where he had been, and where he was going. That was what made the wind the wind, and him so immutably solid. He did not have it in him even to coddle a pretended glow. Still, he made one last attempt to save what little warmth the alcohol had engendered in him. He bolted across the wide stone terrace, running to the shelter of the visitors' entrance.

Once inside the building, Ernie took off his overcoat and made his way slowly downstairs to his locker. He combed his hair by the lavatory mirror and held a Lifesaver in his teeth while he rinsed his mouth, so his breath would be clean. He was careful not to get any cold water on his face: that might make him alert, and alertness was sometimes indistinguishable from anxiety.

The first secretarial cubicle outside the Guides' Lounge was occupied by a relief typist. Ernie asked the girl at the desk to call Kiiko.

"Hello, Ernie." A wedge of laughter jagged out at him from the Lounge before the door closed behind her. He supposed they had been laughing at him, all those girls inside. He didn't much mind their thinking him ridiculous, smirking at his attentiveness to Kiiko. It mattered only that Kiiko, for once, take him seriously.

"How are you?" he said.

She stood there, in the cold white fluorescent lighting of that hallway, leaning up against the poster on the wall, looking as golden as if she sat in a room softly spotted with candlelight. Her eyes glowed black, and there wasn't a crease in the smoothness of her round face. Most of the girls, no matter how young, were cruelly caught by the lights in the utility sections of the building, designed in the most practical fashion to accommodate reading and paper work. But not Kiiko. The formation of her bones and the placement of her features were such that no sign of a wrinkle by her mouth, no shadow beneath her eyes, appeared, even in the harshest of overhead lights. Even when she smiled there was no hint of a line in the corner of her mouth. Or when she chewed, as she was doing now, nipping tiny fragments from a tuna fish sandwich poking out of a wax wrapping.

"Excuse me for eating in front of you, Ernie," she said. "But I fell asleep and I've only a few minutes before I must go back on duty."

"Aren't you feeling well?"

"I'm feeling fine," she said softly. "Only a little tired."

"Is anything wrong?" he said with concern.

"No. I watched television very late last night. That's all."

"If that's all it is," Ernie said.

"I told you. Did you want to see me about anything special, Ernie? I left my Coke inside and the sandwich is very dry."

"Go get it," he said. "I'll wait."

"No, it isn't necessary. Please. If you don't mind, I go back inside now."

"All right," Ernie said.

He tried to smile, to show her it was important to him that she sit down and eat her lunch as she wanted to, and that he didn't mind her dismissal—polite, it was always so sweetly polite—but a dismissal all the same. One side of his face felt frozen, and only the right side of his mouth that went along with the pretense. What was intended as an understanding smile became a half-smirk, and he despised himself for his inability to seem as lovely as she.

"Is something the matter?" Kiiko said.

"Nothing. You better go inside and finish your lunch."

"It's all right," Kiiko said. "I have the sandwich here. I am not so thirsty. I can get the drink after. What is it, Ernie? You look upset."

"You should eat a hot meal. You're so tiny. You can't get strong on tuna fish sandwiches."

Kiiko smiled. "Is that what you're upset about? My not having a proper meal?"

It was the perfect opening. Even while knowing he did not always come up quickly enough with the right words to say, Ernie knew that this was the time to extend the invitation for dinner. But he was angry with himself for having shown he was upset and annoyed with her for remarking on it.

"I'm not upset. Stop thinking people are upset because they're concerned about you," he said and walked away.

Sipping on her Coca-Cola, which she had stupidly left on the radiator, Kiiko did not giggle with the other girls. Nor did she impart to them any of what had happened with Ernie. But what had happened? Nothing. He had asked after her health, which was usual. He had expressed concern, which was also usual. What was not usual was the expression on his face. For a moment he had looked grotesque, like a man afflicted with indescribable pain. Ernie was sweet, and Ernie was a little sad, and Ernie was a bit of a fool at times. But pain had seemed somehow beyond him. The embarrassing knowledge that a big clumsy turtle could writhe in discomfort beneath his seemingly impenetrable shell she found oddly disturbing. A creature who was capable of subtleties of feelings could not be so easily considered a creature—it was possible he was a man. And although Kiiko had been trained to subjugate her own wishes to men's, she had reserved for herself the privilege of subjugating herself only to those men she respected. And, more important, she had learned how to seem as if she were humbling herself, all the while keeping the upper hand.

With Ernie she had not even pretended. She had been polite about his feelings, but never really concerned about them. Now, for the first time, she felt concerned. If he were in pain, whatever kind of pain, he was far more subtle than she had suspected. And being more subtle, he was deserving of more kindness than she would have extended to the turtle she thought him to be. So when the girls made their jokes about Yearny Ernie, Kiiko did not join in the laughter. Not even to be polite.

At five-thirty, going up the circular steps to the main floor, she saw him waiting, his knuckles pressed white on the balustrade.

"Oh Ernie," she said with pleasure. "I'm so glad you waited for me."

"I didn't . . ."

She interrupted before he embroiled himself in nervous denials. "I'm sorry I could not have a chance to talk to you before. What was it you want to ask me?"

"I . . ."

"Come," she said, her hand inches away from his, pulling him by untouching fingertips. "It's so busy here with the people. The concourse is quieter."

He followed obediently behind her, staring down at her tiny dark head from what seemed a dizzying height. "The information desk," Kiiko said. "We can speak by the information desk. At this hour of the day no one wants to know where the world is going. Now," she said like a schoolteacher, turning to smile up at him. "Please," she said softly, like Kiiko.

"I only wanted to ask . . . I want to invite you for Christmas dinner. Home. With my mother and me. You shouldn't be alone on Christmas."

"Oh Ernie, how sweet of you. But I'm not going to be alone. The family I boarded with when I first came to the States has asked me to spend Christmas with them. But you are so kind to ask."

"Oh."

"I wish you had asked me before. But I thank you so much anyway. And your mother."

"When did they invite you?"

"Last week," she said.

"Did they ask you if you had some place to go?"

"What do you mean?"

"Did they ask you if you had any place to spend Christmas?"

"I suppose so," Kiiko said. "I don't remember exactly."

"Try," Ernie said. "Try to remember exactly what they said."

"Ernie, I'm very bad about conversations. It's all I can do to remember my own English. Much less anybody else's."

"Who are these people?"

"I told you. A family I boarded with when I first came."

"What do you mean, boarded?"

"Boarded. Rented a room."

"You didn't know them before or anything?"

"How could I know them? I was eighteen, and I was never out of Japan before I came here. And they had never been any place but New Jersey."

"So they weren't really friends."

"Not when I met them," Kiiko said. "But we are friends now."

"It's not the same," Ernie said. He was talking too quickly, but he couldn't stop himself. "It's not the same being friends with people and renting a room from them. I bet when they called you they said I bet you haven't got anything to do on Christmas. Wasn't that what they said?"

"I don't remember, exactly. What do people say? I hope you're not busy, or are you busy . . . ?"

"You see?" Ernie said. "They were afraid you didn't have anything to do on Christmas, so they felt sorry for you. They were making a gesture, because they felt sorry for you, because they knew you didn't have any family and they were afraid you didn't have friends. But they were wrong, don't you see, so you can call them and tell them you're sorry, but you're coming to our house."

"Ernie, I can't do that. I already accept their invitation."

"But it wasn't really an invitation, don't you see? It was a gesture, because they felt sorry for you. I'm not asking you because I feel sorry for you. I want you to be with us Christmas. I'm your friend, so you call them and tell them not to expect you, you're spending Christmas with a friend. You'll see. They'll be very pleased."

"I'm sure they'd be pleased to know I have other friends," Kiiko said. "But they are friends too. I can't cancel the appointment."

"You could," he said. "You don't want to. You don't even want to try."

There was no way to explain to him, Kiiko could see that; she had never seen Ernie so frenetic, or heard words coming from him with such speed. He stood nearly two feet taller than she did, but looking up at him, Kiiko had the feeling that he was pitiably small. "I'll try," she whispered. "Of course I'll try. Let me call them and see if there's any way to get out of it—and then I can let you know."

"Are you sure?" Ernie asked. "Are you sure you'll try?"

"Of course," Kiiko said. "If I can do it without hurting their feelings."

"You won't hurt their feelings," Ernie said. "I'm sure you won't hurt their feelings. They were only asking you because you didn't have any place to go. But now you do." He took a piece of paper from his inside breast pocket and started writing something on it, leaning against the information counter. Kiiko could see his hand was shaking.

"Here's my number," Ernie said. "As soon as you find out you can come, call me."

"If I can come," Kiiko said. "I'll phone you either way."

"Oh you'll come," he said, "I know you'll come. And don't worry about letting me know, even if it's the last minute."

"Won't that inconvenience your mother?"

"Oh, don't worry about my mother. She'll be tickled pink to know you're coming, even at the very last minute. Tickled pink."

"What girl?" Ernie's mother said.

"A girl from work."

"That girl you call long distance?"

"What long distance, Ma? How much is it?"

"It depends on what her prefix is."

"Eldorado 5."

She picked up the telephone directory and wrinkled her forehead, scanning the pages. "That's three message units."

"I'll give you the money."

"Plus overtime. The initial period is five minutes. It's an additional message unit for each five minutes of overtime or any fraction thereof." She closed the big book with a bang. "And you say you're not interested."

"I told you I'd give you the money."

"I don't care about the money, Ernie. It just seems wasteful, all those message units on a girl you're not interested in. And if you are interested, I don't know why you couldn't come out and tell me. You don't have to hide a thing like that from your mother."

"I'm not hiding anything. I told you I wasn't interested, and I'm not. Not the way you think."

"And that's why you're bringing her here for Christmas dinner.

Boys always bring girls they don't care about home for Christmas dinner."

"I didn't say I didn't care about her. I only said not like you think. She's a sweet girl, Ma. Only I'm not a boy. I'm thirty-nine years old."

"You're still plenty attractive. *Plenty* attractive. I'm not surprised she wangled an invitation out of you."

"She didn't wangle anything. I went out of my way to ask her."

"And you say you're not interested."

"I didn't think she'd have any place to go for Christmas. It seemed the Christian thing to do."

"Is she Catholic?"

"No," Ernie said.

"With all the Catholic girls who live in the same message unit area, you have to find a Protestant from Eldorado 5."

"She isn't Protestant either."

There was a sharp intake of air. "A Jew?"

"I don't know what she is. A Buddhist maybe . . . she's Japanese."

Ernie's mother covered her eyes and was silent a moment. "Why does she need Christmas? How do you know she even believes in Christmas? How do you know she believes in anything, a . . . a . . ."

"She doesn't have to believe in it, Ma. She's in America and we have Christmas. She ought to be with a family."

"She ought to stay with her own." She wiped her forehead. "Where's her family?"

"I don't know," Ernie said. "I think they're dead."

"You don't even know?"

"I don't like to ask her. She's very shy." The real reason he didn't ask was because he wanted to believe they were dead. She was an orphan, that was how he thought of her, that was what made her so in need of his protection. He didn't want to hear that they might be alive.

"Pretty shy," she said. "So shy she gets you to ask her to your mother's house for Christmas."

"She didn't get me to do anything. It was my own idea."

"Watch out for her," she said. "The worse ones are the ones that make you think everything is your idea. You better look out for her. Maybe it's good she's coming. I can watch her, very carefully. Women know about other women. Better than men, believe it. I'll watch her, and then I'll be able to tell you what's what. You're going to need plenty of help, I can see that. You've waited too long, Ernie. You're a good boy, and you didn't wait all this time to make a mistake."

"For God's sake, Ma, I only asked her for dinner."

"Christmas," she said. "You may not know how serious it is, but I do."

"Don't start imagining anything," Ernie said. "Kiiko may not even come."

As it turned out, she didn't. Ernie's mother celebrated the occasion by making a baby suckling pig instead of turkey. But Ernie couldn't eat a thing.

About four-thirty when his stomach finally quieted down, he took the subway into Manhattan, went to The Grotto, and got drunk with Ned Baimbridge.

VI

FOR Ursull, the Christmas season held none of the deceptive magic it seemed to have for most of the other girls who worked as guides. When she was a child, she remembered, there had been about it an aura of anticipation, because it meant presents, and a certain degree of relaxation in the stiffness of her father's attitude. But as she grew, and was sent away to school to be educated, Christmas became only a hiatus in her study schedule, an almost unwelcome interruption of the academic performance that had made her such a great favorite with the nuns. The sternest of the Sisters would betray regret at her departure for the six weeks' holiday; the softest would caution a safe journey, eyes filling with tears, and hug her with the irrational affection of a mother who fears that any separation might be permanent. She was the bright, sweet child that none of them would ever have: she understood that from the time she was very young. It seemed unfair, somehow, to leave them for parents who seemed so curiously unmindful of the child they had.

Not that the Hernans were at all displeased with Ursull; on the contrary: at the start of each new holiday her father would inform her how well she was looking, and how pleased he was with her progress, much in the same manner he gave his semiannual report to the stockholders of his bank. Then he would kiss her formally on both cheeks and send her off with her mother. And although Frieda Hernan spent the holidays in forced hovering over Ursull, lavishing clothes and sweets and outings to puppet shows, for all her loveliness she was not as clever as the least demanding of the nuns. Her love, although welcomed, was a little too unconditional and unearned. The triumph, for Ursull, would have been winning some display of affection from her father. And this, in all her Christmases, and all her holidays, she had never been able to do.

She did not love him any the less for his inability to be won. She had never been a disappointment to him, of that much she was sure, and she intended never to shame him. Gradually she had come to accept that this was the way things would be between them always, and if it pained or disappointed her, she was not aware of it. What she was aware of, vaguely, was that Christmas connoted no particular feeling of family or sentiment. So when Señor Almadon, one of the Argentinian delegation to the UN, called to invite her to the Christmas party aboard the Italian liner *Castelgondolfo*, saying it was her father's special wish that she spend the holiday time with a close family friend, she was distinctly surprised.

She accepted at once, of course. She was fond of Almadon, who had been a regular visitor to her home in Buenos Aires throughout her childhood. Besides, she had not seen too much of him since being in New York, although the city now served as his headquarters. And though she did not particularly relish glittering diplomatic parties, she was always well-received at them, and that pleased her. But mostly she accepted because in all her life she had never declined any of her father's requests, no matter how indirect.

Once, when she was ten, her father had remarked that she looked particularly pretty in a dress of mariposa blue; and Ursull had put it on every day for a week, until her governess had to hide it from her, saying she was beginning to resemble more a sprig of garlic than a butterfly. And when, at thirteen, she had expressed wonder and admiration at the Catholic girls in the convent school who were planning to become novitiates, it had taken but one dark and pained expression on her father's handsome face to drive all thoughts of belonging forever to the Sisters from her mind. So she regarded her acceptance of Almadon's invitation as a genuinely happy gesture, rather than a duty.

She had no intention of telling him about Gerd; but her mind and senses were so full of him, that fearing she might speak without meaning to, she invited Bo to come along to the affair. Bo was certain to monopolize the conversation and amuse Almadon, which would preclude any of those dangerous party silences that Ursull might inadvertently fill with thoughts it was too soon to think about, and far too premature to send home.

For her part, Bo was giddy with anticipation at the prospect of what was to be, in her mind, an international ball. Despite Ursull's protestations that the party would be like all parties, no more stimulating and no more glamorous than any large reception Bo might ever have attended, Bo refused to believe her. The possibility of boredom in the midst of fezes, saris, and other accouterments of intrigue seemed as likely as a famine in the middle of Horn and Hardart.

She bought a new dress for the occasion, green velvet in honor of the jaded attitude she was soon to acquire, she was sure, and deliberately plunging in deference to the jaundiced appetites she was determined to whet. Not that it was her intention to hop into the sunset with the first shiek that oiled her way, but it was the season to be jolly, and there was no harm in seeing if she couldn't drive men mad. Besides, she and Mary Kate and Alec Ingells, the foul and attractive young actor, had been having terribly intense discussions of what it was like to have grown up since the Second World War, under the Terrible Shadow of the Bomb, and how it was inevitable, under the circumstances, that morality should be shot all to hell.

Her own morality, she was ashamed to admit (and consequently never did), had not been affected in the least by the Terrible Shadow of the Bomb, and she continued to think and function the same way she imagined she would have if she had been born after World War One, and lived under the Terrible Shadow of the Machine Gun, or whatever was the new horror of that period. But she supposed that was attributable to her small-townness, and love from her parents, and all the things that Alec regarded as so contemptible. So rather than confess that she felt herself an anachronism in the Age of Anxiety, she began to work up some feelings of anxiety that she was so little representative of her Age. All of which resulted in her decision that if she could not be totally hell-bent for destruction (which Alec seemed to regard as the normal modern state), she might at least leave herself open for a little trouble. Consequently, she bought the dress.

The party itself was scheduled for the evening of Monday, the twenty-eighth of December, and all through the day Bo felt edgy and distracted. Birgitta seemed absorbed in some problem of her own, and rather than risk endangering her newfound amity with Ursull by a surfeit of her company, Bo chose to lunch with Kiiko, and bask in her premature serenity. It was Bo's wish to absorb some of Kiiko's gift for silence, so that she herself would not spoil the party by her terrible compulsion to talk. Still, the compulsion did not miraculously disappear over the cafeteria luncheon, and in very few minutes she found herself racing through accounts of how inadequate she felt to qualify as Alec's symbol of the generation born in the Second World War.

"How funny you are," Kiiko said in quiet amusement. "Why have you got to be the symbol for anything? Are you Yoshinori Sakai?"

"Pardon?"

"The Olympic torchbearer in Tokyo last summer. The boy born two hours after the bomb fell in Hiroshima."

Bo looked down at her salad plate.

"I don't understand your wish to be a generalization, Bo. It seems to be the hope of most young Americans to conform to non-conformity. And the Japanese as well, I must say, since most of the young people are so busy imitating Americans."

"But not you," Bo said.

"Not now," said Kiiko. "But two years ago at home I was quite busy trying to be like my contemporaries—unmannerly, sometimes rude, unsentimental. After all, as terrible as war is, it teaches you to have character; and we had never suffered the actual, present pains of war. We cannot remember the humiliation, the black markets, the experience of holocaust, the rumbling of hunger in our stomachs this moment, now.

"We were educated in schools and colleges that were eons ahead of those our parents attended. And now that a generation has grown up *knowing* the Emperor to be mortal, we can afford to have a 'crush' on Princess Michiko, who plays tennis, and was a commoner, and married the future Emperor. She can become the greatest popular figure for the women of my generation."

"Including you?" Bo said.

"At one time." Kiiko shrugged. "But that was because I was so busy being 'modern' I did not bother to be selective."

"And who do you admire now?"

"It is hard to say. When you grow in a country that used to be possessed by hero-worship, it is difficult to acknowledge that you have any heroes at all. But I admired Kennedy. And very much, Dr. Noguchi."

"I don't know who he is."

"But there is no reason why you should. Do you know the American scientists who win Nobel prizes, and devote themselves to medical research? You spend so much time being apologetic, Bo. We are the ones who are supposed to say 'so solly, please.' " Kiiko smiled. "There is no need for either of us to rush into being clichés."

"The wisdom of the Orient," Bo said.

"I think not." Kiiko shook her head. "My generation of young people and students has been rioting and having wild beach parties and generally behaving badly enough to show that even that phrase has no permanent foundation. What has foundation is life, the practical solution of problems, some humanitarian view of the universe—all those sweet-sounding phrases that our age has been so quick to dismiss as foolish, and old-fashioned. The old-fashioned values are there because they have proved their worth, and you come back to that view when you get over the great necessity to be 'new,' and 'different.' That much is universal. It isn't wisdom, Bo, and it isn't the Orient. It's called growing up."

As she dressed for the party that evening, Bo tried to remember everything that Kiiko had said, but the truth of the matter, she realized, was that she was far more interested in Alec's appraisal of the times. She confided as much, as she put the last of her makeup on, to Mary Kate.

"Well, that's only natural under the circumstances," Mary Kate said, appraising the neckline of Bo's dress.

"What circumstances?"

"You're not ready for moral rearmament yet. The main thing on your *psyche* is getting laid."

"Honest to God!" Bo picked up her coat and moved to the door.

"Tits up!" Mary Kate shouted behind her.

To Bo's chagrin, the party seemed as if it would turn out exactly as Ursull had predicted. Although there was a certain amount of dazzle in their being picked up at Ursull's apartment by Almadon's limousine, once inside they were driven down to the docks in the depths of the West Forties, and exited into the cracking cold of night winds coming through open spaces on the piers.

"Hurry inside," Almadon said to the girls, as he leaned over to give some last-minute instructions to his driver.

Heels clicking on the frosted, slippery cement, the two rushed for shelter inside the vast lower anteroom of the Pier 42 building.

"Bo," Ursull whispered as they got inside the doorway, touching her arm with a gesture of unaccustomed camaraderie. "If he asks . . . anything, you will not mention Gerd?"

"What about him?" Bo said.

"Nothing. . . . Of course there is nothing to say, I don't mean to give it any importance. But Almadon is so curious to let my family know what I am doing. I wouldn't like him to pick up any information that might seem—significant, when it really isn't. So you won't mention him?"

"Mention who?" Bo said, trying for some of Kiiko's charming inscrutability, but realizing the subtlety was lost on Ursull, who seemed too preoccupied to appreciate humor, she smiled. "I've forgotten all about whatever his name was," she said, and squeezed Ursull's hand.

Two ladies from the UN Hospitality Committee stood shivering at the foot of the protected gangway on the second story, leading up to the ship.

"Your invitation, please," said the policeman who stood beside them. Señor Almadon reached inside his breast pocket.

"Ah, but there's no need," gushed one of the ladies, a withering blonde, smiling lavishly. "The good Doctor Almadon is very well known to the Hospitality Committee."

"Madam." Almadon bowed nearly from the waist, and kissed her gloved fingertips. "It is amazing that the committee is not renamed 'the Graciousness Committee.' 'Hospitality' is too mild a word."

"He's heaven," Bo whispered to Ursull. "She's about to faint right onto the gangway."

Ursull smiled as she followed Bo up the narrow wooden walkway. "All the more remarkable in that he hasn't the least idea who she is."

"How do you know?"

"He would have introduced us instead of being so elaborately complimentary."

"Well, that makes him even more heavenly," Bo said. "I guess they all know who he is, though. Those poor hungry ladies who are all set to zero in on an eligible Latin."

"He isn't eligible," Ursull said. "He has a lovely wife and four children."
"In New York?"
"In Buenos Aires."
"So then maybe he is eligible—at least according to them. After all, with the wife there, and he is attractive . . ."
"And very wealthy, so his wife comes to New York one week out of every month, or he flies there."
"Oh," Bo said quietly. Not that she had any wish to become involved with a married man, but he was amazingly good-looking for a contemporary of somebody's father.
"Now come, my lovely ladies," Almadon said, hurrying up behind them, a hand on each of their shoulders, impelling them onto the promenade deck of the ship. "I am sure the party is barren for your absence."
"It seems awfully quiet," Bo said. "Are we early?" There was no one on the deck with the exception of some ships' officers who smiled constantly but seemed unfamiliar with English, or the possible direction of the party.
"We are fashionably late," Almadon said. "I wanted to come precisely on time so you could fully enjoy the party, but I'm afraid the entire party is being held unfashionably early."
"Which way is Main Deck?" said a flustered lady in a mink jacket, to the officer standing by the LOUNGE sign.
"Per la ascensore," he said, smiling terribly wide.
"He wants us to take the elevator," Ursull said.
"Which way is the elevator?" the lady said, and was answered by the same enthusiastic but thoroughly uncomprehending smile.
Ursull asked the question in Italian, and was greeted by an answer so lengthy and effusive that Almadon and Bo started to laugh.
"You have your first admirer of the evening," Almadon said, as the elevator doors closed and he pushed the button for Main Deck. "I thought he would follow us into the elevator."
"Italians become very excited if you speak Italian," Ursull said.
"You underestimate yourself, my dear. You are extremely lovely, even to a man who is not an Italian. You and your friend both."
"Thank you," Bo said, as the elevator began its slow descent.
"It is not a compliment, it is an appraisal," said Almadon. "The wonder to me is that I should be lucky enough to be able to escort

both of you to this party, when New York is so full of energetic young men who would be most anxious to accompany you anywhere."

"You are too kind," Bo said, falling into his same formal speaking pattern. "And you are also too optimistic. The number of wonderful young men floating about in New York City is grossly overrated in the popular imagination. It's all you can do to find a decent escort, much less a potential romance."

"You jest," said Almadon.

"I wish," said Bo.

The doors opened onto Main Deck, with two grinning officers standing in front of the purser's office. "After all," said Bo, as Ursull went to ask them where the party was, "it's not everyone who can stumble onto a man like Gerd."

Her face went bright red, as she realized what she had said. And although Ursull had not heard her make the slip, Almadon had. Bo hated herself in that moment, and wished she could learn once and for all to have a good time and relax, and not feel this inane necessity to fill every moment with her mouth.

"Like who?" Almadon said.

"Oh no one," Bo said. "A cousin of mine in Cleveland that everyone has a crush on."

"Gerd?" said Almadon. "That's a German name, isn't it?"

"I don't know," Bo said. "Is it?"

"Is your family German?"

"I don't know what we are," Bo said. "Scotch, Hungarian, a little mongrel thrown in. We never get too worked up about background in Cleveland."

"That's one of the nicer things about your country, I would imagine," Almadon said.

"I certainly hope so," said Bo, and dashed toward what she hoped would be the furore of the party.

It was terribly disappointing of course. The minute she checked her coat with the attendant outside the Main Lounge, she felt flooded with embarrassment. There she was, all eyes upon her cleavage, she was sure; not that she was misshapen or anything, quite the contrary. But as her glance scanned the room she saw at once that she was terribly overdressed. There was not another fully exposed bosom in the place, and scarcely more than a few naked collarbones and backs. Most of the women were wearing dress suits or high-necked wool dresses, almost as if they had come directly from the office upstairs to the Christmas party at a big advertising agency, which is what, she supposed, this was in its own way. After all, most of these people worked at or had business with the UN, which, for all its noble purpose, was a business like anything else, employing people, having a good year, or a bad.

There was a liquor punch by some wilted hors d'oeuvres, and she drank it, making a face, but not wanting to seem obtrusive by asking for an unmixed drink. A stern, burly Yugoslav, who was not her dream of romance but at least had no wife and children in Zagreb, muttered to her that if she had come early she could have had the hot canapes, and that she would have enjoyed.

"It makes no difference," said Bo, a little slurringly. There was more liquor in the punch than she had imagined. "If this were the Yugoslav Embassy party, we could all be drinking vodka, and that I would have enjoyed."

"We do not serve vodka at our parties," he said testily. "We are Communist, but we are not Russian."

"I'm terribly sorry," Bo said. "I wasn't testing your commitment. I was only saying I like vodka."

"We don't drink vodka," he said.

"I apologize," she answered. "What do you drink?"

"Slivowitz," he said, and walked away.

"I am not a hit at this party," she murmured to herself.

Almadon was very cordial, introducing her and Ursull to all those who seemed as though they might be of interest to either of the girls. But after two hours, Bo realized it was exactly as Ursull had predicted: a large reception, like all large receptions, crowded, undirected, and, in the end, terribly boring. "And even more," Ursull whispered. "It is exactly like all parties on a ship—no visitors being able to find the room on Main Deck, and by the time they do, the ship is ready to sail. But alas, there is not even to be a sailing tonight. Are you ready to leave?"

"Whenever you are," Bo said, and aimed herself for a final salute to the punch bowl.

"You're beautiful," a young man whispered behind her. She knew he was young without looking, merely from the timbre of his voice, which she guessed in the crowded hum to be softly accented with the tones of Central Europe. "If I had seen you when you first came in, the night would have had meaning for both of us."

"And is it too late?" she asked quizzically, turning to meet what she knew would be his frank and forthright stare.

It was a little less forthright than she had imagined, veering slightly to the left of her forehead, but she supposed that it was because he, too, was unaccustomed to the whisky punch, being a fair-skinned Moslem and forbidden alcohol by the Koran, probably.

"Don't know," he said. "Are you wiz zomebody?"

It was possible that he was French, having slipped into a Chevalier accent, although Bo could not imagine it, the French having to train for such a long time for the diplomatic service, and he so very young, and handsome.

"Only a friend," she said. "Señor Almadon." She blushed to herself to think how glibly she had told Almadon that romance could not happen. "And a girl I work with at the UN." She blushed even harder to think how foolishly she had accepted Ursull's pronunciamento that there would be no one at this party who would bring about a change. The world was full of adventure, and at a party given by the UN. . . . the possibilities were as wide as the world itself.

"She young, or what?" the young man said.

"I beg your pardon?"

"Well, I only thought if she was young, I could fix her up with one of my buddies. I came here with a couple of buddies."

Scotland? Bo thought. The IRA? Australia? Where was the culture that had given rise to this young man. "Forgive me," she said aloud. "I can't quite place your accent. Where are you from?"

"Dartmouth," he said.

"Oh for God's sake," said Bo, and went to get her coat.

VII

ALL through dinner, Birgitta seemed to bounce between joyous hilarity and an almost studious pensiveness. It was the second time Mason had brought her to this particular East Indian restaurant—too brightly lit with a lunchroom garishness—but with excellent food and a restrained clientele. She seemed to be delighting in the cuisine, but then, in the month or more that he had eaten dinner with her regularly, he had never seen her indifferent to a meal. Even things that he himself found difficult to manage, like a particularly greasy *couscous* at a North African bar they had discovered on Twenty-Eighth Street, Birgitta approached with the daredevil gluttony of an iron-bellied adolescent.

Nor could Mason attribute her strange lack of ease to the presence of Quilo Harabey at dinner with them. Quilo, almost from the beginning, had been appointed unofficial delegate to their relationship, a post they had commemorated by buying him a Shriner's fez and a YMCA sweatshirt, which he good-naturedly donned whenever they went to his apartment for drinks, or when, as tonight, there was little likelihood of Quilo's bumping into any of his fellow diplomats from the UN. Quilo was a solemn, seemingly pompous African, but Mason had quickly seen through his reserve, and attributed his manner more to the singsong quality coming through his archly British diction than to any personality traits. Making jokes did not come naturally to Quilo, but at least, as Mason pointed out to Birgitta, he kept putting on the sweatshirt to let them know the appreciation of their humor was there.

"He's probably a riot in Watusi," Mason had said, and Birgitta laughed with him, as, eventually, did Quilo.

If anything, Quilo tonight was unusually relaxed, his eyes projecting more merriment than Mason was accustomed to seeing. He spoke with minimal solemnity, and the stentorian tones he used even for polite and casual conversation were considerably lightened.

"What are you so happy about?" Mason directed his question to Quilo, even though the thing he really wanted to know was why Birgitta seemed depressed. "Don't you think he seems a little too happy, Birgitta?"

She nodded abstractedly, her mouth full of food.

"In seven or eight weeks," Quilo said, "perhaps before, if the Assembly Session is over in time, and I can make all the arrangements, I go back to my home to fetch my sweetheart." He grinned enthusiastically. "Even now her family is making the preparation."

"You sly dog," Mason said. "How you do keep a secret."

"So when next I return to the United States, I will bring with me my bride. Provided, of course, all goes well."

"Well, I think even a bungling diplomat like yourself can manage a routine thing like a wedding." Mason chuckled. "Don't you think so, Birgitta?"

"I don't think you ought to put him down when he's discussing something so important to him," she said.

"Oh, it's all right," Quilo said, his teeth gleaming white. "I am almost used to the strange mind of our friend by now. And even he could not still my enthusiasm for my sweetheart."

"Oh I don't know," Mason said. "Why don't you let me try?"

"Stop," Birgitta said.

"Listen, he happens to be fairly enthusiastic about the future of Africa, and he still manages to make some nifty boo-boos."

"What is a boo-boo?" Quilo said.

"A mistake."

"Ah well," Quilo said, his smile still broadening, "that is because we are human. But it is because we are human, also, that we marry, so if anything our humanity will enhance the glory of the event."

Mason shook his head, sadly, and then sighed. "You're in too gay a state of mind, my friend, for me to be able to offend you. So . . ." He smiled and extended his hand. "Let me instead offer my congratulations."

"They are welcome," said Quilo.

"I'm sure you'll be very happy," Birgitta said.

"That is kind of you."

"I withdraw what I said before." Mason picked up his napkin and wiped his lips. "There is no conceivable way even you could mess up a simple wedding."

"Ah, but it is far from simple." Quilo waved his hand. "The wedding itself will be a very elaborate affair. And the bride, although she is the loveliest girl in the village, is getting a man they consider in our country . . . what is your expression? Quite a caught."

"Quite a catch," Mason said.

"Exactly. So even though I would take my sweetheart as a bride for no consideration but her own loveliness, it is a question of her family's honor that they provide her with a suitable dowry."

"Have you finished eating, Mason?" Birgitta asked. Seeing him nod, she reached for his plate. "Is it very dear, the dowry?"

"Not by American or European standards. Or even some African ones. But it will be expensive for her family, because they are not among the wealthier of their tribe. So they will have to work exceptionally hard to collect the proper number of cattle, the amount of cloth required . . . that sort of personal treasure for the bride."

"But if you're going to live in New York . . . ?" Birgitta said.

"It makes no difference. It would not be needed even in an African City, but these are village people, and the token must be presented, even if it is not to be used by the couple. Customs die hard, you see, and it is well to keep them alive, especially in the case of family pride. I have already caused somewhat of a problem for them in their community by choosing her as my sweetheart, instead of one of the daughters of the richer families. They will have to go on living there, even though we might be gone, so it is for their happiness as well as my sweetheart's that they be able to show they can provide for her. And they will."

"I'm sure they will," Birgitta said.

"Oh there's nothing to worry about." Quilo smiled. "All of their distant relatives and faraway cousins are contributing something, for the family's honor. And what they cannot manage, my brothers are providing, under cover of darkness. But," he grinned wide again, "it must all be done slowly, and with a great deal of caution. . . . It is one thing, stealing gold, or even sneaking it into a treasury . . . and quite another secreting a goat onto a man's property in the middle of the night."

Mason and Birgitta both laughed.

"And of course it must all be managed cleverly, and slowly, so all the animals do not turn up at once and seem too much of a miracle. Especially to the parents, who would be highly insulted if they knew I am helping."

"I underestimated you," Mason said. "You are a first-rate diplomat."

Birgitta, still smiling, exchanged Mason's barely touched food with her empty plate and started sprinkling salt on it. "We must all celebrate together when she comes." She forked some food into her mouth, and mumbled one syllable.

"When?" Mason translated. "She wants to know when."

"It depends. How long it takes me to make all the arrangements here, how long it takes to get the prescribed number of gifts together . . . Fortunately, my sweetheart is delicate. Her health is strong, you understand, but she is small for a village girl, and quite dainty. Her appetite is also small, which means it will not take much to feed her, and that too determines the size of the dowry. It is not for that I love her, but it is a stroke of luck, her appetite. If my sweetheart were to be like our Birgitta, the heavens know how long it would be before we could marry. It would not be quite so simple a matter, my brothers smuggling in elephants."

What started in Birgitta as laughter changed quickly to a short choking cough. Her eyes grew glossy, as she stopped chewing and turned away.

Quilo looked at her curiously. "I did not mean to offend you," he said, a wrinkle of concern on his smooth wide brow. "It is what comes of my trying to make a joke."

"Don't be foolish," Mason said. "You couldn't hurt her with a bulldozer when it comes to eating. I insult her all the time and she just keeps chomping away, happy as a vulture. Don't you, honey?"

She didn't answer. A faint flush began working its way up her cheek.

"It just went down the wrong way," Mason said. "Didn't it? You want me to hit you on the back?"

She shook her head, and reached for the glass of wine.

"That's right. Drink it down," Mason said. "It just got stuck in her throat, that's all."

"I was joking," Quilo said. "You are a wonderfully constructed young woman, not the least bit fat. Your appetite is health, and that is how it should be. It grieves me that my sweetheart does not have more of an appetite, truly it does. Perhaps I chose the wrong word, when I said she was dainty. You see?" He hurriedly took a large alligator wallet from the inside of his jacket, and extracted a picture from between his identification cards. "She is not what you would call dainty, so much as compact, that is perhaps a better word." He offered the photo to Birgitta. "As you can see, she is certainly not lacking in flesh. When I said dainty, I meant only in comparison to most of the girls in her tribe, who stand much taller, and are much fuller in the back and hips. I didn't mean, certainly, in comparison to you."

Birgitta examined the photograph in her hand. The girl's face was young, and very dark, with exceptionally wide-set eyes. She was completely naked, except for a string of beads hanging from her waist. "She's lovely," Birgitta said.

"I don't often show the photograph in America, of course. People here are poor about concealing their shock—I even encountered some difficulty in having a snapshot made into the large photo in my bedroom. The picture was taken at her puberty rites, to show all her points of beauty."

"Lovely she is, indeed," Mason said, taking the photo from Birgitta and looking at it before he handed it back to Quilo. "You're a lucky man."

"Thank you," he said, returning it to his wallet. He smiled uneasily at Birgitta. "But you can see, can't you, that she is far from fragile? I meant nothing by what I said." He looked angrily at Mason. "It is your fault for always saying I am too serious. I try to make a joke, and I am clumsy and offensive."

"Please," Birgitta said. "You didn't say anything wrong. It was a very funny joke."

"Then why did you become upset?"

"It was what Mason said," she murmured, looking down at her plate. "Something got caught in my windpipe, that was what it was."

"I hope that's so," Quilo said. "If not, I beg you to accept my humblest apology."

"Oh come on," Mason urged. "This isn't the General Assembly. Don't make such a big deal."

"All the more reason," Quilo said. "Birgitta is my personal friend. You understand, don't you?" he asked her. "I think of you as my friend."

"I understand, and I'm very grateful. It's nothing you said, I promise."

"Then what was it?" Mason said. "All that business about brides . . . Surely you're not sentimental about ritual sex in darkest . . ."

"For one who was so anxious to let something drop," Birgitta flashed at him angrily, "you can be pretty persistent, and damned annoying."

"Now I'm making you quarrel," Quilo said.

"Nobody's making us anything," Birgitta said coldly. "Except your friend here who seems incapable of letting things go."

"If you'd be happier without me . . ." Mason said, making as if he were getting up.

Birgitta ignored him, fixing her glance on Quilo. "Is there anything I can do to help you? You'll want to get everything ready, before you bring her back?"

"Oh yes." Quilo nodded. "I am already looking for another apartment. The one I have now is quite suitable for me alone—many of the diplomats are living there, because it is so convenient to the UN. But I would wish to live in a building that was not so big, and one that was closer to the markets. It will all be terribly new to her, of course, but I imagine if she can do her own shopping, she will feel much easier." He drew a small pipe from his overcoat, and began filling it with coarse tobacco.

"Why don't I help find an apartment?" Birgitta said.

"That is most kind, but the embassy has already been helping me. And one of the ladies from the Hospitality Committee has been out many times."

"Every little bit helps," Birgitta said. "I could get the papers this weekend, and stop in at some of the new buildings, and . . ."

"It really isn't necessary," Quilo said. "I appreciate it, but I think we have already settled on something that will be quite suitable, if we can work it out." He lifted a lit match to the rectangular bowl of his pipe, and sucked in the flame. "The management has already been in some discussions with the Hospitality Committee, and they think we will get the apartment, provided my wife dresses in some sort of tribal robes so the other tenants will not confuse us with American Negroes."

Birgitta looked away.

"Of course," Quilo continued, with a wry smile, "I would have enjoyed seeing her in Western clothes, and the other will take some doing, as she lives in the warmest part of the country where the national costume does not consist of much more than you saw at the puberty rites. Still, I think we can manage. I am in the midst of working something out with the wife of my good friend from Ghana."

"Next case," Mason said.

"We'd better go," Birgitta said emptily. "It's late."

They walked Quilo back to his apartment on Forty-Fourth Street, and Birgitta shook her head at his threshold offer of a drink. But she took his hand warmly, and wished him much happiness, and reiterated her hope that they could all celebrate together when he returned with his bride.

"We will," Quilo said. "Be assured we will." He shook hands with Mason, and went into the swinging glass door of the apartment building.

Birgitta was very quiet as they moved to the corner. Mason asked her if she wanted to take a cab, but she shook her head, walking slowly, her shoulders slightly hunched against the wind, her face partially hidden in the collar of her bright blue coat.

"I don't know where you get your energy, chickadee," he said. "You're not so much younger than me, how come you make me feel like an old man?" He smiled at her, but she did not see the smile in the darkness. When he peered around her shoulder and put the smile so it was almost in front of her eyes, she looked away. "I don't know, I'm about finished by the walk from the restaurant, and you're still raring to go. It's enough to give a healthy American boy a feeling of inferiority."

Her eyes crinkled slightly above the collar of the coat.

"Come on," he urged her. "Let it come out. Don't be afraid to show you're having a good time."

"Look who's talking," Birgitta said, but she laughed anyway.

"So what do you think?" he said. "You think if I fueled up like a Swede truckdriver, I could foot it all the way to Seventy-Seventh Street?"

"Shut up," she said, and punched him on the arm.

"Ingemar Johanssen." He did a brief, light-dancing shadowbox toward the lamppost. "All the time I thought you were a Swedish lady, and here it turns out you're Ingemar Johanssen in drag. I should have known all along."

"There was a simple way of finding out," Birgitta said.

He seemed not to hear her. "That's nice isn't it, about old Quilo? He's such a stick, honest to God, I never knew such a sweet man that seemed like such a stiff. I like to think of him hangdogging around his lady. Maybe that'll take a little of the rod out of his backbone, and he'll be able to relax."

"That's all most people need, is to feel wanted," she said softly. "Anybody if they don't feel wanted, can be ill at ease."

"Ill at ease?" He chortled. "Ill at ease? Man, I have seen him completely and thoroughly at ease and he is still a stiff."

"Then maybe he wasn't really at ease," Birgitta said.

"Oh he was. Believe me, he was. The first time we went out together, I took him up to Harlem. We went to clubs, bars, the whole Thomas A. Cook, and that man was out of his head with controlled joy. There were a couple of moments there I thought he was actually going to blow his cool. But he has no cool to lose. He is cold."

"I don't think so," Birgitta said.

"Well, honey, you can see things in the black heart that not even us perceptive pickaninnies can find."

"Maybe he was embarrassed," Birgitta said. "Maybe he was being gracious, but he didn't really want to go to Harlem."

"Didn't *want* to go? He begged me. I mean it. He really nagged till I took him. There was no mistaking the expression behind that sub-Sahara stare. Oh no, he wanted to go. He's such a goddam farmer."

"Then maybe he was sorry once he got there."

"He wasn't sorry. He thought he was in Hollywood, for God's sake. All those pretty girls, he kept saying, all that music. Goddam farmer thought he was in Hollywood."

"Why do you keep seeing him if he's such a farmer?"

"Quilo? I love Quilo. He is the epitome of the noble savage. Rousseau would have adored him—Thoreau would have flipped his pond. The only problem with Quilo is he's so busy showing how far he's come from being a savage, he comes on a little too noble, even to himself. Like a kid in a rented tuxedo who's still got manure on his shoes, so doesn't dare look down. But I love him."

"You're very hard on the people you love," Birgitta said.

"Why shouldn't I be? I'm easy on the ones I hate. Easy as pie. Yassuh, nozzir." He lifted an invisible tray on the upraised palm of his hand, and shuffled it slow motion up First Avenue.

"I changed my mind," Birgitta said. "Call me a cab."

"Okay . . ." Mason stopped, mid-shuffle.

"You're a cab," they said in unison, and laughed.

He stepped out from the curb and scanned the thinning traffic up First Avenue. "There's one," he said, and put two fingers between his lips. His whistle was sharp and clear, and the car with the small yellow light on top veered from the right-hand lane in his direction until it was within a few feet of him. The driver narrowed his eyes, and pulled away.

"You better try," Mason said, and stepped back on the curb. "They might stop for you."

"We'll take a bus," she said, and pulled him to the opposite side of the street.

The bus was almost empty, except for an elderly woman dozing in the front seat, her head rocking against a shopping bag that seemed to be filled with old newspapers and celery tops. "Let's sit in the back," Birgitta said. "I don't want to wake her, and I feel like making noise."

"You're in a peculiar mood," Mason said, grasping the back of the seat with one hand, holding Birgitta's elbow with the other as she smoothed her coat beneath her.

"Am I?" She looked up at him, innocently. "You can sit down, now. There's plenty of room."

"I noticed it during dinner—even before he made that crack about your eating. You kept bobbing up and down like a yo-yo."

"Whee," Birgitta said, bouncing exaggeratedly with the motion of the bus. "I'm a yo-yo."

"Stop being silly, now, please."

"Why?" Her blue eyes crinkled at the corners. "Will the neighbors talk?"

"I just hate to see you flying around on such a forced high," he said. "All you'll do is make the plummet twice as fast when you start to fall."

"Can't you stand it for anybody to be happy?" she said, the smile glazing over on her face.

"Not that happy. Not that fake happy." He clutched at the metal handrest on the seat in front of him. "I worked too many cuckoo hutches not to know what happens when the highest flyers get brought down."

"I'm not crazy," she said, tears welling up in her eyes. "God knows I should be after this past month and a half, but I'm not crazy."

"Easy," he whispered.

"Well, now you can be happy, because I'm not happy anymore." The tears edged over her high cheekbones, and rolled down the sides of her face. "Does that make you happy?"

"No, Birgitta." He handed her a handkerchief. "Not at all. I didn't want to bring you down."

"Well you did," she snuffled, unfolding the handkerchief. "This is clean."

"That's all right," he said. "Use it. That's what it's for."

She stared at it thoughtfully, and then blew her nose. "How much does it cost you, having this washed and ironed."

"I don't know. Fourteen, maybe fifteen cents."

"Oh dear," she sobbed, and buried her eyes and nose deeper in the white cotton.

"Now what did I say?"

"Fifteen cents," she wailed. "And I've got ten washing machines in my basement."

He smiled, and curled his hand gently a few inches behind her bowed head. He held it there, for a moment, uncertainly, and then let his arm come to rest on the back of the seat, well behind her huddled, shaking shoulders. "Now come on . . . I've got a fine laundry, been dealing with them for years. Wing Lee's hand pressing and washing. You wouldn't want me to take my business away from them? Chinaman's got to live, too."

She blew her nose again, and wiped it with exaggerated gentility. Then she looked up at him. "I used to take Olaf's shirts to the Chinese laundry down the street from us. The first time I went there, he was pressing a pair of shorts, with one of those irons that plugs up into the light socket, and I was so pleased. I thought, finally here's someone who will iron Olaf's shirts properly—he wasn't very fussy about most things, but he couldn't stand the laundries that machine-pressed his shirts, they were always putting wrinkles in." She reached over, tentatively, and touched the points of his collar. "You know what I mean?"

"I know," he said and lifted her hand, gently putting it back on her lap.

"Anyway, one morning I had to go to work especially early, to cover the early shift for Bo, so I took the shirts over about eight o'clock. And I caught him. Chow Mein, or whatever his name was. There he stood with the ironing cord still plugged up into the light socket on the ceiling, and a blue pair of shorts stretched out on the table half-ironed, and the truck right outside the door with two men bringing in huge bundles of shirts from the machine-pressing plant."

Mason laughed.

"I told Bo, and she said there was nothing left to believe in anymore. Do you think there is?"

"Sure," he said. "Sure, there's plenty. My Chinaman still presses his own shirts. He hasn't gotten smart yet."

"I wasn't talking about Chinese laundries," Birgitta said.

"You feeling better?"

"Sure. Much better." She crumpled the handkerchief and put it in her pocketbook. "I'll wash this one anyway, if you don't mind. Fifteen cents is fifteen cents. . . ." She toyed with the catch on her purse, opening and closing it. "I'm sorry about before. You didn't bring me down. I've been like that all evening."

"I know," Mason said.

"Birthdays always make me like that. All anticipating, and overexcited."

"Why didn't you tell me it was your birthday?" he said.

"It isn't. It's yours."

"My birthday's the fifth of May."

"Well that's a nice date, too, but you never told me—so I decided to make it today. I baked a cake."

"You're stupid," he said, smiling.

"We haven't had any occasions for so long—it's been at least three weeks since Christmas, so I figured we were due for something."

She turned her head toward the window and peered out into the darkness. "Did we pass Seventy-Second Street? Did you notice if we passed Seventy-Second Street yet?"

"No."

"Oh, it's all right. It's up ahead. . . ." She looked down at the purse in her lap, and kept buckling, and unbuckling. "I even have a present for you. . . ." She waited.

"Olaf's gone," she said, and buckled the clasp, holding it closed. She turned slowly and looked over at him. His jaw was set very square and tight, and the skin seemed to be straining over warm brown knobs beneath his ears.

"Well?"

"That shouldn't have been a present for me," he said, finally. "That should have been for you."

"What's the difference?" She shrugged. "I haven't been to bed with him since I met you."

"I didn't ask you to—"

"This is our stop," Birgitta said, getting up and pulling the cord. "We better hurry."

He walked the two blocks to her building in silence, Birgitta humming a tune deep in her throat, and dancing with occasional lampposts. An old Czech storekeeper, in a dusty cap and an overlarge dull gray sweater, pulled the iron gate across the glass front door of his magazine, candy, and sausage store, and peered over at them with nearsighted indifference. The avenue was very still, except for the faraway yowls of battling alleycats, and the whoosh of air brakes from an unseen truck.

"Come, slowpoke," she said. "It's cold."

They turned off the avenue, to Seventy-Seventh Street toward the river.

Two stories above the street, an old woman sat on the fire escape outside her window, looking up at the stars, and fanning herself with a newspaper as though it were the middle of July. A baby cried somewhere, or perhaps it was another cat. Mason could not tell. He was not used to such silence in the street, and it was oppressive.

"Come," she said. "Come, we're here."

He hesitated outside the brick and glass entranceway, glossily canopied in managerial eagerness to make a good impression. Apparently it had not been impressive enough. More prominent even than the canopy, brick and glass, was the enormous sign standing on the sidewalk: 2/3/4/5/ ROOM APARTMENTS AVAILABLE. . . .

She pulled him by the arm, a little girl dragging a too-big pet, before he could see the name of the desperate rental agent. "I thought you were the one who was tired," she said.

"I don't think I ought to come up."

"But he's gone. I told you. He's been gone for a week, but I was saving it as a surprise—for your birthday." She smiled at him so openly and ingenuously, he heard his throat crack dry.

"I'm tired," he managed to say. "I'm very tired."

"But your cake . . . I made your cake."

"For a minute," he said. "I'll come up for a minute."

"Good." She beamed. "For a minute."

In the lobby, from habit, Mason looked quickly around to see if there was any sign of the doorman, giving him looks darker than his own skin. But he was nowhere around, and the doors to the self-service elevator were already open in front of them, Muzak jangling out into the barren marbled hallway.

"Come," she said. "I'll be the operator. You don't even have to push a button."

"I thought they turned that stuff off at night." He squinted up at the ceiling where the music seemed to be originating.

"They do," she said. "At eleven. It's only ten-thirty."

"It feels later."

"That's because you're an old man," she said, stepping out of the elevator, jingling the keys in her coat pocket as she went down the hall.

"Well . . ." She threw the door open. "Here it is. What do you think of it?"

"I could tell better if you turned on the light."

"How clever you are." She ran to the wall switch, and bathed the tiny foyer in a muted gold light. Closing the door behind him, she took his coat and hung it in the hall closet, beside her own.

"Now come," she said, taking his hand. "Close your eyes and let me lead you, so I can give you a wonderful surprise."

He hesitated.

"It's only the cake," she said.

The main room was still unlit, so he did as she directed, closing his eyes, letting himself be led across the carpet and around a corner. She told him when to sit, and instructed him not to peek until she said so. Through his lids, he was aware of a tiny flash of light, and then another, like two distant tiny rockets, close together but eons apart in an infinite sky.

"You may open them now," she said.

She stood directly in front of him, her face shining in the light from the one candle blazing on top of the loaf of French bread. "Happy Birthday."

"Is this my cake?" He grinned.

"Only half of it," she said, and carried a deep covered copper pot, a tiny flame shimmering beneath it, to the table in front of him. With a potholder mitten, she lifted the top. "Look."

"I see dark," he said, peering over the edge.

"Oh. I suppose I'd better put on the light." She drew down an overhanging chandelier, a wheel of wrought-iron candles, and turned a switch, illuminating the dining alcove. Inside the pot, swirling in dark red script on pale creamy gold, was a shaky, liquid HAPPY BIRTHDAY MASON.

"It's magnificent!" he said. "What is it?"

"Fondue. Cheese fondue. Anybody can bake a cake."

He laughed. "You are a remarkable girl. Truly a remarkable girl."

"I have to admit I had a little trouble finding a dark enough cheese to make the inscription."

"How did you manage?"

"You won't be disappointed?"

"Nothing you do could disappoint me."

Birgitta hung her head. "The man at the Deli gave it to me. He put purple food color in the cream cheese for a bar mitzvah."

He smiled.

"Well, don't just sit there admiring it." She broke off the end of the French bread, still dripping with its candle, and handed it to him. "Dip it in and eat."

"I wish you had told me before I had all that dinner. I couldn't eat a thing."

"You're not hungry?" she said.

He shook his head. "But I suppose you are."

"I am," she said, turning away slightly, blowing out the candle on the bread, and the warmer beneath the pot. "I am very very hungry." She smiled, and lowered herself slowly to her knees, running her arm inside his jacket to his back, pulling him toward her as her face pressed into the front of his shirt. "So much so, that if don't take care of me, I may die."

"Stop it," Mason said, his voice shaking. "Please. Don't make me hurt you."

"I won't," she whispered against him. "I won't."

"Birgitta, please, I'm asking you."

"Yes?"

"Get away from me. Please get away from me."

She pulled him tighter against her, and her cheek found the softness of his skin inside his shirt. "Goddammit," he said, his hands coming up like iron grips on her arm and shoulders, flinging her away. A surprised gurgle escaped her throat, and she fell backwards in a clump on the floor. "I asked you, goddammit." He rubbed his eyes furiously with his hands. "I asked you."

"You asked me what?" she said. "To get Olaf out so you could be with me?"

"NO! NO! You listen, but you don't hear. I wanted him out of here for *you*. For *you,* not for *me*. I asked you to stay away from me."

"Every night?" she said. "Is that what you were asking me at dinner every night? To stay away?"

"I told you to make other dates. I didn't tell you to only see me!"

"But you called," Birgitta said. "Every day you called, and asked me to see you."

"Only if you were free. Only if you had nothing more important to do," Mason said.

"Free? I was certainly not free. I had nothing to do, nothing at all, if I could see you."

"That was a mistake," he whispered. "I didn't want you to do that."

"I wanted to. I want to. I WANT! I WANT!" She lifted herself to her knees. "Can't you understand that?"

"Better than you," he said huskily.

"Of course," she said. "Better than me. No one can feel or understand anything as well as you. I had forgotten."

"I'm sorry. Let me help you up."

"I can manage." Her knee buckled under her, and she reached for the edge of the table for support, pulling the chafing dish to the floor.

Mason shook his head. "You are clumsy," he said, smiling warmly. "You're beautiful, but you're clumsy."

He went into the small kitchenette, and got some paper towels, and started wiping up the spilled cheese. She watched him, almost trance-like, tears falling slowly, dully down her cheeks, like tallow wax from a candle, as she stared stupidly, telling him he didn't have to do that, and thanking him, and saying she wished she were dead.

"There," he said, piling the dirty towels in the paper bag by the sink, washing his hands and drying them on the red and white dish-towel. "It's all clean. Like it never happened."

"Only there's no fondue," she whimpered.

"There'll be others."

"That's what they all say," she said. But she let him help her up. The last moment, before she completely had her balance, she rocked gently toward him.

"No, baby," he whispered against her hair.

"Why?"

"I've told you why."

"No you haven't. You've only told yourself, and thrown words at me. Nothing you said means anything. Not to me. Please . . ." She turned her lips toward his.

"Cut it out. Goddammit. CUT IT OUT!"

"You're a hypocrite," she screeched at him. "Do you know that? You're the worst kind of hypocrite. Quilo can think of me as a woman—just a woman—no white, no black. A woman. He said if my bride were like Birgitta—not white like Birgitta but with an appetite like Birgitta. Why can't you see me like that? What do you think it is if it isn't bias?"

"Sense," he said softly. "Good solid sense."

"Well, it's not. You're lying to both of us, honest Abe. It isn't sense at all."

"I told you I shouldn't have come up here."

"Is your estimate of yourself really so low, you've got to humiliate me? Is that going to make you a big man? Humiliating me?"

"I'm not humiliating you," Mason said, straightening out his collar. "You're humiliating yourself. I tried to stop you. I told you not to."

"Oh you are thoughtful," Birgitta said. "You are the most selfless, thoughtful man. Always thinking about others, and *nobody* ever thinking about you. That's shocking. Simply shocking. Here's you, so perfect, and here's me, not even acting the good hostess." She grasped the edge of the room divider and moved outside the kitchen-ette. "The least I could do is show you the rest of my apart-ment. Won't you come in? Let's pretend we're starting all over again. Why Mason, how lovely to see you. Won't you come in?" He followed her into the living room, and moved toward the window seat as she switched on a lamp. "What do you think of my little place?"

"It's nice," Mason said, surveying Birgitta's apartment. "Very nice. Clean and crisp, just like you."

"More like Olaf," Birgitta said, switching on the indirect lighting pole behind the desk, and easing herself into the sling-back canvas chair. "When he first moved in here it was a perfectly usual studio apartment. He got the idea of partitioning off the kitchen and that side of the room and making it into a separate dining alcove—and he measured and designed, and then we went down to the lumber yard, and got the wood. He installed it himself. And then he designed the bookshelves and stained them, and mounted them on the wall behind the bed. It does look wonderful, doesn't it—the whole wall arrangement looks built in."

The bookshelves went from ceiling to floor on either side of the bed, almost down to the pillows in the center. Lights, of various intensities, emanated from behind different shelves. A reading light from the overlarge shelf that doubled as an end table, softer lights from beneath, the wooden platform mounting under the bed—all controlled by a switch at the right side of the mattress. The bed itself was kingsize, covered with a multicolored wool throw. It looked enormous.

"He must have been very handy," Mason said.

"Yes, he was," she said coldly. "Is there anything else you want to know?"

"Look lady, you don't have to get angry with me. I didn't ask to come here." He stood up from the window seat, more planks that the clever Olaf had erected to hide the radiators in front of the triple bay windows, covered with warm blue velvet that did nothing to take the chill from Mason's back. "These windows don't close completely," Mason said. "There's air seeping in somewhere."

"It's better than suffocating."

"You ought to speak to the superintendent about fixing them."

"He is not as handy as Olaf," Birgitta said.

"Well, I'm sure you can work something out."

"Why don't you sit on the bed if you're cold?" Birgitta said.

"I'm all right here." He sat down stiffly.

She leaned far back in the chair, caught in the sling of canvas, one foot beneath her buttocks, and the other leg curled up over the metal rim. "These chairs are expressly designed for comfort once you're in them, but they are extremely difficult to get out of," she said. "I assure you you'll be quite safe on the bed."

"The playground of the western world," he said.

"Is that what offends you?" she said coldly. "That I didn't save myself for you?"

"Nothing offends me," he said. "I offend myself."

They were both silent for a few moments. Mason turned and looked out the window, peering below for lights and searching above for stars. He could see neither. The apartment was on the fourteenth floor of an elevator building by York Avenue, and had been advertised as having a view of the river. Birgitta had told him it was true, for almost three weeks after she signed her lease, until they started construction on another elevator building directly behind it, one story higher. Now the view was obscured by the blank face of a retaining wall, and the sky was hidden by the neighboring penthouse.

"They really hooked you with this place," he said.

"I don't mind it," said Birgitta. "The rent was really quite cheap as long as I was splitting it with Olaf."

"I didn't tell you to make him move out," Mason muttered.

"Of course not. All you said was you couldn't come up here while I was living with another man. Thank God he's gone, I say. Now we can be together as we really are, at ease, relaxed and comfortable, without the pressure this man feels in public places."

"I didn't ask to come," Mason said.

"And where were we to go? You refuse to take me to your apartment."

"You'd really like that, wouldn't you? You'd really like that fine. Shucking and jiving all the way to a Hundred and Tenth Street."

"You don't have to live in Harlem. You could live in the Village or on the West Side . . ."

"I know," Mason said. "But it makes everything so much easier. Cabdrivers won't stop for a black man, you see, because they don't want to take him all the way uptown. You can wait maybe one, maybe two hours before a taxi will stop for you, and then it's almost always a black man who wants to go home or a cabbie with a license to carry a gun. So I figure, as long as he's finally stopped, this brave liberal, why should I break his dark heart and tell him to take me to West End Avenue?"

Birgitta rolled her head back against the metal frame of the chair and stared at the ceiling. "Why don't you buy some acid?" she said. "You could put it in a bottle like nosedrops and carry it with you all the time. Burn yourself somewhere—not a fatal spot, just some place extremely sensitive like the crook of your elbow, or the inside of your thigh . . . that would be a good place. And every time the pain started to go away, you could just dab a little on to start the agony again. That way you could be a little easier on yourself, Mase. You could have the pain all the time, constantly reminding you of pain, only you wouldn't have the problem of having to come up with the words to torment you. That seems a little much for any man, having to supply both the agony, and the words to remind him of the agony."

Mason laughed. "Oh lady fair, if that were only the case. If you only knew how many times I have honestly tried forgetting—even actually forgotten for a moment, only to be reminded by something or someone a lot less sympathetic to me than me."

"But why with me?" Birgitta said. "Have I ever said or done anything to make you feel this way?"

"Nothing," he said. "Except be a snow princess."

"You have a problem," Birgitta said.

Mason smiled. "True, true. But then, so do you. Whuffo you wanna mess with me, honey? Plenny a Charlies round hyar like to slip it to you. Why don't you save us both a lot of grief and spread your lily thighs for the white folk?"

Birgitta got up from the chair with some difficulty, raising herself with her arms, easing her hips over the edge, and went toward the kitchen. "But I've had so *many* of them. And I've never tried a big buck nigger." She batted her eyelashes at him and smiled sweetly as she passed the partition into the alcove. There was a clink of glasses and the sound of bottles being moved around, as her voice drifted over the partition. "You see, I've read Norman Mailer too, Mase darling, and I know you black boys are insatiable and your parts are absolutely *enormous*. You wouldn't want me to miss out on that, would you?" She came back, carrying two small glasses filled to the brim with a transparent white liquid, and offered one to him. "Aquavit?" He took it, and she settled onto the window seat beside him, still using the same mocking, cloying tone. "Then too, I've read all those other books, and seen *Birth of a Nation,* so I know how you dinges lust after us white women."

"Okay," he said. "Cut it out."

"What, honey? My lady parts? Is that what you want me to do, so we can keep up this sweet relationship, meeting every night in integrated bars, laughing for a few hours because you seem to be able to forget my color if not your own? Eating dinner in African and Indian restaurants, where I'm the freak, so you can feel more or less at ease? Bringing me home and leaving me in the lobby of my building, kissing me chastely on the cheek if the doorman isn't around, or holding my hand lightly in the taxicab if the driver is one of your people? Who should perform my hysterectomy, a white surgeon or a black? Or should I take a quick hop to Sweden and see my father, and say, you're the specialist in endocrines, Doctor. Give me something to shut off my juices—because I have great hungers and nothing to feed them."

"I didn't ask you to stop seeing other men. I didn't tell you to get rid of Olaf."

"You said it was wrong, living with a man I didn't love."

"That was honest."

"For whom?" Birgitta said. "For me or for you? I wonder, sometimes, if you have any concept of what real honesty is. Or isn't everything you see colored. Black frontlash. There's a phrase for you. Use it in your magazine. There isn't an ounce of moral indignation in you that isn't as biased as the people you despise."

"That isn't true," Mason said. "You're attacking me and I understand, but it isn't true."

"That's very liberal of you," she said. "Making an attempt to understand me."

"So see other men. Let Olaf move back in."

"I doubt that he would," Birgitta said. "He may be white, but he still has his pride."

"I'm sure you could break him down." The glass in his hand was shaking. Drops of the transparent liquid splattered onto his trousers. "I'm sure he loves you. He would have to love you."

"I don't want him back," Birgitta said quietly. "That's one thing you don't understand about amoral women. When we care deeply about one person, we can't care lightly about someone else."

Mason stood up. "I'm sorry," he said. "I'd better go."

"When will I see you?" Her voice was anxious.

"I don't think we better see each other anymore."

"Not even in the dark?" Birgitta whispered. "If we saw each other in the dark no one would have to see us. No one would have to know we were together."

"You glow," he said. "Especially in the dark."

"If you came here . . . If you only came here. If we spent time together in this apartment, no one would know." Her tone was pleading, and she could not look up at him.

"You don't deserve that," he said.

"I'll be good," she said, like a frightened little girl. "I won't ask you to be with me alone anymore. We'll keep it the way it was."

"We can't. Not any more."

"Then make love to me," she said. "Make love to me, just this once."

"I can't."

"A farewell gift of the generous spirit?" Birgitta said. "Couldn't you find it in yourself to give me that?"

"I don't want to make it more involved," he said.

"More involved? Oh my God, you sound like a twenty-one-year-old schoolgirl. That girl I work with—Bo . . . I suppose she's a typical American virgin, wouldn't go to bed with a man because she thinks that would make it 'involved.' Involved? What could be more involved than what we already have? You stimulate me, you make me laugh, you make me angry, you make me cry, you make me more alive than I have ever been, and you think making love to me would mean our relationship was *involved?* Dear God in Heaven, what could be more involved than one human being who is empty without the other one?"

"I could tell you," he said. "But you're too angry now to believe me."

"You're right," she said. "You are unbelievable. My angry Negro intellectual who is also a twenty-one-year-old Puritan maid."

"I'll get my coat," he said.

She did not look as he went to the hall closet. She could feel him moving around in the tiny foyer, and picture the easy flow of muscle beneath the light wool sports jacket. She heard the swish of material, as his long arm reached into his overcoat sleeve. She covered her ears and tried to press all her senses into numbness but she could feel him and picture him with eyes and ears closed, and it was too much for her.

"Oh please." She ran to the entrance hall and threw her arms around him, and pressed her lips to his throat. His hands involuntarily circled her head, and he stroked her silky hair.

"You smell so clean," he whispered. "You smell so pretty and clean."

"Please don't go," she wept. "Please don't leave me."

"I have to, baby. If I go now, we'll both get over it. If I stay, we won't be able to."

"Why would we have to get over it?" she said.

"You know the answer to that. We have no real future, you and I. If I had you with me, it would be that bottle of acid, for both of us. The pain would be there all the time. Only not just for me. I can't punish two people like that."

She shuddered, and he patted her back to warm her, but she drew away. When she looked at him, the tears in her eyes seemed to have hardened into crystal.

"I see," she said. "This way we're just punishing me."

"Believe me," he said. "It'll be easier now than afterward."

"Why?" she said coldly. "You really believe the legend about yourself? You really buy that nigger myth? You think once I get a taste of your big black body nothing else will ever satisfy me again? I have news for you, Mr. Reporter. They have bigger and better ones in all shapes, sizes, and colors, all over the world. And I've had plenty, so I know. It depends on the person, you see. Even pallid Olaf was well hung, because he had a little manhood in him. But you're so piss-ass noble, it's probably no bigger than my pinky."

"Good night, Birgitta. I'm sorry." He turned to go.

"Go ahead!" she screamed after him. "Be a martyr. Only when you make your noble sacrifice, be sure it's yourself on the altar, and not someone else."

The door closed behind him.

An hour later, her eyes swollen half-shut from weeping, she went down to the street and hailed three different taxicabs. When the last driver stopped, and she saw through her heavy, stinging lids that he was young and reasonably attractive, she invited him up to her apartment. She did not even offer him a drink before taking off his clothes, and her own.

VIII

THEIR courtship, after the near-disaster of their first theatre date, had developed with all the charm and predictable sweetness of a fairy tale. And Ursull tried to remind herself, whenever she became a little cautious or wary of Gerd, that some of the most enchanting fairy tales, like the most cynical philosophies, had originated in Germany. That this incredibly handsome, brilliant and witty prince should have appeared out of a crowded nowhere to claim her, was no longer a source of great wonder to Ursull; Gerd had so continually assured her she was a princess, she had begun to believe him, if only because, as a good pupil, she responded to constant repetition. That their romance was preordained, and could only end happily ever after, she still had some doubts. But they were beginning to crumble under the battery of his loving protestations.

"Is there anything more positive than a German in an argument?" she would ask him.

"Nothing," he said. "Except a German in love."

The one unqualified miracle that was still left to Ursull was the fact that their relationship had survived their first Saturday date, and going to the Miller play together. Although not a believer in love at first sight (which Gerd swore he had recognized and acknowledged the moment he joined her tour) Ursull was still a subscriber to the notion that the course of true love must run smoothly at least for the length of the first formal rendezvous.

From the moment they entered the theatre, he so resplendently golden and tall beside her, and she, stretching comfortably to her full height, neck held high, dark and regal in deep maroon velvet, she had felt a sense of deep malaise. He was at first disappointed, then angry, with the location of their seats, and after being unable to contact his ticket broker on the phone, had settled reluctantly into the middle of a rear row, his long legs cramped against the seat in front of him. As soon as she opened the program, she was sure that in his present mood the play would be a mistake.

It was. The difficulty was not only in the subject matter, dealing with German guilt and responsibility in the extermination of the Jews, which content he might have anticipated, or at least been aware of—it was the play itself. It was slow, and grim, and excessively wordy, and had been played with no intermission. She had felt her own buttocks begin to deaden underneath her, and could not bear to think what stiffness and tingling was going on in his legs, if not in his mind. Had there been but the faint possibility of moving, and temporary escape—not so much for the Jews in the play who were undoubtedly doomed—but for Gerd, there might have been some hope. As it was, she could imagine no worse possible choice for a first date, unless, possibly, she had asked him to take her on a guided tour of Auschwitz.

True, he was a German. Obviously, in his physical appearance, he was the Hitler ideal of pure Aryan. And since his father's company was so successful and had been so for a long time, there was every possibility, even likelihood, that his family had been Nazis. She did not relish the thought; but the grim irony was that most anti-Nazis had not survived, except by fleeing Germany—and there was suspicion even among the refugee German colony in South America that some of its leading citizens, professed anti-Nazis, were indeed really Nazi war criminals who had escaped toward the end of the war. She could not hate Gerd for being born a German—it would have been as insane and illogical as hating a man for being born a Jew. Besides, when Hitler had come to power, Gerd could have been no more than an infant. Could she despise him for having grown up in a country once afflicted with an inexplicable madness, any more than she could hate a child for growing up healthy in a country ravaged by plague? Of course not. He, at least, was blameless, and incredibly beautiful.

All this she tried to communicate to Gerd in the darkness of the theatre by taking the hand that rested near her elbow. But after a while even her fingertips were numb and damp, and she sat covered in confusion, not wanting to add to his physical discomfort by keeping hold, and not daring to take her hand away lest he confuse her gesture with disdain. Finally, she leaned over and whispered to him that her arm was asleep. He nodded coldly and released her hand, wiping his palm on the legs of his trousers.

It was a fiasco. Afterwards at dinner he made fitful attempts at being lighthearted and amusing—but they collapsed in mid-gesture. And she, trying with equal desperation to help him, only made it worse and more painful for them both. He had taken her directly home, shaken hands stiffly in front of her door, and promising politely that he would phone her soon, disappeared from her life forever.

Or so she had thought. She did not have much time to brood about it, however. Sleep, ringed with regret, did not come easily, but it came. She was awakened from it by the ringing of the telephone by her bed.

"Hello."

"Ursull?"

"Yes."

"This is Gerd. Did I awaken you?"

"Yes, but it's all right."

"I know it is," he said. "At least you had some sleep. I had none at all."

"I'm sorry."

"So am I, but that doesn't matter now. I waited as long as I could, but it is past nine o'clock, and that is late enough. Too late, if we are to have the entire day in the country."

"I see," she said coolly, but she was smiling.

"How soon can you be ready?"

"An hour?"

"It is too long. I will be outside in fifteen minutes."

"You can't get here so fast."

"I am already here. My car is parked across the street from your entrance, and I am looking at your window from the phone booth on the corner."

"And what if I told you I couldn't go with you?"

There was a silence on the other end of the phone. "I would drive away and never come back again. Until perhaps tomorrow."

She laughed. "I'll be ready in a half hour."

"Fifteen minutes," he said. "Please, no more. Last night was perhaps the worst of my entire adult life, and to erase it from memory will take all the beauty of a very long day. The sun is shining, but it is still winter. It will be dark by five o'clock. Fifteen minutes. Please."

"Fifteen minutes," she said, and hung up the phone.

It gave her enough time to make herself fresh, and wash the sleepy uncertainty from her eyes, and see the full joy of her smile in the mirror above the basin. It also gave her enough time to pick and discard five different sweaters, and finally select the pale blue that would make the whites of her enormous black eyes seem just as blue by contrast, and the skirt to match, and long woolen stockings and flat-heeled walking shoes: they would walk, and whisper, that much was certain. She put on no makeup, because that might take a few minutes, but her features stood out clear and in case they stopped in somewhere softly lit for dinner, she put a lipstick and an eyeliner pencil in the pocket of her camel's-hair coat.

It did not give her time enough to fix her long black hair in an intricate knot behind her head, or even a soft braid around her ears, but that was all right: if they were to walk and whisper, there was the chance that he might like to see it in the wind, so she brushed through it with strong strokes, once, and circled it gently behind her neck with a pale blue satin ribbon. She had never been so completely aware of herself before; but, smiling with pleasure at her own reflection, she realized it was because no one else had ever been so completely aware of her. There were her parents of course, and her teachers at school, but she had never believed them—and Bo and the girls at the UN, but they were just being kind—and the many young men who had wanted to woo her; but they, of course, hadn't mattered.

She looked at herself and realized, for the first time, that someone could fall in love with her quite easily. And closing her eyes for a moment, she desperately wished that he would.

He did. The moment she approached the small red sports car he told her that a man with less self-control than he might be driven quite mad at the sight of such beauty so early in the day, especially after having slept not at all the night before. Such a man, finding himself hopelessly in love with her, might declare himself at once. But Gerd, with his admitted restraint and innate caution, waited until six o'clock that evening.

They were sitting on a small mossy bank near a stone bridge in northern Connecticut. (Gerd wanted to place a marker there so they would be able to find it again. Though his sense of direction, like all his instincts, was unerring, he admitted that he found himself slightly unhinged, and consequently, lost.) They had found the place by accident, though Gerd insisted, smiling, he planned on its being there, near a thickly wooded residential section off the main road. There was a sign near the small lake, saying trespassers were forbidden, but like everything else he had been accustomed to all his life, his habit of obedience had been undermined. It would be another matter entirely, he told Ursull, if it said trespassers would be shot, as he had more reason than ever to wish to stay alive. But in his present state, he insisted that no one could mistake him for a trespasser, and certainly not once they saw who was with him. She belonged in the softness of the countryside—such beauty would be welcome, and wanted, anywhere—even when all else was kept away.

They walked on the bridge over the narrows, where the stream emptied into the lake, and Gerd said it was lucky the water was frozen, or he might find himself dangling his feet like a schoolboy in July instead of an aging executive in December. The sky darkened around them, hidden partially by the trees, and they found some pebbles to throw, a soft blanket he had covered her legs with on the ride up to sit on, and the mossy place on the bank to settle, and talk, and look at each other, unaware how quickly time was passing. He touched the back of her neck, gently, and took the pale ribbon from around her thick black hair. It fell down her back and around her face like a soft dark cloud, and a few strands of it blew across the negligible distance between them, and touched his lips.

"It's so dark," he whispered.

"It's late," she said. "And it is winter, as you said."

"I wasn't speaking of the sky." He reached over and traced his fingers across her cheek, back to her ear, and his hand closed around a thick coil of her hair. "Sometimes you are aware all day that night is coming—inevitable, predictable. There are many kinds of anticipation: for the person who is afraid, there is dread; for the person who is eager, impatience. And for someone like me, so very reasonable, my life so well-ordered, I face it as a fact. Yes. Night exists. It is coming. I am aware of it all day. But when it happened, I didn't even see it happening. Do you understand?"

"I'm not sure," Ursull said.

"I am," he said softly. "I'm in love with you."

He kissed her once, sweetly, on the mouth, his lips unexpectedly soft. Then he took her firmly by the shoulders, and raised her to her feet, stooping to pick up the blanket and drawing it tight around her. "Are your hands cold?" he said, and not waiting for an answer, kissed her palms, before tucking them inside the blanket's edges. "I must take good care of you," he said, his arm around her shoulders, hugging her to him as they slowly walked back to the car. "I always knew you existed, but you still come as a surprise."

Eventually they found the main road, and he drove more slowly than he had on the journey coming. He made her snuggle down in the bucket seat so she wouldn't have too much cold wind on her face, although she kept assuring him she liked it. It didn't matter, he said, smiling, next time he would put the top on the car so she could be properly sheltered, as befitted a priceless treasure. With his right arm he held her to him, his hand loosely capping the radiant wonder of her hair.

They stopped to dine at an unexceptional restaurant near the New York border, but Gerd exclaimed it was the finest dinner of his life. He saluted it with the finest wine the place had to offer, a moderately good Reisling which he said they could not drink too much of, because he was drunk enough on his emotions, and still had to drive.

Ursull through all of this was thoughtful, battling her own confusion; it was not that she disbelieved him—she herself had found unaccustomed magic in the day. And, for all her great reserve, she felt that if she opened her heart she might indeed find herself confessing she too was in love. So it was entirely possible he had fallen in love with her as he said. The worst cynic was a frustrated romantic, so it was conceivable that not having lived long enough, or sought hard enough, to suffer frustration, a person could afford to be completely at the mercy of romance.

What confused her was what had gone before, and what now would come after. The way the first evening together went, was, in her concept of love, the barometer of an affair. No matter how well she knew a young man, or how pleasant he seemed to be, it was their first evening together alone that mattered. And if it had not gone completely well, which it seldom had, there being so many small things that could mar an otherwise perfect evening, she might continue to date the young man in a friendly enough fashion, but realize it would lead nowhere. Consequently, none of her brief courtships had survived. Of all the dates she had ever accepted, or which had been arranged by parents or friends, the first evening with Gerd was unquestionably the most unnerving, uncomfortable, and in all ways, the most disappointing. That such a beginning could turn on its own weathered stem into a blossom of love astonished her. She did not rule it out as a possibility—she had been too good a student of philosophy to discount the seemingly illogical. But that this was to be her great romance seemed highly unlikely.

The other thing that troubled her was, if he was to be her lifelong lover, what were they to do now that they knew they were in love? Love had a beginning, which boded well (as theirs hadn't, but she was willing to let that pass for the moment), a middle, where each lover was unsure of the other and himself, and the end, where, freed of their doubts, the lovers could at last confess their feelings. But he had already done that. Or at least pretended to, and she could not think anyone so straightforward and honest, guilty of sham. True, she had not confessed her true feelings, and that at least could torment him for a while, keeping him on tender tenterhooks.

"I do not love you," she could say, and watch his beautiful face shatter, but that she could not stand to see. Besides, it was a lie. At least she thought it was a lie. Being more or less inexperienced in matters of the deeper heart, it was possible she did not know what love really was. But she was not stupid and her intuitions were excellent, and even without a basis of comparison, she had a very good idea this was as close as she would come.

She would not pretend indifference: she was not cruel, nor was she a good-enough actress. What she would do was say nothing to him for a while. That would make him wonder. That would keep them going. Going where? That was the problem. Would they marry? It seemed most likely: as little as they knew of each other, it was apparent that they were ideally suited. And marriage was the final curtain, once the end had been attained, and they'd confessed, and there were no obstacles, as there obviously wouldn't be between Ursull and Gerd. Either marriage, which was probable, or tragedy, which, looking at his warm golden-gray eyes glowing from the candles and the wine and the sight of her, was out of the question.

No, the only thing to do to fill the middle act of their perfect play was to say nothing. She could look warmly but speak coolly, and confess nothing at all. And when, finally, Isolde said I love you to Tristan, magnificent strains could swell from the orchestra pit, a stirring enough climax to warrant the final lowering of the curtain without either of the lovers having to die.

But at the threshold to her apartment her plans were somewhat revised.

"I won't ask to come inside," he said, his hand circling her mouth so her lips opened like petals toward his face. "All I would want if I came inside would be to make love to you, and there will be time for that. Today we have fallen in love, and that is a very full day for any man, and any woman. Making love, that we will do the rest of our lives." He drew her face toward his, and as their lips touched, his hand moved to the back of her head, pressing it gently forward. His other hand reached inside her coat, and skirting her breasts lightly, came to rest on the small of her back.

"I love you," he whispered, against her mouth. Then his lips were on her neck and his warm breath was in her ear, and she was turning her face frantically to find his mouth again with her own.

"Ursull . . ." he said, and his hands were behind her, urging her body toward his.

She pressed herself harder against him, and when her body could strain no nearer even with the helping insistence of his hands, her own arms were around his shoulders, impelling him closer.

"I love you," he said again, against her hair, and her throat, the words a warm windy whisper across her fiery cheeks.

She struggled for something to hold on with her lips, but his face was nestled deep in her throat and she could not find his mouth. And so the words escaped her.

"I love you," she said. She certainly did not mean to say it. She hadn't even known she would say it. The whole thing came as a great surprise to Ursull.

But then, of course, so did Gerd.

In the days that followed, Ursull tried to atone for her inexcusable breech by tormenting herself with as many doubts as possible under the circumstances. Gerd was delightful, Gerd was beautiful, and Gerd was more demonstrative and attentive every day. But she made an effort. When she could no longer question his sincerity, she tried being anxious about her own desirability. And when her mirror stubbornly refused to reveal a single flaw, she took to asking unsure questions of her co-workers.

Bo was no help at all. Every time Ursull would turn to her, asking if she thought anyone could possibly be in love with her, Bo offered reassurance. Anyone would be a fool who wasn't, Bo said, filling Ursull with despair. Even Birgitta, who could be counted on for some cynicism, was absorbed in her own problem, and kept telling Ursull it would be fine, she was lucky: everything for her and Gerd would be simple, and easy. Ursull had no problems at all.

Finally, after four or five days, Ursull abandoned her abortive attempt at anxiety. Gerd, apparently, had not noticed—or if he had, had chosen to pay no attention. He adored her; it was a miracle, but seemed highly in order. He refused to be anything else but overjoyed.

At the beginning of the weekend, however, she did manage to create something of a problem. Every night during the week he had taken her to a long, wine-filled dinner, or a movie with a light meal afterward. When he brought her home, he would kiss her for a few moments outside her door, never asking to come inside, and never again repeating his reason for not asking. Ursull had been somewhat relieved—not that she believed she would not be able to control him, but she was not altogether sure she would be able to control herself. She had never considered herself cold: she had accepted it as a fact like any other that sometime, with someone, she would probably feel passion. But she had never suspected, other than intellectually, the extent to which she would feel it.

Her first physical contact with him had rocked her to her foundation. Although she had done no more with him than she had done with any young man, with Gerd she had done it eagerly—even aggressively. Her behavior shocked her no more than her thoughts, which she took to be as licentious and salacious as those of a depraved man. Sometimes she visualized him without his clothes, and when she felt him next to her, it was all she could do to keep from asking him not to leave, not to leave at all, but to come inside the apartment, and go straight to bed with her, and not leave their future in the future any longer. It was always with mixed regret and relief that she watched him go down the stairs.

So when he called for her in his car outside work Friday afternoon, and she saw the grocery bags on the floor, she felt a brief wave of apprehension.

"What are those?" she asked.

"Food, wine. Everything we will need."

"For what."

"For the weekend."

"Are we going away?"

"We're going to your apartment," he said.

She was quiet all the way home, her pulse pounding so noisily in her ears, she was afraid he could hear it.

"I think we better have an understanding before we go upstairs," she said when he had parked the car.

"We have an understanding." He reached across the steering wheel, and took her face in his hands. "If we don't, nobody has ever had one."

"Please, Gerd," she said, and pulled away from him. "I don't mind cooking dinner for you. I'd enjoy cooking dinner for you. But that's all."

"I see," he said, smiling.

"Do you agree?"

"We shall discuss it later," he said, and got out of the car, reaching in for the grocery bags.

Ursull's parents had wanted her to take an apartment with some other girls: she had made many friends in college, and there were three daughters of Argentinian businessmen and diplomats in New York whom she knew quite well. But she had demurred, explaining that she hadn't had a room of her own since she was at home. All through school she had boarded with other girls, and when she married, there would be an end to privacy. They finally agreed, trusting her not to let it come before.

As she ascended the stairs, with Gerd close behind her, humming the kind of tune she supposed men whistled in the shower, she bitterly regretted her decision, wishing that there were three or maybe four other girls inside the door, making any attempt on his part impossible. But she knew, even as she wished it, that her thinking was ludicrous. If he was not to be manageable, no number of girls or even full-grown, wart-nosed, duennas would keep him away. He had a place of his own, a suite in a hotel, where he did not think it would be proper to take her, but where she knew, if he insisted, she would go. If his wish were merely to seduce her, there were any number of places where he might try, and, unless she manifested a good deal more control than she felt, succeed.

The apartment looked warm, and softly lit, and, she noticed with a shiver, highly conducive: she had tired of stiff-backed chairs and wooden benches to improve posture at school, so almost everything was fluffy pillows, and deep feathery settees, and thick rugs. There was even a fireplace that worked, and she had prepared it only that morning with kindling and logs, almost as if she were expecting him. He might find it difficult to believe she liked to lie in front of fireplaces by herself, late at night when he was gone and she was burning with the glow of him.

"Magnificent!" he exclaimed, going directly to the fireplace. "You are a superb housekeeper. Do you take care of all this yourself, or does someone come in and clean for you?"

"I do it," she said, beginning to empty the provisions onto the sideboard of the three-quarter kitchenette.

"Splendid," he said. "In our home in Berlin you will have many servants, but it is well your knowing how to run an orderly home. Sometimes servants try to take advantage, and not do all they should, if the mistress is not herself immaculate." He struck a big wooden match onto the front of the fireplace.

Her spine stiffened, as she felt a shudder go through it. She wasn't sure if it was the sound of the match, like sandpaper scratching against metal, or the word "mistress."

"But why do you stay in there, Ursull, when I am making this lovely fire?"

"I have to prepare dinner."

"It is just past six. We have time. We have . . . much time. Come, sit by me. We can read our future in the flames . . ."

If it were to be settled, it would have to be settled before she was beside him, touching. If he really cared for her, he would have to agree before their bodies were close together. The responsibility would have to be taken by him—because once his arms were around her, she wasn't sure she could be responsible.

"Please, Gerd. First we must talk."

"You have been too long in America," he said, smiling.

She came out of the kitchenette and sat in the single chair near the fireplace, primly, her legs drawn together like a schoolgirl's, and her lips pressed tight like a schoolteacher. He was sprawled on the floor in front of the sofa, one elbow resting on an ottoman, his face three-quarters toward her, eyes shining gold from the reflected flames, and some inner amusement.

"I think you know how I feel about you," she said.

"Ah, it is to be a seminar." He shifted himself to his haunches, and sat as stiffly as he could on the floor.

"But I don't like the tone of the conversation."

"Then why don't we stop talking?"

"Please," Ursull said. "Don't make jokes."

"I am not to make jokes, and I am not to be serious." He raised his palms in defeat. "What does that leave me?"

"Why can't we continue just as we are?" Ursull said plaintively.

"But my darling, that is exactly what I intended."

"I thought . . ." She hesitated, and a warm flush covered her forehead, probably from the reflected heat of the fire. "Before, in the car, you said . . . you said, something about the weekend . . ." She looked down at her hands, clasped tightly in her lap. "I'm sorry if I misunderstood."

"You didn't misunderstand," Gerd said. "But that doesn't mean we can't continue as we are. As we are, we are two young people in love. We are going to be married. Our whole lives will be spent together in unbelievable happiness. It began when I knew I loved you, and it will end when I die. There will be no change. Except that we will love each other more, the more we love each other. You see?"

"You change words around," Ursull said. "That is all you change."

"But it's you who makes me deal with words. Come. Come here by me, and I'll show you."

"I can't," she said. "Not until you've agreed."

"To what?"

She took a deep breath, and did not look at him. His tan shirt beneath the beige sweater was open at the throat, and sprawled there in the fire's glow he looked all one color, and she could imagine him naked. "There will be no more between us than there has already been."

"Never?" He smiled, and the whiteness of his teeth was the only contrast on his whole body.

"You know what I mean."

"No. No, I do not." He moved toward her on the floor, and raised himself to his knees in front of her, slowly unclasping the locked fingertips in her lap. "Is there any doubt in your mind that I love you?"

She had tried very hard all week, creating some doubt, but it was impossible. "No," she said.

"And do you think for a moment that a man like me, when he loves, as I love you, would let you go?" He unclenched the pressure of her wrists, and slowly kissed her right palm.

"I don't know."

"I hope you are being coy," he whispered against her wrist. "The woman I love could not possibly be that stupid."

She had a strong impulse to touch the thick yellow hair only a few inches from her fingertips, and press it against her breast. But there was enough strength left in her to subdue the desire. Instead, she feverishly began pulling at the binding on the arm of her chair.

"We are to be married," Gerd said. "You know that as well as I do. All this week I was tempted to carry you away, but we both have responsibilities: we are adults, and we have jobs to do, for a while at least. So I waited until today, with three clear evenings and days in front of us. If you want, we could fly some place tonight, and be married. I have known since Sunday how it would be. The only question is when.

"We are young, Ursull. We are healthy. We are intelligent, but we are both German enough to be superstitious. What we have we will not find again with anyone. We know that now, and we could act on it now.

"But it is quite another thing with parents. Parents are fearful of impulse in their children. Families take time to get used to an idea. I am not sure how it is with you, but my family is important to me, and important in the community. I am the eldest son. It would not do, for their present happiness and mine, to say, Dear Papa, I met the only girl yesterday, and today we are married."

"It is the same with mine," Ursull said.

"Are they poor?" Gerd asked.

"No. Quite the contrary."

"Then they will want to give you a proper wedding. They will want the perfect setting for their jewel. We must give them time, although we need none for ourselves. You have written them, of course, about me?"

"Not yet."

He lifted his lips from the crook of her elbow, and gazed at her face with a hurt expression in his eyes. "What were you waiting for?"

"I don't know. I didn't know if there was anything to tell them, yet. I was waiting for . . . I'm not sure . . . for it to be settled."

"We have waited for each other all our lives," Gerd said. "Don't you think it is settled? I wrote my family the day I had lunch with you at the United Nations. I have met an exceptional girl, I said. And the next day I told them your name. And the day following I told them you were of German parentage. And the day after that, I described how beautiful you were. All this before we had ever been together alone. Have you no sense of preparation?"

She laughed, and both her hands clasped his neck, and she hugged him to her chest without thinking. In a moment she was covered with confusion.

"Please," she whispered. "Please don't."

"Why?"

"I do love you. But we mustn't, Gerd, please. I'm . . . I'm a virgin . . ."

"But what else should you be?" he said. "Have you ever loved anybody before?"

"No."

"So? Has no one ever wanted to make love to you? Are you deeply religious and consider it a sin? Have you never felt any passion? Or were you waiting for a husband?" he asked like an angry inquisitor.

"A husband," she whispered.

"I am your husband," he said, his voice becoming, suddenly, as searching and gentle as his lips. "Before God, I am your husband. The only question is, how soon before our parents. You will marry me? You are married to me?"

"Yes," she whispered weakly. "Yes."

"Then I take you, with joy . . . as my bride."

That night, after they had eaten a long and luxurious dinner, and drunk wine, and made love in the bedroom, and made love again in front of the fire, he lay asleep, in a golden naked glow on the beige carpet, one hand curling through his tousled yellow hair, like a slumbering child. But he was not, Ursull noted with pleasure, a child at all. She ran her fingers once, greedily, over the wonderful length of him. Seeing he did not stir, she kissed him softly on the shoulder and went to the desk.

She took out a piece of paper from her stationery box, and glancing back over her shoulder, she smiled, and hugged herself once, in pure pleasure. Then she began the letter to her mother and father, carefully working in, among other chatty items of parental concern, the single sentence that she had met an interesting young man.

IX

ON the third day Birgitta did not show up for work, Pauline, the supervisor, added something extra after completing the morning's briefing. She told the assembled girls that unless Birgitta appeared at the office that afternoon, with some reasonable explanation, she would have no recourse but to dismiss her. Pauline, for all her seeming harshness, had an inside like a marshmallow, she told them, and much as it grieved her, she could not condone such irresponsible behavior.

"After all," Pauline said, touching a wisp of her thinning brown hair, and trying to put it back in line with the girlishly cut bangs, "you girls are somewhat in a position of public trust. We make no particular demands on your private lives—but when your comportment starts carrying over into your work, we've got to draw the line."

"I'm sure she's sick," Bo said. "Birgitta's been late, but she's never just not shown up before. She feels very strongly about her job."

"Birgitta feels strongly about many things," Pauline said coldly. "I've looked the other way any number of times, but I certainly will not pretend to be blind." She drew her blouse collar in primly and brushed imagined lint from her suit front, always the signal the briefing was coming to a close.

"You said you weren't concerned about her personal life," Bo said. "I'm sure there has to be a very good reason— She would never have just stayed away, and not even called in."

"Unfortunately, I am not blessed with your deep feelings of security where the Swede is concerned. And this is not some . . . sorority where girls will be girls. Besides, I don't have to answer to you, Miss Bowman—you are all answerable to me, and I in turn have a responsibility to the organization. And that's all for this discussion. I just wanted to put you girls on notice, so no one could feel I was being unfair to Birgitta."

"It might be a little fairer putting Birgitta on notice," Bo said.

"I assure you I would be happy to, if I had any idea what particular apartment she was gracing this week." Pauline turned her back, and started into her glassed-off cubicle.

"Bitch," Bo murmured under her breath, waiting until the fading, waning woman was out of hearing. "Birgitta always used to tell me she was a dried-up, jealous prune, and I thought she was exaggerating."

"Hush, Bo," Ursull said smiling. "Pauline has the insides of a marshmallow. You heard her tell you so herself."

"Some marshmallow," said Bo. "They don't make marshmallows that consistency."

"No?" Ursull said. "When I was ten I had what you call a pen pal in Massachusetts, and when she went away to summer camp, she sent me for my birthday a package of the things her mother sent her. A salami, some crackers, and two boxes of Campfire Marshmallows. It was a very thoughtful gesture, but she did not put nearly enough postage on to reach Buenos Aires except by the slowest possible freight, so I didn't receive it until the following January. The salami was withered, and the crackers were stale, but the marshmallows seemed to me perfectly in order. . . . Of course I had never seen a marshmallow before. I tried to bite into one, and it was like sweet cement—I chipped my front tooth." Ursull smiled. "My mother was very upset, but I wouldn't let her throw them away—I kept trying to eat them. I thought it was some weakness in me—not to enjoy something that a friend of mine found so wonderful. Fortunately, nothing was lost, as I chipped so many teeth that they all had to be filed down, so I looked all right. But I never wrote to her anymore, I was so disappointed in her peculiar taste. According to my experience, Pauline is exactly a marshmallow."

"Is Brigitta ill?" Kiiko asked.

"I'm sure she is," Bo ventured, as they started walking upstairs to the main concourse. Actually in the past three days she had phoned Birgitta many times, but no one had answered. Although she knew Birgitta had been planning to make Olaf leave, it was inconceivable that he could have done anything violent out of rage and disappointment. Olaf was not emotional—that was one of the things Birgitta had found so objectionable about him at the last. Bo had thought of phoning Mason—but that would have been interfering and presumptuous of her. The fact that Bo was both interfering and presumptuous was beside the point—it frightened her, the idea of phoning a Negro and asking him if he was shacked up with her girl friend. If he wasn't, he would doubtless be highly indignant, thinking she considered him an immoral black. If he was, he might consider it a sign of some race prejudice on her part, not realizing that she would ask the same question, with a great deal more ease, of practically any white man.

"I think perhaps she has run off with a theatrical producer I introduced her to," Marie Claire said. "I know a great many theatre people, because when I was raped by the Arabs in Tangiers, I escaped by concealing myself in the costume truck of the road company Comédie Française."

The other girls ignored her.

"You must try and reach her, Bo," Ursull said. "You know how much she values her job, and I am afraid the marshmallow will do what she said."

"Bitter old bitch," Bo mumbled.

"It isn't her fault," Ursull said kindly. "It is not the fault of the marshmallow if it is too long exposed to air, and not being used as it is meant to be used, it grows hard and stale. We can't all have our wrappers removed when we are fresh, and that is a sadness."

Bo looked at Ursull sideways, astounded. Was it possible? For a moment she lost her ability to speak, and almost to think clearly. It staggered her imagination, which on even a dull day could be counted on to be moderately wild. But that Ursull, cool, collected, serene Ursull, could be speaking in personal terms of love, and sensual experience, was incredible. No, Bo decided, taking a firm grip on her mind. Ursull might have warmed up a bit lately, but her use of the language was still a trifle stilted. Like all foreigners, who treated English with the respect due only the unfamiliar, Ursull was not yet free enough to make a straightforward point in conversation. Rather, she tended to ramble through fields of allegory. And life, like conversational English, lay a trifle away from and below her: a little demeaning, and a little too real.

Ursull's statement about marshmallow was only allegory, Bo concluded, and nothing more than allegory, offering absolutely no hint of personal experience. It was a shame, but, shame that it was, it was a relief to Bo. If Ursull could once leave the groves of Robert Graves and come inside the portals, where the people were, then perhaps Bo was being unnecessarily aloof. And Alec Ingells with his absurd actor's posturing might be right in thinking Bo childish and absurd. For special as she might seem in Cleveland, to her father, and sometimes even herself, Bo knew that she was no Ursull.

The morning's first visitors were coming in the front doors, moving slowly, undirectedly, toward the information booth for directions and tickets to the General Assembly, and some—presumably a little more alert—following the signs pointing to the tour area or trailing after the guides. The girls walked like an undisciplined but highly attractive platoon, Kiiko breaking from their ranks to greet Ernie, who just happened to be in the same spot he was in every morning, where the girls would pass.

"Excuse me," Kiiko whispered, as, extraordinarily light-footed as she always was early in the day, she bobbed away from them—a tiny black-topped cork in a navy blue sea. "There's Ernie."

"Fancy," Hillary said, but Kiiko had moved too quickly to hear her.

"It is so sweet," Ursull said. "The way he pretends to be there by accident. Always waiting for her."

Marie Claire pulled her jacket tight down around her hips. "I find it not so sweet as sinister," she said. "The two Arabs always waited for me in the same spot in the Casbah as I walked to school, and I too imagined they were looking out for my welfare."

"Well, they were," Bo said.

"Par*don?*"

She said it in French the way she always did when she knew she was about to be offended. But Bo didn't really care—her patience with Marie Claire was beginning to wear quite thin. There was no need for her to intrude herself and her fables into a conversation that centered momentarily on Kiiko, and a day that looked to focus on Birgitta. True, Bo intended to intrude herself on it, but that was quite another thing, done out of friendship and good intentions and the temporary chance to forget about her problems with Alec. "I'm sure they were thinking of your welfare," Bo said. "They must have known how important it would be to you later in life to have a collection of rape stories."

The most remarkable thing about Marie Claire, as Birgitta always pointed out, was her refusal to become insulted. Confronted with sarcasm, she chose to take it innocently, and directly challenged in a momentous lie, she would ignore the moment and the skeptic completely, often coming back later the same afternoon to reinforce and even embellish her fable.

"Do you really think so?" Marie Claire said. "I believe you just like to see something good in everyone."

Bo quickened her step, and nodded to Ursull to come away from the rest of the group so they could speak alone. It was something she could do with much more convenience in the Lounge, or even between tours. But it pleased Bo, the idea of engaging with Ursull in blatant camaraderie, even though no one might notice but Ursull. It also delighted her that she could become involved in a problem that was not her own, that she could make her own. And, of course, there was Birgitta, of whom she was genuinely fond. It would be only fitting for Bo to charge in to the last-minute cavalry rescue of Birgitta, at her sexual Little Big Horn.

"Would you cover for me before lunch?" she whispered to Ursull. "I want to go to Birgitta's apartment and see if I can find her. I don't want Pauline to notice I'm taking extra time."

"Of course," Ursull said.

"And if I should be a little late getting back . . ."

"I'll cover," Ursull said.

Bo left the building a few minutes after eleven, signaling to Ursull, who was sitting at the far side of the Lounge, that the moment had come—waving the coat she had secreted from her locker, so Pauline wouldn't see. All the way uptown in the cab, the noise of the traffic seemed a bugle call to Bo's cavalry rescue. At her first sight of Birgitta, however, Bo's own role in the drama was forgotten.

Birgitta had come to the door only after Bo had rung the bell repeatedly for ten minutes, the groggy fear of her whispered "Who's there?" filling Bo with a genuine feeling of alarm. Three times she had answered her own name, and three times there had been a baffled whimper from inside. Finally, the door opened.

It was only by the outline in the doorway that Bo knew it was

Birgitta. Her eyes were swollen almost completely shut, giving a weirdly Chinese caste to the usually wide, frank blue eyes. Two triangles stood out above her cheeks like great welts, running sideways, widening from their thinnest point at the corners of her eyes. Her nose was red and distended and even her warm, beautifully shaped mouth hung bloated and slack. Her hair was damply tangled, and she shuddered, round-shouldered in a wrinkled silk robe.

"What happened?" Bo said, closing the door behind her.

"I'm a whore," Birgitta murmured, and stumbled drunkenly to the unmade bed.

"Have you been drinking?" Bo said stupidly.

"Not really," Birgitta whispered. "I've been crying. See what happens to us when we cry too much, we aging whores?"

Bo walked toward the kitchen. "I'll make you some coffee."

"America. Coffee fixes everything." She threw herself in a weary huddle on the bed and bit thoughtfully into her forearm. "When I was very young, I could cry with no hardship whatsoever, you know that? And five minutes later I was as fresh as before. Maybe a little red-eyed, but that was the extent of it. And then when I was twenty-two, I had a crying jag that lasted for almost a day, and weeping gave me the appearance of a Moslem. Now I am nearly twenty-five, and grief has made me an Oriental. I spoke to a doctor about it a few months ago—I regarded fits of crying as one of the luxuries of being a woman. He said the swelling had something to do with tear duct displacement, and bodily fluids. Apparently there are some people who haven't got enough water in them or something, as they get older. They swell up for days. I made up my mind I wouldn't cry anymore, I couldn't afford it—but I bitterly resented having to give it up. So for three days I've been having what you might describe as an orgy, you see. A predictable result when one has spent so many years being ascetic. At least in that area."

Bo lit a match under a pot she had filled with water, and forgot to blow it out, burning her finger. "Have you got instant, or do you want me to make regular?"

"I don't care what you do," Birgitta said. "Oh Bo dear, I didn't mean that the way it sounded. I meant the coffee."

"Don't worry about it," Bo said. "I'm not here for my feelings."

"If you really want to help me, you could look in the bathroom and see if there are any more aspirin. I think my head is splitting, I'm not sure."

"They're here," Bo said. "In the kitchen."

"Oh," Birgitta mumbled as Bo brought out the bottle and a glass of water. "I thought that was saccharin—I've been taking it in my coffee. I have been drinking coffee, you see, like a good American. Not that I thought it would help, but I wanted to put some liquid in myself so I wouldn't have all this tear displacement, and I kept gagging on water. But, as you see . . ." She swallowed two pills and gulped down the contents of the glass, shuddering. "No matter how much I put in, it doesn't replace what's been used up. Sort of like an aging whore who keeps putting, what is that called? . . . alum on herself, but she still sags like an old purse."

"Stop it."

"I'm sorry. I keep forgetting how many things still come as a shock to you."

"I'm not shocked," Bo said steadily. "I just think you've punished yourself enough."

"For what?" Birgitta said. "Do you have any idea what I've done?"

"For whatever you've done," Bo said.

Birgitta breathed deeply and rolled over on her back. "I apologize for thinking you were a Puritan, Bo. A Puritan would say I hadn't even begun to suffer for my sins. Do you know what I did?"

"I don't care," Bo said. "If you want to tell me, you can, but I'd rather you put cold water on your face, and got dressed."

"What for?"

"Pauline said if you're not back by this afternoon, she's going to have you fired."

Panic cut through the bloated features. "I can't go out. I can't go there. I can't let anyone see me."

"You don't look so bad," Bo lied. "You can put on dark glasses, and tell Pauline you had an allergic reaction or something, and that's why you haven't been in. You're better off if you go in like that. She'll believe you, and then she'll probably send you straight home again."

"I can't go out," Birgitta said, her fingers on her throat. "He might see me. I told him I was only using the apartment for the night, that I didn't live here, but I don't think he believed me. He might be watching the building."

Bo did not ask who might be watching. She had never seen Birgitta in such a state of anxiety, and it filled her more with frightened awe than curiosity. The girl on the bed flailed slowly, like a beaten, featureless fish, except her eyes were almost indiscernible, and the cry in her throat was wretchedly human.

"Honest to God, Bo, I've never done anything like that before. I swear. I don't answer the phone, but it keeps ringing. All day and all night it keeps ringing, and I think, oh my God, he took the number when he was here. He saw the number and he keeps phoning me. You won't believe how it's been ringing."

"I've been calling you a lot."

"At three in the morning? And four, and five? And have you been ringing my bell? In the middle of the night, is it you who keeps ringing my bell?"

"Maybe it was Mason," Bo said.

Birgitta covered her face with both hands. "It wasn't Mason. He isn't coming back. He isn't ever coming back." And then the tears began anew, as she began to tell Bo what had happened at their last, their final meeting. She screwed up her face like some hideous enraged child, whose agony was not as pathetic as its show of pain was ugly. And yet, in spite of the distorted not-really-Birgitta face, and the fact that Bo did not honestly consider the loss of Mason to be mourned —especially not by Birgitta, who could have anyone in the world, once she was herself again—Bo felt her insides churning in sympathy and confusion.

"I want to die," Birgitta moaned, her shoulders shaking convulsively. "I really want to die."

"Well, that's only because you look so terrible," Bo said, smiling gently.

Birgitta raised her face from the pillow and peered at Bo. She looked confused for a moment, and then laughed, too hard. The laughter shuddered backwards into sobs.

"Birgitta, you've got to stop. Please. You're not accomplishing anything by this. So you cared about him, fine. Maybe you were even in love with him, I don't know."

"I was, I am."

"That's beside the point. It didn't work, it can't work. So that's it. People are disappointed in love all the time, and they don't just fall into pieces."

"How do you know?"

"I'm not stupid," Bo said. "I might be inexperienced, and I may even be a bit of a prig about myself, but I can see things. I'm not blind. If everybody in the world who loved somebody who didn't love them back crumbled into bits or started dropping dead, there wouldn't be a population problem. This entire planet would be strewn with chunks of people, and corpses. So you loved him and it didn't work. But life goes on. I know that's a homily, but homilies are homilies because they're true, and the truth of it, the terrible truth, is that life goes on. Life *does* go on. Unless you're some sort of nut, of course," she said, and went over to the bed, touched the wet, feverish face and smiled. "If you stopped crying and gave your eyes a chance to make a comeback, you might meet somebody tomorrow."

"I want Mason," Birgitta whimpered.

"You're a crybaby, you know that? You want somebody and he doesn't want you, so you throw a tantrum."

"He does want me," Birgitta said. "He does. He's just being noble. The Black Man's Burden."

"Then let him be noble. Be a little charitable about it. Whether or not you can see it at this moment, he is doing the right thing. The idea isn't whether or not you can become involved with him, it's whether he can afford to become involved with you. So at least he's being kind. He told you before anything happened. If he was a son of a bitch, he would have gone to bed with you first, and then left you. This way, at least, you haven't lost anything—so you can't get really hung up."

"Oh Bo," Birgitta whispered. "Sometimes you sound like you understand something, and I find myself listening to you as if you knew what you were talking about. And then you go on too long—and I realize what a baby you are." Birgitta reached for a soggy Kleenex and blew her nose. "Why is it everything hinges on sex in your young American imagination? Two people find each other, and care about each other and become deeply enmeshed—and it doesn't all revolve around sex. In the beginning of a relationship, there's a marvelous tentative quality when you haven't been to bed together, that some men and women can't sustain on any other level. It's like a perfectly balanced fencing match—lunge, thrust, withdraw. And that keeps young and giddy couples going, because they haven't the intellect or the emotion to make it happen in any other areas.

"When you first sleep with a man, it isn't the end of a deep and meaningful relationship. You grow. You grow better and richer and more relaxed and more excited. Or some, because they have made it too important, or because one or the other partner isn't all that stimulating, grow bored and restless. But it isn't the end of a relationship.

"Nor, in some cases, is it the beginning. Mason and I were so deep inside the other without touching, it made me afraid. Do you see? We have been to bed with each other's thoughts, and each other's feelings, and that is something that happens rarely. All that we haven't explored completely is each other's bodies. And he spares me nothing by denying me that, don't you see? I might be able to face losing a man I have loved completely, in every way. But I can't live with never having touched him."

Bo was silent for a few minutes. "Get dressed," she said finally.

"What for?"

"So you don't lose your job."

"I don't care about the job."

"Maybe not today. But you will tomorrow, when it's lost."

"I could dress," Birgitta said. "But I can't leave the apartment."

"That's nonsense," Bo said.

Birgitta grunted wearily. "After he left the other night, I picked up a taxi driver. A taxi driver! Not the first one I ran into, of course, I was very selective: I stopped two others and let them go away. 'Drive on,' I said, like they were some medieval coaches.

"I think I was crazy when I did it, I don't know. Maybe it's an excuse, but I don't think so. I've never picked up a man before. Oh yes, at a party, or something, but everybody does that, that's what they go to parties for. But I swear to you that in my whole life I never went to bed with a man I just met. Unless we had been properly introduced by someone of good family, of course." Birgitta smiled wanly. "You see, my promiscuity is highly exaggerated—to you, and even to myself.

"But this taxi driver—I don't know who he was, or what he was, and I brought him here. God knows you can't blame the man, because you know what he thinks I am, and for good reason. . . . He didn't want to leave. I finally had to threaten to call the police before he'd go. He said he'd be back, though. And he has been. That's him, at the door, all night long. And on the phone. What can I do?"

"Change your phone number," Bo said. "Move from here. Get another apartment if you have to."

"But what will I do if I ever have to get somewhere in a hurry?" Birgitta said, tossing her head like the other Birgitta, but with only a shadow of that girl's smile. "Ah Bo, be wise. If you ever let down the iron gates of your chastity, never be wanton with a taxi driver. If you want to avoid him afterwards, it puts a terrible crimp in your means of transportation."

"Start getting dressed," Bo said. "I'm going to go back and tell Pauline I've seen you, and you're ill. If she insists on seeing you, I'll come back and get you, and we'll go out together."

"You're so sweet," Birgitta said. "You think you can protect me from my phantom cabbie?"

"He'll leave you alone if you're with somebody. Anyway, he probably isn't even around."

"But could you be sure? How could you guess, as you raised your hand at the corner, if that was him bearing down on you now, or parked on the other side of the street? Pity the lady who's afraid of every shadow. But pity more the lady who doesn't know who might lurk behind the steering wheel." She made a fitful attempt at laughter, but Bo could see that Birgitta was genuinely frightened.

"I'll be back for you," Bo said. "Get dressed."

Kiiko did not have much appetite. More than eating lunch, what she wanted was to lie down on one of the sofas in the Lounge and take a nap. The girls sometimes would get quite involved in bandying about the psychology none of them had majored in in college, Freudian versus Jungian versus Adlerian theory; and although Kiiko never joined in the discussions, it was her amused but firm conviction that at moments such as these, all of them were wrong: sex, food and shelter, power—none of them were the prime motivation for man; if a person was tired enough, his basic drive was sleep. He could be frustrated, starving, and totally unimportant, but the thing he really wanted was rest. Still, she knew she was not as tired as she imagined, and she had promised Ernie she would have a sandwich with him in the coffee shop. So, sighing softly, and stretching to the greatest length her tiny body could manage, she slipped into her shoes and went to meet him.

It was the first time she was having lunch with him; he had seemed so bitterly disappointed that he could not walk her home that evening, she had accepted his invitation immediately. Ever since the incident at Christmas, when the pain she had seen in his face eradicated the foolishness, she tried being especially kind to him. And it did no harm to seem pleased, as well as aware, that he was around. When she smiled up at Ernie, he seemed to stand a good deal taller, and, his carriage improved, his eyes losing some of their weary, frantic look, he seemed a great deal more attractive, and even, sometimes, young. And the most curious part of it was, that he was not bad company, Ernie wasn't—not for waving to in hallways, and for being seen safely home. He was polite, and attentive, and prompt. All of these things were more a pleasure than a handicap in being seen to your door.

And that was all he would ask to do: see her to her door. He had asked it three days after Christmas, when she had apologized for not being able to have Christmas dinner with him, and said again, as she had on the phone, that she hoped his mother hadn't been inconvenienced. It was nine-thirty in the morning when he asked it. "Can I see you home?" he said, like they were both at a party and it was very late at night. At five-thirty he was waiting for her, his overcoat buttoned wrong, so it hung down longer on one side, the old-fashioned hat on his head making him look unnecessarily like somebody's father. He had escorted her, her private policeman, speaking only when she spoke, holding her elbow gently and impersonally as they crossed streets. He had offered to take her home by cab if she wished, but she didn't live that far away, and her complaints about her feet, she confessed, smiling, were highly exaggerated. Besides, going home was not the same as taking out tours.

Every afternoon when they reached the tiny brownstone where she lived, he always tipped his hat politely at the street door and watched as she got safely inside. There was no hint of his wanting to be invited upstairs for a drink, no indication of expecting any more than that walk. And he never again suggested her coming home to his mother's for dinner.

He was waiting for her now in the coffee shop, his shoulders hunched tensely, his arm hugged protectively around the back of the seat next to him at the counter. When he saw Kiiko come in the door, he relaxed a little, and made a not entirely successful effort at an easy smile.

"I didn't know if you were coming." Ernie stood up.

"I said I would."

"I thought maybe you changed your mind. They're very busy here. I had a hard time keeping the chair."

"I'm sorry if I'm late." Kiiko lifted herself onto the leather-backed stool as Ernie dropped into his. "I started to fall asleep."

"Are you ill?"

"I love to sleep," Kiiko said. "I'd rather sleep than anything."

"That's not right, a girl as young as you. Maybe you ought to see a doctor."

"I'm fine," Kiiko said. "I am naturally lazy, nothing more."

"Have something hot. That'll perk you up." He handed her the menu, sounding like a television commercial, which was where he had probably heard the expression.

She studied the card and started to order a tuna fish sandwich. But Ernie looked so disappointed she said she would have a hot roast beef sandwich, the same as he ordered.

Ernie fidgeted for a moment and then made an attempt at looking and sounding casual as he asked why Kiiko wasn't going straight home after work.

"Nothing very exciting," she said. "A friend of mine wants me to see some plays in Greenwich Village, and they start early, so I have to go directly from here."

"A boyfriend or a girl friend?"

"Oh, it is a boy, but he is not a boyfriend. He is a friend who's a boy."

"There's nothing wrong with your having boyfriends. You're a young girl. You ought to have plenty of boyfriends."

"Why?"

"Well . . . You have lots of time of course, but it never hurts to have boyfriends. And then when you want to get serious and settle down, you can pick the best one."

"I'm already serious, Ernie." She smiled at him. "But I have no plans to settle down."

"I don't mean right away . . . I mean when the time comes you want to get married."

"It won't."

"A lot of girls say that. A lot of girls, especially now, feel very emancipated, you know, modern, and they say they don't want to get married, but they change their minds."

"Perhaps," Kiiko said. "I, for one, am not at all emancipated, and not very modern. But I won't get married."

"You just say that now. You'll meet somebody, and then you'll see how fast you'll change your mind."

"Perhaps," Kiiko said. "But I don't think so."

"What do you want to do then?"

She had told him any number of times that she intended to go back to Japan and teach but he either did not think her answer important enough to remember, or he had asked simply because it was conventional conversation. Whatever the reason, Kiiko did not mind telling him again. It was something to say, and although silences did not bother her, they seemed to discomfit Ernie.

"You can still get married and teach, both," Ernie said. "I don't see that that changes anything."

"It's a special school in the country, where I'm going. You must devote your full time to the children. Teaching them during the day, and caring for them at night."

"There must be plenty of regular schools in Tokyo and places, where they'd be glad to have you. Why would you want to go somewhere like that?"

"My father runs it," Kiiko said.

Ernie stiffened slightly. He had deliberately never asked her questions about her family, and when she mentioned them in conversation, he would not pursue the discussion. Usually, she dropped it, being no more anxious to volunteer personal information than he was to find out. Today though, she seemed anxious to talk. He did not try to change the subject. Instead, he bit large chunks of his sandwich and swilled it down with gulps of coffee, hoping the gnashing and swallowing sounds from inside him would blot out her voice.

"He could have been a great professor anywhere—at any of the great universities in the world. But after the war he founded this special school—it's a combination rehabilitation center and . . . orphanage, I suppose you'd call it. Only that's not the important part. What matters is that these children, these bright, gifted children, be given all the educational benefits of children who have homes, and money, even though ours are . . . somewhat unusual."

A piece of beef lodged in his throat, and his face was crimson with the effort of swallowing.

"Are you all right?"

"Fine," Ernie said after a moment. He signaled the waitress for more coffee, and another sandwich. "What do you mean, unusual?"

"They are what some people might call defective. But it is a wrong word. There is nothing defective about their minds, or their capacity to learn. Most of them have unusual intelligence. Truly unusual. If they can grow up without being made to feel abnormal, there is every likelihood they will make outstanding contributions. And they need teachers badly."

He did not have to ask what the children's abnormalities were: his fevered imagination was clotted with pictures of maimed and deformed Japanese babies. He tried to quiet the queasiness in his stomach by swallowing more food, like a frightened ship's passenger in a storm who believes that putting more in his belly will keep it from heaving.

"Why would your father ask you to teach at such a place?" he said.

"He never did. I think it was something he hoped for, but he never expressed the wish. The decision was mine. When I became eighteen, I told him I would like to come to America for a while, to improve my English, before returning home to begin as a teacher. I think he was very pleased."

"Don't you know?"

Kiiko shook her head. "He was never one to express emotions easily. Besides, I think he wanted not to seem too happy, in case I should later change my mind."

"Why don't you?"

"Why should I?"

"That's no life for a young girl. It's like being . . . a nun."

"Aren't you Catholic?"

"I'm not religious."

"Still, I have never known a Catholic who did not love his nuns."

"The ones I knew were all old."

"I don't believe that's so, Ernie."

"Is that what you want to do? Marry yourself to some Japanese Christ?"

Kiiko looked down at her plate. "I want to help the children."

"Well that's nice. That's very nice. But it's still not a life for a young girl, raising children that aren't her own."

"Why not?" she said quietly. "My mother did." She was silent for a few moments, and then watching him, began to laugh softly. "Goodness, Ernie, what an appetite! Do you always eat such a lunch? I can hardly finish even half my sandwich. They give you so much food."

Ernie, who had been about to order another sandwich, dropped his hand miserably. The roast beef in the coffee shop was sliced very thin—not like the grotto. It was well done, and hot gravy could not disguise the fact that it was leftover and cold. But he merely shook his head.

"It wasn't criticism, truly," Kiiko said. "I have nothing but admiration for such a wonderful appetite. I was only thinking, if you enjoy such a big lunch, you might be wiser to eat in the cafeteria. They give you much more food, for almost the same price."

"I don't like the cafeteria, it's too noisy."

"Where do you usually go at lunchtime?"

"Nowhere special," he said, blushing furiously for fear she would know he was lying, not knowing why he had to lie at all.

Somehow, Bo managed to convince Pauline that Birgitta was ill—very ill. She had a terrible case of food poisoning, Bo said, and was so swollen she was hardly recognizable.

"Why didn't she call?" Pauline asked.

"She hasn't been well enough to call anybody," Bo said. "Not even a doctor."

"That's pretty foolish," Pauline said, almost kindly.

"I know," Bo said. "But have you ever been really sick in a place that wasn't home?"

"Yes," Pauline said. "I see what you mean."

"I'm getting my own doctor to go up there and have a look at her this afternoon. If it's all right with you."

"For God's sake, what kind of woman do you think I am? Why wouldn't I want a doctor to see her?"

"I meant, if it was all right with you, I'd like to go with him. She's really pretty shaky, and I thought it might be better if I were there."

"Try not to take more than an hour," Pauline said.

The office of *American Crisis* magazine, if it did not have the gloss of what Bo imagined to be the headquarters of Time-Life, Inc., and the stone cold grandeur of its building, was at least located in downtown Manhattan. Not that Bo had anything against going to Harlem, she was sure, but considering that Pauline had granted only rigid leeway, the less time she took for travel, the better. The magazine was on Park Avenue South, in the Twenties, in a building also occupied, Bo noticed from the directory in the elevator, by purse and shoe manufacturers, and a wholesale chandelier distributor. The elevator man nodded to her when they reached the fourth floor, and told her to turn right at the end of the corridor.

The hallway was battered, but clean, and the smoked glass door to *American Crisis* had, except for the recently repainted gold lettering on the door, the look of an old-fashioned dentist's office. She went inside with only a mild feeling of malaise, and giving the surprisingly crisp-looking young colored girl at the switchboard her name, asked her to call Mr. Williams.

"I don't know, sir," the receptionist said into the headset. She turned to Bo. "Who are you with?"

"I beg pardon?"

"What company are you with?"

"Oh. I'm not a publisher or anything. Would you tell him I'm a friend of Birgitta's."

"It's personal, I believe, Mr. Williams. Miss Bowman is a friend of Birgitta's."

He came through the Dutch door in a moment, his arm already halfway into his coat. He was tall, moderately dark, and his face was interestingly put together; still, Bo felt a degree of disappointment. Not that he was not an attractive-looking Negro, but from the extent of Birgitta's anguish, she had half expected Harry Belafonte.

"There's a coffee shop around the corner," he said to Bo. "You'll be more comfortable there than my office."

"I don't mind," Bo said. "If it's easier inside . . ."

"It's not very private. We'll be better off around the corner." He told the receptionist if anyone wanted him, he'd be out for a while, and to take messages.

The luncheonette was fairly empty at that hour of the afternoon, and no one paid much attention to them as they sat in the back booth.

"Have you had lunch?" he asked.

"I don't want anything, thank you," Bo said.

"Two coffees," Mason said to the man behind the counter.

"Okay." He faced Bo. "Why did she send you?"

"She didn't. She doesn't know I'm here, and she'd probably be angry if she did know. But it doesn't make any difference. Birgitta's in very bad shape."

"So's the world," he said.

"Don't you care about her?"

"I care about a lot of things," he said. "But I can't do anything about them."

If he had been a white man, Bo would have gotten very annoyed and told him so, in no uncertain terms. But as it was, she controlled her anger, and tried to speak as gently and intelligently as she could. "You don't understand, Mr. Williams. She's ill."

She was rewarded by a look of deep concern on his face.

"What's wrong?"

"She's worked herself into a terrible state. She's been in hysterics for nearly three days, and she can't pull out of it."

He stared at his fingers. "We all have our problems."

"Mr. Williams, I know you're supposed to be a little testy and very bright, but I don't think you have to equate your problem at this point with Birgitta's. There's centuries of history and people who are responsible for yours. The only one who gave Birgitta hers is you." It surprised her that she had said it, even though she thought it true. But as he had tried to come on the same as any white son of a bitch, she saw no reason to treat him differently. Curiously, he seemed to warm to her anger.

"I'm sorry about that," he said. "I really am. But I don't think I'll help by going to see her."

"I do," Bo said. "If she doesn't shape up, she's going to lose her job. I kept the supervisor from firing her today. But if she doesn't show tomorrow, I'm afraid that will be it. Birgitta isn't just working at the UN for larks, you know."

"I know," he said. "I know a lot of things about Birgitta. But I know a little about myself too, Miss Bowman. I'm not her husband, I'm not —what she wants me to be, and I'm certainly not a doctor."

"A doctor couldn't help her," Bo said. "You're the only one who can help her."

"That's nonsense."

"I honestly wish it were," Bo said. "But a doctor won't be able to convince her to leave the apartment. Even if he could pull her together, she wouldn't go outside."

"Why?"

"You better ask her that," Bo said. "I'm afraid if somebody doesn't do something, she'll flip completely."

"People don't just flip unless they're very weak or very self-indulgent. Birgitta isn't either of those."

"I'm afraid it isn't so simple. Flipping, I mean. Or Birgitta."

"Why won't you tell me what the big problem is?"

"It isn't my place."

"That's very class-conscious of you, Little Girl, but I think maybe you got a bit of a tendency to dramatize."

"Well that's very perceptive of you, Big Man. It so happens I usually do. But this happens to be a fairly dramatic situation."

Mason smiled. "Okay," he said. "You have clutched me with your curtain raiser. I'll go see her."

"That's very white of you," Bo said, annoyed.

"Good for you." He laughed. "You're okay. I like you."

Bo got up and started putting on her coat. "I hope you aren't just being condescending," she said.

Birgitta took a long time opening her door. At first Mason thought her hesitation was because she didn't really believe he had come, no matter how many times he repeated his name. When she opened the door, he knew differently.

"Oh baby," he whispered gently. "You look just terrible."

She started to laugh—deep clutching little sobs of laughter. He closed the door behind him.

"Don't look at me," she said, raising her hand to her face. The gesture was confused, and she seemed to have not enough fingers; she looked like a fat lady caught naked, with only a tiny washcloth, and a number of things to hide. "I don't want you to see my eyes."

"What eyes? You don't have any eyes. Pissholes in the snow, that's what you got."

She turned her head away slightly, but the smile was vaguely recognizable as Birgitta's. "Stupid."

"The pot calling the kettle," said Mason, throwing his coat onto the chair.

"The pot calling the kettle what?"

"The pot calling the kettle stupid." He sat beside her on the bed, and gently smoothed the cap of her matted white-gold hair. "I must say, though, I'm touched. No man has ever been more deeply mourned during his lifetime." His hand moved to her cheek, fingertips trailing along the swollen ridge under her eyes.

"Why are you doing this now?" she said stiffly.

"Doing what?"

"Why are you touching me now?"

"I don't know," he said. "I guess it's because you're funnier-looking than I am."

"Oh Mason . . ." She turned and threw herself into the cradle of his arms, and hiding her face from him, told about the taxi driver. And moaning her shame into his lap, the warm full-bodied woman lay trembling like a small, skinny child.

"Yeah?" he said, when she had long ago finished speaking. "And what else?"

"What else?" She looked up at him, confused.

"What else did you do?"

"Nothing."

"Well hell, girl, you going to start bragging, at least come up with a couple of stories."

"Stop," she said. "Stop pacifying me."

"Pacifying? That's the trouble with all you goddam neutrals. You finally do something a little bit violent, and you think it's the end of the world. So you have to make up for it the rest of your life—maybe even after. Look at Nobel, for God's sake. Comes up with a piss-ant thing like TNT, and forever more they're giving peace prizes."

She smiled. "Of course you would try and make me feel better."

"Well, if this tack doesn't help, I could try the opposite one. Like maybe telling you some of the things I've been doing since I met you . . . After I'd leave you."

She looked at him curiously.

"You want to hear, honey? You want to draw up a dossier of my vilifications? I'll tell you one instance of self-and-other-people abuse, and then you can tell me about your taxi driver. Then I'll hit you with a new one, and you can tell me about your taxi driver. And then I'll tell you still another hair-raising tale and you can tell me about your taxi driver. Of course, by then your story might start to sound a little stale, and—if you'll excuse the expression—pale by comparison. But that way, at least, we can start sort of a . . . Mutual Laceration Society. If that's what you want, you let me know."

"No," she said. "I don't want that."

"What do you want?"

She didn't answer.

"Well, so long as you're being so self-effacing, I'll say what I want."

"What?"

"I want you to go inside and wash your face."

"Why?"

"Well, I'll tell you." Mason sat her up gently and cupped her chin in his hands. "I don't mind kissing a white girl, but I don't like them to taste salty."

Finally, wonderfully, they made love. Afterwards, she huddled against his body, her face moving slowly back and forth across his chest, cheek caressing in mute gratitude and relief the dark velvet above his ribs. He whispered softly to her not to move, and padded barefoot into the insular, walled-in dusk of the apartment to the kitchen, returning with some ice cubes wrapped in a towel.

"What's that for?" she asked.

"Your eyes. It'll help take down the swelling."

"It's useless."

"Yeah, I know. But try anyway."

She pressed the pack obediently to her face. "It'll be days before I look right again. Provided I don't cry anymore."

"Oh, please God, don't do that." He smiled. "I'm going to have to be very good to you. It's a terrible sword hanging over a man, not to be able to raise his voice, or be a little bit nasty. Or beat up on a lady."

She laughed. "It's not that bad. You can beat up on me if you really want to."

"Oh no. I take no chances. I'm going to keep you away from sad movies. And move all the furniture out of the way, so you won't stumble on anything."

"Stop," she said, and her shoulders shook.

"And I'll have to watch that too. Don't let her laugh too hard either, because that can bring tears."

"You're ridiculous."

"Well hell, I know that, and you know that, but nobody else can see it straight off. Whereas you . . . Strangers looking at you, seeing us walk down the street together, could hardly help but turn to each other and say: 'What does a fine-looking young man like that see in a girl like her? Why, it's Beauty and the Beastie come again.' "

"They'd be right," Birgitta said.

"Of course." He started putting on his clothes. "But then they might not understand you were once really a princess, and a spell of weeping had turned you into a frog."

"Is it that bad?"

"The ice'll take it down."

She seemed to realize for the first time that he was getting dressed. "Where are you going?"

"For a hearty Swede, you have a remarkably empty larder. If I rightly remember the lady you used to be, your taste buds ought to be exploding any moment now."

"Don't go." She lowered the towel. Her eyes were beginning to open, and what little he could see of them showed fear.

"I'll be right back."

"Don't go."

"Honey, please. There's nothing to be frightened of."

"But I'm not hungry. Really."

"I can live with your uncertainty," he said, buttoning his shirt. "I cannot live with your unsatisfied appetite."

"Please don't go."

"What are you worried about? I said I'd be right back. So I'll be right back. I'm done with leaving you."

Her fingers twisted the end of the towel, already beginning to drip from the melting ice. "What if he comes?"

"Who?"

"The driver."

"He won't."

"Yes he will. I know he will."

"You know?" he asked. "Or you're afraid he will?"

"Both."

Worry knitted his forehead. "Birgitta, I know you've been upset, and I understand. But you don't hold that out as a threat. To yourself, or me. I told you I'm not leaving."

"It isn't a threat," she said. "I'm not doing it to hold you. I swear. I know he'll come. He's been coming every night. Calling and coming, ringing my phone and ringing my bell."

"You sure?"

"I wasn't imagining it, Mase. I haven't cracked up, you know. Only chipped a little."

"Okay . . ." He stepped into his shoes. "I'll come right back. If the phone rings, you answer. And if it's him, invite him over."

"Are you crazy?"

"Only a little chipped," he said, smiling. "Tell him to wait a couple of minutes, you want to put on some makeup or something. You'll know what to say."

"I don't understand."

"You got a key?"

She nodded toward the mail table. "There's an extra one. It's . . . it's extra."

"Fine. I'll come back as fast as I can. I'll use the key. If the bell rings, don't answer. I want to be here when he comes."

"What are you going to do?" she asked.

"Don't look so anxious. I only want to greet him."

The phone did not ring while he was gone, she told him as he piled the groceries on the dinette table. Nor had the doorbell.

"Okay," he said. "So we'll be ready if it does. But we won't wait for it."

They did, though. All through dinner, their conversation was tentative and expectant, and both found themselves listening for something through hollow silences. Birgitta ate more than she had since their last dinner together, but her appetite was oddly restrained. They watched the news on television, but neither of them seemed engrossed. Finally, they gave up even the pretense of wanting distraction. They just sat there, in the darkened living room, with only the small light from the kitchenette, waiting.

At nine-thirty the doorbell rang.

"Ask who it is."

She went to the door, reluctantly, and whispered her inquiry. There was no response. The doorbell rang again.

"Maybe he can't hear you," Mason said.

"He can hear," she said. "He never says who it is. I don't . . . I wouldn't recognize his name." She looked away.

"You owe any money?" He was beside her in the dark entrance foyer.

"No."

"Then it ain't no bill collector," Mason said, unbuttoning his shirt. "They're the only ones I know ring like that. Tell him just a minute."

"Just a minute," Birgitta called out through the door.

"You got a light in this vestibule?"

She nodded.

"Turn it on," he said. As she did so, he handed her his shirt. He stood, naked to the waist, trouser belt unbuckled, and only socks on his feet. "Now you get inside."

"But . . ."

"Just go in there and stay out of sight. And don't say anything. Okay?"

"Okay."

"How do I look?" He grinned at her, and inhaled deeply, throwing his shoulders back and expanding his chest. "I look like a fierce black?"

"Pretty fierce," she said.

"Go inside."

She moved obediently out of the tiny foyer, and he waited a moment, giving time for another insistent pressure on the bell. Then he opened the door.

"Yes?" Mason asked, stretching himself lazily.

"I . . ." The man outside looked startled, and extremely confused. His eyes searched the door, and came to rest on the letter. "I . . . guess I've got the wrong apartment."

"You got the right apartment, mister. But you got the *wrong* idea." Mason's voice was much deeper than normal, and he strained it all the way into his belly, remembering the radio voice of Kingfish.

The man outside was fairly dark-complexioned, probably an Italian, Mason figured. But his coloration turned first Nordic, and then high American Indian. "I . . ." He started to back away.

"Now hold on dere, buddy." It was better than Kingfish, Mason realized with perverse pride. "I'se glad dat you made dis hyar call. I been hopin' to git a chance to speak to you . . . I been meanin' to tell you ta keep away from mah sistah."

"Your . . . your what?"

He was perhaps overdoing it. The fellow might be a little young to remember Amos and Andy. "My sister," Mason said.

"Your *sister?*"

Nordic again. A veritable Swede. "Dat's right. I don't like your messin' aroun' wid her. You evah come neah her again, I gonna kick the shid oudda you."

"Oh." He turned an unclassifiable gray. "Oh," he said again.

"You undahstan?"

"Sure . . ." He nodded like a jack-in-the-box gone mad. "Sure sure, I understand." He started to back off down the hallway.

"Hold on dere," Kingfish boomed.

The fellow scampered back in front of Mason, looking back nervously over his shoulder as if he were being pursued, although facing his pursuer. "Yes?"

"I jest wanna be *sure* you undahstand. I really got nothin' against white men, undahstand dat."

"I understand." He bobbed his head wildly.

"Ya see . . ." Mason took a long, artful breath, and released it slowly. "I don't hold it against our Mammy. I can't help what mah mothah did. Ya know what I mean?"

"Sure," the fellow agreed, eagerly. "Sure."

"Howevah . . ." Mason drank in a final, massive dose of air. "I'm goddamned if I'd want my sistah to marry one."

X

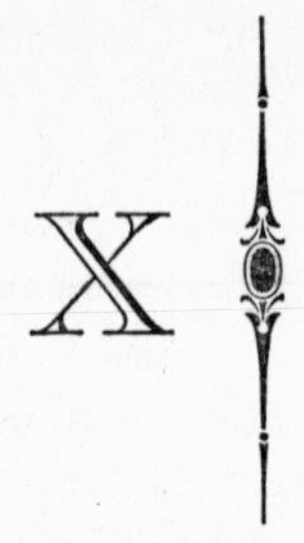

SOMETIMES, when the nights on Seventy-Eighth Street grew longer than even winter could account for, Bo and Mary Kate, after unsuccessfully exhausting all other means of speeding time's passage, would settle into a fervid discussion about sex. Their talk encompassed both the finer and grosser points of the most romantic and animal aspects. And eventually the conversation became an informal, but nonetheless intense debate about the importance, or unimportance, about crude vs. polished erotic technique. Both girls were a wellspring of accumulated information, all the more remarkable in that they had only a smattering of, or an occasional rubbing up against, personal experience. But neither of them particularly wishing to acknowledge that fact, and both fearing the other would consider her contribution adolescent, the debates soon lost their intellectual gloss, to become tinged with emotionalism. Mary Kate, quickly losing patience with what she considered trivia, would try to focus the argument on what she believed to be (incorrectly, Bo was sure) the crux of the matter: size.

"Bullshit," Bo said, since it was just the two of them. "The size has nothing to do with it, and you know it."

"I know no such thing," Mary Kate countered. "If a man has an ineffectual one, there can be no sexual satisfaction."

"For a cow, maybe."

"For a woman," Mary Kate insisted.

"Well of course, if his thing is nonexistent, that's one thing. But I'm talking about a normal one."

"The bigger, the better."

"Bullshit," Bo said again.

"You know perfectly well that the women in harems are hung on their eunuchs, because having their testicles cut off makes their things enormous. So the women all get hung up."

"That book is very misleading, Mary Kate. I don't care if it does have an introduction by a psychiatrist. It's just pornography, and you know it."

"It cost seven-fifty."

"What does that prove? Just that you're a sucker for buying it. And even more for taking it in, like it was some kind of gospel, for Christ's sake. All it is is hard-cover pornography, with foreword by a supposed MD."

"They couldn't advertise it in the *Times,* if that was all it was. And a medical man wouldn't endorse it."

"Have you checked his credentials? They're just masquerading filth under the guise of enlightened textbooks, that's all. The publishers don't know how to compete anymore since *Fanny Hill.*"

"Bo, you amaze me. This isn't anything that just started, for God's sake. It's not some new revelation, for sensationalism or anything like that. It's been fact for a long time. The fact that the books are now available is after the fact. The mystique of big things goes back over hundreds of years. Thousands maybe."

"But it is *mystique,*" Bo ventured.

"All mystiques, like all myths, have their roots in truth."

"Bullshit. They have their roots in ignorance and superstition, like you're displaying at this very moment."

"Ignorance and superstition? You call William Faulkner ignorance and superstition?"

"Mary Kate, if you knew how to interpret stream-of-consciousness, you'd realize he wasn't writing about his own ignorance and superstition, but the other Southerners."

"But there's a reason why they have the superstition, and it's valid Negroes have enormous—"

"I don't want to get into that," Bo said.

"Why not?" Mary Kate looked genuinely astounded. They were always getting into Negroes, and it had never bothered Bo before.

"The whole idea is stupid."

"Did you read *The White Negro*?"

Bo shifted in her chair. "I liked him better when he wrote about war. He knew something about war. He doesn't know beans about Negroes, he just wishes he could be one. And if he were, he would be very disappointed. The only change would be in his skin. His thing would still be the same size."

"You're crazy," Mary Kate said. "Did you ever see pictures?"

"I saw *The Sky Above and the Thing Below,*" Bo said. "They didn't look particularly big to me."

"In comparison to what?"

"In comparison to anybody's."

"Most of them were wearing carrots," Mary Kate said. "You couldn't really tell."

"Penile sheaths. They weren't carrots, they were penile sheaths."

"Where'd you get that expression?"

"I went to see it with a student psychiatrist."

"There is no such thing," Mary Kate said. "The least there is is a medical student who plans on going into psychiatry. But an undergraduate psychiatrist does not exist."

"He planned on going to medical school. And he *was* a Psych major."

"In Ohio? I want to wish you a lot of luck with his information."

"Mary Kate, I don't believe sometimes how insulated you are."

"The word is insular. A penile sheath is insulated."

"Well then, you're insular. Your own father studied medicine in Ohio."

"But he did practice in Europe during the war, you know. *After* being an army doctor at home, where, by the way, he was the official examiner for a countless number of inductees. And of whom, incidentally," Mary Kate smiled smugly, "he happens to have a great many photographs. I've seen them."

"And?"

"To the knee," Mary Kate said.

"Really?" In spite of herself, Bo was terribly curious.

"Except for a couple of the taller Negroes of course. Theirs fell well below."

"I don't believe you."

"I'm not in the habit of spreading misinformation of which I'm not sure." Mary Kate lay back on the sofa, and sighed.

"I still say it depends on the individual."

"I agree with you."

"You do?" Bo said, surprised.

"Of course. Some more highly sexed Negroes have bigger ones than other Negroes. But the least of theirs is more than the average white man's."

"Bullshit," Bo said.

They seemed to have come to somewhat of an impasse. Bo, feeling both relieved that the discussion was over, and sorry she could not rely on the validity of either of their information, went into the bathroom and started to set her hair.

"What are you doing in there?" Mary Kate yelled.

"Well the door's open, so it couldn't be anything too offensive."

"What are you doing?" Mary Kate appeared behind her in the doorway. "Why are you setting your hair? It's only eight-thirty."

"I thought it was later," Bo said. "It feels later. Maybe you should take the living room tonight, and I'll go to bed early. Read a book or something."

"But you *can't*. Alec is coming over."

"To rehearse?"

"Something like that."

"Then you won't need me." Bo continued twisting the rollers into place although she stopped wetting her hair. "You can close the door and have the living room all to yourselves."

"But I told him you'd be here," Mary Kate pleaded. "I said you'd be home all night."

"Honest to God," Bo said, a bobby pin clasped in her teeth. "I wish you'd stop shoving him down my throat."

"Well—as long as that's as far as he gets . . . you have nothing to worry about."

"Gross," Bo said. "There is no disputing it. You are a gross personage. And an eminently fit companion for the sex-obsessed Alec. I don't know why both of you don't leave me alone and find each other. It would be a perfect merger, a marriage made in bed."

"I don't want you to marry him, for heaven's sake, Bo. But sooner or later you will have to shed your protective Cleveland coloration, and Alec is good practice material. He's broody, and interesting, and quite attractive in a sulky kind of way. And he does care about you."

"He cares about my thing."

"Well, what's so terrible about that?" Mary Kate said. "Would you rather have some suitor who was blind to it? Would you rather go to concerts and art exhibitions with a man for years and years, and then one day find yourself in bed with him and he leans over and says 'Hmmm, what have we here?' Besides, I don't really think Alec is as sex-obsessed as you think. He's always behaved perfectly with me, and I've seen him around most of the girls in class and he doesn't come on with them." Mary Kate sat down tentatively on the edge of the bathtub. "Maybe you bring out some kind of perverse reaction in him because you're so cold."

"I am not cold at all," Bo said, flushing furiously. "But unlike *some* people I know who are aroused by smut which they send away for at exorbitant prices, I cannot be titillated by an interminable discussion about sex."

"I'm not going to let you attack me just because you're on the defensive."

"That's very wise of you," Bo said. "As I was saying, there has not been one occasion in my brief but stormy relationship with Mr. Ingells when the entire evening hasn't hinged on talk about sex. An intellectual approach to the glands is not only a bore and a drain, it is self-defeating."

"I thought you were the one who considers technique so important in bringing it to its full peak; and technique, you said, is a result of intellect, sensitivity and memory."

"In bringing what to its full peak?"

"The glans," Mary Kate said.

"I said *glands*." Bo rolled her eyes backward. "I don't know why you always have to think so graphic."

"Well, you shouldn't talk with a toothbrush in your mouth. It's as bad as food. Anyway, maybe if you'd relax a little instead of always insisting on brightly lit places where he couldn't possibly lay a hand on you, you'd give your idea of romance a chance to happen."

Bo rinsed her mouth cleanly, wiping it with a towel, and turned to face Mary Kate. "Last night, my dear, your Alec Ingells and I had just such an evening. . . . We went to an Italian place—dark, dimly lit by candles in Chianti bottles. There were violins, on records of course —I wouldn't let him take me to any place expensive, not because it would make me more seducible, but because I don't think he can afford it— You see, I do look out for him in my own cold way.

"So there we were, in this very romantic darkness, and I was feeling pretty relaxed and schmoozy and all—the wine was cheap but gorgeous, and Alec had shaved for a change, and was looking very good, I must say. So as I'm eyeing him over the pizza, he suddenly looks at the platter and says, 'Have you ever thought what it would be like, fucking an anchovy?' "

Mary Kate laughed.

"Well it may be very funny to you," Bo said. "But it put a bit of a damper on my feelings."

"Well, you have to try and understand him, Bo. Alec is a very intense person—I told you how talented he is. He desperately wants to go into analysis, but he feels he isn't an important enough actor yet. So he has a tendency to overanalyze everything, by way of preparation, to lead to his own greater understanding. You get what I mean? There isn't a thing in the world he doesn't try to dissect."

"Including a pizza," Bo said, opening a cold cream jar.

"I didn't mean that, I was talking about feelings, reponses, conflicts between people. That's why he might show this tendency to . . . dwell on certain aspects of your relationship. Overarticulate before the fact and all. God, I remember one week we were preparing a scene from *Hansel and Gretel* as a change of pace. *Hansel and Gretel* of all things! And before we could even start dropping bread crumbs in the goddam forest, Alec insisted on a three-hour discussion on sibling rivalry."

Mary Kate plopped her hands on her knees, where they rested. " 'Alec,' I said, 'this is not a question of deep-seated Freudian conflict between a brother and sister. These are two little kids whose parents are starving to death, so they want them to Get Lost. Do you understand, Alec?' I said. So you know what he said? He said, 'Well, if that isn't the apotheosis of parental rejection, I don't know what it is.' So I told him what it is, is a children's story. And you know, he refused to believe me?"

The downstairs doorbell rang.

Mary Kate went to press the buzzer releasing the front door. "Take off the cold cream," she said. "The bridegroom cometh."

"I have no wish to see him," Bo said, picking up a Kleenex.

By the time Alec had reached the fifth floor landing, the elevator being so slow, Bo was in bed with a book. She also had her brassiere on under her nightgown; and although her hair was in rollers, she had covered it with a bouffant red snood she considered both piquant and sad.

"Where's the kid?" she heard him mumble through the closed door.

"She's in bed," Mary Kate answered.

"Beauty!" Alec clapped his hands together. "If I give you a quarter will you go down and get a soda?"

"I don't take very long to finish a soda."

"Okay," Alec said. "How about fifty cents for the movies."

"How long has it been since you got into a movie for fifty cents?"

"Shit." Bo heard the jingle of change. "I didn't figure I'd have to spring for anything tonight. Let me see how much I got with me."

"Mary Kate!" Bo shouted.

Mary Kate opened the door. "Yes, Bo?"

"If you *dare* to leave this house I will not be your roommate ever again."

"Beauty!" said Alec from the living room. "My roommate's thinking of cutting out to Chicago, and like that, you can come sack in with me." He stuck his head into the room and peered at her.

"Son of a bitch," he said. "Butterfly McQueen works again."

Bo touched her cap, and then brought her hand quickly back to the page of the open book. "This is my bedroom, Mr. Ingells, if you don't mind."

"Mind? I think it's sensational." And with that, he did a running jump through the air and came to rest, spread-eagled, on top of the covers and Bo.

"I guess I'd better go to the movies," Mary Kate said.

"You do no such thing!" Bo shouted, red-faced, as she swacked out furiously at Alec and rolled out from under him. "You horrible animal. You unleashed boar."

"That's boor, baby." He grinned up at her, resting the back of his head against his hands.

Bo flushed even deeper, bringing her arms up to cover the naked scoop in the neck of her nightgown. "That too. Boor, boar, bore, spelled both ways."

"What you hiding, little chicken, the fact that you're wearing a bra- zi- ay? That's okay, I'm sure your titties hang sweet and high, but there's no reason not to hoist them up there so you don't sag before your time."

Bo ran into the bathroom and locked the door. Fortunately, she had undressed so hurriedly she had left her clothes hanging on the hook behind the door.

"What you doing in there, sweet thing? Putting on your diaphragm? That's good. Be sure and use plenty of jelly—I got a powerful seed."

"Oh shut up, Alec," Mary Kate said. "Sometimes you do go too far."

"Not in this instance," he said. "Why, I ain't hardly begun."

"Shut up and come into the living room."

"Don't be ridickalus. I'm plumb contented, right where I am."

Bo could hear the bouncing of bedsprings, and her blood seethed, she was sure. He was loathsome, there was no doubt about it. At least there was no doubt about it tonight. She threw the rollers into the sink and ran a comb once through her hair.

"Yessirreebob," Alec was saying as she opened the door. "Plumb contented."

"Well, well, Mr. Ingells," Bo said. "What scene are we rehearsing tonight, *Tobacco Road*?"

"God's Little Acre." He patted the bed beside him. "And here's where it is. Come on, honey."

"Up your giggy with a Mello-Roll," said Bo, taking her coat from the closet.

"That's one hell of an idea." Alec chuckled. "But it's much more Tennessee Williams than Erskine Caldwell."

"Bo . . ." Mary Kate followed her to the living room door. "Bo, where are you going?"

"To the movies," Bo said. "I am not as hard up as Alec Ingells. For cash," she shouted. "Or anything else."

Ernie's mother had taken to sitting in the living room evenings, staring at the wall. After she finished serving him a big, silent supper, she would scrape the dishes, pile them in the sink, and go into the living room, fixing the old oak blanket chest in the most advantageous position, and her eyes on the wall. At first, there had been a few pictures hanging there: an old wedding portrait of herself and Ernie's father, a photograph of Ernie in the Air Corps, and a print of a bowl of daisies, reproduced and mounted in a redwood frame. But one by one she had taken them down, until there was nothing left but a few holes, one nail she hadn't been able to pry out, and a ten-foot expanse, floor to ceiling, of slightly peeling Dusty Rose.

She would not even look at television anymore. Every evening, Ernie would do the dishes she told him not to bother with, and after hanging the dish towel neatly on the rack behind the sink, go into the living room and turn on the set. But she paid no attention. He started bringing home *TV Guide,* and on Sunday mornings, he would go out and buy all the newspapers that contained a separate and complete illustrated TV section, so she could really plan a program well in advance, for her entire week of watching. But all she would watch was the walls.

"Ma," Ernie said. "Why aren't you looking at TV?"

She didn't answer.

He patted the back of the big armchair in front of the console. "Why don't you sit here?" He fluffed up the bottom and back cushions. "Come on."

She looked at him as though he were crazy, wanting her to move from the comfort of the wooden blanket chest.

Ernie turned on the switch, and looked at his watch. Then he picked up the three catalogs he had placed temptingly on top of the set, and turned the pages. "It's nine o'clock, Mom. You know what that means." He moved the dial to the proper channel. "Come on, it's your favorite program."

She didn't turn her head.

"Why won't you at least look?" Ernie pleaded.

"To tell the truth," she said, "I haven't got the heart."

Ernie was baffled. The one thing in life his mother had seemed to enjoy in the last few years, besides cooking, was television. And the food was for his mouth, it was his eating that seemed to give her pleasure, she hardly touched a thing. But the programs, those she devoured like a greedy child. Now that she had stopped watching, Ernie did not know what to do for her. He was home every night for dinner, and ate even more than he wanted, and made loud noises of appreciation. But it didn't seem to satisfy her. She would still go in and look at the wall. No matter what he did to please her, she wouldn't watch television.

Actually, she was watching, only Ernie didn't know it. The minute he was out of the house on his way to work in the mornings, she would rush to the chair in front of the TV, to see the Morning Matinee, the Late Morning Matinee, the Lunch Matinee, and the

Late Lunch Matinee. During the commercials she would anxiously switch dials, and watch a little of the game shows. The only bad thing about mornings was there were so many commercials she sometimes had to go all around the dial before finding a station that wasn't broadcasting one; but even when all did, she worked it out by finding the commercial she liked best and watched that. She sat there with the eagerness of an alcoholic going through the motions in public of being on the wagon. By five-thirty, when she had to think about preparing dinner and making the beds, she had had enough to keep her going until the next day. And, as much as she loved her boy, she could hardly wait for him to leave the house in the mornings.

It was the evenings she wanted him home.

For a time now, Ernie had been going out after supper and coming back at twelve, one o'clock in the morning. Ernie's mother knew where he was going. She had talked about it to her sister Maureen in Bellport, talked about it at great length. Much as she worried about the message units, the peace of mind Maureen gave her was worth the anguish.

"Mr. Ernie's seeing . . ." she said into the phone. "My Ernie's seeing . . . Oh, it makes me sick to even say it."

"What is she?" Maureen said. "A tramp?"

"I wish. At least a tramp has a heart of gold. She's . . . a Jap, Maureen."

"A what?"

"A Jap. A Japanese. From Hong Kong."

"That's China," Maureen said. "The part that isn't Communist besides Formosa."

"Wherever she's from, what difference? A Jap girl. Can you imagine? My poor Ernie, he thinks he's Red Buttons."

"So keep him away from her. Pretend to be sick."

"Don't you ever watch any programs, Maureen? An invalid mother, that's a sure way to drive a boy into the streets, straight into her arms."

"So then act crazy. If you're acting crazy, he'll be too worried to leave you alone."

"How do I do that? I'm no Olivia De Havilland, Maureen. I'm a mother. I don't know how to have fits."

"You don't have to have fits. Just act funny. Don't do anything he's used to, leave dishes in the sink, things like that."

"Not even cook?"

"Especially not cook."

There was a pause. "I couldn't do that, Maureen. I'm a mother."

"Oh . . . Well, maybe you could stop talking to him."

"We don't say much to each other as it is," she said. "Ernie's never been much of a talker. He just sits in his room the little he's home while I watch TV."

"You watch a lot?"

"Till my eyes fall out. It's all I've got, now that I have no more son."

"So stop watching television."

Ernie's mother felt a pang in her stomach, like somebody had died. "Why?"

"Then he'll know something's wrong."

"He never even knows I'm watching. He doesn't pay attention."

"He would if you stopped. He's bound to notice something is peculiar."

"You think so?"

"I *know* so. Television is like having another person, you know what I mean?"

"Yes," she said, miserably. She had come to think of the set as her friend. She even told Ernie that one night, when he was putting on his coat to go out with that Jap. "A boy's best friend is his mother," she had told him, "but a mother's best friend is her television set." He had gone out anyway.

"So if you have another person in the house," Maureen said, "you may not pay any attention to them while they're there, but if they leave, you notice, right?"

"I suppose so."

"Stop watching television," Maureen said.

"What'll I do?" she asked, desperately.

"I don't know . . . read."

"I haven't the patience."

"Then don't do anything," Maureen said. "It'll probably be better if you don't do anything anyway. It'll make it more dramatic."

It was, Ernie's mother had thought, a brilliant suggestion. For the first two days she stopped watching she cleaned a lot, scrubbing old pots and pans and the kitchen ceiling. But Ernie hadn't been home to see, and by the third evening, the place was immaculate. The next night he was home, and she had tried just sitting in the armchair, but she didn't know what to do, being so close to the set: the temptation to lean over and switch on the knob was unbearable.

It was the fourth night that she decided to sit on the oak chest, staring at the wall. It was certainly dramatic, as Maureen said. And there was no doubt that Ernie noticed. He started bringing home TV magazines, and three, four times a night he would ask her didn't she want to turn on the set. He was certainly noticing, and even worried: there was no doubt about that. There was no doubt either that Maureen was pretty smart. It was, Ernie's mother had to admit, a very good idea.

The only problem was, it didn't work.

He would notice, he would worry, but at nine or ten or even eleven o'clock, three or four nights a week, he would put on his overcoat and his hat and go out into the night after his Jap. Ernie's mother said to herself if she wasn't so concerned about what would happen to her boy, she would wish herself dead. Sitting there, on that cold hard lumber, her legs and back like lead, she felt that she was mourning not only the loss of a son, but the death of her best friend: a friend who could be brought back to life with the merest flick of a switch. But she didn't dare. She might become so absorbed, she wouldn't hear his footsteps in time to turn off the set. He would think she was all right again, and then all her weeks of self-denial and suffering would have been for nothing.

"You sure you don't want me to turn it on, Ma?" Ernie said, as he came out of the bedroom.

She shook her head sadly.

Ernie stood in the doorway for a moment, watching her with puzzled eyes. Then he went to the hall closet.

"Ernie?"

"Yeah, Mom."

"What are you doing, Ernie?"

He came back into the room, his overcoat on his arm. She could feel her heart tumble into her lap.

"I have to go out for a little while. Do you want anything from the drugstore or some place?"

She shook her head.

"If you want to, if I'm not back soon . . . maybe you could watch a little TV."

"No." She swallowed the eagle's egg that was in her throat. "No, I can't."

"Why not?" Ernie smiled at her, a sad little smile, fuzzy around the edges.

"It's not in me anymore, Ernie." Tears welled up in her eyes, and when she leaned over, one fell all the way to the floor, with a great plopping sound, it seemed to her. But if he heard, he gave no sign. And he couldn't very well see the tears with his back to her, going out the door as he was.

"Take care of yourself, Ma," he said, without ever turning around, and shut the door behind him.

In a few minutes, when she was sure he was gone, she got up from her bier. And taking the *TV Guide* from the top of the set, she went into her small bedroom, locking the door as she hadn't done since Ernie was a small boy and Joe was alive and they were afraid the child might wander in and see what parents did. She lay back on the bed, her left hand on her heart, her right hand clutching the book firmly, as she studied the listings of that day's programs, and tried to imagine what they would be like.

Ernie stood in the hallway, a few feet away from her apartment. From where he was, he could observe the door perfectly, but he knew, after careful study, that behind the slight niche, flattened against the wall as he was, with only dim light in the stairway casting a concealing shadow, there was no way Kiiko could see him.

He had started coming there at night after Christmas, the second time she let him walk her home. The same faulty latch that had caused him to fear for her safety allowed his easy entrance into the downstairs. Finding out the number of her apartment had been only a matter of a swift sideways glance at the mailboxes. So no one would have any idea, as he climbed first the front stoop and then the stairs to her landing, that he had no business being there.

And if anyone thought that, they were wrong: Ernie had very important business. He had to protect her, and the only way to protect a vulnerable young girl in New York was to be there when she needed him. She was too smart and too good to go any place where harm might come to her, so the only time it could happen was when they brought her home.

He always knew the nights she was going out—sometime during

their walk from work he would ask her nonchalantly what play or what movie she was seeing, and she would answer that she wasn't going anywhere, or, she would name a play or a movie, or even say, "Oh, we're not doing anything special, just going out to dinner."

And then he could be waiting. Then he could be there in time, and not a moment too soon, either. Because something was going to happen to her, he knew it as surely as he knew himself. Only it wasn't going to happen, because he would save her.

The nights she stayed home, he didn't bother to be on call: He trusted her not to invite anyone into her apartment. But the other nights he worried, and rather than worry and not be sure, he worried down the hall.

There was one fellow she seemed to see more than the others: a slight, well-dressed young Oriental whom Ernie could have broken in half with one hand. But there was no need. Like Kiiko, the boy was quiet, and well-mannered, always shaking hands with her politely at the door, and saying he would call her in a few days. Nothing more. Ernie was always glad to see her coming home with him. He was not so glad to see her with some of the others. Some of the others seemed dissatisfied with the handshake. And some showed their dissatisfaction, leaning over and trying to kiss her sweet little mouth, as Ernie tensed himself, waiting. But she handled them well. She turned her head aside quickly, and whispered "No, please," and if any of them got ugly about it she told them she didn't think they had better see each other again, and then they retreated, saying things like "Suits me," and other stupid, young punk expressions.

Ernie could have ripped them into shreds for hurting her feelings that way, but at least they were out of her life and wouldn't bother her anymore. That was the important thing. He didn't like their hurting her feelings, but her feelings at least would mend quickly. She was better off with them gone, and smart enough to know that: and that would quickly bring healing tissue to the tiny violation of her pride.

Ernie pressed back into the shadow, and smiled because she was so safe. And in Brooklyn, Ernie's mother, reading the synopsis of *To Each His Own,* on the Late Show, wept.

XI

"MAMA'S are so funny," Ursull said, leaning over and pulling gently at the golden hairs on Gerd's chest. "They have instincts like bears."

"Mama Bears?" He smiled at her through the smoke from his cigarette. "Papa Bears? or Baby Bears?"

"Goldilocks." She tugged at one long strand, and then watched it curl back around her finger.

"What are you doing to me?" he said. "Are you trying to make me bald?"

"I want to make them straight. I can't understand why the hair on your head is so straight, and these should be so curly."

He craned his neck slightly, kissing her temple. "I'll have them removed. We could shave them, or strip them away, if you want."

"Oh no, please." She touched his shoulder with her lips. "I love them. The rest of your body is so smooth. I look upon these as . . . an oasis. A tiny forest in a marble desert."

"Then I will have transplants, all over, and become hairy like an ape."

"Don't do anything," she whispered. "I adore you as you are. Your body is perfect."

"It's all right for a man," he said. "I prefer yours."

They kissed once gently. And then, without turning his head, he stubbed his cigarette out in the ashtray on the bedtable and brought his hand back over the smooth rise of her hip.

"Oh no, don't," she said, as his lips pressed harder against hers. "Not yet. I have something important to tell you."

"What?"

"I can't remember," she said, and sought him, openmouthed.

"Was it about your mama?" he asked, after a moment.

"Oh yes . . . Mama." She raised herself on one elbow, and smiled down at him. "She is so funny. I have been so careful, writing her about you. One sentence here. One sentence there. All hardly noticeable by themselves, you know, we wished to make everything gradual. It is cold in New York, et cetera, et cetera, but don't worry I have plenty of warm clothes and have bought some beautiful sweaters, and I met an interesting boy, and the Ramirez sisters called me to meet their young uncle, but their cousin was such a bore I said I was busy. And then a week later, I wrote I saw such and such a movie, and described the entire plot in great detail; and then, so incidental you might easily miss it, yesterday I went to tea with the boy I told you about. He is quite attractive and bright. The next letter, I mentioned your name. Four such letters, that is all I wrote, and this morning, what do you suppose?"

"You received a cable from your mama. 'Who is this boy?' "

"How did you know?" Ursull said, surprised.

"Your mama is not so quick as my mama. I received my cable two weeks ago."

Ursull laughed. "My mother is extremely quick. You are a better correspondent, that is all."

"So what shall we tell her, this quick mother of yours?"

"That we are in love?" Ursull asked.

"Not just yet," Gerd said. "She sent a cable because she feared such an answer. First you must calm her fears, reassure her that I am just another young man, and when she thinks she has worried about nothing, then you will write her we are in love."

"You're cruel," Ursull said, and nipped the soft flesh of his shoulder.

"I am sensible," he said. "Which is something that you cannot say about mothers."

"How do I do this? How do I make you seem just another young man? You are not just another young man. You are magnificent."

"That may be so." He smiled. "But that may be also because you love me. If you write about me objectively, I may appear quite ordinary."

"Impossible."

"Well, we must at least try."

"How could I be objective about you?" Ursull said, her eyes shining.

"You must approach me coldly, like a banker, as if I were making a loan application. Facts. Nothing but facts."

"Nonsense," she said, "I couldn't do that. I have no experience with loans."

"What do you have experience with?"

Ursull thought for a moment. "Schools," she said. "Only schools and universities, I'm afraid."

"Fine," he said. "Then we will approach it as if I were making application to a university. Nothing very personal, that will come with the interview . . . Where I was born, when, educational background, religious affiliations, sports . . . clubs . . ."

"Do you belong to many clubs?" she said. "I thought it was the English who joined clubs."

"The English, you will remember, picked up many of their best habits at Heidelberg."

"Why don't you have a scar?" She traced a line from his cheekbone to the side of his mouth. "I should adore you with a sinister dueling scar."

"I shall get one tomorrow."

"No," she said. "If you haven't already got it, I don't want it. Did you belong to a fencing club?"

"Certainly," he said. "But I was too vain and too good to get slashed."

"What other clubs?" She touched his mouth, and pulled her finger away as he bit at her.

"The usual ones. A tennis club. A skiing club in winter. My father's banking club. An academic society for exceptional scholars."

"And when you were a boy?"

"Hitler Jungen." He felt her pull away slightly. "Does that bother you?"

"I don't know," she said. "How did you feel about it?"

"I loved it," he said.

"You loved Hitler?"

"I didn't know Hitler. I only knew the organization, and it was wonderful for an eight-year-old boy."

"All that hatred?"

"You don't understand, Ursull. Then we did not know it was hatred. What we knew was that they gave us uniforms, like men. . . . Like grown men, even the girls. Wonderful uniforms, with many, many pockets. You know how children love pockets. Pockets with flaps that buttoned and unbuttoned. Pockets in the pants, pockets on the jackets, one on each breast, and two inside the jacket, and even . . . there was even a pocket on the side of the sleeve. That was a very special pocket. That was where we kept our identity cards and our card of membership in the *Jungen.* You have no idea what a feeling of importance that gave us, a card in such a pocket, like a grown man.

"A piece of string, when it was buttoned into a pocket, made it a treasure. Treasures were not so plentiful in those days, you know. And a card—our own card with a number, a photograph, a fingerprint . . . Can you imagine how exciting that is to a child, to be fingerprinted? It was like a game. A fascinating, adult game, and we had to be very important, obviously, to be allowed to play. At least that was how it seemed at the time."

"I see."

"Do you, Ursull? Of course you must. You are an intelligent girl. Children are children."

"I suppose so," she said. She paused for a moment. "And what did you think about what they taught you?"

"Who thought about it? Does a child question the words of his teacher? He might be a superior or an inferior student, but he doesn't question what is told him of history, geography, mathematics, does he? Do you know many pre-adolescent skeptics?"

"No," Ursull said. "No, of course not. What did they teach you?"

"Oh, you know, all that rubbish about the inevitable supremacy of Aryans . . . They showed us skulls—pictures of skulls: the Jewish skull, of course had a smaller space to accommodate the smaller brain. The Negro skull was flat and inferior, from centuries of having their brains shriveled in the sun. And the Oriental skull had room only to accommodate a brain the size of a pea."

"But you knew it was rubbish."

"Not then, of course. I didn't realize it then, but of course now I know."

"And what about Hitler? How do you feel about Hitler?"

"He was a fool," Gerd said.

"Really?" She swallowed hard, greatly relieved.

"Of course he was a fool. If he hadn't been so stupid about the Jews, Germany would have succeeded."

She did not pursue the discussion. Succeeded in what, world domination? Stupid about the Jews, how? In despising them, or exterminating them, thereby incurring too much anger abroad? He had been eight years old, that was all. A little boy who loved pockets. Like any normal boy, but in a country gone insane. And that was not his fault, where he had been born. The important thing was he had grown to splendid manhood, and she loved the man he was, and forgave the child he had been through no fault of his own. It mattered only that he did not believe any of those things anymore. All the years of brainwashing, and yet he had been able to rise above it, the brilliant, perceptive young man that he was, and see it as the nonsense it was. And if he had not been able to free himself completely from the teachings of his youth? If, indeed, the child was the father of the man?

Ursull looked at him in the dim glow of the bedlamp. If the child was the father of the man, it did not matter. She was in love with the man, and not the father. She threw herself on top of him with a ferocity that astonished both of them, and tried to blot out her thoughts with love.

The balcony of the 86th Street movie house was not very full; it was the middle of the week, and quite late at night, and except for scattered couples who Bo supposed had too much leisure time or not enough to say to each other, or waifs like herself who had been driven into the storm by sex maniacs, there was not much call to go to a neighborhood theatre. The desperately lonely and the perverts would be downtown, she had reasoned solemnly, as she debated with herself whether or not to spend the extra quarter for the loge. And deciding she would be goddamned if she was going to spend more money than necessary because of that miserable Alec, on a picture she had no wish to see, she bought a balcony ticket.

A light streamed from high above her, illuminating not only the screen, but the center section of seats around her; and she noted with twenty-five cents' worth of regret that the loge below was shrouded in darkness. But as the picture was even more routine than she had imagined, there was no need to lose herself in it completely, so she watched with the lights on-half interest she usually reserved for television.

The movie had been advertised as highly sexual and shocking, but in light of her recent adventures with Alec, she found it neither, although she had to admit the girl wore bedsheets a lot, in itself exceptional for an American film. To the average viewer, who had not been exposed to the courtship of a satyr, Bo supposed all those crotch shots of the girls in whorehouse row might have seemed stimulating, but being pretty jaded, Bo knew she was not really a proper judge. She looked at her watch, and was disappointed to see it was only ten-thirty. Alec would probably still be there, waiting for her; she decided to stay till the end of the show.

About three seats to the wind, plotwise, a man sat down in the aisle seat, only one seat away from hers. It struck Bo as a little peculiar, considering the balcony was almost completely empty. She had an impulse to get up and move farther down, where there were a scattered couple or two. But glancing out of the corner of her eye, she saw he was a Negro, well and cleanly dressed. If she changed her seat, and there were no reason for it, which she was sure there was not, he might think her prejudiced, which she was certainly not: Mason Williams was probably as decent a young man as any she knew, and if Birgitta wanted him and could cope with the problems, he was doubtless exceptional. So Bo stayed where she was.

Some minutes later, after the all-important pornographic book and perverted sex scene the *Times* had so despised, Bo became conscious of an odd noise coming from her right: a whisking sound, like the hurried scrape of an emery board against fingernails. She shifted uncomfortably, and tried to place what it was.

If he's scratching his fly, Bo thought, I'll get up and move. She looked over.

He was not scratching his fly. He was watching the screen in total absorption, his left elbow leaning on the armrest, little finger of his left hand rubbing along the ridge of his upper gums. And with his right hand, he was pulling the skin regularly but disinterestedly back and forth across his organ, which lay fully exposed in his lap.

It wasn't as big as all that. Bo hadn't seen very many, it was true, but there had been instances when boys in parked cars had pleaded with her to at least touch it, and she had acceded to their request: it didn't seem very much different from most of those. The most striking aspect about this one, at the moment, was that its head was aimed directly at her. So if, in spite of the nonchalance with which he was stripping away, he was anywhere near climax, she would probably be caught in a seminal spray.

The speed with which Bo moved surprised her: it could not have been more than a second between the time she had seen what was going on, the thoughts running abstractly through her mind, and her getting to her feet and passing into the left aisle. True there had been twenty or thirty seats on the left, and only two to her right, but what was she supposed to have said, "Excuse me, sir, would you mind lifting your thing, I'd like to get through?" Likewise amazing was the calm with which she descended the steps, her mind racing, but her tread deliberate and slow. What should she do now? Go to the usherette, and say, Excuse me, ma'am, but there's a pervert jerking off in the balcony? The usherette was sixty years old at least, and would probably faint, provided she understood what Bo was talking about. And if Bo went down to the manager's office, by the time they got back he would probably be gone, and they would think she was some kind of nut who imagined that about everybody. If she left the theatre, he might follow her, which in his present state was highly dangerous. Not that he could necessarily be distracted from his present pastime; but if her departure cast a pall over the proceedings and brought him down, so to speak, he might follow her in a cab and see where she lived; even if he didn't try anything right away he might come back the next time he saw a dirty picture.

So all she did was go into the one populous row of the balcony where people were, and excusing herself to the first couple, sat between them and the second. The girl on the right looked at her peculiarly, and Bo had the funny sensation for a moment that the girl thought her some kind of pervert coming into the one crowded row with a whole empty theatre to choose from, wanting to grope either her or her escort, or maybe even both, who knew anymore? She was tempted to lean over and explain, confiding her experience to the lady, but decided she was better off letting it go.

In a few moments, Bo was relieved to see the Negro leaving the balcony, by the exit on the left. He was wearing a beige gabardine raincoat, very smartly cut, and she was delighted to see it move out of sight. She waited a few minutes, long enough for him to have gotten away from there, to make sure he would not be lurking around some place outside.

Unfortunately, she miscalculated. Very shortly he returned, his raincoat over his arm, and made his way up the steps again, behind her. So he hadn't been leaving at all. He had worn the raincoat to hide what was going on in—or out of—his pants, and finished himself off in the bathroom.

Bo got up, and excused herself to the couple on the right. The woman glared at her, but it didn't matter anymore. She passed by the aged usherette, walked slowly down the stairs to the main floor, and looking back to see that no one was coming down the stairs after her, she made a dash across the marbleized outer lobby of the theatre.

She caught a cab directly in front of the marquee, and although she kept glancing out of the back window to make sure there was nobody trailing her, she still made the driver go four or five blocks out of the way, doubling back from Seventy-Fifth Street, and around Park. He kept looking at her in the rearview mirror.

"I hope you don't mind," she said. "I'd explain, but it's very complicated."

"That's okay, lady. It's your money."

She asked him to wait until she was inside her door, and tipped him extra. And with a final nervous glance up the quiet sidestreet, she let herself in the front door.

In the elevator, she started to tremble. By the time she unlocked her apartment door, her face was drained of color and her knees were actually shaking. When she saw Alec sitting on the couch, she walked over and slapped him across the face.

"Baby," Alec said, holding his cheek stupidly. "What did I do?"

"It's all your fault," Bo said. "Driving people out of their own apartments, for God's sake, into movies in the middle of the night so people can come and masturbate on top of them practically."

"Where'd you go?" he said. "Forty-Second Street?"

"Eighty-Sixth," she said.

"Jesus. Is nothing sacred?" He got up and put his arms around her, gently, hugging her and rocking her shoulders. "Poor baby chicken."

"Where's Mary Kate?"

"She's asleep. She decided to use the bedroom so I could wait up for you out here. I wanted to make sure you were all right."

"Oh sure," Bo said. "I can imagine. Look who's looking out for me. Attilla the Hun is suddenly Mother Cabrini." She peered up at him. "Well what's the real program, Mother? Now that I've had a terrible experience, you want to give me an even worse one?"

"No chance," he whispered. "I'm sorry. Honest to God. I was only kidding before. And I'm sorry. I won't do it anymore. I've got to look out for you. You're incident-prone, honey. That's for sure."

"How you planning to look out for me? With binoculars? Or you going to tie me to a fourposter and mount me at regular intervals?"

"No more of that." He brushed the gingery bangs away from her forehead, and kissed it lightly. "I'm going to look after you like a father. Your own father."

"You don't have to be that careful."

"Yes I do. I value you. I really do. As a person."

"As a person?"

"That's right."

"A girl person or a person person?"

Alec smiled. "A person person."

"And what about the other stuff?"

"What stuff?" Alec asked.

"The sex business."

"It's over. Closed shop."

"Really?"

"Really."

"No come on?"

"None," he said.

At first Bo did not believe him. When she did, she found to her own confusion that she felt somewhat disappointed.

Ernie pressed closer to the wall. The building was made out of tissue paper, and he could hear every step, every sound that had been going since he began his vigil. But this was the first time he had become fully alert. Even where he was, standing on the fifth floor, with the footsteps just starting up to the first landing, he recognized the tread: light and uneven, like the uncertain earth-walkings of a hummingbird.

The boy with her was heavy-footed and lumbering; if he was young, he was too fat, Ernie could tell that from the shortness of his breath, starting up the second long flight. A young boy didn't wheeze like that, not so easily. Even Ernie had kept himself in good enough shape not to feel the climb until just at the last. They weren't speaking to each other, Kiiko and her date. Was it out of Kiiko's regard for him, seeing he was having a tough time with the stairs? Or had he done something to offend her?

Ernie clenched his teeth. With the Oriental boy, she chattered like a magpie in her singsong tongue, anxious to say all the nice things she could to him before they reached her door. But even with some of the others, she talked all the way up the two last flights—more talking than was usual for Kiiko. And Ernie understood why, he was sure: she appreciated the evening, was pleased with their company, and wanted them to know it; but she intended to dismiss them the moment they got to her apartment. Not wishing them to be offended, but not wanting them to stay, she made sweet and polite farewell, always in motion. She was running away from them, in a way, all the time her words dipped warmly toward them. Kiiko was not a tease. She wanted no protracted good-byes at her door, because that might seem to them to invite something she would never accept.

That she was not speaking now, worried Ernie. It was always an effort for her, meaningless talk, but she usually forced herself while climbing the stairs. If her silence now was not because the boy was uncomfortable, then she was annoyed with him. And Kiiko did not become annoyed easily. What had he done to upset her—young punk Fat Boy.

Ernie saw the dark, shiny little head, bobbing up toward the light of the landing, and he felt a shiver of happiness go through him. And then he saw the boy. His crew cut was velvet smooth on top, but his hair separated at the roots, damp with the sweat of his scalp. His forehead glistened with great, ugly drops of moisture, above the thick eyebrows. He had blowzy lips, like Baimbridge, and a fat thick neck, reddening upward to the ears from his open collar. Ernie had been right about him, without seeing him. He was a pig, and she was wise to get rid of him as soon as possible.

"Okay," the boy puffed heavily, "what's the story?"

"Good night, Teddy," Kiiko said.

"What is it with you, Kiiko? You've been like a stick all night. Is it my fault that the theatre had technical difficulties? I wanted to see the play too."

"We could have waited," she said. "I'm sure they fixed the lights right after we left."

"I didn't feel like sitting there for two hours," Teddy said.

"You didn't feel like sitting there at all. You only took me to that theatre because you knew your friends were having a party a block away. If you wanted to go to a party, why didn't you just say so?"

"I was afraid you might not want to go."

"And if I didn't? Wouldn't it have been fairer to extend the invitation you meant? Was it better like this—fooling me into going to a party I didn't enjoy, and you didn't enjoy either?"

"I would have had a good time if you weren't such a stick."

"Then why take me? Why not go alone?"

"I wanted you there, Kiiko." The surliness left his face, and he came toward her with a hopeful expression.

"Good night, Teddy." She turned her back to him.

"I'm sorry if you didn't like it. I'm sorry if I tried to fool you, Kiiko. I only took you there because I thought—well I thought maybe—with that group, you could—loosen up a little."

"Good night, Teddy." Her key was in the lock, and she started to turn it.

"Why are you always so formal? Politeness is one thing, but—why are you always so unbending when it comes to . . ." He put his big hands on the back of her shoulders.

Ernie saw Kiiko go rigid. His own spine stiffened, and his hands tightened into fists.

"I don't think we better see each other anymore," Kiiko said.

"What is it with you, for Pete's sake? I never even made a real pass."

"Good night," she said, without turning, and pushed the door open.

"Well Christ," Teddy said, seizing her right arm. "If I'm going to get punished for something I only thought about doing, I might as well go ahead and do it." He turned her roughly, his mouth swooping down like a devouring hawk toward her lips; but she turned her face toward her coat, and he touched only the harsh wool of her collar. His left hand tore at her coat, and he thrust his arm rudely inside. As the fragile material of her silky dress came away from her shoulder, Teddy clamped his hand against her tiny breast.

She gave a startled cry. Ernie saw himself dashing out toward her, a white flash of vengeance, tearing the hideous hand away, fading the red sting of those clumsy fingers from the paleness, the unbelievable paleness of that breast, by the sheer power of his esteem. But to his own horror and amazement, he saw at next glance Kiiko and the boy were still standing exactly as they had been, the brutal hand like a rude hammer on that porcelain cup. He had not moved. He had done nothing at all. His blood hammered in his ears and he could not breathe from the tightness in his throat; but he couldn't move; his hands were useless clenched fists that hung stupidly at his side, and his legs, his mobile, powerful legs, would not move at all.

He started to open his mouth, to shout to the offender to let her go —but the sound lodged in his chest. What good would it do to shout? Shouting would only frighten her—as would his presence, his pointless, ineffectual presence. He tore at his palms with his fingernails and wept soundlessly, begging whatever power it was that held him captive to let him go. He had lived only to protect her, and now he was unable to move.

But he saw to his great relief and shame, that Kiiko was not so helpless as he. She pushed the boy away with a power that was astonishing in such a little girl, and her hand cracked across his cheek. "Get out of here," she said, striking out in pathetic little flurries of fists and nails. "Get out of here and never come back."

His surprise lasted long enough so she had time to slam the door in his face. "You bet I'll go!" he shouted, when he had recovered himself. "And don't worry about my coming back. Believe me, I've had enough of you without any of you."

He ran his fingers through his hair, and wiped the back of his hand against his cheek. "What the hell you think you got down there that's so special anyway?" he yelled. "Plutonium?"

He backed off toward the stairs, but apparently felt he had not said enough. "I've seen plenty of your little products, sweetie, they're a glut on the market. The secret is cheaper parts, and cheap labor, but American workmanship and quality still beat them by a long shot."

Satisfied, he started down the stairs.

Whatever paralysis had seized Ernie was suddenly gone. The rage and helplessness lodging in his gorge spewed up into his mouth, and he tasted it, his tongue moistening the dryness around his lips. He waited until the footsteps were two or three flights below him. Then he started down.

In the street, the boy turned right. That was good. On the left there were three solid-front apartment buildings, but on the right, between Kiiko's house and the corner, were three brownstones, and two small stores, separated by an alleyway. Ernie let him get only a few paces past the alley, before calling to him.

"Teddy?"

The boy turned, a puzzled expression on his face. He was still bristling from the encounter upstairs, and this was not his neighborhood.

"Yeah?"

"How are you, Teddy?"

He narrowed his eyes. "Do I know you?"

Ernie laughed. "You son of a gun."

"I'm sorry, mister, I don't recognize you."

"Well come over here," Ernie said. "Come over here under the light where you can get a better look at me."

"What light?" Teddy asked.

"This one. This one right here," he said and brought his fist crashing into the beefy boy's face.

The blow staggered him, and he started to open his mouth to yell, and that was when Ernie hit him in the throat, and brought his knee into the stomach so he wouldn't yell and would double over both. He did just as Ernie wanted, collapsing as nice and neat as if Ernie had requested it aloud and the boy was eager to comply.

He wasn't as heavy as he looked: Ernie didn't even have to strain himself, dragging the half-unconscious boy into the alley. It made him feel almost kindly toward Teddy, his going along with everything so nice, and he patted his cheek in almost a friendly fashion as he propped him up on top of one of the garbage cans, back against the red brick wall. Only patting him nicely didn't seem to be bringing him to, so he slapped back and forth hard across his face, holding the two sides of the boy's coat together across his chest with his free hand so he wouldn't start slipping around, making a lot of unnecessary noise.

The boy's eyes tried to focus. "Hey," he said heavily. "Hey, what you want, mister. You want my wallet, it's in my jacket. Lemme . . . lemme get it, I'll give it to you."

"I don't want your wallet," Ernie said benignly. And jerking him abruptly forward he brought his fist into the side of his neck. As the boy went sprawling sideways, Ernie's left hand clubbed into his ribs.

"Jellyfish," Ernie said disgustedly, as the boy lay sputtering, face down, on the alley pavement. Little muddy sobs started hacking out of him. "Blobby jellyfish."

"What do you want?" the boy said. "Please. Tell me what you want."

"Get up," Ernie said. "Get up if you can, you blobby jellyfish."

"What do you want? You know my name. You're not just some mugger."

"Get up and I'll tell you."

Teddy looked up at him through eyes streaked with tears and dirt. "If I do, will you tell me—and then let me go?"

"I don't make bargains with jellyfish."

The boy lay there, trying to hug the ground.

"But if you don't try to get up, Teddy boy, I'm going to break your balls."

He raised himself slowly to his elbows and knees, and then lurched drunkenly to his feet, toppling the lids from one of the garbage cans.

"Shut up," Ernie rasped, grabbing him by his collar. "You want to wake the neighbors?"

"Please," Teddy gasped. "Please. What do you want?"

Ernie whirled him around, brought the hated face in tight next to his own eyes, so he could see how ugly it was all striped and blotchy with fear. "I want you . . ." Ernie whispered hoarsely. "I want you to leave . . ." He stopped himself just in time. The punk just talked like a punk. He didn't have enough guts to straighten out, or enough sense to listen, and his arms young as they were, were flabby and afraid to strike back, at anything but little girls. Tiny little soft girls, with creamy porcelain breasts.

If Ernie told him to leave Kiiko alone, the punk would probably come back for her. Another night, sometime, when maybe through some terrible fluke, Ernie would not be there to protect her. Or when —the thought hit him like wind-lashed icicles and his skin burned from the force of it—when, like tonight, oh Jesus God, he had stood there, immobilized like a pansy.

"Stay out of this neighborhood," Ernie screamed, slashing out at him with both hands. "You hear me? Stay away."

"You're crazy," Teddy whispered, from behind the makeshift shelter of his arms.

"Stay away," Ernie screamed, and finding a weakness in the cage, drove the butt of his palm past the quivering elbow, hard against the side of the boy's head.

Teddy slumped to earth.

"Do you hear me?" he shrieked. "Do you hear me?"

Ernie thought Teddy was just being stubborn. Stupid and stubborn, that was all he was. But when Ernie leaned over to hoist him up from the ground and saw the delicate stream of blood dribbling from the boy's ear, he realized Teddy would not hear anyone so easily again for a long time.

XII

THE woman who lived down the hall from Birgitta was not a bigot. When she phoned the police to report the girl, she did not even mention the fact that the man was a Negro.

"Eighteenth Precinct, Connors," the officer said on the other end of the line.

"I'd like to report a couple living in sin."

"Who is this?" Connors asked.

"Do I have to give you my name?"

"If you want to lodge a complaint, lady."

"Well, it's not as if I wish to bring an action against them, is it? I just want you to do something."

"An action is with a lawyer, lady. This is the police station. Maybe you ought to call an attorney."

"But I thought the police were to protect our public safety. Is that all you do, arrest the wrong people for murder?"

There was a pause. "All right, lady . . . What is the nature of your complaint?"

"There's a man and woman living in sin, at 440 East Seventy-Seventh Street."

"And?"

"And what?"

"And what do you want us to do about it?"

"Well, you must do something. After all, public morals are a public trust. I'm not a busybody, officer. What people do is their own business, provided they keep it their own business. But when a couple live blatantly together without being married, and actually show off about it—something must be done."

Actually, they had been extremely discreet. In the beginning, when Mason had first come to stay with Birgitta, they never came home together. Or if they did, they never entered the apartment at the same time. Nor did he leave with her in the morning when she went to work—or the rest of the time either, the lady down the hall knew, from peering through her peephole, where she stationed herself all day, eating sandwiches and not even answering the phone, leaving her post only to void her bladder when the need was really pressing. She knew he went in there—she saw him no matter how sneaky he tried to be. It seemed an insoluble puzzle, until one morning, when she set her alarm for six o'clock and without even brushing her teeth, went straight to the door. She saw him leave the apartment at seven-fifteen. Obviously a truck driver, or a narcotics peddler. Why else would he leave so early? the lady thought. It never occurred to her he was trying to avoid being seen. Still, after that she left her door slightly ajar so they wouldn't think they were fooling anybody.

Sometimes, with her ear pressed to the wall, she could hear them talking, or, when she was very lucky, one of them would drop a pot or a pan to the floor. Then she could buzz down to the doorman and tell him the people next door were being extremely noisy, and having a boisterous party, and it was too late for that kind of goings-on, according to her lease. Unfortunately it was never much later than nine or ten at night, and the doorman told her so. So there was no real way she could complain to the landlord. The police, however, were another matter entirely.

"What exactly do you expect us to do about it?" the officer repeated.

"You're a policeman. You know your duty in these cases."

"What cases? Have they done anything to you? Do you think they're going to rob you, or threaten your life, or what, lady? I'm not doubting your good intentions, but we have to be specific about charges in these cases. If we went around picking up everybody that their neighbors didn't like, we'd be open to an awful lot of suits for false arrest. Do they have a criminal record, or what?"

"I'm sure the man does," she said.

"What kind?"

"How should I know. You're the policeman."

"Yeah," he said.

"Couldn't you come and scare them, or something?"

"For what?"

"For illicit fornication. I've read all about the vice trials. You're always picking up girl witnesses and charging them with illicit fornication."

"That's a little different."

"Why? Because you want to get that Virginia What's Her Name? Is that all you really want, to make trouble for important pimps? Or do you care about public safety, like you say?"

"How are they endangering public safety, would you mind telling me that?"

"Fornicating so blatantly, in public? If that isn't a threat to the morals of the community, what is?"

"You've seen them? What do they do, leave their door open, or did you drill a hole in the wall?"

"What did you say your name was, officer?"

"What did you say your name was, lady?"

There was a silence. "Well, I can see that the police's attitude toward morality is sheer sham. Nothing but sham. The only reason you probably arrest anybody, is that they don't come up with a payoff."

"Look, lady. I don't want to get into an argument. We've got a pretty busy schedule here. Tonight we had four assaults, eighteen robberies, and a murder. I don't mean to make light of your problems, but unless there's something really terrible going on there, we can't afford to send out policemen to check out every complaint that some nu . . . somebody calls in. Whose apartment is it, the woman's or the man's?"

"If it were the man's they wouldn't have given him a lease. And if they had known what kind of girl she was, I assure you they wouldn't have given one to her."

The officer paused. "Is she over twenty-one?"

"Her age is not the question here. It's that she's affecting public morality. She's living in *sin*."

"Well, yeah, I know that, you mentioned it a couple of times. But sin is not the same thing as crime. If she's over twenty-one, as long as she's paying her rent, I'm afraid there's nothing we can do about it."

"This is an outrage," she said. "I intend writing a letter to the *Journal-American*."

"Yeah," he said. "That sounds like a swell idea. Why don't you do that?"

The phone clicked against her ear. The lady looked furiously at the receiver before she slammed it into its cradle. Then she went over to her typing table, and moved the brochures and the piles of addressing aside. She was several weeks behind with her mailing service, but she could not worry about that now. Inserting fresh paper into the typewriter, she sat down and composed her first letter, to the *Journal-American*, with a copy to the *Daily News*, signing it OUTRAGED CITIZEN. And feeling her mind and her fingers click into top precision performance, she sent off a second one, a trifle more specific, to the landlords of the building signed OUTRAGED TENANT.

Birgitta and Mason, taking turns soaping each other's backs, heard the furious clicking through the bathroom wall.

"She's off again," Birgitta said. "I must confess I've been a little worried about her these past few weeks. I thought she'd been murdered or killed herself, it's been so quiet."

"That kinda lady never has enough longings to kill herself. Only people who want something bad enough to know that it's missing kill themselves. And they don't get murdered either. Ladies who peep under their beds never find prowlers."

"Why are you so hard on her? You've never even seen her."

"She's seen me," Mason said. "She busted her butt trying to get a load of me. Now she has, so she leaves her door open to let me know."

"Well then, you've wrought a beautiful change in her life," Birgitta said. "She has about four locks and bolts on her door, and she uses them all. When I used to pass her door on my way to the incinerator, I would no sooner set down my foot on the floor near her, than I would hear all of them clicking and chaining away. She won't open the door for anybody. Not even Gristede's. . . . The poor delivery boys, every time they ring her bell, she screams 'Who is it' like she's expecting Lon Chaney, and then tells them to leave it outside the door. Last Halloween she hung a huge shopping bag on her knob for the Trick and Treaters, with a note pinned on it: *Children: Help yourselves.* Of course children don't trick or treat in New York very much, and there aren't any in this building. It was still there the next day."

"That's kind of sad," Mason said, gliding the soap over the arch of her shoulder blades.

"I thought so too. I didn't want her to feel bad, so I took it. For three days we lived on Hershey bars."

"Piggy," he said, and brought the bar under her arm, to her breast.

"No fair. I haven't done you yet. First clean, then play."

"Tyrant," he said, handing her the bar. Then they both revolved slowly in the tub, and his back was to her. He reached behind him, and she slapped his hand under the water.

The persistent typing continued. "What the hell does she do in there, anyway?" Mason said.

"I'm not sure. In the beginning, I was afraid she was a writer. I couldn't stand the thought of anyone that weird and hidden being creative—it made me feel so useless living next to this Gorgon of creativity. Twelve, fourteen hours at a stretch, she goes sometimes, the hermit lady."

"A lot of very good writers have been hermits."

"On Seventy-Seventh Street?"

"Times change. You can't always cloister yourself in New England. Even Poe wrote 'The Raven' on West Eighty-Fourth Street."

"How do you know?"

"There's a plaque on the building. Two fifty-five West. A friend of mine moved in there, once the neighborhood ran down."

She batted him silently on the back of his neck. "Shut up," she said. "It changed since Edgar Allen Poe even before your friend. Anyway, there are so many better places a man can hide than one of these big, sterile buildings. University campuses, like Cozzens. Or even the village. Being hidden is one thing. But isolated like that —isolated from any kind of feelings, like she is. I can't imagine a writer as cut off as that lady."

"Maybe she used to have a life, when she was young."

"That's the strangest part," Birgitta said, rubbing the lather down to the slim line of his waist. "She isn't really old. Everything she does is so old maid spinstery. But I saw her in the elevator once, and she can't be much over thirty."

"Is she pretty?"

"Not really. Although it was hard to tell. She was wearing a scarf on her head, and dark glasses, and her coat collar was pulled up over her chin, and she had on high boots, up to her knees. It was very spooky."

"I don't know," Mason said. "Maybe she was scared once by a European movie."

"It was in the middle of August," Birgitta said, scooping up handfuls of water, letting them run down his back. "It was well over ninety degrees. Turn around, your back is done."

He faced her, and she started rubbing soap on his chest and shoulders. "Hey," he said. "This doesn't seem quite fair."

"I'm still washing."

"Yeah, I know, but you have a front, too. Why don't I have a cake of soap?"

"Up there," she said, not looking at his face. "In the shower dish."

He raised himself half out of the water, and sat down again, the thin wafer in his hand. He dipped it into the water and brought it under her left breast, drawing it slowly up over the fullness, circling around and stabbing the edge of the soap gently into the pink center of her tiny nipple, watching it swell.

"Cut it out."

"Don't you want to be clean all over, like the man said?"

"You're not cleaning."

"Who say? Who says I'm not?"

"I say."

"What do you know?" he said, switching the soap to his other hand. "You're a girl."

"Oh."

"Yeah," he said softly. "You certainly are."

There was a silence, disturbed only by the gentle lapping of the water, as his hand moved out of sight, and the clattering, from next door. "You certainly are," he whispered.

"Stop," she said weakly. "Don't do that."

"But you have to wash there just like any place else. When you were a little girl, didn't your mama tell you that?"

"You're not my mama," she said.

"Yeah," he grinned. "I know. Isn't it wonderful?"

"We'll drown."

"Yeah," he grinned wider, "I know that, too."

The flat cloudy surface of the bathtub water slowly became a tiny gale-whipped ocean. And then it was still. The typing from next door had stopped, and there was silence.

"Do you suppose she heard?" Birgitta whispered.

"Hell no," Mason said. "And if she did, she probably figures you like to play with boats."

"Poor lady," she sighed, "what does she know?"

"Right," he said, and kissed her wet hair.

"Poor lady," she said again. "I almost wish . . . If I were really unselfish I'd let you go in there and do it to her."

"Yeah," he said. "I bet she'd love that."

"She would. That's the sad part of it. She may not realize, but that's what she really needs."

"Don't be so generous with my body," Mason said.

"I'm not. I only said if I could be I would be. But I'm not. She can't have you."

"I'm sure she'd be very relieved," Mason said and smiled. "I guess we better think about getting out, or we're both going to turn into prunes."

"I suppose," Birgitta sighed.

"Don't regret. The best is yet to come."

"Yes?" She smiled expectantly.

"We've still got to get dry."

Ever since the bad experience of the movies, Alec had been treating Bo like a sister. An honest-to-God sister, she had complained to Mary Kate, who laughed at her and told her to remember the nature of her previous complaint. That was beside the point, Bo insisted. She realized now she had been behaving like a foolish little virgin, and now that she had admitted her own foolishness, she could also afford to be frank about her virginity. It wasn't sacred after all: Virginity for the sake of virginity was not quite the same as art for art's.

It was fine if you were immature, and trying to save it for your husband or something like that. But Bo was nearing her twenty-second birthday, she had seen a little of life, and was tired of hanging on to it like a dead prom corsage pressed in an old scrapbook. Her youth perhaps was not exactly withering, but her virginity seemed to her as both outdated and stale, a shriveled piece of paper in the casebook of her life, growing distinctly yellow around the edges. She had no intentions or thoughts of marrying just to finally unload it, and the burden of holding on to it was quickly becoming greater than fear about its loss. Especially since Alec had become increasingly attractive and appealing to her ever since he had stopped making his pitch.

"But I care for him!" she shrieked to Mary Kate, in the city silence of their apartment.

"You care for his thing," Mary Kate said.

"Oh shut up. You don't have to torment me with my own former stupidity. I've confessed I was wrong. I've confessed it to you, and to Alec. So why don't you both leave me alone?"

"I thought Alec was. I thought that was why you were complaining."

"Oh shut up. You have no understanding. So it took a while for me to straighten out, but I've come around. You know that. I've come around! Only now that I've come around, he won't come around. Why won't he?"

Mary Kate was silent.

"Oh now don't pull that—I didn't mean for you to really shut up."

"Maybe he figures he scared you so badly, Bo, and he really likes you so much—he does have a degree of nobility in him, every actor does, otherwise they wouldn't all want to play Hamlet. So maybe what little better nature he does have is finally coming to the fore, and he's only doing what's right by you."

"But it isn't right. Not anymore. I can't stand it sometimes, he's so beautiful. He's been wearing a lot of those nylon pullovers lately, and you know how he's always loved tight pants, and he just lies there in that goddamned studio of his, looking up at the skylight, lolling on that old mattress, rocking his legs back and forth, and I think sometimes I'm going to go out of my mind if I can't touch him. But how can I touch him if he won't touch me? He won't touch me!"

"Well, maybe he doesn't realize you have come around. Why don't you let him know?"

"Let him know? I've done everything but take off all my clothes and scream 'Take me,' for God's sake. I keep reaching for his hand, and sitting close to him on the mattress, putting my face next to his and rubbing my thighs against his legs and mooning. Last night I pretended to fall asleep so I'd have to spend the night with him. And you know what he does, my Prince Charming? He rouses Sleeping Beauty, only not with a kiss even, for God's sake. He drops a goldfish down my exposed breast which I have exposed solely for the purpose of arousing him, and as it's flipping away in the depths of my innocent brassiere, he laughs at me and says, 'Come, Chicken Little, single bedtime.' '

"Well why don't you tell him how you feel?"

"I'm embarrassed," Bo said. "I mean, after holding out so long if I offered him my thing on a platter, he might not even want it anymore."

"It's a chance you should take."

"I can't afford to," Bo said. "If he just doesn't want me anymore that's one thing. If I give him the chance to tell me, and he tells me, I'll perish. I can stand suspecting it, but I couldn't stand having it confirmed.'

"You're a coward," Mary Kate said.

"Well! Aren't you clever. Whatever gave you that idea? Anyway, it's too much to ask a woman, even a woman who was such a fool she refused to allow herself to become a woman . . . I can't offer my body like some slut, and then be turned down. I do have some pride, you know. Like this, I'm in great agony, not knowing. But if I knew for sure he didn't want me, I wouldn't be able to see him anymore— I couldn't stand seeing him, not if he felt that way. And I really couldn't stand not seeing him, because I love him so. At least I think I love him. How can I be sure if he won't go to bed with me?"

"God, you're horny," Mary Kate said.

"You have no soul," said Bo, and tore up a few old magazines.

"So why don't you simply try to seduce him?"

"What do you think I've been doing?"

"Maybe you haven't tried hard enough."

"I told you I've done everything but actually get undressed and jump into bed with him."

"Well maybe that's what you'd better do," Mary Kate said.

Bo didn't say anything; she decided, instead, to sleep on it. The dreams she had were so graphic, that when she awakened she realized she had no choice but to follow the wisdom of Mary Kate's counsel. She did not discuss her decision with Mary Kate; nor did she intend to entrust details of her program to Alec. He would find out soon enough what she was up to, when he was up to his ears, so to speak, in her.

It struck Bo as a trifle coldblooded, taking twenty pills, one a day, against that day, thirty-two days off, when she would give herself to him, irrevocably. She had absolutely no intention of trying the act before she had tested the pills at least one moon's worth, and it did seem a little deliberate for an act of spontaneous passion. Still, it was a lot better than lying to a gynecologist about being married (the G.P. did not ask anyone her status—it was, after all, only a prescription, and he didn't have to go probing around inside to find out whether indeed you were Mrs. So and So, and if so, what size). Besides, the thought of constantly equipping yourself with that thing on the chance that it might happen was too much to bear, as was the thought of a child. (Too much to bear, Bo thought, that's fairly funny.)

The pills made it all much easier, and if when taking them she did feel a vague queasiness, which she strongly hoped was emotional, it was preferable to the prospect of fooling around with that thing. The fitting was the least of it. The lies, the deception (self-deception was easy, it was trying to fool those people at Margaret Sanger that must have been really hard). And she was sure that everyone, even those who considered themselves liberal and enlightened, wanted to lie, even to the liberal and enlightened people at Margaret Sanger. Bo had once heard a story about four girls from Smith who took an apartment in New York for dirty weekends; a boyfriend of one had gotten drunk and called the apartment at four o'clock in the morning, disguising his voice, saying it was the police, and there had been a surprise raid on the Margaret Sanger Institute, and they'd gotten all four of their names and sizes from the records, the girls were not to leave the apartment, the police were on their way, and they were all under arrest. Naturally he had meant it as a joke, and Bo supposed it would have been fairly funny if the girls hadn't flown into a panic, and one of them, being disoriented and half-asleep, thought she was back in the dormitory and jumped right out her ground floor dorm window, only to realize too late that she was in, or rather out of, a third floor New York apartment. Actually she hadn't been killed, except in the version told at Vassar: she'd only broken both her legs and chipped her elbow. But still and all it wasn't funny. Not even fairly.

No, Bo thought, popping the round pink pill into her mouth, and enjoying a brief shudder of uneasiness. Pills were the best way, there was just no contest.

A contest for what? she stopped to wonder briefly. What was the prize?

The day after he gave the boy a beating, Ernie had been afraid to go into work: he felt sick, and tired from being sick most of the night, with his mother outside the bathroom door asking him couldn't she please come in and hold his head. And he had also been afraid, not that the boy was dead—he had checked carefully that the boy wasn't dead—but that the police might have gotten to Kiiko to question her, and that Kiiko, seeing him, would know what had happened. Ernie hadn't wanted to leave the house at all that day. But between his own nagging feeling of confusion and stupidity, and his mother's seeming almost anxious to get him out of the house, he finally got dressed and went into the city.

He was halfway across the UN Plaza before he realized it was Saturday.

But he hadn't gone back to the alley. Stupid as he felt he was, he was too smart to return to the scene. The only possible link the police might be able to find between him and Teddy would connect only if he stuck his big, dumb face into the garbage cans.

By Monday he felt almost all right. And pretending to himself that nothing had happened, he gradually became convinced nothing had. Kiiko did not appear troubled, so he did not need to be. Her well-being was all that mattered.

It was not until several days afterward, when she told him he wouldn't be able to walk her home after work, that the gnawing started again, on his insides.

"How come?" he said to her, as she moved across the concourse toward the Dispatcher's Desk. "What're you doing, going to a play, or what?"

"Nothing so pleasant, I'm afraid," Kiiko said. "A friend of mine is in the hospital, and I have to go there right after work. Visiting hours are over so early."

"A girl?'

"A boy I used to see. I feel terrible. He's been there some time and I did not find out until last night. I saw another friend of his, and he told me."

"Is he very badly . . . sick," Ernie said, taking a great deep breath to still the shaking inside himself. He had almost said "hurt," and she had said nothing to indicate why the boy was in the hospital. He had to be more careful not to give himself away.

"Nobody seems sure. He had a concussion and injuries to his ear. Hal did not know for certain whether he will regain his hearing."

"Hal . . . Is that your friend's name?"

"Hal is his friend. Teddy is my friend in hospital."

"I'm sorry."

"You are most kind," Kiiko said.

"Were you . . . are you in love with him?"

"No," Kiiko said. "No, of course not."

"I didn't mean to pry," Ernie said nervously. "I only meant . . . You seemed so upset."

"It is very upsetting when it happens to someone you know. All the time I read in the papers of violence in New York, and it is unfortunate, and terrible. But it is never so bad, somehow, when it happens to strangers."

"And this . . . Teddy. Is he a very good friend of yours?"

"A good friend, yes."

"But you weren't in love with him?"

"I told you," Kiiko said.

"Was he . . . was he in love with you?"

"Teddy likes a good time," she said softly. "Teddy is just a boy who likes a good time."

Ernie realized, suddenly, that he hadn't asked what had happened to Teddy. Later on, when she thought about the conversation, she might remember that he hadn't asked.

"What exactly happened to him?"

"He was beaten," she whispered. "Brutally beaten. You read of it all the time but it never seems the same when it happens to strangers."

"Robbed, or what?"

"Nothing," she said. "Only beaten. It happened right near my building right after he brought me home, apparently. I keep thinking I could have done something to help him, yes? Perhaps if I had invited him for coffee, and he had stayed a little longer with me—or if he hadn't insisted to bring me home. You understand?"

"Nothing you did would have changed anything," Ernie said. "These things just happen."

"You are good to try and make me feel better." Kiiko sighed. "But I am not the one who needs compassion, Ernie. Nothing happened to me."

Ernie felt dizzy. Nothing had happened to her, yes, that was true. But it hadn't been the fault of that punk kid that nothing had happened. He deserved it. Ernie wasn't going to tell her that, but it tore at his insides, all that feeling sorry for a rotten punk kid.

He saw the dispatcher motioning for Kiiko, and heard her whispering good-bye, conscious of her moving away, like the wish blown free from a dandelion. He closed his eyes for a moment, and turned, making his way unsteadily back to the main entrance.

Somehow, he managed to get through the morning. By eleven forty-five his stomach was screaming. By the time the noon siren blasted across the city, it sounded to him like an all-clear signal, freeing him from some threat he didn't understand. Once away from the environs of the UN building, he broke into an open run, all the way to The Grotto.

What he finished his third roast beef sandwich, he was still vaguely out of breath. Feeling something he could not quite classify as appetite, but wanting only to make it go away, he raised his head above the shelter of the booth to catch Charlie's eye, and order again. He hadn't been aware of the presence of the hated voice until it boomed across the bar at him.

"What Ho! Watchdog of the Wickies!"

Ernie shrunk back down into his shoulders, but it was too late. He heard the heavy-footed shuffle approaching and raised his eyes to see Baimbridge's grinning face.

"I thought you had deserted us, oh guardian of the goo. . . . It's been so long since I saw you, loving friend, I figured you had disappeared from the face of the earth, sucked down in your prime in the luscious quicksand." He balanced his drink in his left hand as he clumsily set himself down across from Ernie, holding on to the table with his free hand. "I thought after our touching discovery of friendship, nothing on earth could keep you from me. Except of course," he licked some of the splashed whisky from his hand, "being up to your eyes in the lovely sticky."

"Leave me alone," Ernie said. "Get the hell away from me."

"Can this be you? Friend of my better days?" Baimbridge clutched his chest in mock despair. "Pal of the Last Noel. Is this the man who hugged me round the shoulders neath the holly—laughing with joy and weeping with despair? Is it he who turns his face from me now, my bosom buddy of yon yuletide toot?"

"I was drunk," Ernie said.

"You *became* drunk," said Baimbridge. "But sober you sought me—to become drunk with me, beseeching me to set you free."

"I never did," Ernie said.

"Deny everything: The first counsel of a clever attorney. Deny everything, no matter how true—especially if true. Deny everything, even with both pairs of panties on the English Department floor, and your face between their legs."

"You're crazy. You're a drunk, crazy man."

"There's that, too, to be considered," Baimbridge said. "But we weren't discussing me. I'm not the pillar of the community who finds me so objectionable. You are the sober Upright who spits in my face hardly a month after eight whiskies set you scratching and imploring me to talk a little Foul Mouth."

"You're crazy," Ernie said again.

"But I've already admitted that, Ernest. A far more scathing self-indictment than your needing a little raunch-lip." Baimbridge heaved a sigh, and settled deeply into the booth. "What is it that could make a man stare at a squatting dog, when he can't look at his own feces? Must we have a proctologist peering up our assholes before we can think about shit?"

Ernie looked down at his empty sandwich plate. "Why don't you go away?"

"Because you need me, Ernie: The evil men think lives with them. The good is oft interred in their bones."

"I'd like a Scotch," Ernie said to the bartender.

"I bet you would," Baimbridge said. "Why do you suppose you came looking for me Christmas Day?"

Ernie flushed. "I felt bad. Some men when they feel like that go out and screw a whore."

"But you came to me," Baimbridge said. "I see."

Charlie set the drink on the table in front of Ernie, and walked away.

"Liquid balls," Baimbridge said. "Drink them up quickly, and when you awaken, you'll be a man, my son. Perhaps."

"Shut up," Ernie said. But to his own surprise, he was swallowing fast.

"Oh, I have known some camaraderie since the fall," Baimbridge murmured. "But never had I a companion of the dirty word like you, Ernest. That is why I wax so bitter-mouth at your turning away from me now. Never in my experience have the sweet parts of a lady been bandied betwixt two mouths with the speed they leapt from yours to mine.

"You were a match, Ernie. More than a match. A challenge! Do you know how long it's been, in my milieu, since I had a real challenge? It was dazzling. Images flew back and forth like ping-pong balls. Ping-pong pussies."

Ernie didn't answer.

"But why do you flush? You should be proud, Ernie. You weren't simply foul, you were creative . . . Do you recall at one point—you were at peak performance after some splendid preliminary workouts—but do you recall your version of 'Love's Old Sweet Song'?"

"No," Ernie said.

"Just a slit at twilight
When the lips are low . . .
And the flick'ring clitties
Softly come and go . . ." Baimbridge sat back and drew from his lips a liquid sigh. "That isn't mere porno, you know—that's poetry. *Innkeeper!*" He held up four fingers, and Charlie nodded.

"What is it, Ernie?" Baimbridge's voice was strangely gentle. "What's the pestilence fouling up your soul?"

"I don't know," Ernie said. "I can't . . . I couldn't tell you."

"Who else could you tell? You know me for what I am. And I know you for what you're not. I'm the only one who realizes how filthy you really are."

Ernie looked carefully at Baimbridge's face. He had never felt such disgust for anyone. Yet, at the same time, he felt impelled to confide in him. If it was true that he had talked with him as Baimbridge said he had, on Christmas—and deep inside himself Ernie knew it was true—there was not much more to be lost. He wasn't going to tell him about the boy. The boy was incidental, Ernie knew that. What was really bothering him went back a long way.

"I killed thousands of people," Ernie said. "Ninety—maybe a hundred thousand. I don't really know."

He stopped talking while Charlie set four drinks on the table, two in front of each of them. Baimbridge, to Ernie's relief, kept the silence.

"Do you want me to call a policeman?" Baimbridge said, after Charlie was back behind the bar. "I know of no fit punishment for so vast and heinous a crime. They could sizzle your brain into sweetbreads, Ernie, and that still wouldn't make you clean. Perhaps it would be better if you tried flushing out your mind."

Ernie swallowed the contents of the first glass, set it aside and sipped on the second. "I've never told anyone before," he said, and began to talk—about the bomb, the death of Eileen, the baby, and his twisted seed—God's revenge. And then he spoke of Kiiko's coming, and knowing he had to protect her, because she was his salvation, rising from the ashes of Hiroshima.

"You're wrong," Baimbridge said, when Ernie, tight-lipped and pale, had finished. "I don't mean you're wrong about dropping the a God, He really might want to wreak a twisted vengeance, though I doubt it. But since *you* don't doubt it, and He's your God, you might be right. You may even be right about the girl—perhaps she is your phoenix . . . Oh don't look so worried about that, Ernie, it's a legendary bird, and birds do not concern us for the moment. At least not legendary birds.

"When I said you were wrong, I meant only you were wrong about never telling this to anyone before. You did. You told me, Christmas night."

"All of it?"

"All of it," Baimbridge said. "In between amiable obscenities, you spilled your tight insides. I wondered at the time what it meant—the soul-baring in the midst of all the garbage. I thought about it, and now I'm sure."

"What does it mean?" Ernie said.

"I'm not a psychiatrist," Baimbridge said. "But as you very rightly pointed out, I am insane."

"I'm sorry about saying that. I'm sorry."

"I'm not. It gives me an advantage. Certainly in your case. Clear-thinking people see twisted things distorted. But twisted people see distortion clearly." Baimbridge curled his fingers around the stem of his martini glass and drew in his lower lip. "If you were Italian, Ernie, you would probably develop *stigmata*."

Ernie's forehead furrowed.

"A circular growth in the palm of the hand," Baimbridge explained. "Like fungus or ringworm, I suppose, I'm not sure, I'm not a doctor. But to the ignorant and superstitious, this . . . fungus, or whatever it is, looks like a scar left by a nail. Say, the nails they used to hang Christ from the cross.

"It's usually got a psychological basis, Ernie, this stigmata. . . . Guilt feelings, identification with Christ . . . taking the sins of the world on your shoulders—or in your palm. It's a messy business, usually reserved for the deeply religious Guilty."

"I've never been very religious," Ernie said.

"Maybe you think you haven't." Baimbridge sighed. "But you have your God—a twisted non-Being who would cast a curse on your sperm for a thing you did but were not responsible for."

"I killed unborn babies," Ernie said.

"How do you feel about abortion?"

"It's a sin," Ernie whispered. "A cardinal sin."

"And you say you are not religious. No, Ernie. You may not be an ardent Catholic, but you have your stigmata."

Ernie opened his clenched fist and stared thoughtfully into his palm.

"In your brain, Ernie. That's where you bear yours— And it's all confused with God and sex and little yellow ladies, and the sin of your murderous pecker. It's there as bright and red as the mark of a nail. Only it's not even in the palm of your hand where the air and the light can get to it. So it's festering. The more you pretend it isn't there, the deeper and rottener it gets . . . until it eats up your whole mind and body and leaves you a jellied wad of blabbering malignancy."

"What can I do?"

"An enlightened man would tell you to go to a psychiatrist."

"My cousin Archie goes to a psychiatrist."

"A prudent man would tell you he didn't know."

Ernie couldn't breathe.

"A glib man would offer you a solution."

"Tell me.'

"You think I'm glib?"

"I have to know," Ernie said.

"Would you listen to a man you knew wasn't prudent—a man you considered a cesspool of Glib—if he tried for one moment to be enlightened?"

"I have to know," Ernie said.

"Go to a psychiatrist, Ernie."

"Will he tell me? Will he tell me what to do?"

"You'll work it out together."

"How long? How soon will I know?"

Baimbridge looked down at his knuckles. "These things take time."

"I don't have time," Ernie said. "I have to know *now!* Tell me *now!*"

"I'm trying to be fair to you, Ernie. I'm trying, on this rare occasion, to do the right thing."

"Tell me. *Please!*" There were tears in his eyes. "Please, you're the only one who can tell me."

"Ah Ernie, I could weep with you. Do you know how long it's been since anyone turned to *me* for an answer? It's enough to make a man forget his better intentions."

"Please," Ernie said. "Please."

Baimbridge heaved a defeated sigh. "Very well." He leaned his head back against the wooden sill, and the harshness edged back into his voice. "You see, it's all tied up with this little Jap girl, this Kinko . . .'

"Kiiko," Ernie said.

"You've built your relationship with her into an obsession . . . and obsessions are unhealthy, even in the most moderately twisted of brains. Your whole history: a sexually passive man, stimulated for the first time by the rape, as it were, of Hiroshima—making you a momentary hero—somebody exciting and excited. The baby, conceived with a woman who did not excite you . . ."

"Eileen?" Ernie stared blankly. "I loved Eileen."

"Perhaps," Baimbridge said. "But I would venture to say she did not excite you. . . . The death of the baby—the articles about the birth defects at Hiroshima—your Catholic guilt—unborn babies, all that rubbish. . . ."

"It's not rubbish.'

"Perhaps not. Certainly not to you. At any rate, it grows . . . the passivity, the guilt . . . And then you see this girl. Japanese? Fine. Hiroshima? Perfect. Guilt, Ernie. She excites you, and the guilt grows. So you convert your excitement into a fantasy of salvation and protection—only the person you must protect her from is yourself. Because what you really *want* is to ravish her; that, and only that, will give you purpose again.

"It becomes an obsession, this protective fantasy of yours. It grows and grows, like a psychic tapeworm, feeding on your shadowy soul, and the dark recesses of your mind. And the more it grows, the greater part of you becomes madness, the lesser portion of you is sane.

"Get rid of the obsession, Ernie. Rid yourself of the obsession, and maybe you'll have a chance."

"How?" Ernie asked.

"Ravish her."

"You miserable son of a bitch," Ernie whispered. "You filthy bastard."

"Wonderful!" Baimbridge chuckled. "How human and how perfect. We're back to abusing me."

"I don't know why I ever listened to you."

"Ah but I do, Ernie, there's the difference. You listened and you listened all the time, not just now. You diddle yourself by letting *me* be vile, hearing me say things you ache to say. So you can go away thinking, '*He's* the one who's loathsome.' I'm loathsome. *I*. Never you."

"I wouldn't touch her," Ernie said. "I'd die before I'd hurt her."

"Maybe." Baimbridge pursed his lips. "I have no doubt that if you continue in this fashion, Ernie, you may prove yourself a man of your word."

"I'll pay for your drinks," Ernie said, getting up from the booth. "That'll square me for taking up your time. But I never want to set eyes on you again."

"Then you better not look in the mirror," Baimbridge said.

Ernie's hands were shaking as he took some crumpled bills from his pocket. "Do you really believe that? Do you really think I'm like you?"

"Not nearly so articulate," Baimbridge said.

"I don't want that," Ernie said. "Not what you said. I couldn't do that to Kiiko."

"Calm down, Ernie," Baimbridge murmured. "Don't be so tough on yourself. It wouldn't be all that painful. As they say in the proverb attributed to the Japanese themselves: 'When rape is inevitable, relax and enjoy it'!"

Ernie clenched his teeth. "She couldn't. Kiiko isn't like that."

"I wasn't speaking of the girl," Baimbridge said. "It was a word of advice to the rapist."

XIII

THE Delegates' Dining Room, although operated by the same concession that ran the cafeteria, was, on the surface, only a distant cousin to that place—not necessarily that much richer, but infinitely more elegant. The room was completely carpeted in a dark shade of blue, cutting both the appearance of vastness, and the noise. The ceilings were low, as they were in the cafeteria, and if not quite soundproofed, at least seemed so from the spongelike white surface, with white lights set at frequent, but moderately softened intervals, into the squares. The tables, set with fresh white linen, held a tiny vase with a single pink-orange artificial rose. At various places throughout the room rods hung from the ceiling, with blue drapes gathered to one side, like a curtain to be pulled if a patient wanted privacy in a public ward. Ursull did not quite understand the purpose of the drapes, but she supposed they were there in the event of someone's wanting a large table closed off, as in a private banquet room.

"I've never eaten in a private dining room," she said to Gerd. "Have you?"

"Many times."

"Shall we ask them to pull the drapes and close us off?"

He smiled. "When you and I have occasion to dine together, in a private room in a restaurant for the first time, we will not close off the world with a nylon curtain. We will close them off with walls and doors and a case of champagne, and no one around anywhere. Except the gypsies, of course."

"Gypsies?"

"One must always have gypsies in a private dining room. To play and sing, and dance. At least, in the beginning of the evening." He reached for her hand across the table.

"What else will we have?"

"Pheasant, I should think. Pheasant, after cold soup, and quenelles."

"And what for dessert?"

"Each other." His eyes glowed yellow. "A private dining room is pointless without an exquisite seduction."

"When will we go?" She smiled back at him.

"Any time. The first day we return to Berlin, if you like. Although I would imagine that first evening my family will want to give a dinner party for us. But we can make them postpone it until we have been settled for a few days."

"After we're married there will be no need to seduce me."

He laughed. "After we're married there will be more need. Nothing will ever be complacent between us, you know that. I shall never be able to make you love me enough."

"Nor I," she said.

"It is too late. You have already made me too deeply in love. I shall never be sure of winning you as completely as you have won me."

She looked around the room anxiously. "I hope you don't mind the choice of restaurant. It seemed most convenient."

He looked only at her. "I find it extremely pleasant."

"It's quite European, don't you think?"

Gerd smiled. "Why, because they have a table in the center of the floor, with a clean tablecloth and desserts? When we tour together, then I will show you restaurants."

"I'm sorry you don't like it."

"I adore it," he said. "I find the view the most beautiful in New York."

She turned to her left, trying to see through the gauzy white material pulled across the length of the windows. "It's a shame they have curtains," she said. "I don't know why they have the curtains pulled. If they were open, we would be able to see up and down and across the entire river. It's such a lovely day. What a shame they don't open the curtains. I'm sorry the place is such a disappointment."

"My darling girl," he whispered. "Why don't you stop apologizing?"

"I don't know," she said. "I feel so . . . embarrassed. Having to ask you to come here like this. To parade yourself like a prize cow. It's insulting."

"Yes it is," he said softly.

But when she looked up, he was smiling at her.

"But only because I had hoped to be considered a prize bull."

"You understand what I mean," Ursull said. "Please don't try to help by making jokes."

"Ursull, this is something we both knew we were going to have to go through. It is something every young couple whose families care about them must go through. There is always an . . . inspection, a being looked over . . . You know that, and I know that. It is not some terrible surprise, but something we both expected."

"By the families, yes. But not by . . . outsiders."

"You said yourself this Almadon is a very close friend of your people's. Yes?"

"I know, but . . ."

"But then there is no but. Your family is not here. They are concerned. Your mother is even more quick to sense what is happening than we anticipated, and like a good mother who is alarmed, she refuses to accept from a daughter that she is in good hands. She must send a good friend to see with older eyes. It is most natural."

"You're so kind," she whispered gratefully. "It is you who should be annoyed and upset, and you are consoling me."

"Why should I be upset? I am having lunch with the one I most enjoy lunching with, it is a lovely day, the restaurant is pleasant enough, and best of all, I shall not have to pay for my pleasure." He smiled broadly. "This Almadon, is he very rich? I don't know about diplomats from South American countries. Are they like dictators, or don't they have that much money?"

"The salaries of delegates are not high. But he has private wealth."

"Splendid!" Gerd clapped his hands together. "Then I shall eat like a horse. A prize horse."

A tall, thin, gray-haired gentleman approached them, smiling, and he kissed Ursull's cheek before turning toward Gerd.

"Doctor Almadon," Ursull said. "May I present Gerd Kraben."

"A pleasure, sir." Gerd was on his feet, shaking hands briefly but strongly with the older gentleman. "Doctor," he said, after they were all seated. "Are you a man of medicine, sir, or is that an honorary title?"

"It has some honor," Almadon said. "Not perhaps quite as much as I would like. I was a student of political history and philosophy, and received the necessary letters to follow my name. Ursull does me the service to use it as a form of address."

"You do yourself too little service, sir," Gerd said warmly. "It is unfortunate that more diplomats do not take the trouble to study the currents of history before they attempt to change its course."

"Perhaps," he said, and signaled for the waitress. "It may not mean so much, Doctor, in Argentina but it means more than in Rome. Have you noticed that? I have never met an Italian not Principe, or Commandante, or Conte, who was not, at very least, a Dottore. A peddler of rags, when he leaves his own street, becomes 'Dottore.' "

"I believe you're right," Gerd said. "But then, I'm not Italian."

"No," he said. "No, you're not."

After they had ordered drinks from the waitress, Almadon turned to Ursull. "Well, my dear. How is everything with you?"

"As it was last evening. When you phoned. I am very fine. Nothing has changed since last evening, when you questioned me so thoroughly."

"I see."

Ursull would not look up, and Gerd could see the red striking out along her cheeks like angry finger marks. "Well, Doctor," he said heartily. "You may minimize your title, but I would say the restaurant staff is not indifferent to your importance. We arrive at the busiest hour, in a room congested with delegates, and have but to mention your name to the maître d', and are shown to this especially fine table right next to the window. Surely that indicates something."

Almadon looked at him carefully. "Only that he is not blind. No matter how important the clientele, there is not a maître d' who would not seat this beautiful child where she could best grace his room. A beautiful woman is a great balm in a fevered world. He had to seat her here."

"I agree," Gerd said.

"And you along with her." He looked back and forth at the two of them. "You make a striking couple."

"I am aware of that," Gerd said. "I know, how very beautiful she is. But I am not ignorant of my own vanity. Part of every man's appreciation of a woman's beauty is how much it does for him. The ugly man appears more desirable. And the handsome man—seems taller—more handsome."

"True," Almadon said.

"I will not pretend to a humility you are already sure I don't have," Gerd said.

"Very wise."

Gerd shrugged. "It would be stupid. You are not here to find out what I am not, but what I am."

"Then tell me about yourself."

Gerd began telling the bare facts of his life, much as they had sketched the biography to Ursull's mother. He spoke evenly, sipping on his cocktail, looking from Almadon's expressionless face to the spreading blush on Ursull's.

"And your family?" Almadon said. "Your father is Otto Kraben, correct?"

"Most correct."

"How would he feel about your becoming involved with a foreigner?"

"But she is not a foreigner," Gerd said, smiling. "She is German. A full-blooded German."

"And if she were not?"

"But it's ridiculous even discussing what does not enter into an argument. And I don't think we are arguing, are we?"

"No, but how would they feel about your marrying her?"

"Please!" Ursull's face was scarlet. "Doctor Almadon! We are not even speaking of marriage."

"But of course we are, my dear." Gerd's voice was soft. "The Doctor knows it, just as your mother knows it, no matter what you may have told her to the contrary. So it is pointless our trying to keep it secret any longer."

"You are already married?" Almadon said quietly.

"We have too much respect for our parents," Gerd said. "And each other. We would not have married without letting them know. I would not have permitted Ursull to deny her mother the pleasure of making a wedding. When I spoke of a secret, I meant only the decision to marry. We wished to keep it secret until enough time had passed to prepare the parents for the news. Since they already anticipate, I suppose the time has come to let them know."

"Then it is definite? Your decision is definite?"

"Absolutely," Gerd said. "We would like to marry as soon as possible, now that the decision is known. We shall write to Mrs. Hernan and my parents this evening. Naturally we would not want to inconvenience Mrs. Hernan. Whatever time she will need to make the arrangements, we will be pleased to give her."

"That's most thoughtful," Almadon said.

Gerd smiled. "Now that the worst is over, now may we order some food?"

"Forgive me," Almadon said, snapping his fingers for the waitress. "I was not thinking. You must consider me totally without manners."

"I consider you a friend of Ursull's," Gerd said. "That is all that matters."

Almadon smiled thinly. "I wish that Ursull would think as much."

Ursull looked, frozen-eyed, into the menu. "Why do you insist on speaking of me as if I were not here?"

Almadon reached for her wrist, but she pulled it away. "Because you act as if you wish you were not here, Ursull."

"I consider this entire meeting preposterous," she said stiffly, and gave the waitress her order.

"You?" Almadon said to Gerd, and waited for him to order. He turned to Gerd after the waitress had walked away. "You will understand, I have only Ursull's interests at heart. She is annoyed with me for asking to meet you, but perhaps you can try to make her understand. I have known this young woman since she was a baby. A precious little girl . . . Her family became my good friends before she was born; it was as if I watched her spring from a seed and grow into this beautiful blossom that sits here at this moment, so silent, so angry with me. If her family had not been my friends, and I had known this child, I would be fond of her. I would still want to know what happened in her life. As it is, with her parents so far away, my friends so far away, and their only child here, where I can see her, but where they cannot—where they cannot know for sure that everything is well—I had no choice but to insist on seeing, on meeting with you both, to determine how things were. I hope you have not taken offense."

"Of course not," Gerd said.

"And I hope you will speak to her later, when she has regained the gift of speech."

"Thank you." Almadon lowered his eyes. "There is no need for anyone to look upon this meeting with resentment."

"I resent only one thing about you." Gerd smiled. "That you knew Ursull as a child, and I did not. That you could see how she was when she was a baby, and I could not. I have so many years empty of

"I shall."

her, I cannot help but be jealous of those who knew her before. I suppose it is the irrationality of lovers. That we will have our entire lives to grow old together seems, somehow, not enough. I am greedy, not only for the present, and the future, but for the past. I should have known her always. . . ." He reached for her cool, damp fingertips and pressed them warmly, but she would not look up. "That she did not always belong to me, disturbs me. I know it is nonsense," he shrugged, and smiled at Almadon, "but I don't understand why we couldn't grow up together."

"No," Almadon said. "No, I suppose you don't."

"I love you, Alec."

"Yeah, baby." He turned face down on the mattress in the corner of the loft, and nuzzled his nose in the throw pillow Bo had bought on sale in Bloomingdale's. "I love you too."

She stood by the window of the loft and tried to raise herself on tiptoe, so she could look at the stars or the street or anything besides the curve of his back and buttocks and thighs, but the sill was too high. Alec never seemed to mind not being able to see out of the windows. After all, he had explained, they had a massive skylight, the enormous studio, like they didn't make anymore—not even in the Village—another small skylight in the closet they used as a spare bedroom, and a john. None of the lofts, even the good ones that people paid through the nose for, had a bathroom already in, and what with the new restrictions on living places, and lofts being a thing of the past, practically, the place was a steal, even if it had cost more than eighty-four fifty a month, which it didn't. If there was no kitchen, it didn't disturb him—he wasn't that big an eater anyway, except when he went out to the Pizza King; and he and his roommate had plugged in secretly to the building's gas line and rigged up a Bunsen burner to make instant coffee. What more did a bachelor need? Certainly not a view, Alec said.

Still, Bo strained to raise herself higher so that maybe she could catch sight of a pigeon on a ledge, or anything ugly. The room was ugly enough—it was big; but besides not being exactly Cordon Bleus in the chef department, Alex and Maurice were not interior decorators either. Besides the mattress, flung uncovered on the linoleum floor, there were three orange crates stacked on their sides, pushed together lengthwise and cushioned on top with an enormous piece of foam rubber, also uncovered, an old ping-pong table that doubled as a dining table for submarine sandwiches, and desk, when Maurice's novel was going well, or Alec wanted to play Scrabble. Books were piled high in the corner they designated the library, and misshapen lamps, unshaded, were placed haphazardly at various intervals around the floor. The whole place looked like a refugee camp in wartime, Bo said, but only twice, because the second time she thought Alec was going to hit her. She had no particular objection to violence between lovers, she was sure, but as they were not yet lovers, she preferred his initial onslaught to be sexual.

She heard him stirring around on the mattress, and scratched nervously on the sill above her chin, trying to raise herself to viewing position by her fingernails. But it was hopeless. There was not even a chair in the room she could use to stand on, to allow her visual distraction. Not a chair, or a pouf, or any of the things she had tried to bring him as gifts, to make it all easier, or at least more comfortable. The first time she had brought him a bolt of material, just a plain bolt of material, on sale, very cheap, she had assured him, to throw over the mattress on the floor, he had flung it, instead, in her face. The effect he had intended was flowing yards of fabric, streaming across her eyes and her outstretched arms. But as the material was still bound together with a cord, it had hit her with an unexpected force, flinging her backwards in a clump, onto the floor. He had been extremely apologetic and soothing, but the soothe had stopped at her shoulders and she almost went out of her mind, she told Mary Kate later. But after Alec was finished atoning, and pacifying, from the neck up only, he explained to her that he had flipped because she was so goddamned concerned with externals. She would be a better person, he told her, if she were less goddamned concerned with externals.

Well, she certainly was concerned with externals, she knew now, straining her legs and her fingernails and her neck like a goddamned Alice In Wonderland trying to look the hell out of the window, because she didn't dare turn around and look at the room. Because ugly as it was, it held a great fascination, seeing as how Alec's externals were stretching and flexing all over the mattress.

Mary Kate, she thought, rehearsing her scene for when she went home, I almost went out of my goddamned mind.

It was too much for ordinary mortal to bear, she knew that now, much too much to bear. Aside from the toll to her fingernails, chipping like dead branches on a tree above her head, she felt as though her insides and her mind were being put through an Osterizer. If things continued so, she would end up a sticky mass of physical and emotional yoghurt. Osterized by society, Bo thought. Liquidized in my flower.

"I love you, Alec," she said, from the depths of her custardy doom.

"Yeah, baby," he said again, rubbing his nose back and forth over the throw pillow he had finally accepted. "Like I said, I love you too."

She left her awkward perch at the window, and came toward him. "You don't understand," she said.

"Sure, baby, I dig."

"What's happening?"

"My nose itches. It's not running or anything. It just itches."

"No, I mean . . ." She sat miserably on foam rubber cushions, and picked a few splinters from the edge of the orange crate beneath. "What's happening with us?"

"What, baby, you bored or something?" He stopped the movement of his head and looked up at her. "I thought you enjoyed coming here, just hanging loose, cooling it. But if you want to *do,* we can go to a movie, or back to your place and watch television."

"I like it here."

"Yeah. So do I." He rolled over on his side and grinned onto his elbow. "This place is a place. I dig it, at night, when all the garment people have stopped making it downstairs, and there's no traffic on the sidestreets, like it's deserted, dead really. Nothing around, anywhere. I like it best at night, especially when Maurice is away, like now, so I can hear myself echo, knocking around. It makes me feel like I was out in the woods somewhere, Oregon maybe, chopping down the big trees, a loner. You know how hard it is, in the middle of New York City, to really achieve a feeling of desolation?"

"I don't think it's hard," Bo said. "I don't think it's hard at all."

"I just lie here sometimes and think about Maurice down there in St. Petersburg, waving his skinny ass around that parental surfboard, charging himself up with a little sunshine, charging his old family up for the tri-annual touch, and then coming back here to write those novels of isolation, and I laugh. I think to myself, man, you don't know what isolation is. Isolation is beautiful, not hateful. And it's only because you've never achieved it that you dread it. But you dread it so much you will never achieve it and find out, and that's the saddest thing about those books that won't come off. Because as long as you're afraid, you'll never find out. You know," he looked at Bo, "he won't even stay in this apartment by himself?"

"No kidding," Bo said, not the least bit interested in Maurice.

"Not at all. Even while he's hitting away at the slippery keys, stoning himself out on the sound of his clickety-clack, he likes to have me around."

"Really?"

"Me or a broad. Sometimes he stashes a chick here for three four days at a stretch, and never even gives her a bang."

"Imagine," Bo said.

"The married lady gave him El Dumpo because she said she was tired of cheating on her old man with a typewriter." Alec stretched lazily, and his hand dropped across his stomach, fingers trailing on the edge of his crotch. Bo stared, fascinated. "That's the trouble with broads—they start pressing, wanting to devour you. It's a hateful feeling—real conquest. Sitting there, knowing they want to swallow you whole. But not Maurice. Maurice just types.

"I laughed for about three days," Alec said. "You have never seen anyone stacked like that one. A brick shithouse pales by comparison."

"What color brick?"

"Knockers like basketballs. Firm basketballs." He palmed them in the air. "She must have been nearly thirty, and they still bobbed around up there like the best apples in the Halloween tub."

Melancholy quickly was giving way to anger. She wasn't interested in Maurice or the married lady or anyone's breasts for that matter except her own. Alec was always suggesting that bosoms, like too-ripe fruit, would eventually start drooping on the vine. Bo was almost twenty-two years old and panic was fast overtaking her. Every night she would check herself in the bathroom mirror, and she was sure she could already detect a slight sag in the left one. It might have been because of the pills, she knew that: the doctor had told her that one of the side-effects of the pills might be a slight swelling in the breast. As long as they had been batting breasts around, she could have asked the doctor how soon hers would begin to fall; but she hadn't wanted to seem too physical, what with getting a prescription for contraceptives and all. So the future of her bosom still hung in the realm of mystique and fear, rather than solid medical information. Still, there was no doubt about one thing: age was approaching fast. At least faster than Alec. By the time he finally made his move, she was sure they would be down somewhere around her knees.

She despised him for not touching her while there was still time, before they left Shangri-La and she withered to pieces before his very eyes. And, sufficiently incensed, she loathed him for mixing metaphors.

"Well, which was it," Bo said, gritting her teeth. "Which did she have, Betty Breast? Apples or basketballs?"

"Basket-apples," Alec said, and started rocking one leg back and forth, easy, from the smooth ball-bearing of his hip.

Bo closed her eyes and tried to clench her imagination. But it was impossible. She could still see him, lolling there, like a goddamned loose-limbed panther that refused to stalk his prey. The rhythm of his rocking pounded in her ears, slow, steady, deliberate.

"You got a headache, or what?" Alec said.

Bo opened her eyes. He was looking at her, frowning. "I hate you," she said.

"Shit, what did I do? A minute ago you said you loved me."

"I didn't know you were even listening."

"Don't be silly. I'm a great listener. I'm about the best audience there is around, even Maurice says so. He no sooner finishes a chapter or even a couple of pages, when he reads them to me, you know that?"

"No I didn't," Bo said. "But I'm thrilled, now that you tell me."

"Sure. He says he can tell just from my reactions what works, what doesn't work. He can cut whole passages on the basis of my facial expression alone."

"No stuff," Bo said. "Isn't he lucky to have you around?"

"Are you being sarcastic?" Alec said.

"Of course not," Bo said. "Please don't waste time worrying about me. Let's talk some more about Maurice."

"Don't you like him?"

"He's all right. I don't know him very well."

"He's a funny kid," Alec said. "If you got to know him better, you'd dig him, really. Maurice." Alec chuckled. "That's the first and funniest. His real name is Morris. Only he says nobody is named Morris anymore but uncles, so he changed it to 'Maurice.' Then we go to see this Shakespeare movie festival, and some commentator at the museum starts talking about Morris Evans, and the whole time Maurice is sitting there mumbling what an illiterate this guy is, until somebody tells him that in England they pronounce it Morris. And Maurice about shits in his pants. Is that too much?"

"It depends who does your laundry," Bo said.

Alec wiped tears of laughter from his eyes. "So the upshot is, he vows never to publish in England. He can't even get arrested by a New York publisher, and he won't publish in England. How about that guy!"

"Yes," Bo said.

Alec rubbed the back of his wrist against his lids, and peered over at her. "I was right. You are steamed about something. What is it, chicken?"

"Nothing," she said. "Nothing at all. Your whole trouble is you're too oversensitive, Alec, that's your whole trouble. Just because we've been sitting here for one solid hour talking about Maurice and Our Lady of the Knockers, and how much you love being alone, feeling desolated, and not once, never once talk about me, or how I'm feeling, or what I'm feeling about, you take the idea into your head that I'm annoyed. I mean, how thin can your skin get, Alec, that you would feel I'm annoyed?"

"I'm sorry," he said, turning his legs and bringing himself to a sitting position on the mattress, yoga style. "Forgive me, chicken. I didn't mean to be so thoughtless. Come. Tell me. Tell me about you."

"What is there to tell?" Bo said weakly. "I love you."

"And I love you," Alec said.

"Oh Alec, cut it out. I don't mean show-biz. I mean real-life."

"Well, sure, honey, so do I. As much as I ever cared about a girl, I care about you."

"Then why don't you *do* something?" she moaned.

"Well, sure." He got to his feet, and came toward her. She waited, not breathing. His fingers touched lightly on her elbow.

"Come on," he said. "Get your coat and I'll buy you a pizza."

Bo screamed. The building was empty at night, and the street was deserted, but even so, the magnitude of the scream shocked her.

"Jesus Christ," he said. "I only touched your elbow."

"Why do you think I screamed!" she shouted.

"Okay," he raised his hands in the air, "I'm sorry. I won't even come close to you again."

"Oh God." She raised her eyes to the heavens somewhere above the dusty skylight. "Oh God, help me. My life is in the hands of a lunatic."

Alec shook his head. "I don't get you, Bo. I don't get you at all. You know how I care about you. You know I'd never do anything to hurt you. I came on with you in the beginning, I admit it, but that's over now."

"Why?"

"Because you almost got hurt on account of me. I scared you, and something terrible almost happened, and I realized then how important you were to me. I mean, I really cared. I've never had that happen to me before, not with any girl, even the ones I thought I really dug. So it matters to me. It really matters to me that I see you, and be with you, and have you around. You know it. You've got to know it. It's important enough to me so my own needs don't matter that much anymore."

"But they should," Bo said. "They should."

"Not on the big scale," Alec shook his head. "I realized it, finally. They don't tip in on the big scale."

"But they matter to me, Alec. Your needs matter to me."

"Well, that's very sweet of you, baby. That's one of the reasons I love you. My needs are important to you now because you care about me as much as I care about you. But I care about you so much that I wouldn't let your caring about me make you do something you wouldn't want to do."

"But I want to," Bo said, studying a crack in the floor. "I really want to."

"No. You just think you want to because you care about me, but I care about you enough not to let your caring about me change your thinking."

"Oh shut up," Bo said. "I'm bored to death with your caring about my caring about your caring about my caring. The truth of it is you don't care about me at all, or you wouldn't be so goddam care-ful."

"Whatever you say," Alec said. "I'll get your coat."

"And then what?"

"Then I'll take you home."

"And what if I said I didn't want to go?" Bo said.

"I'd know you were lying, just to make me feel good."

"Then you'd be stupider than I thought."

"I don't want to argue with you anymore," Alec said.

"Why not? I want to argue. I mean, I really *want* to argue. Sincerely. You wouldn't want to deny me anything I really want, would you? Please. Argue with me a little."

Alec shrugged. *"No bole el pina,"* he said.

Bo narrowed her eyes, seething. "Isn't it enough you mix metaphors in English?" she said. "Must you also wipe out Italian?"

"Spanish," he said. "It means 'it's not worth the effort,' in Spanish." He went into the broom closet, and lifted her coat from the top of the mop.

"Not quite," Bo said. "The phrase you are groping for so clumsily is *'no vale la pena.'* Val-lay la pain-ah."

"That's what I said." He slipped his arms into his fleece-lined leather jacket, holding her coat in his teeth.

"I'm afraid not. You said 'no boh-lay el pee-na.' Loosely translated, I believe that means 'Don't ball the pineapple.' "

"Whatever you say." Alec held out her coat.

A thin band of sweat or steam, she wasn't sure which, had accumulated under her bangs, and she wiped at them angrily before thrusting her hand into the armhole. As the coat slipped over her shoulders, she could feel his breath at the back of her neck, and his hands on the top of her arms. "Please," she whispered. "Hold me."

"I can't, baby. I don't trust myself to stop there."

"That's all right. Really. It's all right if it doesn't. Hold me."

"Uh-uh." He backed away from her and moved toward the door.

"Why?" Her lips was trembling, she could feel it, and sufficiently impressed that her lip was actually, legitimately trembling that she managed to get real tears in her eyes, something Mary Kate could do at the least provocation but that Bo had never before managed to master, she turned so he could see, too. "Why?"

"I'd hate myself in the morning," Alec said not even looking at her, and pulled on his black leather gloves.

"Go fuck yourself," Bo said.

"Maybe," he smiled, "it might be better."

His smile shattered her heart, and her resolve to never speak to him again. "Better than what?"

"Balling a pineapple," he said, and stepped out into the hall.

When the doorbell rang at nine-thirty in the evening, a brief look of panic flitted across Birgitta's face, and she reached for Mason's hand. When she touched it, the panic disappeared.

"Bad girl," he said.

"I'm sorry. I just thought for a moment . . . I'm sorry."

"Women weren't made to think. Go. Cook me something."

"I'd better answer the door."

"Cook."

"Will you answer it?"

"I ain't in my Kingfish frame of mind." He patted his belly, and rolled off the bed. "You get it. But ask who it is. Anybody wants to ring your bell, you tell them to do it in the daytime."

"Who is it?" Birgitta said, through the closed door.

There was a muffled sound from outside.

"Who?" she said again. She heard Mason go into the bathroom.

"The manager," the man said from outside.

"Would you mind coming back in the daytime?" Birgitta said. "I'm not dressed."

"I'd appreciate your getting dressed, Miss Nils. It will only take a moment."

"Wait," Birgitta said, and went back into the living room. Mason was standing in the doorway by the sink, rubbing a towel over his forearms. His trousers were on, and his shirt was hanging on the doorknob. "What do you want me to do?" she whispered. "It's the manager. Shall I tell him to go away?"

"You can do whatever you like," Mason said, reaching for his shirt. "I don't know why the hell he can't come back in the daytime."

"I'm not here in the daytime," she said.

"So much the better."

"He said it would only take a moment."

"So let him in if you want to." Mason buttoned his shirt. "You've got nothing to be ashamed of, have you?"

"Of course not."

"So stick your chest inside your robe, and I'll stick the bed inside the spread. And invite him in and we'll have a party."

"Please don't get angry with me, Mason. I only asked you a question."

"You're afraid," he said. "You promised me you wouldn't be afraid of anything, and you're afraid."

"No I'm not. I don't like people coming around here at all hours, that's all."

"Then tell him to screw. He's not the police, for Christ's sake. He's got no right to come here without phoning you, telling you to put your clothes on, and hide your buck in the closet—routing you out in the middle of the night. They're no goddamned Gestapo."

"That's right," she said. "So why are you making it into a crisis? It's probably something perfectly simple, like they want to paint or change the tile in the bathroom."

"Let them write you a letter."

"Why must you make everything a crisis? A single knock on the door, and you're imagining all kinds of things."

"I'm imagining nothing. I told you to do what you want."

"Don't be mad at me," Birgitta said, kissing him lightly on the mouth. "I'm on your side."

She went back to open the door.

"Yes?" she said to the young man standing outside. She had opened the door only slightly, and her body blocked his view into the apartment.

"Miss Nils?" He took off his hat, and held it awkwardly against his briefcase.

"That's right."

"I represent the management of this building. My name is Roan. I'd like to talk to you if you don't mind."

"I don't mind in the least," she said. "Talk."

"I think you'd prefer it if I came inside."

"How do you know?" She smiled. "How can you tell what I'd prefer?"

His forehead got quite red, especially across the place where the pressure of his hatband had been. "I think we'd better go inside. I have something quite personal to discuss with you, and I don't think you'd want the neighbors to hear."

"Which neighbors?" The smile froze on her face. "The lady down the hall who's watching us through her peephole?" Birgitta waved her hand gaily at the little glass in the door. "Hi, dear, how are you?" There was a tiny, almost imperceptible click, and the tiny white eye went black. "Say," Birgitta said, looking back at the man. "How come she has a peephole and I don't?"

He cleared his throat. "I'm . . . uh . . . I believe, she, uh . . . had it put in herself."

"Well, then you wouldn't want me to take this little tête-à-tête inside where she couldn't watch, would you? I mean, after she's gone to all that trouble. That just wouldn't seem Christian, do you think?"

"Please, Miss Nils. *I* would prefer it if I could talk to you inside."

"Then you'll just have to be unhappy," Birgitta said, smiling. "For a teeny weeny while. Say whatever you have to say, please. And say it here."

"Very well . . . uh. You . . . uh . . . leave me no choice."

"I hope not."

"Miss Nils, we . . . uh. We've had . . . uh, complaints from some of the tenants in this building. . . . Some, uh, letters. They, uh . . . they uh say you've been giving some extremely noisy parties."

Birgitta looked at him blankly. "Really? I haven't been. That is, I haven't been until now. But if they're so lonely and unhappy that all they have to do with their time is write letters to you, I'd be pleased to start throwing a few . . . parties, that is, and invite those poor people. If you'd be so good as to let me have their names?"

"That, uh, won't be necessary."

"Whatever you say." Birgitta shrugged. "I was only trying to be neighborly. . . . Well, if that's all . . ." She started to close the door.

"I'm afraid not. They, uh, also state that you have for some time been, uh, living with a gentleman."

"Really?" Birgitta said. "How would they happen to know that? I mean, if there were anyone staying here, how would they know whether or not he was a gentleman? Have his manners been under surveillance, or only his morals? And mine of course. I know you wouldn't want me to leave out my morals."

"I, uh . . ."

"Birgitta?" Mason called out from inside the apartment.

"Yes?"

"Why don't you ask the gentleman to come inside. It must be drafty out there in the hall. He sounds like he's taken on a chill."

"All right," Birgitta said. "Won't you come inside, please?"

"Thank you."

Birgitta started to close the door behind him, and then remembered. She leaned out into the hallway, and waved toward the door at the end of the corridor. "Sorry, doll, " she said, and went inside.

Mr. Roan, his hat still clutched in his fingertips, against the lock on his briefcase, followed her from the foyer into the studio. He stood, for a moment, rocking up and back on the balls of his feet, before she told him to sit down.

"This is Mr. Roan," Birgitta said. "He's from Welcome Wagon."

"How do." Mason grinned wide and held out his hand; Roan shook it, the line on his forehead deepening. "Right nice of you people to come to call. Won't you set a spell?"

Roan looked around the room, at the big bed, the window seat, the deep canvas chair. Finally, he moved toward the straight chair by the desk.

"Now then, Mr. Roan." Mason slung himself deep into the canvas. "What can we do for you? I suppose that sounds funny, coming from me, to you, your being from Welcome Wagon and all."

"I'm not from Welcome Wagon."

"You're not?" Mason looked puzzled, and turned to Birgitta curiously. "Why would you tell me he's from Welcome Wagon when he's not from Welcome Wagon?"

"I was making a joke," Birgitta said, biting her smile away from her lip.

"Well, that isn't nice," Mason said in a tone of quiet reprimand. "I mean, do you think that's nice, making a joke at the expense of our friend here? Why, just look at him, he's so embarrassed he probably wishes he were dead. Do you, Mr. Roan? Wish you were dead?"

"Certainly not."

"That's the spirit. Don't you ever lose that gumption, a nice young mean like you, your whole future before you. Don't you ever wish you were dead, no matter how big a fool you seem."

"If you don't mind . . ." Roan said.

"Hey, come on, let me take your coat. You don't really look comfortable, hunched up there like that."

"No," Roan said. "I prefer to keep it on."

"By the way," Mason said, "that is really *some* coat. Who's your tailor, Mr. Roan, do you mind my asking? I sure haven't seen many coats cut like that. Not in the past ten years, anyway."

"May I please just state my business?"

"Why sure," Mason said. "What business you in?"

"I represent the management of this building, and—"

"You hear that, Birgitta? A young fellow like him, still wet behind the ears, and he already represents a whole management. Doesn't it kind of give you a thrill, living in America? Son of a gun." Mason slapped his knee. "There's democracy in action for you."

Mr. Roan sat quiet for a moment, his fingers nervously curling the brim of his hat. "Shall I continue?"

"Continue?" Mason clapped his hands. "Shit, baby, of course you can. You can continue and continue, straight to the top. That's the beauty of the land of opportunity. Only we're going to have to do something about your hat. I mean it's a sensational-looking hat, I haven't seen one like that since Ralph Bellamy played comedy leads, but they're going to have to fix the sweatband if they want your business, cause it presses too tight above your eyebrows, and when you get nervous, or tired I guess, I mean I don't know if you're nervous or just plain fatigued, but whatever it is, when that happens you get this mean red mark on your forehead, I mean *mean*. If I was Mickey Spillane I might describe it as an angry red gash, you know?

"Not that it makes any difference to me, you understand. Some of my best friends have angry red gashes." He took Roan's hat and crumpled it between his fingers. Then he dumped it into the wastebasket.

"Now see here . . ." Roan said, but Mason shook his finger in front of his face.

"Uh-uh. We don't say, 'now see here,' anymore, Mr. Roan. 'Now see here' is kind of old-style Ralph Bellamy, like the hat. The hat is gone, Mr. Roan. Gone."

"Miss Nils, I would very much appreciate your asking your . . . uh, friend, to please stay out of this."

"Out of what?" Birgitta said.

"I came here to speak with you. I would appreciate being able to speak."

"Speak," Birgitta said.

"Yeah, honey, do," Mason said, easing himself back into the chair. "I for one can hardly wait to hear."

Roan cleared his throat several times, and Mason made big yawning motions with his mouth.

"Now then, Miss Nils. It has come to our attention, through, uh, complaints from some of our tenants, that you are involved in an . . . uh, unorthodox living arrangement."

"Say it, baby, speak out loud and clear." Mason smiled. "She is harboring a black man, and it ain't the village smithy."

"May I finish?"

"Mason, please," Birgitta said. "It isn't his fault. He's only doing a job."

"I appreciate your understanding," Roan said. "At any rate, there have been these, uh . . . complaints. Nothing formal has been lodged, you understand, and the building wishes to bring no formal action against you."

"How you mean, formal?" Mason said. "You mean you'd wear dressy sheets?"

"Stop," said Birgitta. "Let him finish."

"As I said, we wish to bring no formal action. We think it would be wiser, and easier for everyone involved, if you were simply to move from the building."

"But I like it here," Birgitta said.

"I'm, uh, sorry about that, but we're sure when you think it over, you'll realize it's much the best way."

"I don't think so," Birgitta said. "My lease runs for another two years . . ."

"Twenty months," Roan said.

"You see, he's checked," Mason said. "I told you this man would go far."

"I think I will be quite happy here for at least another twenty months," Birgitta said. "When the time comes to renew, then we can talk about whether or not you want me. Meantime, I intend to stay."

"Well, I'm sorry you see it that way," Roan said, and got to his feet. "If you insist on sticking to that attitude . . ."

"I insist," Birgitta said.

"Then we will have no choice but to begin action to evict you. Eviction proceedings are a matter of course for a realty company. It will be a relatively simple matter for us. You are the one, I'm afraid, who would suffer."

"Now hold on . . ." Mason said. "Let me get you right. You going to try and get rid of this dear little child?"

"That's right."

"On what grounds?" Mason said.

"I think that's fairly obvious."

"You got a copy of your lease on you?"

"Why?"

"I'm interested in what kind of leases you have. Does she have some kind of a morals clause, like a big bitch movie star?"

"It may not be in the language of the lease. But society is quite clear on this point."

"Oh yeah, sassiety," Mason said. "I get it." He turned to Birgitta, and smiled. "You see, honey, this whole thing is based on a misunderstanding. This man is going on the assumption that I'm boffing you. He thinks I'm jumping on your bones without benefit of clergy, and *no one* in New York does that. That's why they want to evict you. They think we're boffing."

"Really?" Birgitta said. "What made them think that?"

"I . . . uh . . ."

"Oh come on, Ralph. Quit stuttering. You know what boff is. Hump, baby . . . screw, fuck. You understand. Only you *don't* understand. Of course not. This is all only part of a sociological experiment, and Miss Nils, being a liberal, has been kind enough to cooperate.

"You see, I belong to this group, it's a club, you could say, sort of, one of those new organizations, only there's no need to get edgy, we are not extremists. No, we are not extremists at all. We are doctors, teachers, writers, historians, a couple of attorneys, one or two bankers —but mostly what we are, is . . . well what we are mostly is black.

"Anyhow, it came to our attention that a lot of the building managements downtown were refusing to rent to our people, just because they were, oh—sort of suntanned Elks. Now, when we asked these managements if this was, indeed, the case, why they like to throw up their hands to the skies with vows it was not, it was not nearly. And still our people, even the ones socked with good hard cash, socked good enough to make them actually *privileged* in any of the communities of the world, couldn't get a place in their own hometown, except in a run-down neighborhood.

"So we decided to make a move. Nothing violent, you understand. Nothing angry. Just a peaceful, pacifist way of getting the lay of the land. Kind of like having lunch last year at a Woolworth's in Florida.

"Now Miss Nils here was kind enough to offer her apartment for an experiment. But that's all. Only an experiment. We ain't breaking no laws, Mr. Roan, honey. And I'm violating no moral code." Mason took a deep breath, and whooshed it out like a laughing bellows at Roan.

"All I'm doing is staging a Sleep-In."

TOGETHER, Gerd and Ursull spent the weekend drafting the letter to their parents, as if it were a prizewinning essay in some contest they had never before been interested in joining, but were now both firmly determined to win. At first they wanted to make it a joint effort, a common statement to both sets of mothers and fathers, signed by the two of them, relating the joy of mutual discovery, and happiness, leading to their decision to marry. But realizing that might seem too cold, too set and after the fact, giving the impression that they had already formed a strong alliance, the two, against the four, they decided instead to make it a personal letter from each to each mother and father. The form was the same for Gerd's and Ursull's— They were so much alike, Gerd had said happily, that the tone could be uniform throughout. "Dearest Mama and Papa," the letter had begun. "I am writing to tell you of the happiest decision of my life, and, I am sure, your life with me." And then they had written a summary of the meeting, the subsequent discovery, and the glories of their life-partners-to-be, Gerd waxing a bit more grandiose and extravagant in his description of Ursull, because he had already praised her extensively in correspondence to his family, and because Ursull would be expected to be modest, even in her appraisal of her beloved. The fact that he was her beloved, Gerd said happily, was tribute enough to his excellence. Her family would know that immediately. The letters had concluded with the same paragraph, about their future plans, and the hope that they could be married as soon as it was possible to plan and organize a formal wedding, as befitted the union, and the parents, so dear to each of them, and thus, so dear to both.

Considering the inevitability and the joy of the announcement of the betrothal, they were both extremely nervous about exact wording. Friday they worked until two o'clock in the morning, and finally adjourned to bed so exhausted and anxious, there was not even the suggestion of making love. Saturday he awakened her with a cup of instant coffee, telling her it was time to resume the Geneva Convention. When she smiled, he told her he was extremely serious: were they not indeed drafting the covenant for the future of the world? Their life together would be the world to him, he said: love had made him a passionate philosopher, proving his own existence. *"Amo ergo sum,"* he said.

"Latin in the morning?" She drew a brush through her long black hair so that it covered her breasts completely and ended in a tangle of dark silk at her hips. "What is so passionate about that?"

"I love, therefore, I am," he whispered into the cool hollow at the back of her neck. "Can you accept the logic of the idea, or shall I prove it to you?"

"We must finish the letter," she said regretfully, her dark eyes meeting his in the mirror. "Let our families see the logic; then you can demonstrate to me."

They worked the rest of Saturday, surviving on cold sandwiches and cheese and white wine, alternated with strong black coffee. In the early evening, feeling their thoughts growing slow and repetitious, they took a brisk walk to the park, and returned to their labor, not terribly refreshed. Again they slept without touching, and it was not until Sunday afternoon that they were satisfied with their effort. They ate their first warm meal of the weekend, and after dinner, Ursull typed her letter at the desk, while Gerd copied his at the dining room table.

He weighed the two envelopes on the postage meter scale he had bought Friday afternoon, stamped them with the proper postage for the fastest possible delivery, and together they drove to the post office where they found a clerk who assured them the letters would go out on the next truck. When they returned to her apartment, his parking space had been taken by a Volkswagen.

"Those Germans," he said. "They are everywhere."

She laughed, but she could see he was tired, the small laugh lines at the sides of his eyes turned heavy with fatigue. Twice the small red car circled the block, but there was no parking space except on the wrong side of the street.

"I should have to move the car by eight o'clock in the morning," he said. "I do not know if I could move myself by eight o'clock in the morning."

"Perhaps you would rather go back to the hotel," she said.

"Would you mind very much?"

"A little," she said. "Not very much."

"We are tired," he said. "It has been a very hard three days."

"Of course."

"But we shall have our whole lives together, you remember."

"I know." She leaned toward him, smiling, and kissed him lightly on the lips. "But I should hate to think if you feel like this now, what our wedding will do to you."

He drew back stiffly, and looked at her. "Do you really think I am so tired, I could not make love?"

"No, certainly."

"Then why did you say that about the wedding?"

"I was joking."

"I think I will come upstairs with you."

"Don't be foolish," she said. "I myself would prefer to sleep."

"You are sure?"

"Certainly. It has been extremely tiring, for both of us."

"I am not so tired," he said. "I am not so tired at all. I was thinking mostly of you."

"Of course, darling," she said. "I understand that."

"Then you would prefer it if I did not stay?"

"I would prefer it."

"Very well," he said, and kissed her forehead. "If you insist."

"Tomorrow," she said. "You pick me up at work, or shall I meet you here?"

"Tomorrow night I must have dinner with a colleague of my father's who is in New York for only a few days."

"Very well," she said, starting to get out of the car, her legs strangely heavy. "Then I will hear from you?"

"Foolish child." He reached for her waist and pulled her back into the car, his hands on her breasts, his mouth covering her face with kisses. "I will see you as soon as I have finished with him. You will wait?"

"Yes."

"I told you only because I didn't want you to expect me for dinner. Did you think I was finished with you?"

"I don't know."

"Did you think I would ever be finished with you?"

Ursull didn't answer. She closed her eyes, and let his touch loose a flow of feeling inside her, drowning the thoughts that had come so fearfully and unexpectedly into her mind. It was the closest they had ever come to a quarrel, and she did not understand. That was what was wrong, she was sure. Things were so perfect between them that she could not cope with a momentary disappointment, and that was childish and stupid. Perhaps anything so perfect was in itself an error, if such an unimportant note could seem so jarring. Very soon, she thought, very soon, they must have at least one lover's quarrel, so she could learn to understand that things did not always go well.

She looked at him in the soft streetlight coming in through the windshield frosted with winter mist. "I don't see how it would be possible," she whispered against his long golden lashes.

"How what would be possible?"

"Quarreling with you."

"Why should you?"

"I was thinking perhaps . . . perhaps we should quarrel, so we would not always expect perfection."

"We have no choice," he said, smiling. "We must learn to live with it, as we would a bad leg." His laughter was in her mouth, sweet and warm.

"Then I was right," she said. "It is a handicap?"

"What?"

"Perfection?"

"Of course," he said, his fingers twisting the thick black coils of her hair. "As life is a handicap. As love."

"I love you," she said.

"And I love you." He reached over and opened the door. "Even if you are perfect."

The letters had been sent out Sunday evening about eleven o'clock. All through the tours she gave Monday, Ursull was vaguely distracted, imagining her letter moving toward Buenos Aires, as an arrow on a map traced the progress of an invading army in an old motion picture. Even with the speed their postage had given it, and all the anxiousness of will with which she urged it toward her parents, there was no possible way it could reach them before Wednesday—or Tuesday evening at the earliest. So when she returned to her apartment Monday after work and found her mother waiting, her joy was mingled with confusion.

"But Mama," she said, after they had embraced, and wept, and laughed at the sight of one another, always their way of greeting privately no matter what restraint they displayed in public. "I don't understand. I'm so happy to see you, but I don't understand. I knew you would phone, or cable, and of course I suspected you might come. But so quickly?"

"We made arrangements as soon as we heard." Frieda Hernan sat down on the chair in front of the fireplace and looked into it emptily, rubbing her hands against the woolen weave of her suit. Her skin, the pale, cool white Ursull had been so pleased to inherit, was still unlined. But as Ursull knelt to light the fire, she noticed that her mother's skin was drawn so tight across her face it seemed almost transparent: pale blue veins stood out beneath the surface, tiny blue rivers etched in the marble landscape of forehead and throat.

Except for the blackness of her hair and eyes, which had come from her father, the girl lighting the fire was a slightly enlarged duplicate of the blond woman in the chair. It was as if a draftsman had constructed a copy from the older model, similar in every angle and limb, but increasing the beauty and size of the original to a slightly greater degree. Ursull had always regarded the difference between them as a decline, rather than an improvement. Her mother, to her, had always seemed the epitome of womanly splendor, and a hand, no matter how exactly alike the shape of fingers, the structure of wrist, that was not as fragile, was like having a gifted amateur copy of a traditional masterpiece miniature. Only since meeting and loving Gerd had she come to enjoy her own size, and to relish every extra inch of height, every additional pound of flesh, as a boon, the greater to feel and give love. And now, looking at her mother in the glow sparking from the kindling beneath the logs, she saw, with a touch of sadness, that the delicacy she had envied seemed overly vulnerable, that the fragility was separated by a very thin line from the cracks and chips of age.

"You look tired, Mama," Ursull said. "I shall have to get you rested before you meet him. He is so wonderful you won't believe it. And I want him to see how beautiful, how lovely and how beautiful my mama is. I'm sure his mother is only a mother, sweet, perhaps, and clever. But I want him to be overwhelmed by how beautiful and young a mother can be. Tonight you will sleep, and tomorrow you have your hair done, and then tomorrow night we will all go out to dinner."

"All?"

"You and I and Gerd."

"And your father?"

"Well, of course Papa, too." It had not even occurred to Ursull that her father had come to New York. There was no doubt in her mind that he loved her, or she him, but there had never been the demonstrativeness between them that there was between Ursull and her mother. Papa was affectionate, Papa was caring, and Papa loved his daughter better than life, so her mother had always said. But he had always maintained a distance, at least in the presence of the child. His pride, and his joy, and his love, came to her mostly through the words of her mother. And always, in moments of decision, whether the decision had to do with school, or a dress, or a party, or her going to the United States, it was with her mother that the decision was made.

In her childhood it had struck Ursull as curious, his aloofness. Her father seemed far more emotional, quicker to laugh, cry, become angry, than her mother; yet with Ursull he had seemed almost diffident. And her mother, in whom restraint seemed much more prevalent, had been the one to kiss and hug and fondle, and weep. She had never really understood it, and after a while, she had come to see it as an incongruity in his nature; and as the good student she was, a fact, although seemingly incongruous, was a fact—no longer questioned, only accepted.

"I didn't realize he had come with you. Of course I meant Papa should come too. Why isn't he here now?"

"He wanted me to speak to you first," Frieda said, not looking at Ursull. "He was . . . He didn't know how to . . . He stayed in the hotel. It has all happened so fast there was no time to prepare."

"I should think not," Ursull said, reaching to grasp her mother's hand, trying to press away the unaccustomed awkwardness. "We only mailed the letter last evening. I still don't understand how . . ."

"Letter?" Frieda looked up. "What letter?"

"The one Gerd and I wrote you, about our engagement."

"We received no letter."

"Then how did you know . . . What made you decide to come? I'm pleased you're here, Mama. More than pleased, I'm thrilled, really. But you did come because of the engagement?"

"Yes."

"But if you didn't get the letter, how did you . . . ?"

"We spoke with Almadon. He phoned us Friday, after he had lunch with you. As soon as he left you, he phoned."

Ursull's cheeks reddened. "I don't like him anymore. I thought he behaved like a meddling old man."

"We asked him to meddle," Frieda said. "We needed to know how far it had gone."

"I don't care. He had no business questioning us as he did, prying it from us, as if it were some terrible secret. It was a wonderful secret, and we were keeping it secret only until the right time had come to tell you, and Gerd's family. There was no need for him to behave like a spy. And if his curiosity was so great, he should have at least respected our right to tell you ourselves. We wanted to tell you ourselves, properly, happily. We wanted you to see it as wonderful as it is, not think we were doing something sly, and contemptuous. There was no need for you to find out like this."

Ursull's eyes filled with tears. "Why couldn't he have kept silent? Why couldn't you have waited and gotten the letter? Then nothing would be like this. Then it would have all been perfect. We could have told you as we wanted, and it would have been perfect."

"No," Frieda said softly. "It could not have been perfect. Not in this world, my darling. Not as long as you live in this world."

"I don't know what you mean," Ursull said, vaguely annoyed. Her mother did not usually deal in abstractions, and coming as it did, at this most crucial juncture of her life, Ursull did not have the patience for it. "I don't understand."

"Of course you don't," Frieda said. "And it's our fault."

"What's your fault?" Ursull said quickly. "Nothing's your fault. Nothing is wrong, so nothing can be your fault. Why do you make such a fuss, why now? I've never known you to make such a fuss about anything." She threw her head into her mother's lap and let her hair fall beneath the maternal fingers, waiting for her to stroke it as she had always loved doing, even when Ursull was no longer a child. "We will soothe one another," her mother had always said, weaving the strands between her fingers, like the fibers of an elaborate tapestry. But she did not touch it now.

"We'll pretend he never phoned you, that wicked Almadon. We'll pretend you received my letter this moment, tonight."

"Pointless," Frieda mumbled.

"Here, I'll read it to you." She ran to the desk, trying to cover her own growing feeling of fear and concern with hasty movement and speech. It was not the way of her mother to grow pale, to speak in vagaries, with subtle hints of sadness. That was more like her father, and it was never a quality that Ursull much admired. "I have the original right here, isn't that funny? The final original, I suppose I should say. We worked on it as if it were a great document—a historical charter really, and Gerd said it was. He said it was the foundation of our new world, and as such, deserved such attention. He is so serious, my Gerd, Papa will love that about him, but you will love his humor. He is not always that serious, you see, except on solemn questions." Her eyes searched the paper, through the crossed-out lines, frantically. "Here. Here's how it begins."

"It doesn't matter," Frieda said softly.

"I like the beginning the best," Ursull went on, unhearing. "We worked so hard to get it right, you'll laugh at what we finally said. 'Dearest Mama and Papa.' " She looked up briefly. "Would you believe we spent a day and a half debating about that, nearly? He was determined to write 'Mother and Father,' but I insisted it was too formal for so much joy, yes? 'Dearest Mama and Papa. I am writing to tell you of the happiest decision of my life, and, I am sure . . .' "

"Don't read it," Frieda said. "It doesn't matter. Don't read it, please."

"What?"

"It doesn't matter. Whatever you say won't matter. You can't marry this boy."

The heat from the fire was enormous, Ursull noticed with surprise. Her palms were sweating, and there were great bands of moisture along the front of her hair and the back of her neck, and her eyes squinted as though facing a great blast of light. "I must let in some air," she said slowly. "It's quite warm in here. Don't you find it so?" She moved to the window, and rested her burning cheek for a moment against the cold, frosted glass. Then she raised it, and took a breath of the icy air.

"That's much better," she said, coming back to sit on the ottoman by her mother's feet. "Don't you find it better?"

Her mother said nothing.

"Oh, but of course you are still used to the heat. It is not yet winter for you. Now, I continue this masterpiece," Ursull said.

"I ask you not to," Frieda interrupted. "Please don't make me listen to any more. I told you it won't make any difference."

Ursull looked up, puzzled. She had been sure she had imagined her mother's saying that. It was all part of that quick dizziness that had occurred, because the room had been too warm. She was sure that had been all it was. "What?"

"I told you you can't marry him."

Ursull shook her head, dazedly. "I don't know, Mama. Am I hearing things? Have I gone mad, or is it you? I don't mean to be insulting, you know I don't mean to, but I can't imagine any other possible explanation for your saying such a thing. Is it Papa? I know he thinks I'm an exceptional girl, I know he is fond of me and prizes me, but does he know about this boy? Does he realize what this boy is? Who he is? Aside from what he means to me, which is the whole world—if I didn't love Gerd at all, he would still be the most desirable person on earth to any father—even the father of the most exceptional girl, which I am not. If he were half what I say, he would still be more than anyone could wish for. And he isn't half. He is twice what I say about him. And you would forbid me to marry him?"

"If I could, I would. But it won't be necessary. You can't marry him. It's simple."

"It is not simple," Ursull said. "I have never gone against your wishes before. But don't tell me I can't marry him. I will marry him, whether or not you let me. Please, I don't want to defy you. Don't say I can't marry him."

"Very well," Frieda said. "I won't. He won't marry you."

"I have gone mad," Ursull said. "You have gone mad, and I have gone mad with you. You haven't even seen him, and you say this? No one has ever loved anyone as Gerd loves me." Her eyes filled with tears. "Except me, as I love him."

"Your father is a Jew," Frieda said.

It cut through the words between them and the heat she had felt the moment before like a jagged sheet of ice, stinging Ursull's eyes, and her brain. "Oh Mama," Ursull murmured. "Oh Mama, how could you?"

Disbelief and shame darkened Frieda's eyes, and her hand moved to her mouth. "My God," she whispered. "My God, what have we done?"

For a moment Ursull did not understand. She stared at her mother's crumbling face, and did not understand at all. What she had said, she said as reflex—from her own shocked confusion. She had spoken only for fear of her own love, lost, not from any true hatred, or contempt. She did not mean for her mother to look so thoroughly ashamed.

"It's all right," she said softly. "It's not your fault, Mama. I supposed you loved him very much."

"It's not my fault?" Frieda said. "It's not my fault? You will forgive me for having married a Jew? You will pardon me for having mixed my blood with your father's? That brilliant wonderful man who lived his life and dreamed his dream only for you. That you would be safe and protected and never have the nightmares of his lifetime. . . . For that you forgive me? For loving him, and sleeping with him, and giving birth to a child that despises him because he has kept her from being a pure-bred Nazi?"

"Oh Mama." Tears welled in her eyes, and she threw her arms around her mother's trembling shoulders. "Please. I didn't think. I didn't mean it, I swear, I didn't mean it. I was thinking of him, only him, Gerd. Not you, not me, not Papa or anybody. Please, I swear. I didn't mean it. I would die before I would be like that."

"You think you would die," Frieda said. "You only think you would die. So many people thought they would die, before they would be like that."

"I love Papa," Ursull said. "You know I love him."

"Of course," Frieda murmured. "Why shouldn't you? You never even suspected: He is so unusual for a Jew. Not at all like *them*."

"Stop," Ursull whispered. "Please stop. Forgive me."

"I forgive you," she said after a moment, pulling her fingers thoughtfully through her daughter's long black hair. "It isn't your fault. It's our fault, for hiding it. For never telling you, as though it was something contemptible. What could you think, except that there was some reason to be ashamed? How could you react, except with shame?"

"You won't tell Papa?"

"I don't have to tell Papa." She sighed. "He knew how it would be, that was why he didn't come with me. He knew what you would say, no matter how much I swore to him you wouldn't say it. . . . No, I won't tell your father. He has been punished enough. God has punished both of us."

"No," Ursull said. "No, please, you mustn't say that. I was horrible, I know. I didn't mean it. I wasn't thinking, only about Gerd, and I am wrong about him. You'll see. You'll see how we are all wrong. It was insane to be frightened, to be ashamed. Gerd is a magnificent man. He isn't like that at all. He is better than I, I swear it. He would not react so stupidly. He is brilliant, and beautiful, and wise, and witty, and kind . . ."

"And a German. Gerd Kraben. Otto Kraben's son."

"He is his own person," Ursull said quickly. "He belongs to no one, except me." She raised her face to her mother's and tears welled over, onto her cheeks. "He is not like anyone, you'll see. No one before, and no one again."

"I'm sorry," Frieda whispered. "I'm sorry you are so very much in love."

"But you mustn't be sorry. There's nothing to be sorry about. It's wonderful, don't you see, it's wonderful to be in love like we are. Nothing can come between two people who love each other as we do. Nothing. Certainly not an idea. An insane, stupid idea."

"Come," Frieda said, taking a handkerchief and wiping the tears from Ursull's face, erasing the lines of salt running down across the edges of the fixed, hollow smile. "Come. We had better go see your father. He will be beside himself with worry over what is happening here. He will imagine all kinds of terrible things."

"But he will be wrong," Ursull said. "You'll tell him he was wrong, won't you? You won't let him know?"

"He knows," Frieda said. "He knows better than I could ever tell him. He has been afraid all his life that something like this would happen. That's why he treated you as he did, his precious beautiful child. Afraid to come too close to you, for fear you would turn away."

"But I wouldn't. I wouldn't turn away. You know that, don't you? I couldn't turn away. I love him. I couldn't turn away from someone I loved. What I did, what I said, I didn't mean, you know that, don't you? It was only a moment, a moment means nothing. It never existed, you'll tell him that, won't you?"

"You tell him," Frieda said. "It would be better coming from you."

"Of course I'll tell him," Ursull said. "I shall tell him I love him, that I have always loved him, that I love him now more than ever." She got to her feet. "I couldn't turn away from someone I love. Any more than . . ." She saw her own face in the mirror, and her voice wavered. "Any more than Gerd could turn away from me."

XV

THE Discothèque, named ROBERT (a long "bob," explained one of the columnists, the haircut being worn by most rock 'n' roll singers), was athrob with more overt sexuality than Bo had at one time imagined she would see in her lifetime. Green lights, then red, and then purple split the ceiling, and colored the faces of the people surging on the dance floor, although their faces were the least important part of the group movement, whirling as in some insane erotic nightmare. The skirts on the girls varied in length from mid-thigh to just below the crotch, and people were packed onto the floor just slightly less than the men were stuffed into their pants. Bo felt all the fascination of a Cleveland Margaret Mead, privileged to watch the initiation rites of the really "In" group of the Manhattan Islands, although she had not the least intention of joining the dance.

To begin with, she hadn't the least idea how to move as the dancers were moving. Not that she hadn't twisted or even frugged in her day, which seemed rapidly to be moving into the ancient past—but these people were so *au courant,* being celebrities, part owners of the club, or the very nose of the Jet Set, that every bar of the blaring music had a special choreography all its own, and she wasn't about to let herself look foolish in front of Alec. It was enough that she was here, having her eardrums blasted and her eyeballs streaked. She had seen how many people had been turned away at the door and, even now, clustered hopefully on the sidewalk outside, hoping someone would make a mistake and admit them, even though they were nothing but a paying customer.

It had been terribly kind of Maurice to invite them, she had to admit that to herself, even though she was angry at Maurice for always being in the apartment he shared with Alec. But apparently Maurice had nothing but kind thoughts for her, so she was wrong to despise him, as the minute his rich friend had called to invite him to ROBERT, and bring some friends, Maurice had invited Bo and Mary Kate. So if Maurice thought of her as a friend, she was wrong to consider him her enemy just because he liked being in his own home. Still, she did not look to her right, where Maurice sat pressed against the wall, huddling out of the lights, talking to his friend Edward, a part owner of the club, which explained his being allowed inside.

Across from her, Alec thumped on the narrow wooden table, eyes averted, staring into the lights reflected in his large vodka gimlet. He was magnificent in tight stretch jeans, with a blue velour pullover, and Bo's heart and her throat and her head ached at the sight of him, and the volume of the rock 'n' roll records.

There was a momentary break in the music, and in the sudden and welcome quiet that was only the babble of voices, she heard Edward speaking. "You want another drink, you pretty thing?"

Bo turned, smiling, to answer him, but she saw he was speaking to Maurice.

"I've about had this place," Alec said. "It typifies the frenzy necessary for the generation growing up today." Odd that he should say that, Bo thought, when there was hardly a person in the place under thirty.

Alec grumbled. "It's so noisy you can't even hear yourself get loaded. I'm cutting out."

Bo felt her stomach turn dizzily. She hadn't even had a chance to talk to him in the noise, and he was getting further away from her all the time, now that Maurice was back.

A girl in a pleated white skirt that barely covered her matching panty briefs stopped by the table behind them, and leaned over to kiss a middle-aged gentleman. Alec grinned as her buttock touched the side of his arm, and made a gesture as though to take himself a handful.

"That's disgusting," Bo said.

"I didn't do it," Alec whispered. "I only pretended."

"I didn't mean you, I meant her."

"I don't think it's disgusting. Ask me, it's letter-perfect."

"You ought to just try and enjoy it," Mary Kate said, raising her voice above the music, which had begun blasting out at them again from fifty speakers. "Myself, I'm using this for observation."

A blond lady passed the table, chattering loudly to her girl friend. "I never should have come here with him," she said, "but they told me he was the best frugger in Fort Worth."

"In class next week," Mary Kate said, "we have to improvise a scene on modern decadence, and I intend to do something on ROBERT. You know, the impossibility of communication between two people in this day and age. A boy and a girl trying to express thoughts of love, with the music blotting out their words and all. But you can use every experience, Bo," Mary Kate screamed. "You just have to take it for what it's worth."

"I'm enjoying every minute," Bo said. "I've never had a better time." And with that she burst into tears and fled from the table.

She had time only to blow her nose a few times and wash her face with cold water before Mary Kate came into the ladies' room.

"Well for God's sake," Mary Kate said. "Are you drunk, or what?"

"A little of both," Bo sniffled. "I suppose he thinks I'm a complete fool. Did he say I was a fool?"

"He didn't say anything. He got all hung up on an orange spotlight and I don't even think he saw you fall apart. Why did you fall apart?"

"I just feel it slipping away, that's all. My one chance at love."

"Oh for God's sake," Mary Kate said.

"Well my chance, anyway. I'm never alone with him, and now, he doesn't even know I'm there in the crowd."

"So why don't you give him a grab? It's crowded enough."

"Oh shut up," Bo said. "You're no help at all."

"You don't want help. You just want to cry and make scenes, even when nobody sees them but me. I don't know why you make everything so complicated."

"Complicated?" Bo said. "It's simple for you to say I'm complicated. You haven't been trying to get seduced as long as I have."

"I haven't been trying to get seduced at all," Mary Kate said. "And why must you go on being so euphemistic. You don't want to be seduced at all. You want to get laid."

"Well what am I supposed to do? He never tries to seduce me anymore. I have no choice."

"Then get laid, dammit, and stop grousing."

There was a loud knocking on the door.

"We'll just be a moment," Mary Kate said.

"So how do I go about it?" Bo wiped her face with a paper towel, and reached for her makeup.

"Lie down and spread your legs."

"You have no class," Bo said. "Much less compassion."

"What I have none of is patience. I have been listening to your song for many weeks now, and it has left the top 40."

"Then what am I going to do?"

"Go back out there and get him drunk."

The knocking came again.

"A second," Bo shouted. "What good will that do?" Bo said in a hushed voice. "Maurice will come home with him and nothing will happen."

"So get them both drunk," Mary Kate said. "Make it a real party."

"You are gross. I am in love, I am not horny."

"You could have fooled me."

"If I was horny, I could do it with a truck driver."

"That might be a good idea."

"Help me!"

"Sure, Bo, anything I can do."

The knocking came, louder and more persistent, accompanied by feminine but unladylike oaths.

"You're a doll, Mary Kate." Bo kissed her lightly on the cheek. "I knew I could count on you."

"To do what?"

"Take Maurice home with you, and keep him there all night."

"Now hold on," Mary Kate said. "I never . . ."

"You said you'd do anything."

"I didn't mean *anything*."

"Then just do a little something. You know. Neck with him a while."

Bo opened the door and walked out of the ladies' room, looking around curiously. "Whoever it was couldn't have had to go that badly if they didn't even wait," she said to Mary Kate. "We weren't there for more than a minute."

"I didn't say I'd do it," Mary Kate said.

"All you have to do is neck with him, for God's sake. Even if I had no eyes for a boy, I'd neck with him if it would help out a friend."

"Yeah, but you're horny."

"Girls don't get horny," Bo said. "Unless they read dirty books."

The music blared back on them as they moved toward the main room, on the other side of the bar.

"You stink," said Mary Kate, as the music reduced her to short syllables.

"You're the only one who can help me." Bo clutched her hand. "Please."

"From the neck up," Mary Kate said into her ear. "Only from the neck up."

"Bless you," Bo said, and went back to the table, seating herself next to Alec. "Let's have a drink," she murmured at his neck. When he did not turn, she shrilled it at him.

"Why?" he shouted back. "What's the occasion?"

"Does there have to be an occasion?"

"Sure." He touched his glass. "I'm not a drinking man. One's my limit. You know that."

Bo swallowed. She hadn't known anything of the sort. "Well, you guessed it, Alec. It's an occasion all right."

"Yeah?"

"Yes. I wasn't going to tell—"

"What?" he hollered.

"I wasn't going to tell, but since you've guessed . . ."

"Huh?"

She leaned over and blurted the lie into his ear. "I'm leaving. Next week. For good."

"Cleveland?"

Cleveland would never do. He was already looking at her a little patronizingly: fondly, but patronizing, as if she were a limped-eared cocker spaniel who couldn't make it among the sleeker city whippets. *"No!"* she shouted. "For Russia."

"Yeah?" He leaned closer toward her. "No shit."

Well of course it was shit, but she certainly had no intention of telling him that. "Does it strike you as so unlikely?"

"What?"

"Does it strike you as so unlikely?"

"It doesn't strike me as anything, I just never thought about it, that's all."

He was clearly all broken up about it, the icy son of a bitch. "Well, you didn't have to think about it. The United Nations did, and I guess they carry a little more weight than you, Alec. I mean, crazy as I am about you, I have this fairly large fund of respect for the United Nations."

"Well, that's terrific, kid. How'd it happen? You hump Gromyko, or what?"

"Very funny," she said, realizing how very funny it was not. Tragic it was, more nearly. If she let things go on as they were, chances were she would probably get to hump Gromyko a lot sooner than Alec. She hated herself for lying to him, but men did that all the time when they had to have a woman. "I'm going to war" they would say, with not even the slightest twinge of conscience. "I'm shipping out tomorrow, Serena, and chances are . . ." (looking away, eyes averted) "I'll . . . never come back." It also disturbed her to be playing the male role in a seduction scene, but she had come to grips with that thought, realizing it disturbed her far less than playing no part in a seduction scene at all.

There was a blessed lull in the music.

"No," she said, "as a matter of fact it's not quite that romantic. I know you don't think of me as efficient, Alec, but the truth of it is I do a very good job at the UN."

"I believe it," he said. "Hell, I do, I really believe it. Mary Kate tells me you give an assbuster of a tour."

"Well, that's sweet of you to say. Matter of fact, the Russian delegation said the very same thing, only perhaps not in that quaint way. They were quite impressed with my manner, and the job I've been doing. So they've invited me to be one of a limited group of young foreigners who will act as official hosts and hostesses at their Centennial this spring in Moscow." Were they having a Centennial? If it was a Centennial, what was it the Centennial of? She breathed a little deeply, hoping he would not ask her these or any other questions, and, if he did, that she would be able to answer them. But she was foolish to worry. If he read the papers at all, it was only the theatrical pages. "We're leaving at once, so we'll have sufficient time to get oriented."

"Or Rushed," Alec said, grinning.

She wondered, for a moment, honestly, how she could possibly be so anxious to give herself to such a clod. Then he wriggled closer to her, and she knew the answer. "So," she sighed, "it's a celebration. Hail, and farewell, as it were."

"Well, shit," he said, signaling for the waiter whom somebody pointed out as a pop-artist who hadn't been selling too well. "I'll drink to that."

Thank God, she thought.

He started to order gimlets for the two of them, but Bo suggested they make it straight vodka. "I'd better start getting used to it plain, the way they drink it back there."

"Well, kid," he said, after the waiter-artist had brought two deep drinks. "Here's to you! Lots of luck."

"Does Vydanya," Bo said, returning the toast.

"Jesus." He wiped his mouth. "That's terrible."

"You're not drinking it right," she said. "You have to gulp it, like beer. That way, it's smooth."

"Yeah?"

"Try it."

The lights and the music seemed to dull the pain she was feeling, and in no time at all she had raised her hand for another drink.

"Easy," he said. "That stuff's dynamite."

"You're a victim of propaganda. Actually it has no more kick than . . ." She snapped her fingers but they made no noise. She looked at them curiously, and tried again. Nothing. A dull kind of squish, but no snap. "Why are we being so stupid?" she said, realizing she was less than steady. "Can't we have a nightcap and go home?"

"Okay."

They raised their fourth glass in toast.

"Little Bo Peep," he said, smiling. "Tooting around Red Square. I can hardly believe it."

"Well, here's to . . ." she said, raising her glass.

"Mud in your ass," he said.

"Up yours," she said, and giggled.

They were silent, both of them, through the music and the next four ounces. Alec looked rather appealing, she thought, even though his features were starting to ooze a little, like the wax on a kewpie doll. She finished her drink and weighed her strategy carefully, etching little witticisms she intended to spring on him, one by one, into the front of her brain. She closed her eyes and peered into the front of her head, trying to picture the words carved in all that marvelous gray matter. But they kept disappearing in a puddle of mud.

"Alec?" she said, opening one eye.

"Yeah?" His own lids looked extremely heavy.

She struggled for that clever thing she had thought of, only a moment before. She knew how she intended to play the scene, strong but vibrant, restrained but giddy, sort of a latter-day Ninotchka waving a swinging Sixties farewell to Melvyn Douglas: Garbo laughs again. But instead, she started to cry.

"Baby," he said. "What's wrong?"

"You won't even miss me," she wailed. "You don't even care that I'm going away."

"Sure I do," he mumbled. "You crazy, what?"

"No you don't."

"Sure," he muttered. "Sure. Yeah sure."

"You don't even want to kiss me good-bye."

"Shit," he said. "You're not leaving till next week."

A well-built girl in the tightest white pants Bo had ever seen, urged her sandaled feet rhythmically through the aisle toward the dance floor, insinuating her graphically portrayed hips at her escort, a tall blond man in a jump suit and dark blue glasses.

"Oh look," Bo said, so Alec wouldn't see the tears streaming down her face.

"Yeah I noticed. James Bond."

"Not him. Her."

"What about her?" Alec said.

"That's Fred Astaire's old dancing partner."

"Don't be ridiculous," Alec snorted. "That isn't her, I used to have a big thing on her, from afar. She must have been six feet tall. This one's a midget."

"She's about five-five."

"Still a midget compared to her. That isn't her."

"Mary Kate," Bo shouted across the table over the music. "Look at her. Isn't that her? Alec says it isn't her."

"It's her," Mary Kate said.

"See?" Bo said, and blew her nose inconspicuously into a napkin. "I told you it was her."

"Son of a bitch," Alec said. "I never would have believed it was her. I always thought she was six feet tall." He settled his ribs into his belly and brooded. "Christ, it just goes to show you. You know what that means? That means that Fred Astaire is probably only five-three. She always looked like a giant with him. And if Fred Astaire is only five-three, that means Ginger Rogers is only five-one. And if Ginger Rogers is only five-one, that makes Ray Milland four-eleven. Jesus Christ, what is there left to believe in?"

"You," Bo sobbed, and stopped trying to control her weeping. "I believe in you, Alec. You represent all that is fine and good and worth having."

"Jesus Christ," Alec said. "I better take you home."

Bo signaled to everybody not to get up, and readied herself to tell them not to bother to leave, to just stay there and have a good time, but nobody else at the table even looked up when they said good-bye. Mary Kate just gritted her teeth and stuck out her tongue when Alec wasn't looking.

In the cab Alec started to give the driver Bo's address but that sent her into greater fits of weeping. When he asked her what was wrong she told him he had said he was taking her home with him, and soon he was so confused he apologized for forgetting. By the time they got each other upstairs to the loft the shock of the quiet, after the noise of ROBERT, and the air, after the smoke they had inhaled for two solid hours, made them dizzily drunk. They stumbled to the mattress in the living room, and fell there, panting.

After a while, when she was sure her stomach had stopped spinning, Bo touched his thigh. "So I'm leaving," she said.

"You just got here," said Alec.

"I mean for Russia."

"Oh yeah, that's right."

"Do you care?" she whispered. "Do you care at all?"

"Oh honey," he said, fumbling for her hand. "C'mere."

"Yeah?" she said happily.

"Yeah sure."

"Oh, Alec . . . oh, Alec."

"Yeah, baby?"

"Take me. Please."

"Wha?"

"Take me," she whispered huskily. "Take me. Now."

"Yeah," he said. "Sure."

"Hey," she said, a moment later. "I didn't mean this minute!"

"No?" he said, looking a little confused. "You said—"

"I meant now, this evening. Not now this very second. Honestly."

"I'm sorry," he said, and sat back up.

"Oh baby," she said, throwing her head across his thighs. "I hurt you."

"No you didn't," he said. "Forget it."

"But I don't want to forget it. Please, Alec."

"Wha?"

"Please. I love you. Make love to me."

"Okay," he shrugged. "Oney I wish you'd make up your mind."

"Not here. Please. Let's go in the bedroom."

"Whuffor?" he said. "Don't you dig foam rubber?"

"No."

"Then let's go on the floor."

"The bedroom."

Alec shrugged. "A mattress is a mattress. But if you want the bedroom . . ."

"Thank you," she whispered. "I knew you'd be good to me."

He was inside the bedroom almost at once. It was several minutes before he returned, looking for her . . . "I thought you wanted to go in the bedroom," he said, vaguely discerning her sprawled, half-dressed form.

"I do," she whispered, one thin tear, all she could summon, trickling down the side of her face.

"Then why the fuck are you still out here?"

"Oh Alec," she sobbed, hollowly.

"I don't get you," he said.

"I love you," she said.

"Yeah, and I love you too. So wha's the big deal?"

"I'm going away and I'll never see you again, and we have but one night to love."

"So? Get your ass in the bedroom."

"Oh Alec," she sniffed. "Don't you realize? This is my first time."

"Shit," he said. "I forgot. You want me to put on a record?"

"I have to have some illusions. Some semblance of a romance, even if you don't care about me."

"I care about you, I care about you," he said. "Come in the bedroom, and I'll show you."

"Alec?"

"Yeah?"

"Please," she whispered, and looked up at him with mournful eyes. "Please . . ." She held out her arms.

"Wha?"

"Carry me?"

He shrugged. "Whatever you say."

It was not as simple as she had imagined, either for him or her. He made terrible grunting noises, and couldn't seem to find the right places to hold her by, either for romance or balance. She kept sliding and pulling on his neck and his throat, and he sounded like he was gargling. One of her legs fell completely from his grip and jabbed rather heavily into his crotch. By the time he finally dumped her, like a great bag of sand, onto the double bed, she was sure it was the last physical act he could manage for the evening. But he seemed to recover himself eventually, panting on the edge of the bed.

"So," he said after a while. "I carried you. You satisfied?"

"Thank you." She looked away.

"So what are you waiting for? Take off your clothes."

"Aren't you going to undress me?"

He held his palms out wearily, and came toward her. There was an endtable next to the left side of the bed, with a lamp on top of it, and she saw to her horror that the top drawer was open, and he didn't seem to see. The edge of the drawer crashed into his groin.

Alec groaned.

"Look out," Bo said a moment later. "Oh dear."

"What did you say?" Alec gasped, holding his side, half-kneeling at the side of the bed.

"Nothing."

"I heard what you said," he breathed. "I heard what you said. You wait until I castrate myself almost and then you say look out. Nobody likes a smart ass, smart ass."

"I'm sorry," she whispered. "Are you all right?"

"No, thanks to you," he muttered. "Now you want to go home, smart ass, or what do you want to do?"

"I don't know." She covered her face with her hands. "I don't know."

"Well decide," he said. "You decide while I'm in the bathroom. When I come out, I'm going to bed. You can be in it, or you can be out of it. Whatever you want."

"All right, Alec," she said meekly.

When he had gone, she quickly got out of her clothes. She debated about leaving on her bra and panties, but it wasn't fair to him, and she had to be fair to him, at all costs. With him love was an act, and with her it was still an automobile after a prom. She would have to get over that as soon as possible, preferably now, if they were to become the great lovers she imagined.

Slipping off her remaining undergarments, she slithered quickly under the rumpled sheets. One arm behind her head, she tried pulling the quilt down, first to her feet, and then to her breast. Finally she folded it back neatly at the bottom of the bed, and pulled the top sheet up to her neck, tight, so it gently outlined the fragile curve of her body. It was still not as effective as she hoped. Sighing, Bo reached over and switched off the bedlamp light.

In a moment the door opened to the bathroom, and he stood there, the light over the sink behind him outlining his naked body. A slight shiver went through her, and she was not sure whether it was a thrill, or disappointment. The bottom half of his torso was not nearly as magnificent naked as she had imagined it would be naked when he was dressed, and she wondered for a moment if he was always lying down because he didn't want anyone to notice his legs weren't all that long. Immediately, she felt ashamed of herself, and loved him all the more for having fairly short legs.

"Bo?" he whispered. "You here?"

"I'm here. Darling," she added.

He switched off the light and came toward her in the darkness. She waited, breathless. And then she heard the clunk, and remembered. She had forgotten to close the drawer.

"Alec," she whispered, reaching for him. "Oh, Alec, are you all right. I'm sorry, Alec. Please. I'm so sorry."

"Forget it," he muttered. "Just give me a minute."

Now that they were safely (dangerously?) on the bed, naked, no further fumblings to be made on her part, and surely (please God) no clumsy incompetencies on his, she let fiction flood her mind, and waited for the fervent moanings, the imprecations, the earnest gropings, the half-tearful, half-joyously ecstatic searching for her secret treasures, and finally, the warm caress, the ultimate surrender, and the thrusting stab of pain before the moment that was a little like dying, only better.

Actually it wasn't like that at all. What little clear perception she had left of what was actually going on, showed him to be going about his business like a busy little bee, intent only on depositing his share of the honey in its proper cell. True, her body was slightly unyielding, which seemed to be no fault of Bo's (she was most earnestly contributing to the scene her concept of her all, which consisted mainly of raking his back with her fingernails, trying to adjust the rhythm of the clawings to his peculiar rocking). Finally he told her to cut it the hell out, take it easy and just relax.

In spite of feeling more than a little offended (in the novels men became particularly passionate when their backs were clawed), Bo tried her best to do as he said. She summoned what was left of her attention, and concentrated on relaxing, gritting her teeth a good deal. She felt herself beginning to perspire from the effort, and earnestly hoped he would not notice.

But he seemed more intent on his project than any effect it might be having on her. She wished for a moment he might say or do something tender, even mumble "baby" as he was forever doing when it was not nearly so important. But all he did was grunt now and then, and curse softly at a specific part of her.

"My goodness," she said finally. "Can't you do something?"

"Me?" he said angrily. "You're no help."

"Then help me," she said, trying for earnestness. "Help me help you." She reached out for his chin, hoping to cup it in loving caress and fill herself with feeling for him that he apparently seemed unable to provide. But the upper half of his torso swung out in a wide quick arc above her, and he was hanging half off the bed, reaching for something in the endtable drawer.

"But I've been taking . . . we don't need . . ." she started to say. Then she heard the top of the jar being opened.

Quicker than she could follow he was back in his place on the bed above her, one arm extended into the air as if waving a flag. And then the arm disappeared, and she felt his hand swooping toward her.

"Fuck it," he said, and shoved a palmful of Vaseline up into her crotch.

"What . . ."

"No vale the pena," he mumbled, and crashed into her.

It didn't hurt at all. She felt neither wonderful nor like dying, only better. She felt absolutely nothing. She could hardly tell it had begun, or that it was over, except that he was lying still and there was perspiration on his shoulder blades. She knew that because she was pressing him against her, to prove to herself that he was actually there, in that position. Which meant they had done it, although there was no proving it from her point of view. She thought for a moment of asking him if he had really gotten inside, but realized immediately how insulting that might sound. She didn't want to give him any worse a time than she already had. And then she remembered, too late, that she hadn't even emitted the sighs that were supposed to accompany pleasure. It was ungrateful of her, if not downright destructive, to let him think he had failed. Briefly, she let rise from her chest a few moans of ecstasy, hoping he would not notice the disparity in time.

"Yeah, yeah," he said into her collarbone, and rolling off her, and the bed, stumbled into the bathroom.

She managed to switch the lamp on without knocking it over, and caught a glimpse of the bed while he was out of the room. There was not even any blood on the sheets. She had not even bled. Not even a shameful commemoration of the act she could not believe had happened.

She turned off the light.

"You want to wash up?" he said, when he returned.

"Not particularly." She wondered if she should say she loved him, even though she didn't, so he would feel, at least, that she was pressing him, and wanted to devour him. That might at least give him a hated feeling of conquest, permit him to hate her because she was like all of them, wanting to swallow him up, and not because she was (oh God) terrible in bed. But she didn't love him enough to give him that satisfaction. Actually she didn't love him at all, and there had been enough meaningless desecrations for one evening.

As he lay down beside her, though, turning his naked back to her, she did manage to summon up a few tears. And in no time at all she was actually sobbing that she wasn't that kind of a girl.

XVI

WHEN Ernie had been at home, lying in his room, on his back, for three days, Ernie's mother figured her tactic had worked. She gave up staring at the wall, and consulted with her sister Maureen.

If it had only been a lover's quarrel, Maureen said, he would have phoned her before the end of three days; so it was over for good. The last time Ernie sat around his room so long had been after Eileen died. So it was the same thing. It was over. The Japanese was as good as dead. The affair was finished.

So it was all right, Maureen assured her, after Ernie's mother brought forward the anxious question. It was certainly all right to go back to watching television. There was nothing for Ernie's mother to worry about anymore.

Ernie was sick. He knew in his heart he was sick, even though he told his mother he didn't want the doctor. The doctor couldn't fix what was wrong with him, so it was crazy even to bother. Not crazy. Stupid. He wasn't crazy. It was Baimbridge who was crazy, and that was what made him sick.

A doctor couldn't wash away dirty pictures. Neither could a psychiatrist. A psychiatrist showed you blots, Cousin Archie said, and waited to see if you saw dirty pictures. But dirty pictures that were in your brain because you jumped into a sewer, like a stupid fool, jumped into a sewer and got clogged up with filth, no doctor could wash those away. Maybe a surgeon could cut them out if he had a big enough knife, and a red-hot poker to sear the place. But Ernie doubted it.

A priest would say he could wash them away. A priest would listen silently, and make him do penance, and give him expiation for his sins, as if a man could be new baptized at almost forty years old. But a priest would assume that God cared about Ernie, and Ernie knew better. Ernie cared about the priests: the priests meant well, and they had always been kind to him when he was a little boy, and it wasn't their fault if they couldn't wash away the filth. Since they couldn't help him, what good would it do to plunge them into the same sewer he had visited? Why expose their ears and their souls to that filth, when it wouldn't do any good? That would be the same as asking Father Coughlin to come to The Grotto for lunch with Baimbridge. Baimbridge would only make him sick, like he had made Ernie.

A shaft of nausea moved up from his belly into his throat at the thought of that crazy, stupid pig, spitting his venom up on the table, puking his filth where Ernie had to look at it. Baimbridge was crazy, he had admitted he was crazy, and Ernie had been crazy enough to listen to him. But that didn't make Ernie crazy. He had been insane to listen, he knew that now, and once you knew you had done something insane, you knew better, you knew right from wrong. You had done something wrong, it was that simple: knowing it had been wrong made you sane. Everybody did something a little crazy sometime in their lives, and when they admitted to themselves it had been crazy, that made them all right. But everybody hadn't been stupid crazy like Ernie. He had been stupid enough to listen, and he knew it, but that didn't get him off the hook, just knowing. Everybody got off the hook, once they realized what they had done wrong, but then everybody else was lucky, and Ernie was cursed. The moment was emblazoned on his memory, and even though he wasn't crazy now, he had those filthy pictures to contend with, a hideous open sore to keep looking at, reminding him of the one time he had been stupid enough to put his hand into a fire.

At first he had wanted to kill Baimbridge. Murder was wrong, and knowing it was wrong meant you were not insane when committing the act—he had read enough about sanity trials in murders to know that. He did not mind the thought of killing him, as long as it was not an insane act. There was no doubt in Ernie's mind that Baimbridge deserved to die. If an area was afflicted with some kind of plague and they found the pestilential rat, killing it was justified. It would be justifiable, and it would not be insane. But killing him would also be stupid. What kept him from doing it was that he recognized it would be stupid. The damage was done, the filth was there, and destroying the person who made it would not make it go away. There was nothing that would make it go away.

For a few days after that horrible, shattering conversation, he had tried getting drunk, but that only made it worse. The pictures became viler, and more naked, and he could hear sounds—terrible screaming, and his own breathing, hideous and loud, like an animal's. Thinking about it was bad enough, and dreaming—dreaming, he would wake up covered with sweat, and a rank odor choking his nostrils. Drinking burned his throat and made days and nights go slower, extending his torment, stretching out time on a rack.

He could not go to work. Kiiko would wonder why he was avoiding her, and he might see her, and he could not stand the thought of seeing her precious little face, and picturing her tiny body broken and violated the way Baimbridge wanted. Not Ernie wanted. Baimbridge wanted, because he was insane. He was more than insane. He was some kind of monster to wish something like that on Kiiko, to say it was inevitable because he wanted it to be inevitable. That was the only possible explanation. The man was some kind of a demon to think thoughts like that about a sweet fragile bud that he had never even seen, but wanted trampled. A man would have to be crazy to think something like that, but crazy was not enough. A man would have to be the Devil himself.

The Devil himself with sloppy lips and fat, stubby fingers, not at all the way everybody pictured him—sleek and dark, and almost handsome in an evil kind of way. The Devil was an Italian, a sleek bootlegger from Chicago with a thin mustache, not a sag-fleshed madman with slime and magnolias dripping from his mouth. Ernie could have stood up to an Italian, he did it all the time when he was a kid. If he had recognized Baimbridge in time, even though God despised Ernie and had abandoned him, He would have granted him the momentary use of God's own lightning to help strike down Satan. But it was too late, even for that. He had not penetrated the strange, deceptive disguise until it was too late. He had not seen in time to rip the evil out at its own evil source. To still the poison while it was in the poisoner's throat, before he spit it into Ernie's ears and shot it with a rattlesnake's tongue into the inner chambers of his brain.

The evil was there, it existed now in Ernie's mind, like filthy writing on a bathroom wall, only stupid children and perverts hadn't put it there: it was scrawled on the tabletop of a barroom, and scarred on his mind by the Devil himself, in the Devil's own words. Ernie remembered how Baimbridge had said it, although he couldn't remember clearly that part of what he had said. The evil . . . The evil men . . . The evil men think, stays, no, lives with them, that was it. The evil men think lives with them. Only it wasn't the evil Ernie thought. It was the evil Baimbridge thought, and said, so that Ernie would think about it all the time, the way he was doing. He knew why Baimbridge thought it: Baimbridge was corrupt, Baimbridge was vile, Baimbridge himself had said so, just as he admitted he was insane. But it still wasn't enough reason to say it. To think it, yes, but to say it? There was no reason to say it, unless he was the Devil himself.

Ernie was not religious no matter what Devil Baimbridge said. And he was not superstitious either, so evil spirits did not roam the earth casting spells, or doing mischief, the way he suspected they still did for his mother. So there was no reasonable explanation for Baimbridge's actions. For three days and nights Ernie lay in his room, trying to drive the dirty pictures from his brain, while searching his soul for a reason, a reasonable reason, why Baimbridge would have said what he did. He could find none. The only explanation had to be that he was the Devil.

He wondered why the Devil, who had so much more important work to do, would have singled him out for so much attention. But since Ernie was important enough to command so much personal revenge from God, as insignificant as he might be, the Devil would consider him a worthy target.

Weeping did no more good than drinking had done. Weeping made him feverish, and the heat only added to the blaze in his head. Praying he knew to be pointless. And cursing the Devil? Cursing the Devil was a waste of time.

So he just lay there, silent, running it over and over again in his mind, trying to blank out pictures with thoughts, only to find the thoughts giving way to the pictures. There was no way to escape, not from the evil, not from the curse, not into the mercy of God. God had no forgiveness, not for him. Men might have nothing against Ernie, but men were not powerful enough allies, not against the strength of Ernie's enemies.

It soothed him, in a curious way, knowing his foes to be so powerful. Men had never despised him. Men had never been his personal enemies, not even the Japanese. That God despised him, Ernie knew, and Ernie had learned to live with that fact long ago. Now, realizing that Baimbridge was the Devil afforded him a degree of relief. He had not understood why a mere man would choose him as a victim, and the thought that he could be hated by a mortal confused and baffled him. When he finally resolved that Baimbridge was the Devil, it gave him some small comfort.

It was true that Ernie had loathed Baimbridge, even before knowing who he really was. But there was nothing Ernie could have done, no earthly reason why Baimbridge, corrupt and vile as he was, would have it in for Ernie personally. Baimbridge, the man.

Ernie sat up in bed, his mind churning. Baimbridge as a man was corrupt and vile, yes. That he knew. Baimbridge as a human being had been destroyed by his own lechery. Lechery. Baimbridge was a man, who, if only a man, had still an extraordinary intelligence, a gift with honeyed words before the honey had turned rancid in the fat-lipped bowl. An intelligence, a career, that had been destroyed by the man's own act of venery. An impure lust that had ravished the life, the future, the fortunes of Baimbridge himself. Why, if a man's bestiality was so rank that it defiled himself, and his family, would he hesitate to strike out at Ernie? But why Ernie? Why Ernie, when the only thought of the man, the mere man, was lechery.

Kiiko. That was the explanation. Baimbridge was so ravaged by his own sated desires, he wanted Kiiko. Ernie had gotten drunk, like a stupid fool, and had told him about Kiiko. How beautiful she was, how frail, how different. And that got Baimbridge excited. It wasn't the way Baimbridge said at all. It wasn't Ernie who wanted Kiiko, it was Baimbridge. The pig was so bored with sensations, he wanted something new, something fresh, and different, like a rare flower floating on a silent pond. Like Kiiko. Only Ernie had stood in the way. He knew that, Baimbridge knew that, like a stupid fool Ernie had told him how he watched her, protected her. So even though he was bursting with greedy appetite, Baimbridge wouldn't dare go near her as long as Ernie was in the way, because he knew Ernie would kill him. Ernie would kill him before he could lay a fat finger on her.

And that was why Baimbridge said what he did. He had tried to frighten Ernie, make him stay away from her—making him think he had bad thoughts about her. And then Baimbridge would have a clear field. And like a fool, Ernie had let himself be frightened. He had fallen right into the trap. Now Baimbridge would only have to stand there, waiting outside the UN, recognize her from Ernie's description, and follow her home. And there was no one waiting in the hall to save her. No one to warn her what he wanted to do. What Baimbridge wanted to do. Not Ernie. Baimbridge.

Ernie got to his feet, his mind racing. The clock on the dresser said five-thirty, but he hadn't wound it for days. He held it to his ear. It was going. There was no way he could make it be before five-thirty; she would have already left work, on her way home. Maybe he was waiting for her now, in the hallway. Maybe he had followed her home yesterday or the day before when Ernie was being such a damned fool, lying there—figuring out that Baimbridge was the Devil, when he was only a man. The filthiest man in the world.

He dressed without breathing, hoping that she would go somewhere right after work, maybe out with that nice Oriental boy who never came near her, or to dinner with one of the girls. Or even to the hospital, to see that punk kid, now that he couldn't do her any harm. Anywhere, as long as she wasn't going home, with Baimbridge waiting for her. He had to be there in time. Ernie had to be there in time.

Quite without realizing it, as he pulled on his clothes, Ernie prayed. He prayed with his mind, and he prayed with his lips, and in the moment before he left the room, he prayed with his hands, that it would not be too late.

"Please, God," he whispered, and then heard what he was saying.

When the door to his bedroom flew open, the syncopated clock was announcing the finish of the Early Show.

"Oh my God," Ernie's mother said, and jumped up from her chair, pushing in the sound button, switching off the set. But it was too late. He was pulling his coat from the hall closet hanger and running to the door.

"Ernie!"

"I can't talk to you now, Ma. I've got to get there."

"Get where? Why are you going, Ernie? Did you think I was watching TV? Is that why it's all right to go?"

"Please, Ma."

"You going to see that girl?"

"I'll call you later."

"But Ernie, I wasn't even watching. I just switched it on for a second to see if it was still running, that's all."

"I have no time, Ma. I have no time."

"Ernie. Look at me, Ernie. I'm going back to the oak chest, watching the wall. Do you see, Ernie? I'm watching the wall."

He opened the door to the hallway. "Do what you want to, Ma. After I'm gone maybe you can look at television."

"I won't watch!" she shouted. "You see? I won't watch. I can't do anything but look at the wall. Would you leave a mother like that, Ernie? Would you just walk out when your own mother is going crazy, looking at the wall? Ernie . . . *Ernie!*"

But he was gone, running down the hallway. She could hear his footsteps sounding in the corridor. And then she heard the slam of the big front door.

For a moment she sat there, her heart beating so fast she was sure she was having an attack, exactly like the woman upstairs who said it felt like a million butterflies beating their wings against her chest, breaking it open from the inside, so she couldn't breathe. She was always describing her symptoms like that, in very poetic language, like Dr. Kildare, so Ernie's mother didn't mind listening, only she didn't take it too seriously. She had been very surprised when the woman had suddenly died, probably because nobody paid any attention. So she sat now, waiting to die unexpectedly, like the woman upstairs, tears flowing down her cheeks at the thought of her neglected grave, where Ernie would not even bother coming with flowers because he was so busy chasing around after that Chink.

She waited for a few moments, but she did not die. And grief for her death melded into anger. When she was good and sure she was not dying, and good and mad, she went to the phone.

"Hello?"

"Is that you, Maureen?"

"Why are you shouting? Before you whisper, now you shout. Why don't you learn to talk like a person?"

"Why don't you learn to keep your big mouth shut, Maureen?"

Ernie's mother said. "If you don't know what the hell you're talking about, why don't you learn to keep your Big Mouth *shut!*"

The hotel where the Hernans had registered was no longer one of New York's first hotels, as it had been in the hurried refugee days of the Thirties, when wealthy Europeans on their way to anywhere else had congregated there. The walls were slightly dingy, and the furniture had none of the smarter reproduction-antique air of the new hotels farther uptown on Park Avenue. But the rooms were still spacious enough to suit Karl Hernan. And it felt familiar, like an old friend who had become a little seedy, but made you feel more welcome than strangers with newer clothes. Such things were becoming increasingly important to Karl, now that he was growing older. Not older, he thought, sitting in the big wing chair in the living room of his suite. Old. It shows. I feel it, and it shows.

It showed to Ursull, too. He could see that, the moment she walked into the room behind Frieda. She ran to him, his beautiful, wonderful child, ran to him as she had always done after long separation, when he didn't have the courage to keep her arm's length away. She ran to him and hugged him like the child she wasn't any longer, as if he were the young man he hadn't been since long before she was born. But he could tell she knew. She knew he was old. She could tell whatever fight had been left in him, by some miracle left in him, was gone.

But that wasn't why she was crying. She wasn't crying because he was old. He looked over at Frieda, his black eyes questioning above the dark head of his child. Frieda nodded. She had told her. The child knew, and that was why she wept. His hand touched wearily on the silky dark crown of Ursull's hair, all she had of him, except the eyes, and the shame.

"Your mother told you?" Karl said softly.

Ursull nodded.

"I'm sorry," he said.

Ursull raised her head, and looked into his face, with her great black eyes. An Indian's eyes, they had always said in Buenos Aires. Quick, alive, searching and laughing. He looked at them now and felt, with great sorrow, that they would never again look other than sad. Sad they would be, from now on. He had taken the joy out of them.

"I'm sorry," he said again.

"Oh Papa, why? Why are you sorry? Are you sorry you're my father, is that it? Would I be alive if you were not my father?"

"I don't know," he said, and tried to smile. "It's an interesting question." He touched her chin, and tried to lift the laughter back into her eyes. But it was gone. "Will you forgive me?"

"For what? For being a Jew?"

"That is the worst of it. I'm not sure for what. For not telling you? Is that what I mean? Will you forgive me for not telling you?"

"Why?" she said. "Why didn't you tell me? Were you so ashamed? That's what I have to try to understand. Is it so terrible being a Jew, that I should be ashamed?"

"I was proud," he said. "My father raised me to be proud. My father was a brilliant man, who gloried in his Judaism like he gloried in life, and books, and science. He was a great scholar, your grandfather. Judah Hermann. A great scholar, a great teacher, a scientist. But you couldn't know that. It was one of the things you could never know, who your grandfather was, because that would tell you who I was—who I had been. And then you would know who you were. And what you were."

"But if you were proud, why would I have been ashamed?"

"You don't understand." Karl shook his head. "I don't even understand, still, to this day. All my life I was proud. And then suddenly, I was afraid. It is very confusing, even to an older person, even to a man thirty years old, as I was, so I know how confusing it must be to you.

"I had a very successful business. I had your mother. The most beautiful woman I had ever seen, anywhere. She kept house for me as a Jewish wife, because she enjoyed my pride. She shared my pleasure. We had one of the most beautiful homes in Germany. The people we entertained, our friends, our good friends, were not Jews or Gentiles. They were Germans. As we were German.

"When it started happening, this madness, we were sure there was some mistake. He means the Poles, we were sure. When he speaks of destroying the Polish Jews, that is one thing. But surely he doesn't mean us. We are Germans. Yes, are also Jews, but we are Germans. He doesn't mean us, we said. All right, he means the Poles."

Ursull looked at him emptily. "Why was it all right? Why was it all right to kill the Poles?"

"It wasn't all right," Karl said. "Of course it wasn't all right. But we were Germans! The best of us and the worst of us were Germans. There is a pride, a history, a heritage in Germans . . ."

"A bigotry?"

"Yes," he said angrily. "Yes, there is, yes, there was, yes, there will always be. It is wrong, but it exists. It is a fact of human nature, like any fact. An ugly fact, but a fact. Still, today, after everything that happened."

"In Germany," she said.

"Yes Germany. And in other countries. All countries look to the East with contempt. The European Jew in Israel despises the Oriental Jew. They don't want to let them in."

"I don't believe you."

"Fine. You don't believe me. I shall send you sometime, you will see for yourself. I despise it in other people, and I despise it in myself, but it exists. I had to come to see that for myself. I had to learn to live with it, because—because otherwise I would have died. We would have all died. I. Your mother. You would never have been born."

"Even though I was German, and not a Pole?"

"Even though you were German. Hermann was a proud and honored name. Hermann was a fortune for Hitler to confiscate. We didn't believe it was happening, but we had to believe it, because they were rounding them up like cattle. Us, like cattle.

"I had some friends, some good friends, Gentile bankers in Switzerland who got my money out of the country before it was too late. A great stonecutter, Caarlin, from Holland, came to my home and used our basement as a workroom for weeks, taking your mother's important jewels and resetting them into decorations on a gaudy little music box, filling it with chocolates and taking it home as a gift to his child."

"He must have been a very good friend," Ursull said.

"He was. He was also a very ambitious friend. I paid him one hundred thousand dollars."

"Was it so important? The jewelry?"

"Of course. Everything was important, because everything was a fantasy. Do you see? Until the last moment, we thought it was a fantasy, a mistake, a terrible mistake. Any moment someone would turn around and admit that there had been some confusion, they hadn't meant us."

"And?"

"They were gone. They were almost all gone. All my friends who had also been sure it was a mistake. They were almost all gone. I waited until 1938, December of 1938, and by then everyone I loved and valued and trusted had disappeared. Where? Why? We still couldn't understand. And even when that crazy man admitted it was a mistake, it would be too late for them."

"And why didn't they come for you?"

"He was smart, the madman. He let me know I was quite right, they didn't mean me, and I was welcome. I was most welcome, only I shouldn't let anyone know he said so."

"Why you?"

"He wanted my money. Many millions in cash. Many millions more in jewelry. Frieda was wearing magnificent imitations Caarlin had made, and they had no idea the jewels were out of the country. Or the money. As I said, he was smart. Only I was smarter. I didn't want to believe in my soul that he meant us, but my pocketbook had known, as early as 1934. It was almost all out of the country by the time he started confiscating. Only *we* were still in Germany, not believing. We were still there, going places, your beautiful mother glorious even in her imitation jewels.

"But soon we realized there was not anywhere we wanted to go. Not in Germany. Our friends were gone, the people we had loved were gone, the things we loved. Only Germany still existed. And we didn't love it anymore. We couldn't, even though we were Germans. So we escaped."

"That easily?"

"Nothing was easy. But it was done. The heart of the world was not as soft as they say, but it was not so hard, either. And the people who did not mean well, at least meant business. They could be bought. Especially when there was a fortune in Switzerland.

"So we escaped. We escaped to Portugal, and then to Canada, and then, briefly, we were here, in this hotel. People we had known only slightly were our dearest friends. People we hadn't liked were our brothers. And then, soon, we couldn't look at each other. None of us. When it became known, how much had happened, exactly what had happened, to what extent, we didn't want to see anyone who knew. Why us? What was so special about us, that we had been spared? And soon, that became our shame. Shame added to shame.

"When we went to Argentina, Hermann became Hernan. A good South American name, yes? It was an easy matter with the passports. An official looking at a passport could easily make an error in copying, especially for money."

"But why?" Ursull said. "Why were you still afraid?"

"I don't know. When you are used to fear, it follows you. It feeds on itself, and produces more fear. And soon it seems more reasonable to hide than to expose."

"Expose what? What had you done?"

"I don't know. I had been a Jew, and been proud of it, only to have the world, the world I respected, tell me it was a reason for shame. When you are told you ought to be ashamed, and the people who tell you you ought to be ashamed are the ones in power, you begin questioning your own values. Are you the one who is wrong? Can it be possible they are right? Is there something to be ashamed of?"

"Is there?" Ursull's eyes filled with tears. "Is there, Papa?"

"No."

"Then why?"

"Perhaps I was ashamed for having lived, when so many, so many better than me, had died." He looked into his hands, and studied them as though they contained a great puzzle. "I'm not sure. Toward the end of the war, when so many Nazis fled Germany to where we were, we were afraid again. Perhaps it is not really over, we said. Perhaps it is only a temporary defeat, and they will spring up anew, even here. Why not in Argentina? It happened in Germany, and there, we were Germans. Here we are refugees, not only Jews.

"When you were born, we were happy again, for the first time. We thought we could build a future for you, like the one the world had destroyed for us. We wanted that future to be as easy as possible. So we decided there was no need to tell you. You were so beautiful, so perfect, so obedient . . . There was never a child like you. We wanted to shield you from everything, especially pain."

"And what have you done? Papa, why are you doing this to me now? Why are you telling me now?"

"You have to know."

"For twenty years you keep this . . . secret, as though it were something hideous, something shameful. Telling no one . . ."

"Almadon knew. A few close friends knew."

"But why do you tell me now? I'm not ashamed. Truly I'm not. I'm confused, because I feel it must have been something dreadful, to be hidden so, yes, I admit that, I am confused. But I'm not ashamed. Only why do you tell it to me now?"

Karl turned his eyes away from his daughter's face. He reached for the drink beside his chair. The ice had melted, and it was a pale sickly yellow. There was nothing to grasp, nothing to reach for, and he needed to take hold of something. Gently he pressed his daughter away from the front of the chair and got to his feet, stretching his tall, tired frame. He went and stood by the window, looking down at the city, the dim candle-bulb from the sconce on the wall casting an amber glow on the white hair at his temple.

Frieda, seeing how old he seemed, how old, and how defeated, came and stood beside him. They did not look at each other.

"Answer me, Papa!" Ursull said. "Answer me."

"I have answered everything I can," he said. "Even what I don't know. Even what I didn't understand myself, I have answered. There is no need for me to answer something you know the answer to as well as I."

"But you're wrong. Don't you see that? You're wrong! What you're thinking is a mistake, Papa. I won't say it, you have to say it, because I couldn't think something like that, not even out of fear. You say it, Papa, so I can tell you how wrong you are. Please. Please. You say it."

"I don't have to," Karl Hernan said, and took his wife's hand. "You answer it yourself, by being afraid."

"It isn't true," Ursull said softly, tears welling in her eyes. "It isn't true, no matter what you think. Gerd isn't like that. He isn't like that at all. It wouldn't make any difference. He loves me, Papa. He loves me, and I love him. It won't make any difference, don't you understand that?"

"I understand," Karl said softly. "This, this one thing, I see very clearly. It is for you to see clearly. For you."

"Gerd is a man. Gerd is a man who loves me. That's all that matters to me, and to him. Gerd loves me."

"Yes," Karl said. "I'm sure he does. He loves Ursull Hernan. But how would he feel about Ursull Hermann? The son of Otto Kraben, and the granddaughter of Judah Hermann. Wouldn't that be a cause for celebration in the Kraben household. In the pure Aryan air of the Kraben country estates. In the clear-blood fortress of Kraben chemicals."

"Then why do I have to tell him? Why does he have to know?"

They turned, both of them, and looked mutely at their daughter. And the pain on their faces seared the tears from hers.

"I didn't mean it," she said. "I swear, I didn't mean it."

"Don't be ashamed," her father said.

"But I didn't mean it. I only said it."

"And if you did mean it?" Frieda said. "What would be so terrible if you *did* mean it? Why shouldn't you think like that, after what we did? What would be wrong about your thinking you shouldn't tell the man you want to marry, when we didn't tell our own child?"

"Do you hear?" Karl said. "Do you understand what your mother is saying?"

"Yes," Ursull said.

"Only now, I will tell you. Now I have to tell you, because you said what you had to say." Her father drew a deep breath, and came toward her. "If you didn't tell him, so what? What would be the harm? To him, nothing. It's a stupid idea, and even if he did believe it, he's wrong. So to him, there is no harm. But to you? To your children? Could you live there, not with a lie, but with an unspoken truth you are terrified someone will discover? Could you raise your children, as I have raised you, in silence? To have them discover, as you did?

"And if someone did find out—there are ways of finding out you know, such things never disappear—how would it be? Then it would not be an unspoken truth. It would be a lie. It would seem to him, always, a lie. He would despise you, perhaps not for being a Jew, but for being a liar.

"A liar. A Jewish liar. In Germany. Could you risk it? In a Germany where no sane Jew could want to live and raise children, because the same thing might happen again."

"It couldn't," Ursull said. "It couldn't happen."

"Of course not," Karl said. "That's what we said thirty years ago."

Ursull was silent.

"But it might not take so long for him to find out, your wonderful fiancé that you wish to shield so. It might not be a husband who one day looks at you with hate. Perhaps it would happen at your wedding. They intend to come to your wedding, your in-laws-to-be?"

Ursull nodded.

"Then perhaps it might happen there. I would be expected to entertain them, these Krabens, yes? Perhaps I will not be allowed to visit with my grandchildren in Germany because someone might recognize me, but at the wedding, I could not hide from these people in my own home."

"Please. Papa . . ."

"Are you sure we don't know each other? We were both businessmen, successful businessmen in Germany at the same time. Is it not possible, have you considered that it is perhaps possible that there was a time we socialized together in the good old days? That perhaps, indeed, we were close associates?"

"Were you?" Ursull asked.

"No." Karl shook his head. "No, I'm afraid not. You see, Otto Kraben despised Jews long before Hitler made it popular."

Ursull stared numbly into her lap.

"Get up, darling," Frieda said. "Get up, and wash your face, and we will go some place for dinner. It's enough, all this talk. You are still our daughter, and we are still your parents. There should be joy between us, even when we have sad things to do. Come. We'll go somewhere and dine."

"What time is it?"

Karl looked at his watch. "Nine o'clock."

"I won't be able to stay long," Ursull said. "I hope you'll forgive me, but there was no way I could know you were coming, and I have to be back at the apartment at ten." She looked up at them, a slight smile on her lips. "You see, Gerd is expecting to see me, and I wouldn't want him to be disappointed. He becomes disappointed so easily, he is like a child, you'll love that about him. But he isn't a child at all, you see. He is a man. A strong, wonderful man. I'd like you to meet him tomorrow. He's sure to be very anxious to meet you, and I know how much you'll enjoy meeting him. But tonight I will see him alone."

"Ursull . . ." Frieda held out her hand.

Ursull pushed it away. "Don't pamper me so. Stop trying to protect me. I don't need to be protected. Nothing's going to hurt me. There's no reason to defend me, when nothing can go wrong. You've protected me for all the wrong reasons, and now there's no reason at all. You see, everything will be exactly as it was. He loves me. He's a stubborn man. This is going to make no difference at all."

Ernie stood behind the break in the wall, the hiding place, the guarding place he had had for so long, and had abandoned like a fool. Like a prissy, weak-kneed fool, just the way Baimbridge had wanted, so he could wait for her, Baimbridge could wait for her, like the horned goat satyr he was. Well, he couldn't fool Ernie. Not anymore.

Kiiko hadn't been home when he got there. He knew she couldn't be home, not even taking a shower, because he rapped so loud on her door a man downstairs had started yelling, asking what the hell the racket was all about. Ernie slipped back into his personal shadows, the shadows Baimbridge had tried to appropriate. There wasn't any point in leaving, Ernie could see that. To begin with, the man downstairs might leave his door open, curious to see who it was, and it was no business of his. It was Kiiko's business, and his business, and nobody else's business at all, especially not Baimbridge who had tried to make it his business.

So Ernie just waited. He didn't care anymore who she was with: one of the girls or even one of the boys who might not be so nice with her. There was no reason to fear any of them.

He had no idea how long he had been standing there. When he heard the footsteps start up the stairs, he pressed himself back against the wall. But the footsteps were hers, only Kiiko's. There was no one with her. And standing as he was, hugging the wall, he realized he might frighten her. She might not understand, if he were to speak to her from the shadows.

He eased himself away, and stepped out into the corridor. But that was stupid. He intended to explain to her why he had come, how important it was that she be careful, but it might strike her as odd, his just standing there. He moved back and forth, seesawing on his own indecision. When her head appeared at the top of the stairs, he was, at that moment, veering back into shadow. So he held himself there, for a moment longer, so she wouldn't be too startled.

"Kiiko?" he whispered, as her key turned in the lock, stepping forward in the hallway.

She jumped as though someone had struck her. "Oh Ernie," she said, a moment later, after she had caught her breath, after the trembling hand had come away from her tiny bosom. "I didn't see anyone. I must have been thinking about something else. I didn't even see you."

"I'm sorry," he said. "I'm so sorry. I didn't mean to frighten you. You know that, don't you? I wouldn't do anything to frighten you."

"Don't apologize, Ernie. I was dreaming, that's all. I just didn't see you. It isn't as if you were hiding."

"No," he said.

He stood facing her awkwardly for a moment, looking at the key in the lock. But she made no move to open the door.

"Kiiko. May I come in?"

"I'm happy to see you Ernie, I was worried about you. We haven't seen you for many days. Have you been ill?"

"Don't worry about me," he said. "I'm fine." He looked again at the door, and then at her. "Can I talk to you?"

"I am happy to see you," Kiiko said again. "But can't it wait? You are coming to work tomorrow, aren't you, and it's late."

"It can't wait. I have to talk to you about something. Please."

A faint blush spread up her cheeks, and she smiled. "I feel so foolish. I am embarrassed, really, but I can tell you. I promised my father I wouldn't let men inside my apartment. It's the one condition he insisted upon when I told him I wanted to live by myself. Do you think that's terribly old-fashioned?"

"I think it's fine," Ernie said. "I think it's just fine." His palms were sweating. "You're right to stand by the promises you make your father." He was beginning to feel a little sick to his stomach, and he wanted her to do something, send him away if she was going to, anything but just stand there, looking at him like that, with so much trust in her eyes, not knowing he had betrayed her to Baimbridge. "It's important, but a promise is a promise . . ." He started to move past her, toward the stairs.

"Ah, but this is foolish. Why shouldn't you come inside? He could not object to you."

He followed her, and watched her switch on the light, too bright and glaring for the obvious cheapness of the small bed-sitting room. She had done her best with small Japanese paper lamps on the bulbs, and pathetic little garden decorations to disguise the sleazy run-down furnishings, but it had not done very much good. There was a basin right by the bed, with a mirrored cabinet over it, like in a cheap hotel room. A slatted wooden draw curtain hung like a window shade over what was probably the kitchen area, and beyond the beat-up chairs in the corner, with the gay little pillows she had thrown on them to no avail, he could see a door ajar with a toilet, and the corner of a tub. Not even a shower. An old-fashioned tub, with the sink in the living room. It wasn't the place for a Princess, and he hated it. For a moment, he hated her for putting up with it.

"Shall I take your coat?"

"All right," Ernie said. "Don't hang it up or anything, though. Just throw it on the bed."

"Then where will we sit?" Kiiko said, pleasantly. "The chairs are only there because the landlord refused to have them moved. But they are terrible. The springs come up and stab you in very unfortunate places." She went to the small closet and hung his coat with her own. "It is wrong, I suppose, to say they are there for show, they are so ugly, but they are certainly not there for sitting."

"It's a nice place. You've fixed it up very cute."

"I wish so," Kiiko said. "In the beginning, when I moved here, I kept making oaths to change things, buy material and recover the chairs. Make curtains for my only window. But everything is so expensive, and I will be here such a short time. It didn't seem to pay, really."

"It looks just fine," Ernie said. "Just fine."

"Besides, I thought, what does it matter, since I have promised my father not to have anyone in, who will see but me? So I suppose I could say, excuse me, but I was not expecting company." She smiled at him warmly, and he looked away. "Please, Ernie. Sit down. If you don't want to sit on the bed, there's a quite comfortable stool there, by the desk. Unless you don't like low places. We are used to sitting low."

"Where do you want to sit?"

"Oh, it doesn't matter. Any place. First, though, I will make some tea. You would like some tea, wouldn't you? It is the least I can offer of traditional Japanese hospitality to my first visitor."

"Ever?" he asked, as she drew up the slatted blind. It was, as he suspected, a kitchen. But not really. It was hardly more than a hole in the wall: a short, half-refrigerator with four burners on top stood on the right with a small oven on the wall above. There was an old, square sink, with a cupboard underneath, and a glass closet just above her eyes with a few old plates and cups and saucers. Not even a draining board, or a place to dry the dishes. She was so meticulous, it pained him to think of her without room to clean and cook and lay out all the food she probably loved to prepare. "Nobody's ever been here but me?"

"Only some of the girls," Kiiko said. "Bo, Birgitta . . . do you know her?"

"Yes," Ernie said. "Vaguely."

"And Ursull, once. You know Ursull. You rescued her one day from a rash intruder." Kiiko smiled as she filled the small metal teapot with water. "Do you remember?"

Ernie shook his head. He could remember nothing, except what Baimbridge said.

"She certainly remembers you. She regards you as a hero."

"And you?" he said.

"I think of you as my very dear friend."

"But not a man," Ernie said.

"A man?"

"You said your father made you promise not to let any men come in here. And then you said it was all right, because it wasn't the same with me."

"Oh, but, Ernie. I did not say that at all. I said only he could not object to you."

"Because I'm not a man. I'm a joke. You say that girl regards me as a hero, and then you laugh."

"I didn't laugh." She looked at him, puzzled. "I only smiled. I smiled not from mockery, but because you are my friend. It pleases me that she regards you as a hero."

"But you don't," he said. "I see."

"Why are you angry, Ernie? What did I say to make you angry?"

"Why'd you let me come inside!"

"You asked. You said it was important. I've been worried about you, Ernie. I haven't seen you for many days. I thought something was wrong. Something is wrong, isn't it? Tell me, Ernie. Did you come here because something is wrong?"

"Why'd you disobey your father? Because you thought he wouldn't know, is that it? Because you thought he wouldn't find out, so it was all right to go against your promise. Doesn't your promise mean anything?" He got up from the bed and started toward her. "What kind of a girl are you, that your promise means nothing?"

"You're angry with me because I did what you wanted? Because I let you come in?"

"I said I wanted it," Ernie said. "You didn't have to believe me. You don't know me. You don't really know me. You don't even know what kind of a man I am."

"I do, Ernie. I do know." Her voice was soft, and soothing, like a breeze on a still, shallow pond, but her eyes were frightened.

He did not hear the voice. He saw only the fear coming into her eyes, and he moved toward it. "You don't know what any man is. There are men around who reek of vile corruption, who stink from it, did you know that? Men who walk around, living right with us, eating lunch with us, walking around free, just waiting. Just waiting for someone like you, so they can hurt, and destroy. You didn't know that, did you? Your father knew it, that's why he made you promise. Why didn't you listen to him?"

"You better go, Ernie," Kiiko said.

"Your father cares about you. Your father loves you. But other people don't. Other people don't love you. Baimbridge doesn't love you. He wants you, he wants to do dirty things to you, but he doesn't love you."

"Baimbridge?" Kiiko said, moving slowly toward the door. "I don't know any man named Baimbridge."

"Oh yes you do. Maybe you haven't met him yet. Maybe you've seen him, only you don't know he's Baimbridge. But he knows you. He knows you, and he wants you. You mustn't let him. You mustn't let him near you."

"All right, Ernie. Whatever you say." She was edging away from him, slowly, along the wall. "I won't have anything to do with him, I promise. Only you better go now."

"What?" Ernie said, his forehead contorted, his eyes not even seeing her face. Just her body. Her tiny fragile body, moving along the wall like a shadow. A spun-glass shadow, that could be shattered in an instant. "What did you say?"

"You better go."

"What did you say about Baimbridge?"

"I said I wouldn't have anything to do with him."

"Nothing? He'll break you, you know. He'll smash you into tiny pieces. He doesn't care about you at all. Not like some people."

"I won't have anything to do with him. I promise."

"You *what?*" He seized her by her small, trembling shoulders. It was like holding a puppy. A quivering tiny puppy. A wave of strength he didn't know existed swept through him, and he pressed her forward, lifting her half off the ground as easily as he would a little bitch puppy.

"I promise," Kiiko said, tears springing to her eyes. "Please, Ernie, I promise. Let me go, please."

"You *promise?* What does it mean, your promise. You promised your father, and you broke your word to him. Why would you keep faith with me? Your father loves you and you didn't care about him. And I . . ." His hand slipped and brushed her breast. He stared at it for a moment, cupping his hand over the perfect miniature roundness, pressing it into his palm. "And I love you," he said, dazedly, "I love you."

"Ernie, please . . ."

His left hand moved behind her back, pressing her forward, closer to him, while his right hand crushed against the yielding mound, as if he would make its impression in the palm of his hand. "I love you," he said, unable to get it deep enough inside his own flesh. He started pulling at the thin cloth of her dress.

"Ernie, let me go. I beg you. Please let me go."

"But it isn't the same thing," he panted. "It isn't the same thing he said at all. I love you, don't you see? That's the difference. It isn't like he said, like it would be with him." He was clawing at her, tearing the dress away from her shoulders, ripping it down toward her belly. And then he saw her breast, saw it clearly, as he had that night in the hall, and the same excitement rushed through him, the same incredible excitement, only it wasn't Teddy close to it now. It wasn't some punk kid rubbing his nose in the paleness of it, some animal Baimbridge who didn't care whose it was, as long as it was new.

She was sobbing. He could hear she was sobbing. Hitting at him with pathetic little jabs because she didn't understand. It didn't matter if she didn't understand. Later he could explain to her. Later he could tell her how it was, how much he loved her, how they could be together always but this was something that had to happen. It had to happen, Baimbridge said it, it had to happen, only he had said it because he wanted her, so he wanted to make Ernie crazy. But Ernie wasn't crazy. She belonged to him. He had to make her belong to him.

"Ernie . . . don't you understand? I can't. Please Ernie, I can't . . . There's something . . ."

He put his hand over her mouth as he fell on top of her, tearing at his own trousers. She struggled against him, uselessly. He wanted to tell her that, that it was useless, but she just lay there whipping around beneath his half-naked thighs. He didn't have time to explain. Her eyes were round with terror, and he couldn't stand looking at them. It was dumb—leaving the light on; he didn't want to see how afraid she was; but he couldn't get up to turn it off or she might start screaming, and he couldn't stand that. He turned her over on her stomach, quickly, as easily as he would a little rag doll, without ever taking his hand from her mouth. And with his free hand, he ripped away her silken panties.

He lay for a trembling moment, as she was, cushioning his fiery center against the soft gentle hill of her buttocks. And then he moved. He could hear the gasp in her throat, even though the scream would not come free in his hand, and he was angry with her. Why was she trying to scream? He loved her, she knew that, he told her he loved her, he had been through all kinds of hell for her, and soon, if she would only stop resisting, soon the last remaining hell, the one he had to go through, would be over, if only she would stop resisting. He pressed against her, harder, upwards, an angry arc; but still she would not yield. Not even a little. He despised her for making it so hard for him when he loved her so.

He pressed again, more insistent now, passion mixing with fury. If only she would do what Baimbridge had said. It was inevitable. It was inevitable. Why did she go on fighting? He had no compassion for her now, not at this moment when she was making it so hard for him, and compassion gone, he thrust with cold unfeeling anger, and found her. She made a terrible sound, deep in her chest, and he could feel it vibrate through his belly. But he didn't care. Not anymore. He had found what he was seeking. He was free.

She had stopped fighting. Now when it was too late, when it was over, she had given up the battle. She lay silent underneath him, not even trembling now. Not even moving at all.

"Kiiko," he said. "You see? Now everything is all right."

She didn't answer. She was angry with him, so she wouldn't answer, and he understood. He understood it fine: she hadn't understood what he was doing, that he was doing what he had to do. But now there would be time to explain. Now he could make her understand, and she would forgive him.

"Kiiko," he said again, and took the palm that had so cruelly caressed her mouth because that was the only choice he had until now, and stroked the perfect little chin. "Kiiko, please. I know you're angry with me, but I'll explain. It'll take a long time, but we have time now. I'll explain." His fingers rubbed along the line of her jaw, and touched her lips. Her mouth was hanging open, slack, and a tiny string of saliva dribbled into his hand.

"Kiiko, please. Don't try to scare me. I know I scared you, but I can explain about that. Please don't do this. I'll explain." He drew back, suddenly, and sat back on his haunches, his fingers tracing over the smooth line of her back, and trailing the golden hills. She was just trying to frighten him. That was all. He wasn't going to be a fool, and actually become frightened. Then Ernie looked down. Beneath her open, oddly relaxed thighs, there was a small pool of blood.

Ernie felt a salt clump of fear in his throat. But virgins bled. Of course. Virgins bled the first time. Eileen had bled like a pig, and he hadn't even done it hard to her. He was stupid to think it was anything more than that.

He got to his feet and went over to the basin, washing his hands, drying them on the tail of his shirt before he closed his trousers. He would be presentable, now, when he approached her. From now on, everything would be presentable, a fine proper courtship, now that he had done what he had to do. He would not even come near her with the intimacy of being partly undressed. Not unless she wanted. Until she wanted.

"Kiiko," he said, kneeling by her unmoving head. "Kiiko, please. You can stop now. I'll leave you alone. Please. Look at me."

She didn't move. He leaned over, and pressed his ear close to her mouth. He could hear her breathing. Strange, choking little sounds, like bubbles from a baby. Slowly, gently, he turned her over. His eyes moved over her face, lovely as he had imagined it would be in sleep, except for her lips hanging open, not prettily. Not prettily at all. A steady stream of saliva oozed from the left side of her mouth. He wiped at it paternally with a corner of her torn slip.

And then he looked at her body. A great bruise spread like a darkening stain upwards to her pelvis, from the strange triangle at the juncture of her hips . . . And then he noticed what it was that seemed so strange. It was not a woman's triangle at all, but a child's. The smooth, gentle slope of a child's uncluttered hill. A child, not yet a woman. A child, not ever a woman.

"Oh God," Ernie murmured, tears catching in his throat. "Oh Jesus God, what have I done?"

He got to his feet and backed away, his eyes brimming over with horror and shame. But there was no place to go. The ugly chairs and walls were behind him, and he stumbled, trapped. In front of him, there was a door, but between the door and where he stood now, lay Kiiko. And he could not pass her. If he passed her, he might look, and he could not bear to see again what he wished he had never seen at all.

There was only one window. The one Kiiko had wanted to make curtains for, but never had. It didn't matter really. The window was not important to the room. It let in no light, and gave no view of loveliness below. Only a five-story drop into an ugly alleyway, cluttered with stray cats and garbage cans. The window wasn't important. It wasn't even very wide.

But it was wide enough for Ernie. More than wide enough.

XVII

FOR several days a pall had settled on the Guides' Lounge. Pauline thought the explanation quite simple: the liveliest of the girls were depressed and disturbed about Kiiko, the quietest ones almost noisy in comparison to Bo and Birgitta. Only Rehahnee, who was wearing a large, conspicuously new and expensive jewel in her nose, buzzed around as usual, giving extraordinary attention to her makeup and clothes. Ursull, who for the past few months had appeared quite animated, had slipped back into an air of preoccupied silence. The supervisor was tempted to speak to her about it: Ursull was by far the most competent of the guides, and that she should be spending so much time after work visiting the hospital was affecting not only her personal attitude, which was none of Pauline's business, but her work, which was. As much affection as she allowed herself to feel for any of her charges, Pauline felt for Ursull; and the unremitting program of work and hospital attendance at Kiiko's bedside were obviously hurting the girl.

"Ursull," Pauline said. "May I speak to you for a moment?"

"Of course," Ursull said listlessly, coming into the glassed-in cubicle from which Pauline conducted her supervision.

"Sit down." She smiled, but the girl did not look up to see the smile. She just lowered herself into the straight-backed chair, correctly, obediently.

"Ursull, it seems to me you've been looking very tired these past few days."

"Yes?"

"I wonder if, perhaps, you haven't been overdoing it. You've been putting in a very long day here, and then the hospital at night . . ."

"Somebody has to stay with Kiiko," Ursull said. "She's had a very bad time."

"I appreciate that, we all understand that. And I'm sure Kiiko is grateful for your concern. But she does have very competent medical attention, you know, and the other girls have been spending time with her, haven't they? Luanna, and Birgitta . . . ?"

"Birgitta has a life of her own," Ursull said. "Birgitta is very—involved. She has a young man."

"I know, Ursull, but don't you, too? I don't mean to pry, but I understood you were seeing someone quite regularly."

Ursull looked away. "I explained to him. I explained to him about Kiiko. He understands that I must spend time with her."

"All the time?" Pauline asked. "All the time you have?"

"My parents are in New York. I must see them, too, when I can. But they also understand about my friend."

Pauline sat down and raised her glasses onto her forehead. "Forgive me, Ursull. I know you are fond of Kiiko, as we all are, but I never noticed you were particularly close. Certainly not so close as to command this inordinate loyalty."

"In times of crisis, relationships sometimes become more important than you have realized."

"I'm aware of that," Pauline said. "But we have to be careful at these times that we don't try to make the other person's crisis our own."

Ursull looked up. "I appreciate your talking to me, Miss Winston, but if you don't mind, as you have said yourself on many occasions, you are our supervisor, not a housemother."

"All right," Pauline said, annoyed with having left herself open to an attack. "All right, Ursull, but . . ."

The phone rang in the Lounge, and Pauline saw Marie Claire waving.

"Yes?" Pauline said, through the glass window.

"It's for Ursull. Tell her it's Gerd."

"Please," Ursull whispered to Pauline. "Tell him I am out on tour."

"Tell him yourself," Pauline said. "I'm not a housemother."

Ursull's cheeks reddened. "I'm sorry. I didn't mean to sound so rude."

"Why don't you take the afternoon off?" Pauline said. "Why don't you ask him to take you somewhere?"

"No, please, I . . ."

"Ursull," she said gently. "Don't make it so hard on yourself. Take the day off. See him."

Ursull smiled wryly. "I suppose I shall have to do it sometime."

"Use this extension," Pauline said. "I'll go outside."

"No, it isn't necessary," Ursull said. "You can stay. I can say nothing on the phone." She picked up the receiver, and Pauline pressed the lit button.

"Hello," Ursull said. "Hello, Gerd."

Pauline got up and walked outside, into the Lounge. It surprised her, and annoyed her a little, that she had felt such genuine concern. The girls responded to her because she was hard, she knew that, hard and unfeeling. There were very few posts at a good salary for an older woman, not too attractive, who could not take shorthand and didn't have a particularly charming manner. They stayed in line because they were afraid of her, and that was why she kept her job. Being a guide at the UN seemed a delightful idea to new applicants, bright, pretty young girls. But after working for a while, the brightest of them realized it was hard on their feet, and hard on their budgets, eighty-five dollars a week, and the best of them would start to drift away, into other departments, into better jobs. And the prettiest of them would get married.

Even the ones who considered it a noble and fairly glamorous idea, working for the UN, soon discovered they could be just as noble and glamorous working for subcommittees or individual delegations, and a lot better paid. It distressed Pauline, every time a new group of trainees arrived, ready for the three-week orientation course, bright, shining, and wide-eyed. She felt like a career army man, a sergeant, who kept giving basic training to new waves of men, only to realize when he got them into shape they would be shipping out to where the real action was. And the only thing a career army man had to hang on to was his toughness. If he became sentimental, he had nothing left at all.

"Miss Bowman!" Pauline said, abruptly.

Bo was lying on the leather couch, a pillow under her head and another over her eyes. She took the top pillow away, warily. "Yes?"

"About this morning!" Pauline said.

"Yes?"

"I know you and your friend Miss Nils regard this place as more or less your country club, where you keep a locker, and eat lunch, and now and then show a visitor around the grounds . . ."

"I don't know if that's quite fair," Birgitta said, from a nearby leather chair.

"I'm not talking to you," Pauline said.

"Splendid," said Birgitta.

Pauline crossed her hands over her stomach like a mandarin doll. "I've grown quite used to lateness and inattendance from the two of you, but even so, I am hard put to understand why, exactly, Miss Bowman, you sashayed in here this morning at ten-thirty."

"Actually, it was ten-oh-five," Bo said.

"Whatever it was, we will agree it was not nine-thirty."

"Right," Bo said.

"What earth-shaking matter kept you, Miss Bowman? What possible excuse could you have for this morning's lateness?"

"My bangs kept curling up," Bo said. "I was trying to make them straight." She covered her face again.

Pauline walked away.

"I don't suppose she'll ask you anymore," Birgitta said, smiling.

"I don't suppose."

They sat there for a while, not speaking. Birgitta absently twisted a runaway strand of her long blond hair, and when the dispatcher finally called for her to take a tour, pressed it back into the bun at the back of her neck and got to her feet.

"You want to go to the hospital lunchtime?" Bo said.

"Not lunch. Maybe after work, I don't know."

"Then I'll meet you in the cafeteria? Twelve-thirty."

"I suppose. I'm not very hungry."

Bo looked at her, amazed. "You sick?"

Birgitta laughed. "Twelve-thirty," she said.

The cafeteria was crowded, as usual, but they managed to get a faraway table in the corner, so they could feel alone. Birgitta picked at her food, as Bo watched her, with concern.

"What's wrong?"

"Nothing," Birgitta said. "I'm sorry I didn't get to the hospital last night. Did you apologize to Kiiko for me?"

Bo nodded. "She didn't seem to mind at all. I think she'd just as soon we didn't come there so much. I suppose she feels under some obligation to talk about it, as long as we're there. And you know how the Japanese are. I mean, in the traditional plays women are always binding themselves around the legs before they commit hari-kari, so when they die their parts won't be exposed. It must be hell to be raped, and then have everyone curious about it. Especially for Kiiko."

"Poor Kiiko," Birgitta said.

"She's going to be all right," Bo said. "The doctors say she's a hundred percent improved already, physically anyway."

"When I saw her Tuesday, she couldn't stop weeping. It was the strangest thing I ever saw," Birgitta said. "She made no crying sounds at all. No breaths. No sobs. Not even whimpering, poor little Kiiko. Just a silent, steady stream of tears. I wish I could learn to cry like that. I would imagine it's a lot less hard on the tear duct displacement. She looked so still, and so lovely, it was very strange. She spoke, and sometimes she even smiled. But the tears just kept flowing. She must have been in terrible pain."

"I don't think so," Bo said. "She told me it was very painful while it was happening, because of her problem . . ." Bo looked away. "But she said the doctors had made her quite comfortable, and she felt almost no pain at all anymore."

"Then it's all the more strange," Birgitta mused. "Granted it's a horrible experience, especially under the circumstances, but Kiiko . . . I suppose it's a foolish thing to say, but Kiiko has so much control. Always. As bad as it was, I wouldn't have thought it could have done that to her. Not so unstrung her. Not completely."

"She isn't crying for herself," Bo said, looking out the window. "She's crying for Ernie. What a lovely girl. What an amazing girl she is, to cry like that for Ernie. My whole life I thought I could cry for other people, I thought I was really capable of empathy, you know? But I've never really wept for anyone, except in relation to me. She isn't sorry for herself, you understand. She's sorry she couldn't explain to him how it was. She thinks she should have made it clearer to him, about not being able to, I mean about the physical problem. She says she told him she could never marry, and she as much as told him her parents had abandoned her and she had been adopted by these people that work with defective children, but she thinks now she should have made it very clear."

"Can you imagine? Kiiko, who finds it hard to tell her name to someone she doesn't know, should have told him that? Should have told the man who criminally attacked her that?"

"Poor Ernie," Birgitta said. "Poor crazy Ernie."

"That's just it. She doesn't think he was crazy at all. She thinks he was in love with her, and something flipped him, and what he did, and how she was, made him kill himself."

"It's possible," Birgitta said. "He never struck me as a violent man. Pathetic maybe, but not violent."

"She even wanted to see his family, to see if she couldn't do something, talk to them, to make it all easier. She phoned his mother, but she wouldn't talk to Kiiko. It's like—in some nutty way, it's like Kiiko feels Ernie is the victim. The only thing that really bothers her, is that he's dead. Can you imagine? My whole life I've made myself some kind of tragic heroine, in everything that happened, even to other people. And she just lies there, all ripped apart inside, weeping for Ernie. She makes me ashamed."

Birgitta put down her fork, and looked out the window.

"I suppose this isn't very appetizing lunch conversation," Bo said. "I'm sorry."

"Nothing to be sorry about. I was hardly listening. Today I am my own tragic heroine," Birgitta said.

"What's wrong?"

"It's my birthday. I'm twenty-five years old."

"We'll have to do something to celebrate," Bo said. "What can I do that will make you happy?"

"Nothing," Birgitta smiled. "Unless you want to marry me."

"My first proposal," Bo said. "I hardly know what to say. But we must celebrate."

"Twenty-five years old and unmarried," Birgitta said. "What is there to celebrate?"

Bo felt a small knot of panic inside her. She had recently suffered her twenty-second birthday, and could not conceive of meeting anyone in the next three years. "You think," she said with great trepidation, "you think girls should be married by twenty-five?"

"When they've met the man, yes."

"And have you . . . have you met the man?" She did not ask with much enthusiasm. Not that she had anything against colored people, but Birgitta was so lovely. And unusual as Mason might be, Bo was sure there were plenty of white men around who could make him pale by comparison, as dumb Alec would probably say, understanding nothing of metaphor.

"Oh, Bo, please don't be coy. The only other person I'm close to who's as unenlightened and childish about intermarriage as you, is Mason."

"I'm sorry," Bo said.

"Don't be sorry. Stop being sorry. Everyone should stop being sorry. You, Mason, the whole world. Stop being sorry and change. I don't mean change how you are. You go on being exactly as you wish. But let me be as I wish. Understand *me*."

"I do," Bo said. "Really I do."

"You understand me in relation to yourself, just as you said you feel grief. Feel joy for me, not in relation to you, but in relation to me. I am *me*. I know what I am, how I am, who I am, and who I want to have with me. I've seen enough, and known enough people, to know when I've met my man. When I've met him, be happy for me."

"I am," Bo said. "If you're happy, then I'm happy for you."

"Well, it doesn't make any difference even if you are," Birgitta said sullenly. "Mason isn't, and he figures prominently in this."

"But I thought everything was fine between you."

"It is," Birgitta said. "As long as I let it go on just as it is."

"So?"

"So I'm not happy letting it go on any longer as it is. I don't want to live with him, I want to be married to him."

Bo smiled. "Forgive me for smiling, Birgitta. It's just that I never figured you for a puritan."

"Neither did I," Birgitta said. "And it would be disturbing to me if it wasn't such a logical, un-puritanical feeling. It's all well and good to be free, and freewheeling. Better than good. It's necessary. But when you know what you have with someone, and that's what you want, then you want it permanently. Marriage suddenly seems sinful, it's such a delicious idea."

"So why don't you tell this to Mason?"

Birgitta grinned wryly. "I've been telling it to him for months now. The only time there is peace between us is when I don't tell it to him, when I pretend I am as pleased with playing house as making a home. We had a terrible set-to last night. I started to cry for the first time since, oh well, you remember, and he ran for the ice tray and started pressing cubes under my eyes so I wouldn't swell and the whole time he said please not to cry, that he'd do anything if I'd only stop crying. And then I said marry me but he said he meant anything but that, so I cried again."

"How'd you resolve it?"

"My cheeks got frozen, and so did his hands. We got stuck together."

Bo laughed.

"I suppose it is funny," Birgitta said. "But I find it so hard to see humor in anything. He's such a pompous, serious ass."

"Then why do you want to marry him?"

"You're stupider than he is," Birgitta said. "No wonder I love you." She crushed her paper napkin in her fingers and held it to her nose, sniffling. "He regards this whole relationship with me as a concession to his beliefs—that he loves me is beside the point. He is an idea man, you see, so emotion is beside the point."

"Don't cry," Bo said. "Please."

"I'm trying not to."

"Why don't you just let it go on as it is?"

"I can't. It is too much a marriage for us not to be married."

"But if it's as good as a marriage, why not leave it at that? For a while, anyway. You're the one who always said that two people who love each other can make their home independent of the judgment of society."

"I only said that because I thought it was true. But it isn't true anymore. We are together, completely together, but that's all we are."

"I don't understand you," Bo said. "What else is there? What else do you want?"

"His name. His children." Birgitta wiped her eyes. "I don't mean to disappoint you, Bo, but it turns out I'm terribly conventional."

"Not exactly," Bo said, but not loud enough so Birgitta could hear.

"And him. My emancipated idiot. With his mad view of morality. Our relationship is moral only as long as we don't marry. Otherwise," Birgitta held the napkin to her eyes, "otherwise, we will be defying society. How's that for logic?"

"I'll get you some ice," Bo said, and got up quickly from the table before Birgitta could tell her it wasn't necessary. It certainly was necessary, not only for the salvation of Birgitta's ducts, but for Bo's equilibrium. It was all very confusing. The more she heard about Mason, the more sense he made, but only from a white man's point of view. He hadn't wanted to sleep with Birgitta, and that was admirable, but not to Birgitta, whose feelings were, after all, important in the matter. And now he was refusing to marry her, which was very sound, but seemed as though it were coming from a bigot who had decided to make concessions. Apparently, Bo stopped to consider, what neither Mason nor she had stopped to consider was that it was, after all, Birgitta's life, so she had a moderate stake in it.

Bo took a glassful of ice from the counter, and waved the girl away as she offered to pour water in it. No, the more Bo thought about it, the more she realized how wrong she was. How wrong both of them were, she and Mason, her ally against Birgitta. We want to do right by Birgitta, Bo thought, but perhaps the time has come to do right by her alone, and not right by her in relation to our idea of what is right by her.

"Here," she said, giving Birgitta the glass, and the napkins she had pulled from the counter.

"Thank you."

"Please don't cry anymore," Bo said. "If you cry anymore he won't even want to live with you in sin."

"Oh yes he will," Birgitta said. "We have both admitted that we couldn't bear to be without each other."

"Don't cry anymore."

"All right," Birgitta said, and blew her nose. "Then let's not talk about me and Mason anymore. And let's not discuss Kiiko, please. Something more cheerful. What's happening with you and your Alec?"

"That's hardly cheerful," Bo said, suddenly depressed.

Throughout her plans and fantasies about her first affair, it had never occurred to Bo that the descent from maiden grace could plummet one so quickly to the category of one-night stand. In all the best-sellers she had read, dealing with all categories of sex life, a girl, when losing (or dumping) her virginity, could be counted on to go through all sorts of trials and tribulations in her affair before the grisly thing resolved itself in marriage (usually to another person, who had not reaped the fruits, or, at least, the first harvest), or madness, reserved for those who had been a bit too free with their favors, before the right man came along; and although they were no longer an easy lay, the fact that they had been was enough to ensure their wandering senseless in a nightgown, broken-minded, at the end of the next to the last chapter, before the good girl went home with her groom from Idaho. But the girls of fiction, no matter how anxious or impossible, lily-white or jaded, never got their just desserts until they had undulated their way through a happy or miserable affair.

No one ever did it to the least appealing of heroines, only to disappear into the very next sunrise. So to be dumped so unceremoniously on the ass end of the act itself was unthinkable. All those heroines, thrashing around a liaison, trying to make it into a marriage, and she, of all people, couldn't even make the goddam thing into an affair.

The curious thing was that Alec didn't figure in this at all. She had no feeling toward him, one way or the other, though she was certainly incensed at the cavalier way in which he chose to ignore what was probably her life's most important step. For a number of days she had sat composing letters to him—injured, brave, coldly hating, warmly loving, angry, forgiving—but, spent after each bout, she would tear them up and go to bed, rehearsing angry speeches to him aloud, until Mary Kate would tell her to shut up and go to sleep, and she would.

But as her passion was now mainly reserved for what she wrote, and her passion prior to their rather bizarre commingling had been directed toward the opportunity to commingle, of her feelings for him she had precious little idea. She supposed that a great deal of her attraction had been not so much in his body as in her mind. And when she thought about it reasonably, which was not too often, she recalled that, taken from its colorful binding, the text of what he had to say was not very impressive.

And of their great night of love? The bloody deed is done, was all Shakespearean murderers would say, their swords wet with the life of Kings and Thanes. And they had a far better command of rhetoric than Alec. So if he chose to merely put it back in his pants, zip up, and never make a mumble, much less an improvisation, over what was, when you got down to it, only a membrane, she could hardly be surprised. He had never claimed to be Lady Macbeth.

Still, if he had any respect for the illusion of disillusion, the least he could do was have the decency to hang around until one of them changed, grew, began to get on the other's nerves, dissipated, found the meaning of true love, realized it was hopeless, died, and, or, et cetera.

"Son of a bitch," Bo said, trying to bend her fork in half. She looked up, rather disconcerted to see Birgitta smiling. She had meant for her to stop crying, but hardly because she was laughing at Bo.

"I suppose the whole time you were laughing at me. All the months I was telling you how I had decided to make my move, the pills, everything. You were probably laughing at me the whole time."

"No," Birgitta said. "No, I wasn't. These things are terribly important when you're young."

"That's true," Bo said. "Not all of us have the advanced wisdom of twenty-five."

"Besides," Birgitta said, "everything you've said—you've been laughing yourself. At Alec, and yourself."

Bo sighed. "I know. But it's still humiliating. Why would he just drop me like that?"

"Because you called his bluff," Birgitta said. "You told me all along how he was. How Mary Kate said he never 'came on' with the girls in class, or her, how he performed in front of you because you were so obviously an unapproachable virgin. The minute you stopped being unapproachable, he moved away. You terrified him."

"How do you know? You only saw Alec, what, twice at my house?"

"Once would have been enough. I was sure immediately. And with what you told me, about Maurice . . ."

"What about Maurice?" Bo said.

"You figure it out."

Bo sat back, dazed. "You think Alec is a faggot?"

"What do you think?"

Bo's head was swimming. "But how could he be a faggot? He *did* it to me!"

"Under what circumstances?" Birgitta smiled. "And how well?"

"Oh my goodness," Bo said, and turned quite red. "Oh my goodness."

"Come," Birgitta started to get up, "we better go back to work."

"Oh my goodness," Bo said.

"Forget about it," Birgitta said. "Make believe it never happened. It shouldn't have, you know, so there's no point in trying to make it even more complicated."

Bo looked up, bleary-eyed, and tried to smile. "You won't tell anyone, will you? You won't tell Mason?"

"Don't be a fool," Birgitta said.

"*Now* you tell me."

She followed Birgitta out of the cafeteria, letting herself be pulled by an invisible string she imagined tied to the blond knot on the head in front of her, so she wouldn't have to look at anyone lest they all knew. By the time they reached the doorway, Bo had almost recovered her equilibrium. The invisible string disconnected, and she saw the object in front of her as a person, a tall, blond, terribly bright and attractive person, who had no problems, no problems at all. As Birgitta said, she knew what she wanted, and she deserved what she wanted, since she was in a position to know. It wasn't as if Birgitta could stumble into something out of ignorance, like some people. There were worse things, there certainly were, than being in love with a Negro intellectual.

They drove up the highway toward Connecticut, looking for the place where it was they had spent their first afternoon in the country, Gerd cursing quietly under his breath that he hadn't made a map as he said he was going to, so they would be able to come back to it always. After a while, he gave up the search, settling instead on a quiet patch of hillside near a reservoir. But it was too cold, they both realized as soon as they tried sitting on the ground. So Ursull suggested perhaps it would be better if they went back to the car.

"I should have made a map," Gerd said.

"It would have been cold there, too." Ursull leaned her head back on the seat. "Papa says you should never go back to places where you were too happy. You're always disappointed."

"Your father is a grave man," Gerd said.

"Yes. With reason."

He tried to kiss her, but she turned her head away, and told him that first they had to talk.

Gerd shook his head. "I don't understand you. All the way up here you refused to speak of whatever it was you must say, and now it won't wait for even a kiss."

"Especially not a kiss," she said.

"You're angry with me," he said. "You're angry because I did not come to you Monday."

"You explained. I'm not angry. You said you had to spend more time than you expected with your father's colleague. Is it the truth?"

"Yes."

"Then I'm not angry."

"And you," Gerd said. "All this week you avoid me, telling me you have to go to the hospital to visit the Japanese girl. Is that the truth?"

"Yes."

"Then I am not angry." He clapped his gloved hands together, over the steering wheel. "Now may I kiss you?"

"No. Because it wasn't all the truth."

"But I read in the papers about the girl. And the man who did it and killed himself. I saw for myself, so I knew you weren't lying."

"I didn't have to go to the hospital. Not as much as I did. I went because it was some place to go. Where I would not have to think about other things. And where I couldn't see you . . . Or my parents."

"Your parents?"

"They're here. They've been here since Monday."

"And you didn't tell me? Why haven't I met them? Why haven't you told me they were here?"

Ursull looked at him, closely. "There was something else more important to tell you first. Something that had to be resolved."

"Yes?"

"I'm a Jew," she said. "My father is a Jew." She waited, watching his face carefully for some flicker of feeling, some betrayal of emotion, but the same strong lines of cheek and bone that made him so spectacularly handsome kept him, at this moment, completely expressionless. "I never knew until they told me Monday," she said, and told him the story, as her father had told Ursull. She did not tell it all, the money, the confusion, the fear, the shame. She told him only about her father's feeling about being a German, and not believing what was happening, and once believing, deciding to conceal it, even from his child.

"So you see," she said, after what seemed a very long time. "You see why I did not want to face you. I needed to put off telling you as long as I could. You see?"

"No." Gerd shook his head slowly. "No, truthfully, I don't. What were you afraid of? That I wouldn't love you anymore?"

She waited, hardly breathing. And slowly, he reached for her face and pulled it toward his own. "Oh Gerd," she whispered against his lips, and tears filled her eyes. "Oh Gerd."

"My beautiful girl," he whispered. "My beautiful foolish girl. How could you imagine this would change anything?"

She held him so tight he laughed, and said she would break his back if she didn't let go, and a bridegroom with a broken back would not do at all. "We'll go some place for lunch," he said. "I think we could both do with a drink, and some lunch."

They drove back onto the highway, relief and love flowing through her. She stretched and laughed and hugged herself and reached for his hand.

"Connecticut," he said. "It is very pretty, this Connecticut. It is a shame they have changed the laws of Green-Witch."

"Gren-itch," she said.

"Greenwich," he said correctly. "Then we could be married this afternoon. But as it is, it won't matter. Three days is only three days."

"Three days?" she said.

"That is all it takes now, in New York. The blood test, and then three days for the license. That is not such a hardship."

"New York?" A vague feeling of fear was building back inside her. "Why New York?"

"Why not New York? It is convenient. We are there. Your parents can even come to the wedding if you like. It will be nice for them, that they can be there to see it."

"And what about your parents?" she said. "What about the wedding in Buenos Aires, and your parents?"

"We shall think of some excuse. We shall explain that your father was here on business or something, that they preferred a small wedding, and as we wished to marry as soon as possible, we decided it would be better if we married at once, in New York."

"I see," Ursull said.

"That way, there can be no . . . no unfortunate incidents."

"You mean, like your father finding out my father is a Jew. That I am a Jew."

Gerd smiled. "You are so foolish. Because your father is a Jew, that does not make you one. You weren't raised as a Jew. You don't think as a Jew."

"How does a Jew think?"

"You know. You have none of those . . . odd ideas."

"About what?" Ursull said stiffly. "From everything I have observed, what little I have observed of Jewish people, Jewishness is a tradition. I have regarded it mainly as a tradition. My father tells me it is a religion, and that it took Hitler to make them into a race. Once they were called a race, once there was a doctrine of genocide, they became a race. And what was left of that race in Europe has been forced to become a nation."

"Nonsense," Gerd said. "Nobody makes Jews do anything."

"Not even go to weddings?" Ursull said.

"What is the matter with you, Ursull? I realize all this has been upsetting to you, finding out you are a Jew; I too would be upset to make such a discovery. But it changes nothing between us, except the wedding arrangements. If you insist, if you're angry, then we shall wait, as we planned, and be married in Argentina. But it seems unnecessary now. We can have your parents, and that should make them happy. My parents will be disappointed of course, but it will be better in the long run of things. When we have children, you can come and visit your family whenever you like. I shall come with you, if you wish. It makes no difference to me, I told you that. But there is no reason to invite trouble. There is no reason to make it known to my father. Your father, too, I am sure, would be happier if my father didn't know."

"And if he did know?"

"It would still make no difference to me. He would object to my marrying you, I suppose, and that would trouble me. But it would not keep me from marrying you."

"I was right about you," Ursull said, softly smiling. "You are an enlightened man. A very enlightened man."

"I am also a man in love," he said. "A German in love. You yourself said there was nothing more positive than a German in love."

"You said that," Ursull mused. "I said there was nothing more positive than a German in an argument."

"Your memory is too good," Gerd said. "I shall have to be dealing with that the rest of my life. I wish you would learn not to remember everything."

She sighed. "So do I." She lay back, adjusting her body to the deep bucket leather of the seat, and stared at his profile. He was very beautiful. Very beautiful, and very sure. She relaxed there for a while, just looking at him, enjoying the sight of him, and the feelings he had instilled in her.

"You are so quiet," he said. "What are you thinking?"

"Are you very close to your father, Gerd?"

"Very close. Closer even than with my mother."

"That's strange. With me it was always the opposite. I was close to my mother, between us there was always warmth, affection, great tears and joy. With my father, there was always a distance. A strange distance. I felt . . . I felt he was almost impersonal toward me. I only found out why a few days ago. But finding out why there is distance, does not close the gap, not all at once. The distance remains. Do you understand what I mean?"

"Certainly," Gerd said, narrowing his eyes against the frosted afternoon sunlight, slowing down the car. "There's a place that looks quite good. Shall we stop here?"

"No," she said. "Please. I want to get straight into the city."

"What about lunch?" he said.

"You can eat after you take me home."

"Aren't you hungry?"

"No," she said. "No I'm not."

"Whatever you say." He pulled the car back into the faster lane of traffic.

"This distance, you understand what I was telling you, Gerd, about the distance between me and my father?"

"Very well," he said. "It is quite natural, I would think."

"Natural between a father and a daughter, or natural between . . ." She let her voice fade. She did not have to finish the question.

"You say you are very close to him, this father of yours," Ursull said, after a moment.

"We have an affection that is rare between two men, even father and son. I think him the most exceptional man I know. And he considers me the same."

"And yet you would defy his wishes?"

"About you? Certainly. Under the circumstances, I won't have to. But if I had to, I would."

"I see," she said. "Then I suppose that explains it."

"Explains what?"

"You are close to your father, and yet you would defy him, marrying a Jew. Being so close, you could afford to drive him away from you, a little. But because I was never close to my father, and I wish to be close to him—because there are years of distance between us that it will take much time, much time, and much understanding to close—I can't afford to alienate him. For this very reason, I could not go against his wishes."

Ursull took a deep breath. "So you see, Gerd, I shall not be able to marry you."

"You . . ." he said. "Why? Why would you say such a thing?"

"It's very simple, Gerd. I respect his wishes. And my father wouldn't want me marrying a Nazi."

Mason wasn't home yet when Birgitta arrived at the apartment, her arms loaded with the bread and cheeses, and the special package with the purple-color cream paste from the delicatessen. So she had plenty of time to make the fondue, and lay out the French bread with the candle stuck on top. At six-thirty she iced the wineglasses and set them on a bucket on the table, beside the half-bottle of champagne. She combed her hair and put on fresh makeup, and slipped into her prettiest, and only, negligee.

When she heard his key in the lock, she was just finishing the inscription in the bubbling center of the cheese. She covered the copper pot with a lid, lowered the flame beneath it, and ran to the door.

"Hey!" Mason said. "What's this? Some kind of celebration?"

Her fingers were around his eyes, and she was telling him not to look, and helping him off with his coat all at the same time. He promised not to open his eyes if she would just keep her fingernails out of them, and he let her lead him to the dining area.

"Son of a gun," he said. "Is it my birthday again?"

"No," Birgitta said happily. "It's mine."

"Why didn't you tell me, dummy? I have birthdays even when it's not my birthday, and you have a for real one and I don't know. I don't have a present for you, or . . ."

"It doesn't matter, I don't want anything from you. Except."

"Don't finish," he said.

"I didn't intend to."

She brought some salad from the small wooden dishes she had placed in the refrigerator, and put out the silverware, Danish ancient, as she called it, and told him to open the wine.

"Unless you don't feel like birthday cake," she said.

"I feel exactly like birthday cake. Chocolate, vanilla, or Gorgonzola?"

"Three different kinds of cheese," she said. "I was fooling around."

She lit the candle on the cake. "You want to make my wish for me?"

"That's for you to do."

"No," she said. "I'm tired of wishing. What I want doesn't seem to mean anything. Maybe if you wanted it, it would happen."

"Blow out the candle," he said. "I don't feel like fighting."

She wet two fingers and snuffed out the flame. Mason said nothing. He busied himself with a cloth napkin, opening the bottle. There was a pop, only a tiny pop, but a pop nonetheless.

"Now we must all laugh insanely," Birgitta said. "Because everything is so gay, and we are all so happy."

"Cut the cake."

She lifted the lid from the pot. "Don't you want to see the inscription, before I cut it?"

"Doesn't it say 'Happy Birthday'?"

"Not exactly," Birgitta said.

"What kind of a birthday cake doesn't say 'Happy Birthday'?" He stood up and peered inside the copper dish. Scrawled across the top of the yellow and orange-gold cheeses, was a runny purple BON VOYAGE.

"What's that supposed to mean?"

"Bon voyage, for heaven's sake, Mason, everybody understands that, even people who don't know French. It means bon voyage." She waved her cheese spoon in the air.

"I don't mean that. I mean what is it supposed to mean? You getting cute, honey? Applying a little of the old lady pressure, like, it can't be marriage, git your slippers out from under my bed?"

"My," she said, "you are sensitive. Of course I'm not throwing you out, Mason. I couldn't do that, and you know it. You're more than welcome to stay, although you might have a little bit of trouble with Mr. Roan."

"Who?"

"Mr. Roan. Your friend from Welcome Wagon. I know he hasn't bothered us, but it might be something else again if you were living here alone."

"Alone?"

"Yes, Mase." She broke a piece of the bread from the end of the loaf, and dipped it into the cheese. "I'm leaving. The bon voyage isn't for you, it's for me. But like I said, you're welcome to stay."

"I see."

"Do you?" She took a drink of her wine. "I wonder sometimes if you do. You're so farsighted, so noble, always looking ahead into the future, the projected history of man. You're so farsighted it's a wonder to me sometimes you don't trip over the furniture."

"I do see. It's just what I said. You're trying to strong-arm me into marrying you by threatening to leave. We can't get married. I've told you over and over again that we can't get married, and why. But you will keep up this goddam irrational feminine shit about feelings and emotions and personal needs . . ."

"And of course feelings and emotions and personal needs are nothing when weighed against societal obligations and sociological significances and that sort of thing, right, Mase? Especially where two people are involved. Two people don't figure in a marriage, do they, Mase? Society, that's what figures."

"I don't want to discuss it," Mason said.

"You know something? Neither do I. It's my birthday. I'd like to have a good time."

"Cheers," he said, lifting his glass.

"Ha ha," said Birgitta, and ate some more cheese.

After a while he looked up from his plate. "You going to just sit there, eating, not saying anything?"

"You said you didn't want to discuss it."

"I don't. But we could talk," Mason said.

"No, we can't. That's what you refuse to see. I could talk, but in no time at all you would make it into a discussion. So it's better if we just don't say anything."

"That isn't true, my making everything into a discussion. We only get into a discussion when you start talking about marriage. If you wouldn't talk about marriage, we wouldn't have to end up in discussions and arguments."

"Then we're at an impasse," Birgitta said. "Because that's all I want to talk about. Marriage and home, and a vine-covered cottage by a waterfall."

"Dey ain't no waterfalls in Harlem, lady. Dat's what you got to git into yo haid."

"Dey ain't no Harlem in waterfalls, sir, and that's what drives you out of your mind. You just won't see that, will you? That your problems, and your people's problems have nothing to do with the problems between you and me. They're our problems! The world's burden has no place in our relationship. You won't see it, and if you could see it you couldn't stand it, because you have to be carrying your cross all the time. Even with me. Especially with me. You can't just see something as it is, like a waterfall, like a relationship between a man and a woman that nothing can interfere with."

"You don't live in the real world, Birgitta. You've got to live in the real world. And the world has problems."

"Not in my home, it doesn't. My home may be in the world, but the world doesn't have to be in my home."

"You're not realistic."

"Oh yes I am, Mason. What we have between us is more reality than most people have all their lives. If that isn't realistic, I don't know what is."

"Harlem is realistic."

"Then go sleep with Harlem. Go make love to Harlem."

"So I was right. You're throwing me out."

Birgitta lowered her voice. "No I'm not. I said you could stay. Only I'm leaving. I'm going back to Sweden."

"Do you want to?"

"You know I don't."

"Then what will it solve?"

Birgitta looked down at her empty wineglass. "Well, for one thing, it will give me some place to have my children."

He swallowed, and smiled. "You planning on getting married?"

"No. I was hoping to, but I'm not planning to."

"Then why *children?* If you want to sound melodramatic, you should say child."

"Well, I would, but twins run in my family."

"You putting me on?"

She looked up. "That isn't worthy of either of us."

"Why didn't you tell me you were pregnant?"

"That's a cheap trick, Mason. An old movie cheap trick. The sleazy tramp from the wrong side of the tracks uses it to land the beautiful rich boy. It wouldn't do at all here. Not for the beautiful and witty blond girl from a fine family to entrap the fiery but rootless Negro."

"How long?"

Birgitta shrugged. "A little over three months."

"Well, why didn't you say something when there was time, so we could have done something about it?"

"For the same reason," she said. "That it happened in the first place."

"You let it happen?"

"No," Birgitta said softly, "I made it happen. I want your babies. I want you, and I want your babies. If I can't have you, then I'll have your babies. But I won't not have your babies and have you."

"Well, maybe it isn't too late. Maybe we can find a doctor who—"

"We won't find any doctor. My father happens to be the best endocrinologist and gynecologist in Sweden, where, I'm sure you know, abortion is legal. It is too late, but even if it weren't, I wouldn't let him touch it, or them, whichever it is. I'd like a boy and a girl, wouldn't you? Then they could play with each other. Twin boys compete, and twin girls get jealous. I'd like a boy and a girl."

"I'd like to die," Mason said.

"Ah well. That's your problem." She got up and went to the refrigerator, and brought out another half-bottle of champagne. "I splurged and got an extra one, just in case. I knew this would be a big party."

"Oh yeah," he said. "You're just full of surprises."

"I'm sorry about not telling you before, Mase dear, but I was afraid you would want to marry me for that reason, or think I was forcing you into it, or you would want to do exactly what you said. And I care about you so much, I might have let you convince me to get rid of them, and I couldn't have stood that, not afterwards. We made these children, and they will be exceptional. I insist on seeing how exceptional they are.

"Besides, I don't believe in abortion. I know that seems kind of priggish, especially coming from me, but I don't believe in it. Not for myself. For the young, or the unfortunate, or those who are unable to care for their children—or people who have been badly used.

But I'm not any one of those. I've got them because I want them. I want them because there was never anyone like you before, and there won't be again, not for me, so not for my children either. I met you at the right time, and that's lucky. I'm lucky, and so are my babies. But I don't know how long we could have gone on like this, and I couldn't have left you for any other reason. And I was ripe. I was overripe. The doctor says I have the greatest pelvis for childbearing he's ever seen. What do you think?"

"I don't know," he said. "I just don't know."

"What do you think they'll be like? Do you think they'll be more like you, or more like me?" She opened the second bottle of champagne. There was no pop, and she looked at it, a little disappointed, before she refilled her own glass. "I kind of hope they'll have your body and my features. That would be nice."

"What's the matter? Mine too Negroid for you?"

"Not at all. But unlike you, I can be objective. And I'm prettier than you are."

"How could you do it, Birgitta? Forget about your feelings. Forget about you altogether. What about the kids? How will they be able to live with the pressure?"

"What pressure? The pressure of being bastards?"

"Cut it out."

"That wouldn't be such a hideous pressure, I don't think. They're kinder about that in Sweden. Girls have illegitimate babies in fine hospitals, and if they can't raise them themselves, they're taken into very good homes. Of course, if you mean the pressure of being dark-skinned with a blond mother and no man around the least bit dark, that might be a little puzzling for them. They might feel a little odd, with everybody in Sweden being so fair. But if there was a big old black man around so they could see how wonderful their father was, they'd probably be perfectly happy, healthy children."

"You want me to come and live in Sweden?"

"Don't be foolish. You don't belong anywhere but here. Neither do your children. I'll go back if I have to, because unwed mothers are not exactly the first name on a party list in New York, but they should be born in America, as American citizens."

"Some citizens," he said. "Yeah, that's some big boon to my children, being born in America."

"And where else would you want them to be, Mase? Forgive

me, but I laugh at you. I laugh at all of you, sometimes. I laugh at the extremist group in Quebec, they're white people, you know, so you won't feel I'm singling out the Negro. They want a separate nation, can you imagine? They want their own country, when they're forgetting a very simple fact. They're Canadians. Whatever is wrong, whatever their complaints, they're Canadians, and trying to be something else is madness. And it's the same with you. Not with you, especially, with all of you. Whatever your problems, whatever needs to be made right, and I know as well as you that a lot does, you are American. An American Negro is more American than he is anything else. There's no place else he can go. Not really. Not and really live. Not Paris for the hip musician, not Africa for the extremist, or whatever part of Texas or Oklahoma or whatever that place is they'd like to have apportioned off. You belong here, and so do your children."

"You want to get married?" Mason said quietly.

"You know I do."

He got up and knelt by her chair, and pressed his head against her breasts, his hands gently holding her stomach. "Oh lady," he whispered. "Oh lady, you sure do load a powerful shotgun."

She touched the dark tangle of hair at the back of his neck. "I won't marry you for that. I told you I won't marry you for that."

"What will you marry me for?"

"You. Me. You and me. But not the babies. And not society. For you and me."

"But the babies exist, honey. You've got to admit that. And society exists too. You see that?"

"Not in my home," she said. "And I don't know about you, but that's where I'm going to live. In my home. That's how we would live with each other."

"Okay," he said. "We would live with each other. But it would be in society."

"So say they looked on us a little strangely."

"Ha!" Mason said.

"All right then, they frowned on us. On any two people. Suppose society was watching a couple, a boy dwarf and his little lady midget, walking down the street. Society might despise them, or fear them, or dismiss them completely, as too horrible to consider. The important thing, the only important thing would be, does he have it for that lady, and does she have it for him? When they go home at the end of that tiny day, is their home perfect? Lilliputian perfect. For them. Not for anyone else.

"Because the truth of it is, Mase, that's all there is. What's between two people. A man and a woman. Everything else is extra. Society is extra. They are what there is, and everything else is outside. Do you see?"

"I see that you think of us together as freaks," he said. "A dwarf and a midget. What kind of happy reality is that? Is that your liberalism, yelling to the world how different we are, that we don't mind being freaks?"

"I wouldn't be a freak, and neither would you. Neither would a dwarf, for that matter, if he loved his tiny lady and didn't go around thinking how lucky other men were to be big. If he loved her, he might only think how unlucky everyone else was, not to be suited to his girl."

Mason got to his feet and pulled her gently by the hand, until she was standing in front of him. He slipped his arms around her. "Jesus, you're an armful for a midget," he said softly. "When do you want to get married?"

"Oh, any time you say," she whispered against his ear. "As long as it's in the next six months."

Late in spring, Bo received a phone call from a girl from Cleveland, a girl she remembered only vaguely but whose father, she knew, was a good friend of Axel Bowman's. She wasn't too crazy about the father, or what little she remembered of the girl, who was terribly much her junior. But as Mary Kate was away for the weekend and she had gotten a call from Birgitta who was just back from her honeymoon, she invited the girl to come over to the apartment for a drink.

The phone call with Birgitta had depressed Bo, not because of anything Birgitta had said, but she sounded so disgustingly happy even though they had been turned away from two hotels in Jamaica, Bo wanted to weep. She herself had met absolutely not one man, regardless of race, creed, or place of national origin, who excited her in the least in she didn't remember how long, and it was hideously clear that life was passing her by. Still, Birgitta had warmly advised her not to panic, that everything happened in time.

Not panicking in spring was a hard and new lesson for Bo, especially since Mary Kate, like a sneaky traitor, had gone back home over one weekend and gotten engaged to the dullest boy imaginable, even in Cleveland. And the worst of it was, she seemed genuinely in love with him, even though he had never heard of Stanislavsky and thought show biz was some new kind of virus.

Even Ursull seemed well on the road to recovery, having returned from Mardi Gras in Argentina to tell of a quite charming young man she had met. Nothing overwhelming, Ursull had said, but interesting enough to prove there was hope.

For Ursull, maybe, Bo thought. But not for her. Still, life was peculiar, you had to say that about it, so there was no point in losing interest.

The girl was not nearly as horrible as Bo had remembered. She shook hands like a boy, but that wasn't her fault: her father had sent her away to one of the better women's colleges. Her name, as Bo remembered, had been Suzanne, but for some reason she was telling Bo now that she preferred to be called Sukie. It was unfortunate, but it was up to her, Bo thought, recollecting the years she had endured as Luanna. It also turned out that she wasn't that much younger than Bo: just twenty-one, which made it only a year. Bo supposed her confusion dated back to the time when Bo was twenty and Sukie-Suzanne was nineteen, and every year seemed so urgent, because you didn't realize how much garbage nothing was lying up there ahead.

"Well, what are your plans, really?" Bo said.

"I'm not sure. Actually this is kind of a magnificent deception. I told Daddy I had to come to New York for this fantastic job interview, only I didn't have any interview at all. I was just kind of hoping I could unearth something while I was here, and then phone back home that I had a job, and a place to live, and then it wouldn't be so hard."

"Hard?"

"Daddy would blow his bald pate if he honestly thought I was thinking of living here. He only let me come for the interview because I cried a lot, and made the job sound so interesting and demanding he was sure I couldn't possibly be qualified."

Bo smiled. "Listen, have you been over to the UN?"

"I haven't had time to see anything. There's so much I wanted to see, only the first minute I got into the hotel room I clutched, and called the only person I knew in New York, being you."

"I didn't mean to see it. I meant to try to get a job there. I work as a guide, and they're taking applications for the group starting in May."

"But that's fabulous," Sukie said. "I knew you were doing something fascinating here, but I didn't realize you were actually working at the UN."

"It isn't as glamorous as it sounds," Bo said, jadedly. "Actually, like anything, after a while it becomes routine."

"Maybe to you, but not to me. Do you really think I could qualify?"

"You graduated?"

She nodded. "January."

"And how are you in language?"

"I majored in French."

"You shouldn't have any trouble at all," Bo said. "And I'd be happy to put in a word for you."

"You would?" The girl looked at her with the most admiration anyone had granted her since Bo became too old to baby-sit.

But she didn't mind. She didn't mind at all. The child needed someone to look up to, to guide her, if she was going to come to New York. She was a sweet thing, really, quite pretty, even if she did have that terrible name: and it wasn't her fault if she was so uncosmopolitan. That credit belonged to Cleveland.

"Actually, Sukie," Bo managed to say it, "if you can find some place to hang on to until June, Mary Kate is getting married, so I see no reason why you couldn't move in here."

"With you?" Sukie said, obviously overwhelmed. "But that would be too perfect. It's like a dream—the answer to a maiden's prayer."

Maiden? Bo thought, and hoped it was in a manner of speaking. She hated the prospect of going through with anyone else what she had been through with herself. Still, time would tell, and at least she was in a position to advise. At least a better position than that swinish Mary Kate who acted as if she knew all and actually knew nothing, and was proving it by marrying the hometown boy.

"But I can't tell you what that would mean to me, Bo. Honestly, no words. It's like a godsend. I told you how my father feels about my coming to New York, but if I were going to room with you! His best friend's daughter. He couldn't object to that! He'd be out of his mind with joy."

"Don't be too sure," Bo said. "Fathers are fathers. They don't want their little darlings out of Cleveland, not even if they're going to be with somebody else's little Cleveland darling. He'll still go into a panic at the thought of your living in New York, associating with all those foreigners at the UN."

"You think?"

"I know," Bo said. "Believe me." She looked at her watch and saw it was almost seven-thirty.

"I'm sorry," Sukie said, seeing the gesture. "Do you have some place to go? Am I keeping you?"

"Not at all," Bo said. "I was just thinking. They have this sensational Hawaiian *smörgåsbord* on Sundays at the Luau, and I don't think it's too late. Would you like to go?"

"Would I!" Sukie said. "You're a doll to ask me."

"My pleasure."

"God, New York. Too much. All these places. Restaurants. Like nothing. All the time, some place sensational to go. Like now."

"To tell you the truth," Bo said, "this is the first time I'm going to the Luau since I got here last September."

"No kidding?" Sukie said, getting up to put on her coat.

"No kidding," Bo said, but knew Sukie would not believe her. Oh well. Let her find out for herself.

"It's just so great about my father, I can't tell you, Bo. You don't know what a difference it will make."

"I know it won't make any difference," Bo said. "He'll still be beside himself." She took her coat out of the closet, and put her arms in the sleeves. "I don't know what it is about parents. They do get very hysterical about daughters alone in New York."

"And with good reason," Sukie said.

"With very little reason, I'm afraid." Bo reached for the lamp cord, and turned off the light. "You'll find out."

She took a final look around the apartment, to make sure everything was in order. Then she picked up her pocketbook and went to the door. "Actually, I suppose, it's because they don't know the city the way we do. The truth of it is"—she opened the door, for Sukie to precede her—"it's all you can do to get into a little trouble."